BY HEATHER ABEL

The Emilys

The Optimistic Decade

THE EMILYS

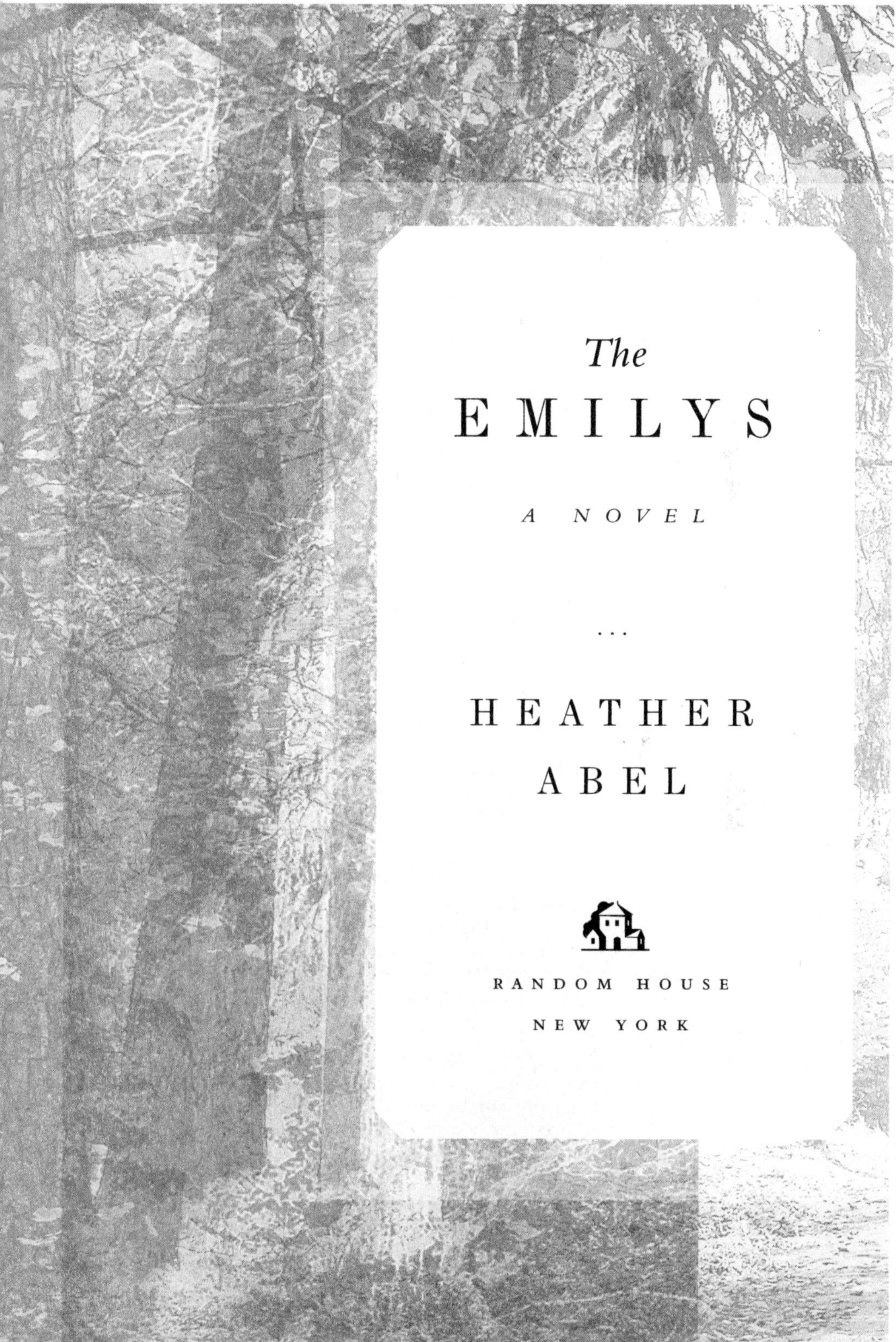

The EMILYS

A NOVEL

...

HEATHER ABEL

RANDOM HOUSE
NEW YORK

This is a work of fiction. Names, characters, places and incidents are the product of the author's imagination or are used fictitiously. Any resemblance to actual persons, living or dead, events or locales is entirely coincidental.

RANDOM HOUSE
An imprint and division of
Penguin Random House LLC
1745 Broadway, New York, NY 10019
randomhousebooks.com
penguinrandomhouse.com

Library of Congress Cataloging-in-Publication Data
Names: Abel, Heather author
Title: The Emilys: a novel / Heather Abel.
Description: New York, NY: Random House, 2026.
Identifiers: LCCN 2025039243 (print) | LCCN 2025039244 (ebook) |
ISBN 9780593979532 hardcover acid-free paper |
ISBN 9780593979556 ebook
Subjects: LCGFT: Fiction | Novels
Classification: LCC PS3601.B435 E45 2026 (print) | LCC PS3601.B435 (ebook)
LC record available at https://lccn.loc.gov/2025039243
LC ebook record available at https://lccn.loc.gov/2025039244

Printed in the United States of America on acid-free paper

1st Printing

FIRST EDITION

BOOK TEAM: PRODUCTION EDITOR: *Annette Szlachta* •
MANAGING EDITOR: *Rebecca Berlant* •
PRODUCTION MANAGER: *Sandra Sjursen* •
COPY EDITOR: *Nicole Ramirez* •
PROOFREADERS: *Courtney Vincento, Megha Jain, Dan Goff*

Book design by Barbara M. Bachman
Title page art by kichigin19 Adobe/Stock

The authorized representative in the EU for product safety and compliance is Penguin Random House Ireland, Morrison Chambers, 32 Nassau Street, Dublin D02 YH68, Ireland. https://eu-contact.penguin.ie

For my parents,
with love

We grow accustomed to the Dark—
When Light is put away—

—EMILY DICKINSON

THE EMILYS

This April

...

IT'S SPRING AGAIN, THE EARTH IN EARLY, URGENT VIRIDESCENCE. The last ice melts on the Connecticut River. Three barred owlets hatch in a white pine. In the garden outside Emily Dickinson's house, trout lilies open. In my house, my daughter watches a sitcom she's seen three times before. Since she left college, she's up late into the night.

I'm awake, too, unable to fall back asleep. All week I've felt that springtime desire to roll down a hillside. I want the new green around me, beneath me. I want to pluck it, press my face into a furl of skunk cabbage. I can't do that, of course, but I can push off my sheets, pull on sweats, head downstairs and out the back door, the concrete cold on my feet. The air is still. The sky moonless. A train moans as it passes through Northampton on its way to Vermont. I listen to a fox ululating in the forest behind my house, but as it comes closer I realize it's not a fox at all. Two women. It's three A.M., so they must be Emilys, although I don't recognize their voices. They're talking fast, interrupting each other, falling into laughter.

A rustle of leaves underfoot, a crack of branch as they near.

I see their shapes through the dark trees. I can't make out their faces, but a spring wind has come into the night, the way that two friends together can create a weather neither could alone. I want to call out to them, but I can't because of a sudden sadness. I miss her desperately. My own laughing friend, my Demeter, the one who doubled me. It's been twelve years, and I still often talk to her, if only in my head. Sometimes I ask where she is and how she is and if she's forgiven me and how is her daughter, who must be twenty-five now, and doesn't she want to know about mine? Mostly, I tell her about my day, all the beautiful mundanities I would share if she were still here. "I saw two women who remind me of us," I say when their footsteps fade into the woods and I'm alone again in the dark.

BOOK ONE

...

The WORM in the APPLE

April—
Thirteen Years Earlier

. . .

i

After weeks of bone-chilling rain, warm gales began. The kind of warmth that makes you say yes when you usually say no. I was cooking when Lev asked to go to a "ground play." It had been such a long winter that he'd lost the word *playground*.

Forget dinner. Forget baths, bedtime. I never did this. But I'd reached what felt like an apotheosis of isolation, and I longed to escape the house I'd lucked into. I grabbed Sonya and her jacket. We headed out to the ground play.

The three of us ate cheese puffs through the town's two blocks of pottery, weed shop, bubble tea, earrings, tattoos, weed shop, T-Mobile, weed shop, Pita Pocket, until we reached a courtyard with chained-up bistro tables—the New England version of a piazza. For the first time in months, there were people in it, enjoying themselves.

"It there." Lev pulled my hand. The playground honestly only gestured toward a playground. Stumps in a lazy spiral. A wooden tetrahedron. Boulders very much identical to the boulders along the river behind our house.

I hadn't remembered that thirty feet of grass separated the piazza from the play structures. Dead grass, the color of nicotine teeth. Sonya refused to step on it.

One child in purple leggings tugging away from my grip. One child with a tin whistle, shaking her frolic of dark brown curls.

"Just this one time?"

"Actually? I'll die if I walk there."

We'd sprung the clocks forward a few weeks earlier, and although it was late, it was not yet fully dark. Lifting Lev in my arms so he wouldn't bolt, I could've looked up and seen a green glow on the branches of the sugar maple, larval leaves as bright as inchworms clinging to the dull branches.

I didn't look up. At the time, I felt every day to be a ladder of crises that I climbed onto in the morning, reaching the final rung at bedtime. I thought this climb would last forever. If I could go back, I would say, Eve, Eve. Look up. The green world, I would say, is constantly changing. It's showing you how. Would you please pay attention?

But we don't go back.

THE MOOD IN THE PIAZZA was celebratory and loud, warm air urging everyone outside.

Ariana Grande singing from a radio tied to the handlebars of an electric wheelchair.

A bus exhaling, opening its doors.

A pamphlet on the ground asking, *What Do Christians Miss Out On?*

My son shouting, "It my turn. It my choices."

My daughter saying, "Actually, I'm not uncooperative. Actually, I go anywhere in the world but grass. How is that uncooperative? That's incredibly cooperative."

Still carrying Lev, I reached for the pamphlet and brushed off a footprint of mud. What *do* Christians miss out on?

Four bold letters filled the center of the leaflet: *HELL.*

I laughed and then wished I had someone to show it to. Humor demands to be shared, which I suppose is why the internet exists. I thought about Henry James and I felt my loneliness, which clung to me like a third child, although I was never alone, and I thought about the way the other mothers at the school gate seemed to look away from me when I smiled at them, and I thought, no, the problem was me, I needed to learn to laugh on my own without devolving into a rumination on loneliness, and I thought, no, the problem was capitalism, or more precisely how a capitalistic country without universal pre-K depends on a mother blaming herself for loneliness as well as, of course, on her unpaid labor, and I tried to remember the precise wording of that Terry Eagleton quote, something about capitalism plundering the sensuality of the body, and then I heard my name.

A woman, around my age, with long black hair was pulling a compact pink rolling suitcase. Beside her, a girl in a sun hat with flaps and large sunglasses with white frames. "I don't feel good," the girl said. The woman kept her eyes on me. "Eve? It's you, isn't it?"

Lev slid from my arms. "Yes?" I was unsure how she knew my name. I knew hardly anyone in this town.

"My god, you look exactly the same. Don't you remember me?"

I tried to place her face or her voice but came up blank. "Wait, from . . ." She was smiling at me expectantly. "Where was it again?"

"Mom? I really don't feel good," the girl said.

The woman gently put her arm around her child and pulled her close. "It's Demeter!"

"Demeter?" I hadn't thought of that name in years. Decades. I looked at her daughter to try to see the girl I'd known, the girl I would recognize, but her face was hidden by the sunglasses and hat.

"D'Errico," Demeter added, as if there could be more than one. "I gotta get her home before . . . We should get that bus." I followed her gaze to a bus rolling slowly forward. "But, my god, I can't believe. Here we both are, Eve. Can you even?"

"So you live here? You live here again?"

"Mom, the bus is . . ."

"We'll catch it, hon." To me she said, "We gotta run, where do I find you?"

"My dad's house." But they took off holding hands, with no sign that she heard me.

"Demeter," I called. Such an ungainly name. People stared. "The same one, same house!"

"Who was that?" Sonya demanded as we watched them climb onto the bus. "Is she your friend?"

Friend had become a freighted concept since we'd moved here from Brooklyn nearly six months earlier, in late October, two months into her third grade, when the cliques and reading groups and jump rope teams had hardened like the earth's winter crust. Sonya hadn't made a new friend yet. Neither had I.

Was Demeter my friend? I'd known her during two discrete but indelible times in my life. The first, a single day when I was six. Later, my twelfth summer, when I last lived in this town.

"For a short time," I said, as I tried to recall that summer thirty-two years earlier, and came up with the back of her head—I was always following her—and the green glint of woods around us. "God, she was fun," I added, but the word felt wrong—dull and generic. "No, animated," I corrected myself.

"What does that even mean?"

"Alive. She was the most alive person I'd ever met."

Sonya sighed and slipped her hand in mine. "Actually, everyone breathing is alive. You can't actually be more or less."

ii

BUT OF COURSE YOU CAN. I HAD FELT, SINCE MOVING BACK HERE, less. We'd moved because I lost my job and then we lost the rent-controlled lease to the one-bedroom Henry James had lived in for nineteen years. Well, only the kids and I had really moved. Henry James was still playing music in the city four days a week, sleeping on a friend's couch.

Henry James is not and has never been named Henry James, I should make that clear. His name is short and Russian, much like him. But he deserves privacy. So, for reasons I'll get to, I'm borrowing this one.

"Demeter? You never told me about anyone named Demeter," he said that Saturday, vodka in a Kermit the Frog cup. Curling against him, Lev pressed an ear to his father's wide belly. From behind his chair, Sonya rested her chin on his bald head, arms around his neck.

"It was just one summer and then I called her my best friend for years but never heard from her again," I said.

"There was a girl, too," Sonya said. "Wearing dark glasses. Very glamorous." And then quietly, with such hope that it made my own chest hurt, she added, "Maybe she'll be my best friend."

"So? Which do you think? I'd guess yoga with that name."

Henry James was referring to our joke—the sort of not entirely inaccurate hyperbole of urban transplants—that everyone in Northampton worked either as a therapist or yoga instructor, jobs with quiet voices and soft, unassuming clothes.

"No, I feel like . . . something else. Something intimidating," I said, thinking of how quick she'd been, how my father had praised her, although I'd searched online for her the evening we came home from the park and found nothing. How had she done the impossible? Walked through life leaving no footprint. "Like a mayor. Or professor. Or architect of refugee camps," I suggested. "She probably won't come by, though. It's been four days."

"She'll come. Wearing her yoga outfit. Trying to get you to her Iyengar class," he said, laughing and pulling Lev to his lap. Henry James never saw trouble where I did. When he returned on the weekends and listened to our stories, the constant runnel of our lives became narrative; his attention seemed to refine and even purify our experience until what had seemed disastrous turned amusing.

He laughed again in bed later—although by then he was stoned and would laugh at anything—about Sonya and the grass. "That's still happening?"

It had started when we moved. The woods behind our house, the YMCA playground, the apron of grass between car and sidewalk, the park with the peacock and three sickly sheep, the park with the small electric train and its teenage conductor. All off-limits.

Although we'd told her it wasn't true, although we showed her pictures of Green-Wood Cemetery in Brooklyn, and Woodlawn in the Bronx, and Calvary in Queens, she remained convinced that the dead from Covid in New York had been moved out of the crowded city and buried under the plentiful grass of Northampton.

"Definitely not," we told her. "Funerals were right nearby. With their families. There's always space in cemeteries. So much space."

"Maybe nobody knew."

"But they don't ship dead bodies without anyone knowing. That's completely illegal."

"People do lots of illegal things. Presidents do illegal things, you told me."

Then the snow and rain fell, and we stopped talking about it.

"Still a thing," I told Henry James. "She says that if I force her to step on grass she'll die like a berry plucked from its vine and eaten by a crow." Sonya had my knack for exaggeration and catastrophe.

"Our funny kid. She'll get over it."

I wasn't so sure. And it started to bother me that Demeter, of all people, whose daughter was probably as much of a wood nymph as Demeter had been as a child, would learn that mine was too frightened to go outside. Everyone knew that nature was uniquely salutary for children.

When Henry James headed back to Brooklyn, I took the kids to Target and let them pick out a Slip 'n Slide, a plastic turtle sandbox, and a wading pool for the backyard, although the temperature was only in the mid-forties.

Sonya made it as far as the concrete steps and took a breath. "I need bug spray first."

She held out her arms as I sprayed on OFF! "Now I need sunscreen."

Once lathered, she said she needed something else. Some other kind of spray.

"There are no more sprays."

She grew angry. "There have to be more sprays. Go look at Target. There's always more sprays." She stomped inside, letting the screen door slam behind her.

"Rurality bites," I said aloud. And then, since humor demands to be shared, I texted each of my friends back in New York. Rurality bites. I waited for their responses with an overblown anticipation, a high note in my chest wanting to be plucked, as if my friends were coming over, coming to see me and bearing gifts, a pot of pasta, an apple cake, but in their stead, of course, they sent pings of response—mini blue heart, static flames, duck, palm tree, haha—and then my phone quieted and I was still on the steps alone, needing to cook dinner.

iii

SHE CAME THE LAST WEEK IN APRIL, WHEN THE AZALEAS PINKED and the cherries gauzed white and the rains returned. A drizzly afternoon, the sky like wet slate. Hearing shouting, the kids and I crowded into the doorway and found them on our lawn: the girl again hidden by a hat with flaps and oversize white sunglasses despite the glowering clouds, and Demeter in a brown snap western shirt and a long skirt the color of red wine. "Come walk with us! That path, from your backyard into the woods? I remember it like yesterday. The weather's perfect." She laughed a little, wiping rainwater from her forehead.

"See, the thing is . . ." I began, and explained my failure as a mother.

But she didn't ask whether I'd tried a sticker chart or set a limit or consulted a therapist. She didn't suggest, as one mother at school pickup had, that Sonya's aversion to grass was the result of too much screen time. "So no grass?" she said. "Okay! We're hanging out in the street. For as long as you want. Who needs grass when God gave us asphalt?"

"Or you could, if you want, come inside?"

She shook her head. "Yeah, not ready to see him."

"Him?" I couldn't figure out who she was talking about.

"Dumb that it still bothers me. Maybe I should just get over it. Tell him he's right about everything. So he's home? Larry's home?"

"Larry? My father? He doesn't live here. Hasn't in forever."

"But you said . . . you said you were in his . . ."

"He rents it out. He moved to England, remember? With Avery?"

"That blond ponytail."

"Gray now. And short. They have two grown children." Why was I telling her all of this? I could hear the rain grow heavier, pattering on the porch roof.

"Oh god. My fucking god." She threw back her head, raised her arms to the clouds. Her shirt was yellow at the underarms. She ran toward us, up the porch stairs, holding her daughter's hand. "I've been so freaked out, Eve. Which is weird 'cause I actually never think about him anymore. It was seeing you the other day." She stared up at me. "He used to tell me how America is a meritocracy and then made me recite the seven colleges I was allowed to attend. 'The more status you have, the more you're respected,' he told me. Me, a kid living in a commune in buttfuck nowhere."

"He said that?"

She held up a finger. "Also, something like, 'You'll need to consistently prove yourself or you're choosing a life of menial labor in which you'll be ignored by the thinkers of the world.'"

"Asshole. And wrong, clearly," I said, feeling a little jealous of my father, how much she remembered him. I wanted to hear about me from that summer. I'd been thinking about it again, it was coming back, her tackle box of beads, the way she'd lie on my arm on the forest floor.

"Well, no. As it turned out, he was pretty much right about me." But she was calm now, all the fluster gone. "And he gave you his house. That's so generous."

"Just for the time being. We're renting."

A lie. He was letting us live there for free.

I explained that we had nowhere else to go—our landlord in New York evicted us after he sold to a condo developer, and I lost my job. Our credit score was wrecked. I was beginning to understand that she hadn't become a mayor/professor/architect, and while I'd been prepared to polish the narrative of my adulthood to keep up with her, I found myself doing the opposite, trying, I realize now, to make us the same, which we never were.

"Damn, I want to see inside again," she said, looking behind me through the open door. She cupped Sonya's cheek. "Will you stay out here with my daughter? No grass. Just the porch?"

"REMEMBER HOW LARRY KEPT six identical copies of his book here?" She splayed a hand on my dusty mantelpiece. I shook my head. I couldn't remember a thing about the house from that summer. "Next to an ashtray with skipping stones he brought back from . . . what was it, Cornwall? And the curtains here were blue with yellow daisies. I can't honestly believe I'm standing here again. I still have dreams that I'm here."

In the kids' room, once mine, she named all seven of my long-extinct stuffed animals. In my bedroom, she conjured Avery's paint-by-numbers—hot-air balloons—and in the kitchen, a particular omelet pan. "I always thought that someday I'd be adult enough to have a pan like that." What pan? I had no recollection. She opened a drawer. "The spices were in here. And the frog soap dish over here."

I was admiring her clothes, the worn glamour of them, and wishing I was wearing certain boots I hadn't worn since leaving New York, wondering if I could slip up to my room and put on the boots without her noticing my absence but also with her noticing the boots. But Demeter didn't seem aware of anything outside her trance of memory, until Sonya came into the house to tell us that the girl was throwing up.

"Fucking sunshine." Demeter ran out to the porch, and I followed.

Low clouds had shifted. Sun brightened the wet leaves of the rhododendron on the path to our house. The girl was leaning over the railing in a milky ray. Lev held her hat with flaps to his chest. I calculated that it had been around three weeks since we'd seen them in the park. "Still sick?"

Demeter rubbed her daughter's back. "It's not contagious if that's what you're thinking. It's just sunlight."

"Sometimes I get . . ." The girl wiped her mouth with her wrist.

"See, we came to Northampton because of it."

"A rash and the shivers."

"To see a doctor for this who can stop it."

"And sometimes my legs ache."

"We're sure they will. Right, baby?"

I didn't ask why the doctor was here in Northampton, which was famous for Smith College, Calvin Coolidge, and weed shops, but not for medical professionals. Sickness. If it's not in your body, in your child's body, if your child isn't shivering in the shower, you push it away. We all do.

The girl said she wanted to go home if that was all right with everyone. She took her hat from Lev and put it on carefully, making sure the flaps touched the edges of her white sunglasses. Demeter said it would probably be best, in the future, to meet at their apartment, which was set up nice and dark.

"What about right now, can we go now?" Sonya asked.

"Soon, tomorrow. Maybe the day after. She needs rest."

Of course, Demeter didn't say "she" but the girl's name. It was the first time we heard it. I'm not going to put it here. I know nobody can track down Demeter by name. I've looked and looked, and she's nowhere once again. But the girl—now woman—well, to give her privacy, I'll call her Persephone. She came with the spring.

iv

WE'D NEVER BEEN TO THE COOLIDGE GROVE APARTMENTS, A PUBLIC housing complex of brick rowhouses, and I was turned around for a long time on its paths, coming upon the same abandoned shopping cart three times before I found the door to 137B and rang the bell.

"Will there be lots of childrens? Will there be goldfishes crackers?" asked Lev, who had his father's appetites and expected a party behind every door.

"Are you sure they even want us to come? Why are you holding a plant? Do people even like people to bring them plants?" asked Sonya, who clutched tight the family heirloom of anxiety.

I, too, doubted the power of the Stop & Shop geraniums dangling in their white plastic hanger. Sure, Demeter and I had once been able to spend every moment together, to sleep in the same bed, but we were forty-four now. Why assume she wouldn't annoy or bore me? Or vice versa?

"Let's leave," I said rashly, just as she opened the door. She wore jeans and a white tank that revealed a dark patch of underarm hair as she pointed to a lightbulb in a yellow cage at the top of a narrow staircase. "Can't turn it off. Fire codes, blah, blah, so Persephone's hiding out."

In the living room: a couch sheathed in plastic, fake flowers on a side table, a large painting of Jesus, blood dripping from his thorny crown. It didn't seem ironic.

"Who that?" Lev asked. I didn't answer, because I was imagining Demeter decorating this room, and I knew we had nothing in common. We were two lines with one point of connection in 1991 from which we'd veered further and further away, an ever-widening void between us. The ecumenical spirituality she'd so delighted me with as a girl seemed to have hardened into something institutional and punitive.

As if she read me, she squeezed my forearm. "Furnished sublet. Highly illegal. If anyone asks, you're visiting Ernesto and Hilda and they're definitely not back in the DR." And then she was crouching beside Lev. "That, my friend, is a historically inaccurate portrayal of the man named Jesus of Nazareth, who, as everyone knows, had brown skin and kinky hair." And then she was brushing my daughter's curls from her face. "Sonya, later will you help me look for Charles Bukowski? He holds office hours in the ravine where we've also spotted bears, and if we're very quiet and the light is right, several dead refrigerators."

In this moment I recognized the girl I'd known. Irreverent, sharp, beautiful—I haven't even described her beauty yet—but more specifically, *nimble,* able to move through physical spaces and conversation like an Olympic swimmer through water, no deliberation, enjoying the glide, the flip kick, her buoyancy.

Persephone's voice from behind the bedroom door: "Charles Bukowski's a woodchuck."

"Also a poet, hon, he'd prefer you didn't forget that." Demeter tugged at a gap in the burgundy curtains.

The door opened. "You're taking too long," said Persephone. For a moment, before Demeter shut the front door and kicked a towel in place to staunch light, I saw her without glasses or hat. Her skin was the color of historical Jesus, many shades darker than Demeter's, her hair thick and wavy. She had Demeter's blue eyes. She jumped onto the plastic-covered couch, cocked her head at my kids. "You two can be the fairy council. We're putting on a play."

WRAPPING A RATTY RED fleece blanket around her shoulders, Demeter led me through the small kitchen and onto a concrete balcony that overlooked a ravine. There was a thin green mist from the fists of unopened leaves studding the high branches of the nearby trees. Down in the tangle of underbrush: wild irises like purple eyes.

"My parlor," she said, insisting I take the single folding chair, sitting cross-legged beside me. I asked about Persephone's sickness, her aversion to light. Was it a scratch on her cornea, a type of migraine, did she need an operation?

No, none of that, Demeter assured. "Can you believe it's called a dingle?"

"The condition with her eyes?"

"What? No, that . . ." She pointed to the ravine. "Real term. Middle English. I looked it up after I asked my downstairs neighbor what the deal was with trash pickup and he said, 'throw it in the goddamn dingle.'"

"Has it been going on for a long time, though? The eye thing?"

She reached up to tap the geraniums she'd hung from the metal railing. "Aren't they perfect here? Yeah, you could say a little while."

It was like this with every question I asked. What had doctors said? Had there been a precipitating event? Her answers were so vague as to basically contain no information. The doctor, she said, would explain everything at their upcoming appointment. I did learn that Persephone was twelve—three years older than Sonya, eight years older than Lev—but couldn't go to school because of the light sensitivity, so it was a miracle, Demeter said, I'd shown up with two kids for her to boss around. Then she pivoted, asking about me. In a quick summary, I grazed over my small successes, shined the spotlight on my larger failures.

She saw through me, again grabbing my arm. "A fucking book! Is it at the library? Look at you! Totally your mother's daughter."

"It came out ten years ago. And I've basically done nothing since."

"Nothing except, what, caring for a child during a pandemic and then a newborn, taking them on walks while your husband taught trumpet on Zoom? Holy shit."

It felt good to hear her repeat what I'd told her. And I have two kids versus her single kid, I told myself. My time had likely been harder than hers.

Her fingers on my forearm were cool. "Sucks hard that you lost your job, but how fucking cool that you were teaching. Professor Yalen, of course you were."

"Adjunct," I clarified.

"You sound like your dad. *Adjunct.* Who cares? I can see you as a teacher. You'd be a fantastic teacher."

I felt flattered. Even better, I felt remembered. In return, I wanted to know about her life, about which she'd been so dismissive. I'd compliment her, I'd show *I* remembered *her.* "So, what about you?" I asked, feeling my reliable engine starting up, humming to life.

THERE ARE WOMEN WHO bend toward men, for whom flirtation and calculations of how to please have become innate, second nature; and there are women who bend toward women. I'm not talking, specifically, about sex. I'm saying my métier was intimate conversation. I knew how to open girls up. It thrilled me to do so. My main trick—although it didn't feel so much a trick as the purpose to which my mind was built—was to find ways to match myself to the other person. I, too, had a difficult mother, tell me more. I, too, went to a school just like that, a camp just like that, lived one block over, loved that book, cried that much, longed for something I couldn't define. I knew those nightmares, that obsession, the wretched, tickling shame.

I learned to do this in middle school, when I would contort myself to extract the sameness, exaggerating preferences depending on who I was talking to. I wanted so badly to know what it felt like to be a girl not raised by my mother. By naming our similarities, however flimsy, I could reassure myself that we weren't so different. And it kept them talking.

This curiosity never left me. What was it like to be another woman? But by that day on Demeter's balcony, it had been a long time since I'd had the chance to find out. With other mothers, waiting at drop-offs and pickups and the benches outside swim classes, conversation seemed fenced in; no matter on what path I ambitiously set forth, we looped back around to an enclosed pasture—what did our kids eat, watch, say, when did they sleep, how did we limit and enrich them?

I worried—as Demeter demurred, "Last thirty years? Yeah, not much, you know. This and that." I worried this dullness was all that was left for me in my forties—oh, time of wine o'clock and Mom's night out.

As I got her talking, this concern quickly became irrelevant, but so were my skills at inserting myself into someone else's story. What could I say about the glory of the Rocky Mountains or her stepfather's fury or her mother's all-encompassing, almost mystical love?

After the summer we spent together in Northampton, Demeter told me, she moved with her mom to a small coal mining town in western Colorado for a Rainbow Family gathering. Mary Katherine soon left that putative family to start her own with Ezekiel—given name Bob Hammer—who existed at the point on the continuum of anti-government sentiment where hippie nudges against paranoid Christian fundamentalism.

Ezekiel distrusted schools, so Demeter stayed home, helping her mother with the three babies born in three years. They sold bread at the farmers markets in Carbondale and Aspen. Whenever she managed to meet a peer, whether the churchgoing daughter of a coal miner or a homeschooled hippie who carved his own lute, Ezekiel would deem them amoral. Her only socializing happened at summer camp in Colorado Springs where she was trained to protect fetuses, because nothing enraged Ezekiel like the murder of fetuses. He made several waterproof signs with photos of late-term abortions, and the family spent long days in front of the clinic in Cortez.

"I used to think about how your dad predicted it," Demeter said. "If I remained ignorant, he said, I'd vote for candidates who cared nothing about me, I'd vote against my interests like all poor people, I'd vote against social services and, well, I can't remember everything I'd vote against, but science was one and abortion was another."

"That's a lot to tell a twelve-year-old."

"I wasn't a typical twelve-year-old is something else he said. In any case, as you might imagine, things came to a head when I ran away at sixteen and returned home the next year, seven months pregnant."

"A baby?"

Pride bloomed on her face. "Micah's his name."

With that, she became older than me, as mothers are who have trudged the unbroken snow of future stages of childhood.

She gave birth in the living room. For the baptism, the family walked to the Gunnison River. She took her time describing the scene. Early spring snowmelt flooded the banks and churned rapids, but Ezekiel, in waders and gaiters and boots, walked with her baby far into the current. His hair was white and long, like Abraham ready to sacrifice Isaac. He talked about how the baby was born into sin, to an unwed and unfit mother who had conducted fornication. Ezekiel would do the Lord's work, he said, and raise him as his own son. Demeter was no longer welcome in his house.

She faked gratitude—*thank you, Ezekiel, sure, dunk my baby underwater*—and left with Micah that night, carrying him for an hour, postpartum bleeding through her sweatpants, until she found a ride to Delta. She kept hitchhiking, all the way to Denver, she said, where she submitted to the shaming of the Salvation Army until she raised enough money to move to New Mexico. She was seventeen. I was taking an SAT prep class, buying new Doc Martens for my senior year at Stuyvesant, feeling marvelously independent when I rode the Amtrak to D.C. to see a band at the 9:30 Club and sleep on a friend's uncle's couch, wondering why I'd never heard from Demeter.

I told her she was wonderful, incredible. I wanted her to know how impressed I was, but then I worried I'd laid it on too thick. She did laugh a little. "I mean, it's not like I had a choice." But she added, "It always was easy to talk to you like this. You were always kind to me."

"Of course. We were friends."

"No, but it's not a given. A lot of people weren't. When you're broke like we always were, a lot of people aren't. I thought your house was a fucking mansion, and you were so generous, shared everything. You were really kind."

Thinking about that summer, I felt myself flinching away from my younger self. Kind? No, I didn't think I'd felt kind back then. Instead, somewhat rotten. Uncomfortably acquisitive. Always paying attention to who got what.

Demeter turned from me to peer between the bars of the railing and then she sprang up, pulling me with her. "He's here."

Pressing her shoulder against my arm, bringing a smell of woodsmoke and sweat, although there was no fireplace in her apartment, she pointed. "Right there." A squat woodchuck nosed out of the brambly underbrush, pausing before an open garbage bag.

"Oh, Charles Bukowski. Do you see how seriously he takes himself? What a pretentious dude he is? God, I'm alone way too much." She leaned her head on my shoulder. They felt so nearby then, those agile girls we'd been—just off the balcony, somewhere in the dingle behind Charles. I carefully rested my hand on her dark hair. It held the sun's heat.

MY GOD, THE GOD of my mother, the almighty of the atheist Jews, he/she/they is a miserly god. A calculating god. A god who, like us, for we made this god in our own image, believes in tit for tat. This god will keep the plane aloft only if you pick up the Cheetos wrapper lying in a puddle of pee on the airport bathroom. This god will award you the job but only as recompense for taking away the lover you wanted more. Pick one. Don't be greedy. After Sonya was born, my milk didn't come in. Her face wrenched with hunger. For nine days my breasts grew ever larger as if I were being inflated by a pump operated by a sadistic thirteen-year-old boy, and I never stopped crying, the wetness of tears on my face and shirt becoming the normal state through which I ate and spoke and read articles about nursing. We fed Sonya with a dropper as suggested by a lactation consultant who spoke of the dire consequences of nipple confusion like an eighteenth-century preacher might talk about the wages of sin. Hungry, she never slept more than forty-five minutes at a stretch, until on the ninth day, at some lukewarm time between midnight and dawn, I dragged her bottom lip toward my wet nipple, which had grown into a little bullet. Instead of pulling away with rage, as had been happening, she suctioned and her throat began to pulsate like a frog's, pulling milk from some deep reservoir, and oxytocin sang euphoria into me.

I promised to never ask anything from the universal storage house, the divine, because I'd chosen. I wanted her above all. What was success? All I wanted was for her to stay alive. It's a stance of scarcity, sure, but back then I believed joy to be scarce.

As the woodchuck wagged its ass with a melancholy air, I risked bartering. I might give up something for more days like this.

Later, when she walked us downstairs, Demeter said, "So next week, that's Perse's doctor's appointment. We've been waiting a couple months. New patient and all, impossible to get in. Hopefully they'll tell us what's wrong, give us some medicine, and we'll book out of here."

"Wait, you're leaving? Back to New Mexico?" I could hear the disappointment in my voice.

"I fucking hate doctors. I fucking hope this is a good one," she said. Then, as if realizing I was there, she swung around and grabbed on to my arms, just above the elbows. "But, man, I'm glad I got to see you again. Little Eve, all grown up. Although you're the same. Totally the same. Isn't it amazing we got to be together after all this time?"

BUT SHE DIDN'T LEAVE. Of course not. Or I wouldn't have this story to tell. The story of Demeter and Persephone and the lost plant, the illness and its cure. The story of everything that changed and all the mistakes I made. What my miserly god gave me and what was taken away, tit for tat.

Ruth

...

She's already a genius, but anyone who finds that satisfactory isn't. *Exeunt,* she adds. *Attenuate.* The pangram came instantaneously today, letters in a beehive rearranging themselves linearly. *Exultant.*

Genius? A bone thrown to amateurs. Don't let it get to your head. Serious spellers know to reach for what's beyond.

A patron passing by on the library steps says, "Yo, Ruth, if you got the Louise Penny I asked for, turns out I actually want the . . ." Ruth nods, keeps her eyes on the screen until she's crowned Queen Bee. The delight of victory must show because a woman climbing the stairs grins back. She's no library regular. There's a pixie excellence to her hair and face. Maybe ten years younger, makes tan Carhartt overalls look sexy.

"Good news?"

"If you're a time-wasting nerd."

"Which I should assume you are?" The woman holds Ruth's gaze. Gorgeous mouth. Ruth hasn't seen her before, but she hasn't been looking.

"I'm more of a . . ." and then her train of thought derails, because, shit, shit, shit, she hasn't stopped her timer. She understands logically that the timer is compulsion atop compulsion. Why would it ever matter to anyone, including herself, how long it takes a fifty-two-year-old woman to spell?

And yet, milliseconds are passing, data of her victory lost to the void of ignorance. She opens the app, presses pause, calculates that it's been, what, four seconds since the woman interrupted? Or maybe longer. Would it be fair to subtract six seconds then? Seven?

By the time she looks up again, the woman's gone.

WHEN HER BREAK IS OVER AND SHE'S BACK AT THE CHECKOUT desk, she considers how she might finish that sentence. "I'm more of a . . ." Because what is she besides a nerd? A librarian, sure, but that's another word for the same thing. What else? Not a wife anymore. Not much of a mom—her son's in Texas. "Hot-but-reclusive butch widow" is how a friend suggested she describe herself on a dating app. Ruth never signed up.

These thoughts are interrupted by Eloise, the leader of the Northampton Ukulele Orchestra, who tells her that Community Room A is still occupied ten minutes into the band's allotted time. Eloise is dressed in her usual cosplay of a mid-century librarian—cat glasses, printed dress (pink poodles wearing sweaters today), elaborate bouffant hairdo. She assesses Ruth in her sweater-vest and Blundstones as if she's shown up unprepared for her own job. "This is unacceptable," Eloise says. "I'm starting to feel like the library isn't a safe space for the arts."

Lately, patrons rarely feel unpanicked. All their needs are pressing.

Ruth nods. She's a connoisseur of nods, meaning transmitted so efficiently that Eloise says, "Thanks. I'll meet you downstairs."

Eleven people of all ages clutch small instrument cases outside Community Room A. Pushing through, Ruth enters the room and closes the door, despite protests from the hallway. Of the thirty chairs arranged in a circle, only four are filled. This happens often: "We're expecting a crowd," a patron brags with self-importance, and nobody shows.

A man looks up from a black laptop. "Almost done here, Ruth. Fifteen minutes, max."

Stephen. But of course. Everyone she knows eventually shows up in the town library. Even her dead wife's ex-husband must take a turn in Community Room A. And who else but Stephen would so casually refuse to leave it?

She hasn't seen him since the funeral—five years ago—and his Iron John woodsman's mien has softened into something more like Santa Claus.

"Just to reiterate, so everyone's on the same page—for causality, we have one vote for 5G, one vote for what we could deem . . ." Stephen pauses to catch up his typing with his words. "Deem a Covid mutation."

Can anyone hurry Stephen when he's like this? His persuasive, podcasting voice. His slow, rabbinical plodding. Well, Ruth can. Twenty-six years ago, she rode circles around him on a yellow and black Kawasaki, shouting, *Man on the land, man on the land, penis on the property.*

"One vote for microplastics in our drinking water."

There's a sharp rapping on the door. Yes, Ruth could kick anyone out of a room, even Stephen, *especially* Stephen. But she takes a moment to remember fucking Ramona in a tobacco barn, then driving her on the Kawasaki back to her housing co-op. Stephen had been kneeling before the communal tomato beds. "Come on in! Mi casa es tu casa!" He couldn't imagine his wife cheating on him with this Korean dyke. Ramona led Ruth to the bathroom where she unzipped Ruth's jeans as Stephen shouted back to ask when Ramona was planning on starting dinner. In the kitchen, Ruth looked him in the eye. "Sorry we took so long."

"I know girls," he said. "Forever gossiping in the bathroom."

"And in summation, while we have no consensus on the cause of the condition that brings us here today, I propose . . ."

Her chest begins to constrict as it does when she wanders too far in the weeds of her memories. Because if Ramona knew what was happening now in Ruth's life, in the life of their son, Orion, she'd be screaming at the top of her lungs. Throwing books from the library shelves.

It frightens Ruth when she can't remember things. Like, how did Ramona throw?

"Out," she says. "All of you. Time's up. Let the ukuleles in."

Ruth heads back upstairs and sees the woman in Carhartts walking toward her. All she needs to do is smile. Or finally finish her sentence. Time-wasting nerd? I'm more of a . . .

But then it comes to her. How Orion would run to the meadow behind their house as soon as he finished dinner, Orion who calls himself Ryan, who's coming home next month for the first time since he enlisted nearly two years ago. The three of them played catch until it grew dark.

Ramona threw underhand. How could Ruth have forgotten? She'd played softball in college. "Imagine," Ramona used to say. "Softball! Before I even knew I was a lesbian."

Ruth's smiling now, but the woman on the stairs has already passed.

May

. . .

i

ON A SLOW AFTERNOON THE WEEK AFTER WE SAW DEMETER, I drove my kids to a grand stone edifice with turrets and vaulted ceilings and absolutely no grass to walk on: the town library. We descended to its basement. The children's section was—perhaps it still is, I wouldn't know, because the era of parenthood that seemed endless finally ended—a concatenation of little windowless rooms away from the gothic grandeur with signs announcing that children must always be within hand's reach. To come here was to deny yourself the precise pleasures of a library—rest and reading. Instead, you trailed your child, if singular, or herded your children, plural, from one room to the next.

We were in the small room with the fish tank when a girl from Sonya's grade appeared with her father. Noticing Sonya stiffen slightly, I decided to avoid an encounter with them, which greatly increased the challenge of the day's herding. Whenever this girl and father entered a room, I'd casually gather Sonya's stack of books, Lev's Playmobil family, and my tote bags and usher my kids into another room. The girl's father had an albinistic blond ponytail and a fleece vest. I'd seen him at school events, and I felt smugly victorious when, after nearly an hour of dodging, we managed to leave through the side exit.

Ascending the stairs, I heard him behind us. "Hey there! This is Fiona and . . ."

"Hi, Fiona," I said, smiling widely as I forfeited the game I'd invented because, of course, *of course,* my child needed friends far more than she needed to learn my aversive behaviors. "This is Sonya. And our little guy is . . ."

He cut me off. "Fiona says y'all moved here this year?"

"Yeah, I think Fiona and Sonya are in the same . . ."

"This is a wild guess, but was it the CP study? Are you pioneers?"

"Pioneers? Like, did we come on horseback to plunder?" He didn't smile. I wanted him to smile. "We drove a Subaru, actually."

"*Climate* pioneers? Did you use the app?"

A woman in a sari and a teenager in a Billie Eilish shirt descended the narrow concrete stairs. I edged to the side, pulling my children with me, but the man stayed where he was, requiring them to squeeze around him as he told me about a computer program he'd written to help people relocate as the world warmed. He was hoping to meet up with some pioneers who'd used his data to come to the same conclusion: That this sleepy college town would be one of the safest bets. He didn't want an influx, of course, which is why he hadn't publicized his choice. But if any of his followers made the logical leap, well, he'd want to know.

I was thinking that if the doctor didn't help Persephone, which wasn't what I wanted, of course, I reminded myself, but if perhaps this help took slightly longer than expected, they'd stay, at least a little while, and I could sit on the balcony with Demeter again and share the humor of this man, this pioneer who moved all the way from Palo Alto, when I noticed his expectant pause. I quickly extracted a noun from his monologue. "Data?"

He nodded as if that were just the question he was hoping for. "The predictive changes over the next thirty to sixty years. Not worst case, just inevitable. Floods in some places, total lack of agua in others, uncontrollable fires, melted asphalt, hurricanes, masses of refugees, air too smoke-filled to breathe, food shortages on a global scale."

Fiona had thrust a leg over the metal handrail and bent backward balletically, her blond hair curtained to the ground, but Sonya was carefully studying this man.

"We have to go." I frowned to show I wasn't a denier, far from it, I was afraid and angry, but also unsure that I could stand to have my child listen to this.

"Hold on," he said with urgency. "Aengus. With an *e*."

I shook the hand thrust toward me. "Eve. With an *e*."

"Oh, so there's another way to spell . . . no, ha, I get it." A small red welt appeared on his neck. I startled when he put a hand on my sleeve. "Want to know, Eve, how I landed on this valley?"

"Well, actually, like I said, we should get . . ."

"Yes, please," Sonya said seriously. "I want to know."

He gave her a surprised, paternal smile. "To start, we're far enough from the rising oceans. Coastal towns will be royally screwed. There's enough alluvial soil to feed a hundred thousand, easy. And we should be able to keep it at those numbers, since we're as far as you can get from the western droughts and the fire hell zones, and still a good distance from the northern borders. With mild legal structures in place, we can limit refugees."

"What's alluvial?" Sonya asked.

"Will we have some uncomfortably hot summers?" he continued, the rash on his neck colonizing more territory. "Sure. But when you compare it to, well, where'd you flee from?"

"We're from Brooklyn," Sonya said. "I go to P.S. 132."

"Went to," I corrected.

"Yikes! The Big Apple. Where to even begin? Flooding, for starters. Real estate depreciated by streets being literally underwater. How does nobody realize the city's surrounded by water? Sewage everywhere. Infestations of vermin. You've escaped just in time."

"WHAT'S INFESTATION OF VERMIN?" Sonya asked in the car. To pass the time before dinner, I'd driven us out of Northampton and up into the western hills where clear tubing linked the maple trees. A drive for the sake of driving.

Rats, I told her, but everywhere.

"Is it true?"

"Is what true?"

"New York will be underwater? What will happen to Grandma? What about Sophia and Marcus and Zora . . ." She began listing former classmates. "DeShawn and Tariq and the other Sophia and all three Maxes?"

By omission, by evasion, by euphemism, by outright denial. How do we lie to our children? "Look!" I pointed at an uninteresting white colonial house. "Isn't it gorgeous? The way the windows are . . . the way the trees frame the . . ."

"But is it? Is it true?"

I drove on. Barns and newly green fields and white churches and black cows and dense evergreen forests and sometimes a stream where the sun leaped on rivulets.

"No. It's not like that," I finally said. Sonya brightened, so Lev and I brightened, too—her happiness always satisfied me, as if I'd solved something important. I could feel my brain, so disturbed by what Aengus had brought up, settle again as we rolled down our windows and sang along to the radio.

ii

STEELY HAIR HELD BACK BY BARRETTES. GRAY SHIRTDRESS. Clogs with socks. My eyes, my height, my mother. She appeared without warning that Saturday, visiting our house for the first time since she moved me out of it when I was six. Irene drove her up from the city in a rented beige Corolla, and I made them tea.

"I remember that poor girl," my mother said, lapping Earl Grey against the edge of her mug. "That unfortunate name."

"I like it." With my back against the couch, my legs reached across the room (they're very long, that's true, but also it's a small room) to the nonworking fireplace in which Henry James had wedged cardboard painted with rockabilly flames in an attempt at winter cheer.

"A hippie's classic lack of forethought. What can a girl do with a name like Demeter? How could you ever just put your head down and get on with things?" My mom looked at Irene for confirmation.

"But she did. She did get on with things," I said. It had been nine days since I'd seen her, and I thought of her and Persephone back in the unflinching brightness of New Mexico. "She's incredible, actually. Impressive. She had her first baby at seventeen."

"That's hardly getting on with things," my mother said.

"Demeter? I don't remember a Demeter. Was she in your high school?" From the folding chair, Irene's red cowboy boots barely reached the floor. With her white hair newly dyed red and her green cape she looked like one of Santa's more Italian elves.

"No, this was my Rome year," my mother said. "Eve spent the summer up here, with Larry, and she wrote this desperate letter telling me everything came easily to Demeter, and she felt stupid."

"Well, I can't believe anyone could make Eve feel stupid," Irene said, gazing at me with the ample affection of the childless.

I felt a stone in my throat. A letter?

"You were terribly jealous of her, Eve. Don't you remember?"

All at once I could see myself at my white desk in the upstairs bedroom, writing with tiny, righteous script on a slip of airmail paper, consumed by envy the way a twelve-year-old can be. Remembering this, I felt silly and a little nervous and horrifyingly naïve, considering how difficult the years following that summer had been for her. "Is anyone hungry?" I asked, changing the subject.

My mother hugged her arms around herself. "What we are is freezing. How can you stand it, darling? We couldn't see our hands in front of our faces when we drove in. Spring is supposed to be joyful, but fog has settled on your town like a fat gray cat."

"I can turn on the heat," I said, pulling Lev's elbow off my knee. He was brushing his doll's hair with my hairbrush.

My mother sighed. "By the time it kicks in, you'll be sick of us."

Sonya brought her tin whistle to her mouth and played an energetic "Ode to Joy," lifting the temperature in the room.

In subconscious mimicry of Lev and the doll, that beautiful way our bodies communicate without our permission, my mother reached out and brushed my curls behind my ear. I stayed still at the surprise of her hands on me. My old trick. Make myself less conspicuous and her mood might not change.

When the song ended, Sonya offered to give my mom a tour of the house.

"A tour?" Irene said. "Did you know your grandma used to live in this very house?"

"For six years that felt like sixty," my mother said, taking her hand from my head. "How did I bear it?"

"She's talking about the first six years of my life," I said, although it wasn't clear who I was telling. "Let Sonya give you a tour."

THE HOUSE IS SMALL, built in the 1920s for mill workers. Not a mansion at all. Two bedrooms upstairs, one in which Henry James, who'd arrived earlier that morning, was napping. Living room and kitchen downstairs. Laundry in the unfinished basement. The short tour ended in the kitchen where I was shoving a tray of pizza bites into the oven. Lev pointed to the back door. "It a yard, but we don't go there."

"Shut up," Sonya said.

"Don't we?" my mother asked.

"Sonya 'cared of grass," Lev said. I held my breath.

"I'm not."

My mother turned to me. "How fascinating! A real phobia."

"Not a phobia. Just a thing about grass. Like a preference."

Nothing captured my mother's attention quite like a child's fears. While pregnant with me, she'd been writing a dissertation about the terrors and grotesqueries of children's fantasies. Soon after I was born, her adviser published her research as his own, claiming he knew she'd drop out when she became a mother. She quit in fury, and the prophecy was fulfilled. Still, she railed against the pablum of picture books and instead told me frightening fairy tales from Japan, Russia, Norway, in which mothers transfigured into ghouls or tree branches or the moaning wind itself, stories that terrified me but also became a part of me, like so much of my mother.

"Why, Sonya? What's so frightening about grass?" As always, my mother dug up the soil of terror. *Did you know?* she'd begin when I was small. *Did you know?* And then she'd tell me about nuclear war and Hitler's gas chambers and women hemorrhaging to death after back-alley abortions.

"She's fine like this, Mom. Really. We have it under control."

My mother kept her gaze on my daughter. "Could it be, Sonya, that it's dark under the earth? Darkness is terrible. Nighttime is the worst time of day. I dread it every evening."

Sonya did not yet have a fear of night. "Nighttime is fine," I said. "It's natural."

Sonya spoke very quickly. "All the time when people were dying, I didn't get it. Where would they go, you know? In Brooklyn there's parks, like Prospect Park or McCarren or Fort Greene, but there isn't any time when absolutely nobody's in the parks, when they could put the bodies down and then put the grass back in a way that we wouldn't know, because I looked and I never saw a . . . like a line in the dirt?"

"It's a problem. What to do with so many dead bodies," my mom said.

"We've explained it," I said. "Plenty of room in cemeteries, right, bunny?"

"I wrote down the number of people who died in New York," Sonya said, kicking the cabinet. "The number is forty-four thousand. Although maybe rounded up or down. You would need a lot of space to bury forty-four thousand people, rounded up or down. And then when we came here, when I saw so much grass here, I figured . . ."

"They took the bodies here?" my mom offered.

"No, they really didn't," I said.

Sonya kicked faster. "We could hear sirens all the time. So probably some sirens were going to the hospital in Brooklyn, but some sirens were taking dead people here."

My mother held out her hand. "Come with me."

THEY WERE OUTSIDE FOR the length of three *Curious George* episodes, enough time for me to boil potatoes and eggs, to steam green beans, mix a lemon vinaigrette, find a dusty can of tuna and some elderly greens. Enough time for me to remove the mail and sticker books and troll figurines and smeared cheese from our table, to lay a cloth, until I was interrupted by Irene, sitting heavily at my kitchen table, as if exhausted by the walk from the living room.

"You look wonderful, Eve. The full catastrophe. Isn't that what it's called? The kids, the mess?" She paused, took an overly breathy breath. "And your mom, how does she seem to you?"

"Good, actually. She seems, well, fantastic."

"Indeed. Top form."

And we laughed with familiar unease, because we both knew there was no way off the top but down. And nobody to catch her but us.

Irene had been my mother's agent and closest friend for thirty-eight years. Twice a week for nearly four decades, Irene rode the subway from Avenue C to circumnavigate the Central Park reservoir with my mother: two aging women, one unusually tall, the other remarkably short, distrustful of the monomania of joggers but never tiring of watching the bird watchers and Tai Chi-ers, and always, always talking. What I mean is, only Irene knew to monitor my mother's moods like I did.

She reached for my hand, her heavy silver and turquoise rings nudging into my bones. "This trip. The way she corralled me this morning, hell-bent. Drop everything, rent a car, I don't care what you've planned for the day, that sort of energy. Be gentle with her today, Evie. I worry we're headed for a crash."

AT LUNCH, MY MOTHER cupped her hands, the tips of her fingers glistening with salad dressing. "See, she needed to know that the flesh is burned away in a great fire, the organs, too, and what's left can fit in two adult hands. A white sandy mixture, I told her, of bone and tooth. Takes up very little space. Much less than a casket. And often not buried at all! She was interested to hear that people display urns on their mantelpieces. We laughed about a *living* room containing the rubble of corpses. She was enamored by the word *urn,* which we agreed makes such a pleasant feeling in the mouth. Try it!" She looked around the table. "Urrrrn. Urrrn."

"Urn," Henry James said.

"Urn," said Irene, glancing at me.

"Urn," I said reluctantly. I could hear the opening notes of *Curious George* from the upstairs bedroom.

"The interesting thing is cremation alone didn't appease her. She wouldn't step foot on the grass until I explained about the soul." My mother pinched a flutter of lettuce, dropped it in her mouth.

I felt the air turn thick. "What about the soul?"

"It's fascinating, really. Somehow she'd gotten the idea that a soul outlasts the body. She worried she'd step on a soul escaping the grass."

"But that's the whole thing about the soul," I said. "It does outlast the body."

"Except it doesn't exist. Which is what I told her."

"Our Joan," Henry James said, stabbing a potato. "Always ready to shatter any illusions."

She beamed at him. "You get it, darling. And as soon as I informed her—no soul, no spirit, we extinguish when our bodies give out—she did it. Onto the lawn! What, Eve? Why are you looking like that? It's not like I told her about deviant sex. Or neo-Nazis. And it was stunning really, how completely she recovered. Isn't that what you want?"

"I mean it is," Henry James said to me. "We want her prancing around the grass. And you saw Sonya when she came in. She's fine."

I rose from the table, feeling my face flush. "You don't know that!"

I also had looked fine when my mother told me about souls. I was five years old, and there was no human on earth as beautiful as my mother. *The worms will eat your body,* she said. *No afterlife. No heaven. No spirits rising in the air. Wormfood, each of us.*

Wormfood, I'd repeated with horror, seeing worms crawling in my own mother's eyeholes.

Wormfood, she'd said happily. Now, wouldn't that make a great title for a book?

And I hadn't been fine. No, not at all.

"Sure Sonya's fine, baby," Irene said, as if to remind me that I couldn't yell at my mother, because she was on the top, the brink, the apex, the pinnacle, with only one direction to go. "Fine, fine, fine," she chanted.

"How about this?" Henry James stood, the short bear-man who rearranged our home with his presence, turning chaos into coherence. He slid his arm around my waist and pulled me close. "How about I tell her that our souls live on in our art? I mean, think about it. Just yesterday, I was visiting with Josef Albers, conversing like two old friends."

"The painter? Still alive?" Irene asked. "And you know him?"

"Died in '76. And yet . . ." Releasing my waist, he danced into the center of the room, arms held high and tawny in short sleeves—he was never cold—his legs wide, the right one stomping and the left shuffling behind, his great stomach leading the way. Snap, snap went his fingers. "And yet I know his *soul.* I know it quite well. Because they exist for artists, don't they? Josef Albers's soul is his paintings. And you, Joan." He came behind my mother and put his hands on her shoulders. "Your soul is, with delicious irony, your *Wormfood* series, all five books."

She gazed up at Henry James. "And yours, darling? Your soul lingers in your recordings?"

"As long as they exist, I'm here. We'll tell Sonya that."

"See, Eve," my mother said. "You'd feel better if you got back to writing. Are you writing? You should be."

"When would I be? When exactly?"

Apparently I didn't hide my annoyance, because Irene began singing, "When when when! Isn't that Shakespeare? When shall we three meet again?"

"In thunder, lightning, or in rain." Henry James played along while squeezing my arm consolingly, but it didn't console. I thought about his days visiting with Josef Albers, his nights playing music while I was playing Chutes and Ladders, and wouldn't I love a little freedom to write, even though I would go crazy missing my children if I had to leave them four days each week? I felt the room fill with menace because we had no souls and I had no time to myself and I pressed my hand on my head, as I did when frightened.

Then it came to me—Demeter at six in a yellow halter top and blue beads, standing on her toes to place her palm on my head. As she talked about my soul, as sure of its existence as she was of the birch branch tapping against her apartment window, all my worry lifted and for a long time it didn't settle on me in quite the same way.

The memory astonished me. I'd been pressing my head like this for so long—for reassurance and comfort and the glint of possibility. And I'd completely forgotten its genesis.

The room cleared of menace and light danced off the tin foil. I must have smiled because my mother stood and touched my cheek. "Look at you, Eve. You're not angry. Oh, I was so worried you were angry. I just say things. They hop right out of my mouth. You'll get back to work. Shove them in the backyard. Write while they're crying. That's what I did with you. And you're fine."

iii

JOSEF ALBERS'S SOUL WAS A GREEN SQUARE, WITH A GREEN SQUARE inside it, with a green square inside that, with a central green square, from his series "Homage to the Square," an homage that had apparently been missing from Henry James's brain, he explained when he first brought me to the Guggenheim to see it with solemnity and jitters as if he were bringing me to meet his parents: an impossibility, since not only had they never left Moscow, they were also dead.

Up the helical ramp, beneath the bright white ceiling, our clasped hands sweaty, both of us nervous.

When we reached the painting, Henry James released my hand and looked down at his brown brogues. He shuffled his body as far from mine as possible, though the painting we stood before was quite small. "So, well, I guess this is it." He laughed dismissively. "Anyway, should we . . . coffee or something . . . early lunch?" I reached over to skim the back of his right hand, the black hairs of which excited me to touch, and he relaxed. Between me and the thrice-blocked square there was no silent explosion, no square peg fitting a square hole, which is how it had felt to him, he told me as we stood there, when he first happened upon it a few months after moving to this country. He'd come to see a Keith Haring exhibit. Hurrying past the permanent collection, he glanced over. Just a blur of green, and yet he'd been swarmed by somatic relief, as if he'd returned to his childhood house and it was waiting for him, untouched by new occupants.

Museumgoers had looked to see who was laughing, he told me, but he couldn't stop, the joke was too funny. His missing piece had been waiting here. In America, up a spiral, behind glass.

He stayed over an hour that day, but we left the painting after just ten minutes, exited the museum into the sensory celebration of hot-dog fug, honking taxis. Jubilant with the success of the meeting, he became more talkative than he'd been on either of our previous dates and also horny, leading me into Central Park and behind a boulder, his hands up my skirt. I began to wonder aloud if anything could give me the visceral fulfillment the Albers painting gave him. What would be my missing piece?

I knew already that it would be a baby, I'd known since I was a teenager, but you can't say that while being felt up on a third date. "What is the thing you care most about?" he asked. "Your dissertation?"

I was a graduate student in English at City College at the time. "Actually," I said, "if my mother didn't, I'd write fiction."

He pulled me to him. "Then this is what you must do. You must."

Eventually I quit the program and moved into his Williamsburg apartment above a bar where he worked whenever the gigs ran out. I began to write. Having a story to think about seemed to rearrange and saturate the entire material world; the internal changed the external so completely. At an art show, a painting's composition would suggest a new structure, or I'd understand that the colors *were* my characters in their purest form. I would see a face on the subway or the way uneven cornices on conjoined brownstones framed the sky and I would understand a plot change. Henry James said that this phenomenon of receptivity was why he never wore headphones like I did. Some days he walked for five or six hours, listening. He couldn't believe how much there was to listen to. "We need a name for this, for when every part of the world is singing, and it isn't singing to you in particular, that would be hubris, narcissism, but because of your attention to your work, you're able to hear the chorus that is always there. What should we call it? You're the English speaker, you're the word person."

I thought about his Josef Albers and I said, "Let's call it Greentime."

I believed that Greentime came to me only because I was living with Henry James, joining his malleable relationship to the temporal world. I taught three sections of rhet-comp and wrote in the evenings when he was out playing music and ate dinner with him at one in the morning. On days off, we'd work until we couldn't, which soon began to happen at the same time, our moods synchronized. Exhausted but antsy, hungry for the world, we'd go to shows, to galleries, to meet up with friends.

When my book was published, Henry James threw me a large party. My mother didn't come. "You don't want people showing up just to see me." For the entire month after my book's release, my mother was sick, either in bed or visiting a series of doctors.

When it was over, her sickness and my book tour, I said to Henry James, "Now I want a baby." I was thirty-three.

I remember that Henry James opened the kitchen window and crawled through to the fire escape. Smoked two cigarettes while I watched him. "There's no way. A baby would be the end of everything." He blamed my mother. "Think about it, Eva, she requires far too much of you already." Then he blamed the deaths of his sister and mother. His mental stability was too precarious, a house of cards that depended upon a lack of responsibilities, days free for Greentime, evenings earning just enough to keep himself in weed, eggs, sardines, and pita. A baby would crack open the Humpty Dumpty, he said. Topple the edifice. Scorch the Greentime. I was growing upset with his analogies.

"This is my life," I said.

"You say that to imply you should have more and more," he said. "So American. But a life is short. And ours has only enough energy and time and money for one thing, our work."

I told him a baby was all I wanted and he told me we couldn't have our lives with a baby and so I left him.

iv

"NOW WHAT?" SONYA ASKED. WE'D CROSSED OUR LAWN TO A PATH through the woods, a dense New England second growth, thin trunks crowding one another like passengers waiting on a subway platform. The woods sloped downhill to a large stream called the Mill River, which is the name of every large stream in Massachusetts.

"Now you play." Lev had already grabbed a stick and was hitting trees with it.

Sonya's face fell. "I don't know how to play here."

I hadn't expected this. I thought the woods would be obvious even to a child of the city once she stepped on grass. Wasn't the urge to touch and become part of the earth innate? "I know a game we can play," I said quickly to cheer her up.

"What is it?"

I thought of hide-and-seek; tag; mother may I?; red light, green light, but I was so tired. My mother and Irene had just driven away. Henry James was napping again. Soon I'd need to start dinner. I lay down on the carpet of pachysandra. It was all I could think to do.

Sonya lay beside me. "Am I doing it right?"

"Can you see the sky through the leaves above you?"

"I can!"

"And the shapes the branches make? And are you very still?"

She nodded. "What's it called?"

"What's what called?" I flicked a bug off my arm. I didn't know what kind of bug or what the trees were named—maple? Oak?—or what sprouts were emerging beneath the dead leaves, and I didn't think it mattered that I didn't know. I thought there was plenty of time.

"The game, Mom. What's it called?"

"What do you think it should be called?"

Outraged, she sat up. "I thought it was a real game. With a name."

"Of course it has a name." I looked up at all the new leaves, sharp green leaves and pale green leaves and scrambled green vines that climbed the tree trunks. "Green."

"Just green? That's not a name."

"Greentime." I regretted it right away, but after a moment of uncertainty, she settled beside me.

AFTER THAT, WE PLAYED Greentime every afternoon while Lev ran around us. My boredom frightened me. I felt my brain dying, although my body seemed healthy. I told myself to use the time to think. What do you want, Eve? I asked. I want to work. But you are working. Isn't childcare labor? Don't you believe in the value of work that has traditionally been done by women? I want to go home, I said. But you are home, I told myself. I want to want someone the way I used to want my mother. Or Henry James. I want to feel that again. Want something else. Your wants are all wrong. I want the phone to ring, I told myself, and just then it did, like the answer to a prayer, Demeter on the phone, after thirty-three days, asking me to come over.

Stephen

...

A FAIRY TALE IN WHICH A WISH IS GRANTED AND IT DESTROYS the wisher:

A woman longing for a man who murders her.

A child asking for candy from an abductor.

Cigarettes. The long game.

(The way they used to feel in the hand.)

Alone on a folding chair in the library meeting room, a Tupperware of scones on his lap, Stephen considers wishes gone rogue. He's early as always.

A man begging for his son to return home. A man begging time to reverse.

Driving on I-84 through Connecticut after dropping eighteen-year-old Kiran at Bard—this was nearly four years ago—he slid into unimaginable despair. Disoriented, he pulled into a pizza parlor and sat clutching a shaker of Parm. The picture of a faltering father. Middle-aged melancholy, how cliché. "It'll pass," his wife, Ritu, said. But that was the precise problem: the passage of time. It all just ended? The family, the noise, the soup, the bickering over music in the car, the jokes, most of which were at Stephen's expense, but who cared? When their older child, Priya, had left, there was still Kiran, cracking them up, needing a ride, listening to records with Stephen, talking endlessly.

Ritu set up an exercise bike in Kiran's room. "Don't you just love the silence?"

Stephen suspects he's a dog, a wolf, an elephant; a pack animal grows bereft without a group. As soon as he'd left his childhood home, he'd headed for communes, co-ops, collective houses, until he created his new family.

Packless, he turned old. Bent down for the newspaper and his lower spine shrieked. His body mutinied, some parts lagging, others rushing, as if even the heretofore well-run collective that was Stephen's corporeal self was falling apart. As all collectives eventually did. The final fight and everyone moves out in a rage, utility bills unpaid. He bought a lumbar pillow.

After two decades as a school counselor, Ritu began a doctorate in education, rented a room in Providence for weeknights. Increasingly for weekends, too.

But Stephen continued to fantasize scenarios that might bring Kiran home. And then, six months into Kiran's freshman year, the second week of March, he watched his son unpack his clothes, filling up his childhood bureau. A worldwide pandemic.

Even as Stephen worked to ignore the dark coincidence of wish fulfillment, he couldn't admit how great he found the months of quarantine. Well, maybe he admitted. Maybe he told everyone. Puzzles on the kitchen table. Catan on the screened porch when Priya visited from Boston. A table has four sides, a board game needs four players, a family should have four people, each holding their own trading empire.

When Bard invited sophomores back to campus, he assumed Kiran wouldn't be interested. Why Zoom from a dorm? They'd ordered oil paints, sourdough starter, harmonicas.

But he went. Stephen emailed links to articles that might appeal to his son but became increasingly aware that he held an obsolete understanding of Kiran's interests. This boy who once told his father everything now said little. On Kiran's socials, Stephen found only canned constructions. *Lowdown tired af. TFW your whole life is a dumpster fire.* "He's depressed," Stephen told Ritu. But when they visited on Parents' Weekend, Kiran shimmered with vibrancy.

His visits home were short and infrequent, but this past March Stephen insisted on his attendance at Ritu's fifty-fifth. It was unusually warm and Stephen carried a picnic lunch up Mount Tom. Kiran napped at the summit while Ritu and Priya took selfies together. Stephen sat beside his sleeping son, eating an orange. So happy, but still not satisfied, he dared wish for more: If only you were here all the time.

A man making the same mistake twice.

About a month later, wearing eyeliner and costume jewelry and unable to stop throwing up, Kiran returned. Light was bothering him.

At the suggestion of their pediatrician, they took him to a neurologist in Boston who found nothing wrong but sent him to a rheumatologist who sent him to an infectious disease doctor who sent him to an ophthalmologist who suggested a neurologist in Boston.

STEPHEN EATS A SCONE as he waits for the arrival of his compatriots in Community Room A. This is the designation—compatriots: *with country*—he accords anyone engaged in collective decision-making. He's made a life of cooperative movements—first the farm in South Amherst where he met Ramona, then the childcare collective after he married Ritu and Priya was born, then a copy shop, a tortilla bakery, a tea company, and now a bike shop. This meant that a significant percentage of his hours on earth have been spent in meetings, and he tries to regard everyone, no matter if they drone on or disregard Robert's Rules, as co-builders of a shared nation.

At last, a fellow citizen walks into the room to join him in the sad land of medical mysteries. Tanya Anguila wears slacks, a white cable cardigan. She cleans a chair with antibacterial wipes, folds a paisley scarf and sets it on the seat. He thrusts his Tupperware of scones toward her. She declines, removing from her purse a small container of cereal.

Tanya's here for her husband, a forensic accountant, now living in their darkened bedroom. The Anguilas believe this illness is caused by a Covid mutation.

Next comes Annie Bordeaux. This week's necklace is a large brass octopus over a crimson tee. Her sister, a painter, has returned to her childhood bedroom in Maine. Annie originally blamed aliens and now is team 5G.

Tim Oliphant walks in and reaches for the scones before he sits down.

Tim is a drummer in three local bands, spanning genres from reggae to shoegaze, and the manager of a pot shop in Easthampton. His girlfriend is now back home with her parents in Tacoma. They blame microplastics in water and food.

"Anyone else coming?" Tanya asks.

They all stare at the closed door. They've met every week for a month now, and nobody new has come forward with this strange illness, no matter the flyers Stephen has left at the food co-op and coffee shops. The enthusiasm they felt in the beginning—there were others out there—is beginning to deflate.

"Let's get started then," Stephen says.

AS TANYA READS THE minutes from the last meeting, Stephen imagines Kiran's friends watching the proceedings. Pay close attention, Stephen tells them in his head. No matter how little seems to happen here today, the collective is the heart of democracy.

How could a boy have so many friends? A couple weeks ago, just after Bard's graduation, which Kiran didn't attend—who knows when he'll finish his last semester—they pulled up to the house in vans and cars. They haven't left.

Despite a thick cloak of irony, faces that say nothing matters, Kiran's friends have turned to hocus-pocus, consulting the compass app on their phone to set crystals around his room, talking about astrology with the minutiae that one usually reserves for political polling data. They're lost, all of them. The pandemic upended their world, tearing them prematurely from the chrysalis of college, confusing chronology, and now they're unable to imagine a future.

With their androgynous hair, their baggy pants, their particularities about tea. Some of them won't eat meat and some will eat only meat, and although Stephen has passed through both phases several times, they aren't interested in hearing from him. They roll their eyes when he stumbles over their pronouns, laugh when he responds that his ex-wife was a lesbian. He is somehow as dull to them as his father was to him, despite the life of invention he's created in these woods. Unlike him, they're hoping to tether themselves to the corporate world—one of them is always at the kitchen island where the Wi-Fi is strongest, saying the most banal and subservient things on Zoom for a job interview.

Is it too much to ask for time alone with his son?

A few days ago, six new friends arrived, announcing they were going to live stream the darkness Kiran lives within. They were, they explained, an art collective. At last.

"I'm sure Kiran told you that I've been a lay scholar of collectives my whole life," Stephen said. But no, Kiran had not told them, and through the wall, he could hear them laughing. Lay scholar. No, *I'm* the lay scholar. Imma show you some lay scholarship right here.

TANYA AGAIN SUGGESTS THEY write an op-ed for the *Daily Hampshire Gazette.* While Stephen agrees that this is an eventuality—he's written dozens of letters to the editor, a literary form he excels at—he cautions the group not to be too hasty. They won't be respected until they reach a more definitive understanding of the situation, a consensus as to causality that could be attained with a few more members.

At this, Tanya calls him a monster. Is he really hoping anyone else suffers the way her husband is suffering? Stephen writes this in the minutes: *Stephen is a monster.*

There isn't much else to talk about. Like Narcissus staring into the pool of water, they've all become infatuated with their own theories, although they posit a few more: mold, pesticide runoff, toxic sludge. Stephen grows weary at the thought of all the toxicity. I can see why you won't leave the safety of my house, he imagines telling Kiran's friends. Why you want your calming crystals and chanting. We've corrupted the very atoms of existence, and the Frankenstein's monsters of our profligacy are coming to get us one way or another.

THEY FINISH UP AND leave early—no need for Ruth to kick them out again. Stephen doesn't want to return home to be ignored by the swarm of youths. At Flywheel, his bike collective, he opens the mail, shoots the shit, takes from a shoebox a few of his rarer bootlegs that might impress, although Kiran's friends insist that even if they were interested in his music there isn't a concert that can't be found online now. At the food co-op, he buys large quantities of innocuous root vegetables for a soup that Kiran's friends will find reasons not to eat.

He enters his house bracing for them. It's not strange that the kitchen's empty—Ritu's still in Providence most of the time—but something's off. He heads upstairs, hearing none of their ambient noise, not even when he presses his ear to Kiran's door. No answer to his knock.

He runs outside and yes, how had he missed it? Their cars are gone. He feels certain that Kiran's left with them, so certain that he scrambles upstairs and doesn't even knock, just opens the door and switches on the light.

"What the fuck, Dad."

Stephen trips over a sneaker, relieved to see his son. "When are they due to return?" he asks, although he already understands they'll never be back, and what felt different about the house was the absence of their clutter, their sweatshirts and tripods and laptops, everything except their chargers, which for months he will find in odd places—in his bathroom, in the basement (they unplugged the dehumidifier), behind a bookcase—and which they'll ask for in frantic texts. He won't send them. In this skewed world where his wishes are granted, he alone will watch his son's isolation grow until he can hear it from every room.

June

. . .

i

THE DAY AFTER DEMETER CALLED, WE LEFT OUR SANDALS MINGLING with theirs on the landing. What did I expect? A room bright with sunshine. A child smiling.

I heard myself say a surprised "Oh!" as Demeter shut the door behind us and we were in darkness. Not total—there was the green light of a smoke alarm dulled by masking tape, and beneath the window, the low-voltage night-light muffled by a black tank top—but darkness still. I think this was the first moment I took Persephone's illness seriously. Before, I'd thought of it—Demeter had led me to think of it—as temporary, a nuisance, easily fixable. "Oh, hello!" I added quickly, drawing out the round sounds, to make it seem that my first "Oh" had been a warm-up for this greeting, but I felt so worried for both of them, worried for a world in which this could happen to a child.

Persephone told Sonya and Lev she'd written a play; they were just in time to start rehearsing. I couldn't discern a note of false cheer, although surely she was upset. When Demeter and I reached the balcony, I saw on her face a firmness. "The doctor wasn't . . . he didn't . . . ?" I said tentatively. "I'm so sorry."

She leaned against the railing, her eyes focused just behind me, seeming to shrug off my sympathy.

I was relieved for the chance to stare at her. I might as well describe her beauty now. Blue eyes like a troubled sea, long bangs she cut herself, black hair to her waist with half a foot of frayed split ends, delicate nose, prominent cheekbones, broad mouth. Large, goofy smile.

Aging face, you might add. Weathered. Too much desert sun. Whatever. As it did when she was a child, her beauty felt like mine. Like it gave something to me. I don't know how to explain this. I'm overly tall and curly-haired with a strong nose and wide forehead, a face that I hated until I was around twenty-four and since then have found delightful—but nothing like Demeter's. I'm no stranger to envying women, and yet I felt at that moment, as I'd felt before, that her beauty opened a door inside me.

She shook her head and looked at me. "Yeah, so the doctor barely let me speak, left after a few minutes, and a nurse drew her blood."

"Oh, Demeter, how awful."

"I've been calling the office. And finally they agreed to give us a follow-up. But the thing is, I don't want to go back alone."

"Do you want . . ." I felt strangely shy to volunteer, although she was clearly asking.

"Would you, Eve? Just, like, moral support."

"Of course, if it would . . ." Then I saw my opening. "But what did he say was happening to her?"

"Same as all the doctors. They all say the same thing."

"Which is?"

The sliding door opened. My son's elfin face. "I hungry. You have cookies?"

Demeter picked up Lev and perched him on her hip. "They tell me I'm lying. Lev, light of my life, what should we do? I have no cookies at all." She pressed her forehead against his. "They all say I'm lying." Then she made a noise, an aggravated, defeated sigh that made Lev laugh. "The thing is, I really, *really* thought it would be different here."

THE MOBIL STATION, SHE said, was just a six-minute walk from her apartment if we cut through the farm run by the vocational high school. I set a quick pace, thinking I'd be nervous to leave my children but found I wasn't. Not with her. I felt instead the sensuality of liberation. The soft wind on my neck, the small brave violets scattered beside the brick apartment building, the lowing of new calves when we reached the meadow.

The headaches began last September, a week into Persephone's sixth grade, Demeter said, breaking the silence, which made two cows lying in tall grass turn in synchrony to stare. Lethargy, too, and an uncharacteristic peevishness. Her pediatrician ordered tests. Not Covid, not Lyme, not strep. Strangely, at night, when fevers usually spike, she'd gain her lost energy, asking to draw, to read, to eat, all of which she was too fatigued to do during the day. Demeter drained her savings bringing Persephone to seven more doctors, all clueless, even when she started vomiting at school. The school counselor said if she missed more days, she'd need to repeat sixth grade. According to ads on the radio, Albuquerque's premier pediatrician was Dr. Fine. Demeter maxed out her credit card on an appointment to which she brought a chart of Persephone's symptoms plotted against various light stimuli over seventeen weeks. He told her that there were two options.

"What were they?" We'd reached the gas station and were standing in front of its mini-mart, in the cherry-sweet vape haze from two teenage girls.

Demeter smiled slightly. "His options? That either she was lying or I was. And he laughed. He fucking laughed and said she had me wrapped around her little finger. That nobody is sick only part of the day. That my child was spoiled, too used to getting her way."

She pushed open the doors.

I caught up to her at the snack aisle. "But wait, what happened next?"

She was crouching, her skirt pooling on the linoleum as she grabbed boxes off the bottom shelf. "Chips Ahoy or Oreos? Which should we get for darling Lev?"

I bought both, along with Diet Cokes for each of us, and a bag of chips we ate as we headed back across the field. She asked what I'd been up to over the past month. I couldn't bear to mention Sonya's newfound grass-walking skill, my child moving further into the world. One of the problems with having been a jealous person, having worshipped a miserly god, is that I worried my own good luck could cause pain the way the luck of others had, at times, hurt me, how my stomach clenched when I'd seen girls with mothers who so clearly adored them, mothers who visited our college, took us out for dinner and asked about our lives. "Not really anything," I said and repeated my previous question. "But what happened, after the terrible Dr. Fine?"

"Child Protective Services is what happened." She licked salt from her fingers. "A man and woman at my door called in by my doctor. If I didn't send Perse to school, they'd find a family to take care of her while I quote 'got help.'"

"Jesus Christ."

"I was so scared. We hightailed it to Olympia. I didn't even hug Micah goodbye, which kills me."

"Olympia? In Washington?"

"Darkest place I know. I spent a month there at sixteen, just before I was pregnant, a little gutter punk. And I swear for the entire time my clothes never dried. My socks grew mushrooms. Persephone and I rented this back room in an apartment owned by hardcore vegans. Sweet couple, but they were always trying to get me to give up burgers—not gonna happen, by the way—and one day the lady told me about this tick in South Carolina that can make you allergic to red meat. She kept going on about the great corrective of nature, leading us from our unwholesome habits, but I wasn't listening, because that's when I realized. The tick."

"What tick?"

"On her neck. At a wedding here in Northampton last August," she said, as my phone rang in my pocket. "A friend from way back. My mom came with us, bought our tickets. And a month later, Persephone's sick."

Sonya's voice on the phone sounded high-pitched and far more babyish than she did in person. "*Puh*sephone wanted to show us the *beya.*"

"A bear? Where are you? Where's Lev?"

"Yeah, a beya. Charles the beya. We went to see and now she's shaking."

I could hear Persephone in the background saying "woodchuck, not bear" and then Demeter snatched the phone from my hand. "Sweetheart, can you get the red blanket from our bed and wrap it tight, tight, tight around her? We'll be there so soon."

Back at the apartment, she ran the bath, and I reached for Sonya and Lev, kissing the sweat in her scalp, his soft knees. Lev wriggled away, but Sonya had been scared and leaned against me. We all squeezed into the tiny bathroom, which smelled of citrus soap and pee. Sonya sat on the bathtub rim, Lev on the closed toilet, swinging his legs. A high opaque window let in enough light for me to see the pale blue tub, the grayish water, and the girl's smooth, narrow limbs like driftwood, beginning to shake again. Demeter held a washcloth to her eyes.

To lighten the mood, I suggested we play I'm Thinking of an Animal. Persephone's was peacock. Sonya's lamb. Nobody could guess Lev's until he admitted the animal he was thinking of was actually a sandwich.

A tick? I kept thinking that a tick was fine, a tick was understandable, treatable. I felt confused, though, that she hadn't told me the first time I came over. Once the kids were listening to the sonorous voice of Zeus via audiobook on the couch and Demeter was on her knees, scrubbing the tub with Comet, I asked why.

"Honestly? I didn't think you'd believe me. Nobody does."

I rested my palm on her shirt, her backbone knobby and warm. "I believe you."

"Do you really?"

"Dem. Of course."

"So you'll come?" She turned abruptly. "You'll come to the appointment next week?"

"I wouldn't miss it." In my exuberance I added, "There's nowhere I'd rather be."

ii

I EXPECTED HER TO DIRECT ME TO THE OFFICE OF A SPECIALIST, but she told me to turn at the familiar sign of an apple with a smiling worm. I knew this place from our own family's visits here—strep tests, hives, splinters—although not this particular pediatrician, young and redheaded, who brought an antsy energy into the room, chewing gum, spinning on a wheely stool. "Mom brought a friend?"

"Eve Yalen," Demeter said from a wooden bench, where she sat with her arm around Persephone. She said my last name slowly, even spelling it for him, which surprised me.

"Just here for moral support." I was leaning against the examining table; its paper crinkled when I gave a little wave. My instinct was to ingratiate myself to authority.

"You thought you needed moral support? Well, I'll say again what I said on the phone. Your daughter is a healthy-mealthy." He kept his eyes on his laptop screen as he talked. "You said you saw a tick on her. Okay. No rash, but I think, well, let's be cautious, let's test. As I told you, all the tests are negative, so not sure what we're doing here. I say, whew, mom, dodged a bullet." He glanced from screen to me. "Yalen? Any relation to the author, um, Jill, um . . ."

"Joan. Joan Yalen," Demeter said. "The *Wormfood* series? You read it?"

"About a thousand times. Loved it. I mean, I *loved* it. Dark as hell, but funny, too."

"Joan's brilliant. Just like her daughter here."

I felt heat on my cheeks. Not because of the compliment, or not entirely, but because it occurred to me that Demeter hadn't wanted me there for moral support. No, it was for my name, because I could align her with brilliant Joan, with fame and respectability. I'd been in this position before, although not with Demeter. But why not? I thought it over quickly, why shouldn't she use my mom?

"Joan Yalen? I'll be darned. Well, Eve Yalen, what we have here is a case of horses."

"Horses?" Demeter asked.

"Horses," he repeated, looking only at me. "You're standing on a road and you hear hoofbeats. What's causing them? Zebras? Not likely." He turned to Persephone. "Have you read *Wormfood*? You like to read?"

"I listen to audiobooks. In Africa it could be zebras."

"Good girl." He winked. "Keep reading."

"She got the tick bite in Northampton," Demeter said, holding out a folded square of yellow paper—the graph of symptoms against light stimuli over seventeen weeks. "What we're wondering is, has anyone else shown up like this? Because there's no other explanation."

He set his laptop on the examination table and rolled his chair close to her. "Here's what I say to kids. Add 'yet' to the end of every sentence. Maybe you say, I can't ride a bike. Or, I can't shoot a basket. Stop. Add 'yet.' Get it? I can't ride a bike *yet.* You don't have another explanation *yet.*" He turned again to Persephone. "Tell Mom to make sure you get outside. Kick a ball. What school do you go to?"

Persephone glanced at Demeter before saying softly, "I don't go to school."

I could almost hear it, how the mood dropped. "What's that?" All levity was gone from his face.

"She'd get sick," Demeter said. "We're telling you." There was a thickness in her voice that sounded like annoyance but that I could tell was fear.

He tapped one of Persephone's knees. "So, kiddo, when you used to go to school, and you complained of an upset tummy, what would happen?"

"My mom . . . she'd pick me up?"

"And then, at home, walk me through it. What next?"

"We'd eat crackers? We'd play some games?"

"You like all this attention from Mom?"

Again Persephone looked at Demeter, but Demeter's eyes were closed, her head resting on the wall. "I mean, I like my mom?"

"How about you remove your hat and sunglasses?"

Demeter opened her eyes. "It's not immediate. The reaction. Could take ten minutes, an hour. Maybe the next day. It's all right here." She unfolded the yellow paper.

"What I'm thinking is, who doesn't want Mom's attention? Who doesn't want to skip school?"

All the muscles in Demeter's neck tensed. "She's not faking it." Her voice was so quiet. "She would kill to go to school."

He rolled backward, pushing off almost violently, and grabbed his laptop. "There's the law," he said. "There's reporting required."

Demeter pulled Persephone close. "Well, we're homeschooling."

"Okay, great." He was looking at his screen, typing quickly. "And the district has your letter of intent and educational plan? Your curriculum? I think I can find it all here if you don't have it on you."

I became aware of a baby screaming behind the thin wall, of my heart calling, emergency, emergency.

"Let's take a step back." My businesslike chirp surprised even me, like I'd been possessed by a flight attendant. "How many weeks until summer break? Two? It's basically summer. That gives us plenty of time to enroll her for the fall. JFK Middle School, that's where she'll go."

"Well . . ."

I smiled at him, the smile of a daughter of a once-famous woman. "How about we make a follow-up appointment on our way out? For September. Persephone will tell you all about her teachers then. Are you excited, Perse? A brand-new school."

"You'll make sure?" He glanced nervously at the closed door, then back to me. "I'll need to see her proof of enrollment."

"You can count on it." I lowered my voice. "Hey, just out of curiosity, what was your favorite *Wormfood*? You know everyone chooses the finale, but mine's book three, weirdly."

A lie. I hated them all. And calculated flattery, too. Guys always wanted to believe they were unusual for loving the third book.

"Seriously? Bring it here." He showed me his pale palm. "Team Three all the way." I slapped him, not as hard as I wanted. "Joan Yalen, man. Some dark nights those books got me through."

DEMETER HELD IT TOGETHER until we reached the balcony and then she lost it, screaming "Fuuuuck" so loudly that Charles Bukowski snuffled away from female pain. "My god, Eve. It was so close."

"She's here, right there." I jutted my chin toward the apartment where Persephone lay on the couch. "She's okay."

"Because of you. That's why. She'd be in fucking custody otherwise."

"No. They wouldn't do that."

"Child Protective Services would've caught us before we left the office. Or whatever it's called here. DCF. He doesn't believe me. Nobody believes me." She started gnawing at her thumb.

I pulled it from her mouth, my palm wettened from her spit. "I do. You know I do, right?"

She looked away; her shoulders shook.

"Do you hear me? I believe you. And I believe Persephone will get better." This wasn't like me. I made caveats. Said the worst would happen. I'd been schooled in crossed fingers, salt over the shoulder, spit three times; only idiotic naïfs spoke aloud their deepest desires.

"But do you really think so? Do you really?"

"I really do." It felt dangerous, but good, too—like sledding down a steep hill. People just talked like this? I tried it again, saying what I wished the doctor had. "This isn't her life forever. We don't know how. And we don't know when. And that sucks. That more than sucks. But I know it's not forever. And that doctor is an asshole."

She turned to me. Strands of hair stuck to her wet cheeks. "No."

"No, he is, Dem. He is."

"No, Eve, you need to put 'yet' at the end of each sentence. He's an asshole *yet*."

iii

USUALLY LEV AND I CAME LATE TO THE SCHOOLHOUSE GATES SO WE wouldn't see the other parents circling up in cliques, like jellyfish in a flat sea. I hadn't lived here for the early bonding years, for newborn group and baby yoga and preschool trampoline parties and Tot Shabbat and kindergarten potlucks. I belonged to no group.

Early for once, I watched them gather, bracing myself with the petty but pleasing thought that my friend was smarter and funnier and more beautiful than any of them, and then shouldered awkwardly into the conversations, one after the other. Everyone was polite, *oh, hi,* and *remind me whose mom you are?* Buoyed by my success with the doctor, speaking in the same efficient chirp, I kept expecting someone to say yes, and then I'd have helped Demeter again. But my question was a buzzkill. Light sickness? Ticks? God no. Wow. Nothing like that. I backed away.

Only Aengus, his long white-blond hair loose, seemed happy to see me. "Eve with an *e*!" He invited me to a party in two weeks. "Solstice. Longest day," he said proudly as if he'd invented the turning of the Earth around the sun. "Annual tradition. The seasons are super important to my family. If you don't mark them, do the seasons even pass?"

I didn't know what to say to that.

"So you'll come? You and the fam?"

Once I agreed, he asked about my summer plans. Travel? Camp? I hadn't thought of camps. Or rather, I'd thought that I couldn't afford camps. He described a complicated schedule, each child at a different avocational site each week. Farm camp, sled dog camp, gymnastics camp, rock 'n' roll camp, rock climbing camp, karate camp, nature camp, etc. He finished with a small, bewildered shake of his head, as if the camps were a burden rather than a great luxury.

I asked if his kids generally spent a lot of time outside.

Worried lines appeared on his forehead at such a question. "Only every minute possible."

"What about ticks? Have they ever been bitten?"

"Ticks? You can't worry about ticks." His smile was pitying. "Nothing you can do about them, so we don't. Worry that is. We pick them off the kids and dogs. Never gotten sick. What makes people sick, the real thing, you should know, is sucking on the teat of distraction. Screens," he clarified.

"That one again," I said.

Aengus raised a finger. "Let me just jot down a note." Squatting, he pulled out a spiral-bound journal and pen from his bag. "Studies confirm that if you write by hand, it's written in your memory as well. Poking at our phones doesn't do it. Neuroscience, especially when it comes to screens, is such an emerging field. It's an exciting time for all of us." He looked optimistically toward the school's double doors as if brain scientists were there, waving to him. He stood up again. He had not jotted down the note.

iv

WE DIDN'T MAKE IT TO HIS PARTY. HOLDING MY PHONE TO CONtrol the music from the back seat, Sonya read aloud Demeter's text—Bonnie canceled!—and I swerved away from Aengus's house and toward the Coolidge Grove Apartments.

This was our fourth visit in the two weeks since I went to the doctor with her. I would have visited whenever Henry James was away. My kids, too, were always eager to climb the turrets and descend into the catacombs of Persephone's imagination. But we were at the mercy of Bonnie.

Shit, Bonnie needs me, Demeter wrote the previous two times we were headed over, and we drove home and played Greentime with desultory dedication. Who was Bonnie? Clearly I'd missed an explanation. I tried to imagine the sort of job that might require Demeter's agile intelligence and energetic presence so urgently yet so erratically. Was Bonnie a lawyer? Museum curator? Dean at one of the colleges? "She drives me batshit, but you know I love Bonnie," she said, assuming familiarity. It seemed the time to ask had passed me by.

On this visit, as the sun dipped beneath the tallest branches of the dingle, I found a workaround. "Tell me," I said, handing her a can of iced tea I'd been planning to bring to Aengus's party, "every job you've ever had."

The heat and humidity had arrived that week, and she rolled her can up one arm as she stared at me. Then she smiled. "You're weird, Eve. Nobody's ever asked that."

But I was interested in everything about her. Well, I still am. I think I remember the list:

Assistant to a weaver in Taos, driving with baby Micah as the sun rose over the Sangre de Cristo Mountains.

Stucco plasterer. Micah in a Pack 'n Play beside the radio.

Day care worker, informally, for the neighborhood kids. They lived in a trailer park where Tibetan flags fluttered in the wind alongside yellow Don't Tread on Me flags. A mostly harmonic truce. Anyone would water your herb garden if you were camping at the hot springs.

Cleaning houses. For years nobody cared if there was a kid stoned out on *SpongeBob* in the corner, but they balked when the twelve-year-old grew taller than his mother. After neighbors called the cops, she started leaving him at home.

Then Persephone was born and out came the Pack 'n Play. Hired by a friend who installed fireplaces, another who owned a frame shop, a third who ran a landscaping crew.

Cleaning houses again. Three great years hired to clean the rarely used third home of an aging musician, taking Micah and Persephone to swim in the heated pool.

And for her soul, she said, she also worked at various times as a:

Costumed reenactor at a historical society; masseuse at the hot springs; narrator of a series of videos by the tourism council; occasional late-night DJ on the public radio station.

But all that ended during the pandemic, which she spent as an Instacart shopper. Micah was in Albuquerque. Persephone on FaceTime so Demeter could watch her remote schooling: cursive, fractions, life cycle of a trout.

Cleaning houses again after that. Now through Airbnb management companies. Feces on the bathroom floor, raw meat smeared onto the counters, all the base animal instincts released by the intimate act of sleeping in the bed of someone you'll never meet.

"Bonnie's a thousand times better, even though she's crazy," Demeter said. "There's only four of us working for her—and she brings all the cleaning supplies. And you know how she always fits me in."

I lifted Bonnie like a dollhouse figurine from her book-lined office and placed her before a vacuum. "Mmm, yeah," I said cautiously, feeling I'd been careless with my imagination. So taken with Demeter's dynamism, I'd ignored what was possible with a kid in the dark, no permanent address, no high school diploma.

"Well, I think that's all." We were at the railing of the balcony and Demeter's face was close to mine, her breath sour but not off-putting.

"Wait, no. Jeweler. I sell the beaded earrings, you know, like we made together? And other stuff, bracelets, necklaces. I have this setup for craft fairs. Black velvet cloth, jewelry hung on skulls my mom finds hiking, very O'Keeffe."

"She couldn't stay away," she said, when I expressed surprise that Ezekiel let her mom visit. "My mom, well, you remember her. She's pure love."

Every few months, Demeter explained, her mom would claim she was seeing a doctor in Denver and spending the night with a friend, and then she'd drive to Demeter in New Mexico. Even though he distrusted doctors, Ezekiel allowed this, because like everyone he was afraid of his wife dying, afraid of loneliness. She'd say a few prayers over Micah, and later Persephone as well, and they'd head out along the arroyo to collect rose quartz and skulls and mica with a small *m*. "We'd hold hands, all of us."

Just then the doorbell chimed its two notes. "Probably Aengus sent a pioneer to tell us to come to the party." I was laughing at my own joke when Demeter dropped her iced tea off the balcony and ran inside. I found her kneeling beside the three kids, her hand on Lev's back. "I need all of you to be really, really, really quiet."

I wasn't nervous as I walked downstairs. The callers could be anyone—Mormons, Girl Scouts, MASSPIRG—most likely a blue Amazon van driving away, leaving behind a cardboard package I'd brandish in the dark room, everyone can talk now! Instead, a man with a large red mole under one eye. The woman, younger, hair in a low black pony, asked if I was Demeter D'Errico, and her darkly lined lips pursed slightly with what felt like scorn.

My pulse grew too loud in my head. Demeter had told me what to tell DCF, but I flubbed my intro. "Eve," I said. "That's me. Eve. Not Demeter."

"Could we . . . ?" She gestured at the stairs. "We'd like a quick chat with her."

My mouth gummy, I pointed to the name on the mailbox. "Gonzales. Hilda and Ernesto. I was just getting their mail. Feeding the fish. I'm her friend."

"Ms. D'Errico's friend?" The woman's eyes were on the curtained upstairs windows. "We just have a few questions for her. And her daughter."

"Oh, not her. Hilda's friend." I blushed when the woman turned her gaze to my white skin, my Jewish hair. "From the center," I added quickly, wondering what center this might be and then it came to me. "The senior center. We volunteer there. Both of us do."

Pleased with my cleverness, I calmed. Lying was like writing, a Greentime of the imagination. "She's on vacation this week. Visiting her sister in the DR. But I know that name. D'Errico? They get mail delivered here sometimes." I shook my head with disapproval. "Hilda thinks it's a scam. Someone saw the address, decided to use it, who knows why. People do weird things."

The peppy tone, the flight attendant's smoothness. I liked this version of me who volunteered at the senior center and wasn't afraid of small talk.

"So you've never seen her? They"—she gestured at the mailbox—"never saw her?"

In the look exchanged by the man and the woman, I could see the relief of an item checked off a to-do list, a file closed.

I watched them walk away, slipped the card he gave me—Massachusetts Department of Children and Families—into my jeans pocket, and ran into the apartment, adrenalized, exhilarated by my success. "They're gone!"

"Quieter," she whispered.

After I explained, quietly, what happened, she rushed for the bathroom and I could hear her vomiting, the flush of the toilet. Even then she couldn't shake the terror; in the living room, she hitched up a slight corner of curtain and knelt there, watching. Sonya reached for the white sunglasses on the couch and silently passed them to Persephone. Beyond the crack in the curtain, the sky blued, then dimmed. The longest day ended. We hadn't marked the solstice, but somehow it turned to summer anyway.

Persephone

. . .

SHE WANTS HER MOM TO COME HOME. SHE *ALWAYS* WANTS HER mom to come home. Her mom said five-ish, and now it's . . . ? She could ask but decides to let Matilda keep the precarious knowledge of hours and minutes to herself.

If she knows, she'll be waiting.

Time alone is either spent waiting (terrible) or forgetting she's waiting (pretty nice).

Sounds can help with forgetting, such as blue jays arguing on the railing of the balcony, the blast of Charli XCX from downstairs, the barking of their Rottweiler. Family sounds. Or when Matilda plays *D'Aulaires' Book of Greek Myths* or the next Irish step dance tutorial or takes notation, but Persephone's too tired for any of this now.

She asks Matilda—her mom renamed the robot voice when she chose an Australian accent—to play the 1990s mix on Spotify, and Matilda gamely responds with Salt-N-Pepa. Persephone pulls off her T-shirt and throws it in an elegant way and spreads the velvet blanket onto the couch in Octavio, pressing her chest with its painful and warm lumps into the soft velvet, moving a little to the music from when her mother was young.

The darknesses have names and offer different forms of companionship and censorship. Octavio in the living room with its covered night-light, where her mom would like her to stay, is masculine and sophisticated. It clears its throat in a fatherly manner and sometimes says "hmm" as it reads an old-fashioned newspaper, the kind made out of paper, but it never finds fault with how she spends her time, even when she's doing this on the velvet blanket on the couch.

Babushka is the bedroom when she twists the blinds just a smidge to see the photos of herself as a tiny baby held by Micah, and Micah as a tiny baby held by their grandma, and Micah in his red graduation gown, and her mom with her friends Cara and Andrea in tank tops in the snow on Wheeler Peak. Babushka is beautiful but sad with all its people from far away. It says, *Well, sweetie, your mom wouldn't have to move if it wasn't for you.*

And then there's Leelu in the bathroom when she turns on the bright overhead light to see herself, just briefly, if she hasn't felt sick that day, as a reward for the hours and hours she spends in Octavio. In here there's a tacky, embarrassed feeling, a reminder of the outside world and all its strangers. Leelu is young and judgmental. Leelu knows the truth.

Persephone doesn't know what she looks like, not really. Leelu's mirror is high and narrow and she can see only shoulders and chest and nipples and chin if she stands on the toilet and leans over the sink—or nose, eyes, hair if she tries out a dance in the back of the room. There's nothing Persephone would like to know more than how she looks, although she'd also like to know the color of the Life Saver she unsticks from a plate on the coffee table and drops onto her tongue.

When she hears footsteps she crawls around hurriedly to find her shirt.

"The Cranberries, really? God, this takes me back." Her mother is hugging her and she smells right and the darknesses are just rooms again. They will eat and talk and hopefully walk outside in the night if her mother isn't too tired from working. "Tell me everything. Did you work on a story? A script?"

Persephone nods. "That's what I did."

"Here, I got you this." Her mother presses something as soft as rabbit fur against her hand. "You wear it like a scarf." She adjusts it over Persephone's shoulders, pulling her hair out of the way so she can feel the velvet on her neck. "It's dark, dark blue, nearly midnight," she adds, before Persephone even has to ask.

"Will Eve and Sonya and Lev come?" Persephone calls over the sound of the sink, after her mother gathers her lunch dishes from the coffee table and carries them into the kitchen.

"No, it's a Henry James day." Persephone tries to imagine him, this father she hasn't met. She loans him a hairy face like the man of the vegans they lived with in Olympia. But this makes her think of the smell of mold. The always rain. Her mom so alone and sad. Her mom is becoming happier here. "Isn't it nice," she says, whenever Sonya and Lev visit. "Isn't it nice to have family friends again?"

It is nice, but it's not *again*. Persephone had school friends when she went to school, but none of her mom's friends have kids near her age. Scott has a son on the fire crew who brings chili for Thanksgiving. Andrea has grandkids in Albuquerque. And Cara and Matteo are just barely out of school. Grown-ups, she thought, never stick together in same-age pairs like kids do, or at least she thought this until she saw her mom and Eve.

With Eve, her mom is bright and chatty and they all go outside together when it gets dark enough. But tonight, after they eat Rice-A-Roni, her mother turns off the music because she has a headache, leaves her plate on the coffee table, and falls asleep right there on the couch.

The kitchen light is still on, so Persephone can't bring in the dishes or wash them or help in any way, except to take the blanket from the floor and cover her mother and brush her own teeth. Just before she leaves the bathroom, her fingers feel for the light switch without her brain telling them to, as if they're an animal with its own desire. A total mistake because once she climbs on the toilet, she sees in the mirror that the scarf around her neck isn't elegant as she had hoped but more like a strangulation. Where does the scarf come from? She sees it hanging in a small shop and then, disconcertingly, she sees it hanging in the closet of a woman her mother cleans for, and she pushes shut this closet door in her mind and jumps off the toilet and switches off the light and quickly tells Matilda to play something, anything.

Stubborn Matilda refuses. She despises vagueness. "Jesus," Persephone says. "Fucking play D'Aulaires."

Her mother must have come to bed, because when Persephone wakes, she reaches out and feels her mother's shoulder. Her mother rolls over, pulling Persephone's hand to her and kissing down her arm until Persephone returns to sleep. But she has that dream again, her first day back at school. She's so excited. Her hair looks good and she's wearing shoes and a backpack, and she's opening the gate to the playground and can see the pink building across the asphalt—she's old enough for middle school and this is her elementary school, but okay, fine, it's still school. But something else bothers her. She's tried this before, hasn't she? Tried and failed to reach the door? She reassures herself that she must have been dreaming then. Yes, those were just dreams. And this is actually happening. Look, she's passing the picnic tables. Look, she's under the flagpole. Her principal, Mr. Rodriguez, sweeps the hopscotch court with a wide broom. Mr. Rodriguez has the wrong face. He looks like the vegan man they lived with in Olympia, but no worries, no problem, she can see the mural of endangered animals that she helped paint in third grade, she's nearly to the door.

Like always she's awake and reaching for her mom. The sheet is warm but empty. She goes into the bathroom to pee and traces the grout in the flower pattern of tile on the wall as she listens to her mom in the kitchen. "Yeah, not even food stamps. I can't be in anyone's system. I definitely can't use this address again." She laughs. "Yeah, that's exactly it. But hungry. A hungry ghost. A Buddhist thing, but it's supposed to be metaphoric."

She's not speaking with the daughter voice, the voice that says, "Oh, Mom, Mom, what should I do?" So she's talking to someone she made margaritas for in the blender or got rides from when her car broke down or kissed in her bedroom—back when she did such things, before they left for Olympia and then here.

Her friend is saying something far away under the Taos night sky.

"No, thanks, really, but we can't," her mom answers. "Not yet. I just think, I really do think I'll find them if we stay."

Her mom believes there are other people like her who puke when they go outside and that they live here in Northampton.

Does Persephone believe this?

Persephone believes her mom will show her a way out of these dark rooms the way she showed her the white circle in the sky and named it *moon* and showed her the lines that formed into letters, showed her how to eat the red of the melon and to float in deep river water, showed her the snow and the snowpants, the rain and the raincoat, the sun and the sunscreen, just like that she'll show her a way out.

July and August

...

i

MONTHS BEFORE I RAN INTO DEMETER, ON A BLEAK WINTER DAY when Henry James was home and the mess and endless tasks of caring for other people threatened to undo me, I went to Target alone and said, enjoy it, Eve, you're alone at Target. I didn't enjoy it, but I did buy baskets, so many baskets, more and more baskets, setting them around the house like buckets under a leaky roof, hoping they would catch the downpour.

Then I went to the library and found every book that might tell me how to improve: parenting books that said I needed to set clearer boundaries and expectations, and ones that said expectations caused nervous system overload and that I needed to regulate my breathing, books about how to organize my time, and other books about how to stop caring about organizing time and do nothing instead, and books about self-care, and books about how self-care was just a capitalistic ploy to make me insecure and acquisitive. I put these books in a basket. Nobody else ever put anything in a basket, although sometimes they'd dump one out looking for something like a missing red sock.

By July, when I told Demeter all this, I owed $46.29 on the overdue books I hadn't read.

"Fuck baskets," she said. We were lying on the balcony. It was too hot to sit up. "Fuck baskets. That's my campaign slogan. Life's too messy for baskets. And those books. Is that what it's like to be raised by Larry Yalen? A constant need to work harder? So punitive. Return the fucking books."

I hate the word *friendship.* It lacks all the heft, the soil, the lightning

I believe the relation entails. It sounds saccharine and cutesy. Shirley Temple with perfect curls, singing about the good ship lollipop.

But that's what came to us. Soil, lightning, friends.

Every day that summer when Henry James was in New York and Demeter was done with Bonnie, she and I lay on the concrete balcony and watched the sunlight on the leaves. When it was too hot for the balcony, we brought the kids frozen orange juice and joined them in the air-conditioned darkness. We played a game she called radio, which was just listening to the radio, albeit on an iPad. You choose a station somewhere in the country and never get up to change the song. Soon we had favorites. Lev's was the Celtic hour on a public radio station out of western Colorado. He would do a wild jig. Sonya preferred a show in Buffalo called Jazz à la Mode. Persephone chose all nine innings of a minor league baseball game—who was even playing? We didn't know, we didn't understand it at all, but we floated down the river of the announcer's enthusiasm, cheering when he cheered. "It's like listening to a play written by aliens," Persephone said.

We paused the iPad—Matilda is what Demeter named it—only when the doorbell rang. The kids knew to be silent as I went downstairs. I never saw the man with the mole and the woman with the darkly lined lips again, although I became friendly with the Amazon delivery driver and left their packages at the door of 137A.

How had it taken me an hour to make dinner before? Demeter scrambled eggs and prepared mac and cheese while I read to her from a book about animal husbandry that she'd found at a Little Free Library and had grown attached to despite, as she said, wanting neither animal nor husband.

The light on the leaves above the balcony was different in early August. Goldenrod. Yellow barged into our life, full throttle, tweenish in its exuberance.

Lev learned to wipe his own butt and to whistle. Sonya learned to French braid and to count in Spanish. Persephone memorized the prime numbers to 733 and figured out how to raise one eyebrow. We felt her brow in the dark. She really was doing it. At night, out came the wheels from the Salvation Army. Persephone took fast to the skateboard, weaving down the only road with streetlights all burned out, looking just like her mom at that age. Sonya slowly pedaled a too-small bike, braking on even the slightest downhill. Lev held my hand while shuffling forward on pink roller skates.

One day on the balcony, Demeter told me about a podcast she listened to while working that said Christians have so many children not actually because of God wanting them to, but because church is such a great babysitter. The moms have time to think and socialize, while someone else watches their kids, teaches them, gives them dinner and cupcakes.

"Are you saying you wish you could go to church?"

She set down her knitting and stretched her arms up like the branches above us. "No, Eve. I'm saying you're my church."

I thought for a moment. "Well, you're my social democratic welfare state."

"Seriously? I'm your Sweden?"

"You're my Sweden."

"You're my safety net."

"There's this picture book where firefighters who are also cats are holding a trampoline for people to jump onto from a burning building. I always think of that."

"You're my trampoline."

"You're my fire cat."

"Whoa, Eve. Look up."

The light in late August. An entirely different beast.

I RETURNED THE FUCKING books. I ghosted the urgent emails from Substacks (*You can't afford to miss my call about the 3 things every parent MUST know about . . .*). I'd forgotten that time didn't have to be adversarial, as long as I had both company and idleness. But it was idleness on the back of Persephone's illness. At home we turned on lights to read books, to hold staring contests, to play cards, all things Persephone couldn't do. How we wished she could! Sonya kept asking us to take Persephone out, to let her see the world, hyping up a fairy house in the bonsai branches in the last room of the library. A canoe the size of a walnut shell, the chairs from a moth's wing. Soon Persephone joined in. She'd only peek, she promised, but it was essential to the script she was writing.

Demeter and I discussed it for days. Was it worth risking Persephone's symptoms to give her a small break from the apartment? We looked at the notes we'd been keeping of how she felt after varying times spent in the living room with its shrouded night-light or under the yellow glow of streetlights. Finally, Demeter sewed large black flaps to a new pink sun hat I bought them.

ii

ON A CLOUDY DAY, I DROPPED THE KIDS AND DEMETER AT THE library's front entrance and continued to the parking lot. I was nervous. I'd always found the basement's dimness gloomy, but was it dark enough? Or would we need the washcloths and Advil and sleep mask I carried?

Story hour was concluding in the Children's section, and the rooms were raucous with toddlers. As I made my way through the bodies, I heard a mother say to another: "You think she's one of them? With the glasses and hat?" I paused, pretending to examine a book about crafting with toothpicks.

"What I think is she shouldn't be here," the other mother said.

I hurried to the farthest room. Lev asked me to lift him up and read a sign to him (REMINDER! CHILDREN MUST BE IN HAND'S REACH OF CAREGIVERS AT ALL TIMES), and I missed the moment when a charge must have gone through the many connected subterranean rooms, an electric pulse, a gossipy murmur, because by the time I put him down there was a small crowd of mothers in the entryway to the last room.

"We're sure she's one of them," I heard one whisper loudly. "From the article."

"An Emily?"

"And at story hour? With all our kids here?"

"Seems like somebody needs to set some limits."

"Start with saying, 'Take off the hat, kiddo. Our job is to keep ourselves healthy. And light is super healthy.'"

What were they talking about? What was an Emily? Sonya was asking me something, but I couldn't focus.

"You just say, 'No, sweetie, we don't wear glasses indoors. No, hats are outside clothes.'"

"Maybe we shouldn't . . . not right now," I said to Demeter, who was scanning the walls for the light switch while deploying a steady river of enthusiasm.

The room darkened. Dusk. The startling cessation of a previously imperceptible buzz. A mother said, "You know what? I'll say something." She wore blue-and-green striped shorts and a yellow rain poncho that fluttered like the wings of a manta ray when she marched across the room. "Excuse me? Hi. So, it seems like that little girl might be an Emily? From the article?" Demeter turned around. "My son, he's really sensitive," the woman continued. "And when I read all about those people in the article, I worried. Kids—you know how they imitate."

I don't want to draw her as a caricature of motherly protection. Still, it's true that her fingers flapped ahead of her as if she could shoo away Persephone in her hat, shoo away darkness and illness, shoo away fear and danger. I felt, like I often did, that every mother sat in her own illuminated spaceship, steering her offspring to safety through the devastating blackness of space.

But Demeter's features were as enlivened by hope as this mother's were by righteous anger. "Excuse me, what article?"

"Well, surely . . . I mean, you must . . ."

Demeter's look was so disarming that she didn't finish, and for a moment I felt a shift in the room as if we were now on a single spaceship together, hurtling so fast through the darkness we didn't even see it, one spaceship of blue and green.

But then the mother pointed to Persephone and anger returned. "You know. About people like that."

"We need you to get her out of here," another mother said.

We elbowed our way through the crowd. On the steps outside, Demeter grabbed my arms. I asked her if she was okay, told her I loved her. "Am I okay?" Her eyes were wet. "Didn't you hear? There are others like her. I knew there had to be."

Ruth

...

i

"DID THEY JUST KICK THAT FAMILY OUT?" SHE ASKS THE CHILdren's librarian as two women and three kids leave through the side door, their egress studied by a jury of mothers.

"It's all in an article in the paper, if you want to know what's what," says a mother joining the check-out line, which isn't moving. "We're just trying to keep this a healthy space for our children."

It isn't an article at all, Ruth learns two days later when she has time to spend with the *Hampshire Gazette* in the periodicals room. It's a letter.

Our blissful little hamlet has always been a place of healing and hope. From visits to the water cures of old to the diligent work of the healing arts community today, discomforts are shed here, sufferers find their balance of health regained.

Misplaced modifier. Ruth scans to the signature to discover the perp. *To protect the ill, we will remain anonymous. The Medical Mystery Collective.*

A coy move. She continues reading:

But could it be that sickness has come to visit us here? Each of us has a loved one who cannot bear daylight or even electric light without pain, dizziness, headaches, nausea, vomiting. They do not know each other. They have never met to discuss symptoms. What is causing this strange photosensitivity?

"Loved one" strikes Ruth as almost too tender for a public letter. It's the singularity of the "one." The particularity. This one, this one is loved.

They've been told that they suffer from IBS, early menopause, tumor on the pituitary gland, anxiety, and more. They've been prescribed antibiotics, inhalers, steroids, MRI scans, pulmonary function tests, echocardiograms, SSRIs. To no avail.

We write this as A Warning and a . . .

A patron asks her to pull blackened pages from the printer's jaws. Exigencies expand. A few days later she returns to the periodicals room and searches for responses to this letter. The first comes from a local MD:

The previous letter writers were cavalier and careless when they speculated a new illness. It's unlikely that these people are suffering from related causes. Nor is four a statistically significant number. As always, medical diagnoses are best left to medical professionals.

A second from a clinical psychologist:

The authors of Monday's letter are describing classic agoraphobia. These four people are choosing to stay inside. Although they experience somatic effects, the root is psychological. Do we say our local hero Emily Dickinson was ill from 5G or from a fungus or from fluoride? No. We say she suffered from agoraphobia.

Thanks to my research on the subject, I put forth the hypothesis that these people suffer from what I'm calling post-pandemic syndrome. As I've discovered through extensive interviews and surveys, isolation and fear left its mark on all of us differently. For some, the result is pathological. I've seen agoraphobic responses around the country, and a cluster like this is not surprising. While we have sympathy for the shut-ins, we must not glamorize their plight by searching for causes that don't exist. We're at high danger for copycat behaviors among a traumatized population . . .

And then the nonprofessionals weigh in. From a patron who checks out British period dramas on DVD: *These people with post-pandemic syndrome or Emily Dickinson's disease or whatever we're going to call it should read the news about India—temperatures of 130 degrees Fahrenheit on a daily basis—or what about the deadly fires in Sonoma? Flooding in Manila? See what real suffering looks like. Then go outside and enjoy our Paradise.*

From Les Cowley, who worked on Ruth's Kawasaki when she still owned it: *Emily's disease? It's a hoax. And you're all suckers.*

From a man in Greenfield, a suggestion that *all of this could be cleared up on the keto diet.*

Followed by a particularly paradoxical letter: *There are now more letters about Emily's disease than there are people with Emily's disease. We should all stop writing about this. Don't pour fuel on the fire of hysteria.*

After this, letter writers move on to other concerns.

Post-pandemic syndrome? Ruth returns the stack of newspaper to its wooden shelf. She knows that patrons are upset. Just this afternoon she was cornered again by the man with the long blond ponytail who nags her to turn off the internet. He's doing the hard work of raising his kids without screens, he says. So why should they be confronted by people online at the f-ing library? How's he supposed to keep them safe?

Fear is all over, she knows that. Safety seems a far shore.

Weird not to want to go outside, though, she thinks when she finally leaves the library in her running clothes. But is it any weirder than what she does? Drives twenty minutes to a trailhead. Secures netting under her visor to keep the throngs of late August mosquitoes from her face. Sets her timer. Feels nothing but disappointment at the top, despite the vast view of a forested valley all the way to the blue hills of Vermont, because she's two point six seconds slower than average.

Driving home in the dusk, she has a memory—not even a memory, a nudge—about photosensitivity. Didn't she once believe she had it? Wouldn't she come home from a run with her head pounding and tell Ramona she couldn't go outside anymore?

The proto-memory recedes as she's driving the tamed curves of the Village Hill development and sees, at the end of the cul-de-sac, someone on her doorstep.

She's been expecting this. You can't find her address online, but how hard would it be for one of the unhinged patrons to follow her home? Not the drug users, no, their desire is both obvious and binary—satisfied or un. She's thinking about the men who become enraged when she's slow to find their CDs or reboot the computers, men without an easy fix to their pain. "Fuck off," she says from the driveway.

"Ruth." A woman looks at her. Red hair in an overgrown mullet. She takes a bite of an apple, a thumb keeping place in a paperback.

—

THE INITIAL EXUBERANCE OF REUNION TURNS AWKWARD. IT'S Ruth's fault. Unused to hosting, she bumbles around her own kitchen. Jessie's funny and charming despite having taken a plane from Oregon and a bus from the Hartford airport. She's on her way to visit her dad in Worcester.

"Wouldn't you fly into Boston then?"

"Hartford was cheaper."

This is never true, but Jessie is filling water glasses and Ruth can't gauge her expression.

"What was your plan if I wasn't home?" Ruth asks, unpeeling the film from a microwaved Trader Joe's meal-sized lasagna in plastic, the only edible vegetarian item on offer, but completely wrong for Jessie, who left a promising career as an assistant professor of botany at UMass to perch one hundred and eighty feet high in the Californian redwood canopy to save a tree.

"If you weren't home? Camp on the lawn out there, I guess. There's a shit ton of lawn. What is this, a planned community? Little weird to find you here."

"I like being close to the library, to town."

An obvious lie. She was the one who loved living in the country, who'd lecture visitors about fox-proofing the chicken coop, woodchopping techniques, running trails. But she couldn't stay in the house, not after Orion left.

"Well, lucky me. You were home." Jessie takes off her sweatshirt, pulls down the tank top beneath.

THE WAY JESSIE LOOKED in 1996: imperious, all-knowing, stunning. Short red hair, long pale neck. Ruth had spotted the flyer in Raos Coffee. *Room Available—Lesbos Only.* When she showed up at the decrepit farmhouse in Leverett—moss on the stones, rabbits on the dirt road, green leaves clogging the windows—she didn't think she'd take the room. Newark to Rutgers to the Lower East Side: She'd never lived in the country. Then the door opened.

All three of them—Jessie, Antonia, Ellen—in shorts and rubber boots, carrying nets, heading to a marsh to look for some green thing. Pickerelweek. Spatterdock. They'd forgotten she was stopping by. "Welcome to the Cunt Collective," Jessie had said, taking off her sunglasses to assess Ruth. "Come with us?"

The way Ruth looked then: leather jacket, motorcycle boots, the Kawasaki to match. Just a child, not quite twenty-five, unwilling to surrender style for the weather. Sweating in black jeans on the way to the river.

Ruth now runs in shoes with toe dividers. She's wearing an old Hot Chocolate 5K T-shirt with a polar bear on it and Orion's gym shorts.

The way Jessie looks now—

Soon after Ramona left Stephen and moved into Ruth's room, she began writing a poem composed of found sentences: male writers describing middle-aged women in their universally lauded novels. (Snippets of it still follow Ruth around, a line or two from Franzen, DeLillo, this from Cunningham's *The Hours:* "She has aged dramatically, just this year, as if a layer of air has leaked out from under her skin. She's grown craggy and worn.")

"See, this is how you know that men can't ever love women, not really," Ramona would say. "They can only love an image, and then mourn the afterimage."

Ramona was twenty-eight and not quite divorced: in the throes of an awakening. Patriarchy, which she'd eschewed in her personal relationship, needed to be pointed out everywhere. Ramona never finished the poem—it grew with every book she read—but she'd stand on a chair to read it at dinner parties. "Listen to this—all the ways to say that women over fifty are invisible at best, repulsively hideous at worse."

Ramona never made it to fifty, only forty-nine.

Ruth is fifty-two, meaning Jessie, who is opening Ruth's refrigerator to laugh at the contents, or lack thereof, is fifty-five.

Jessie now?

Ruth forces herself to look away from the beauty that is Jessie now.

UNLIKE RUTH, WHO WORKED MINDLESS HOURS AT RAOS COFFEE, all three botany grad students of the Cunt Collective were ambitious, but Jessie's discipline outpaced the others. When Jessie's redwood was felled, her friends waited for her to return—to her senses, her job, the East Coast. She never did. Ruth is honestly hazy on Jessie's life, because Ruth's last decade was so terrible as to render everyone else's somewhat fake.

Sitting on the couch, Ruth drinks a beer while Jessie catches her up. She lives alone in Eugene, works as a substitute teacher. Bio, chem, physics.

This life sounds sad, but Jessie appears to be the opposite. Borrowing Ruth's laptop, she plays a video: thirteen people rappelling from St. Johns Bridge in Portland to stop an oil icebreaker on its way to the Arctic. Jessie points at a bright green anorak. "That's me. Hung there all night, twenty-nine hours, until the criminals left."

Ruth looks from the video to Jessie. "How?"

Jessie's explanation includes context about tar sands oil, Ojibwe water protectors, the necessity defense. "I was seriously depressed about the world for like ten years. It infiltrated basically every moment. We didn't talk then, you wouldn't know. Middle-aged woman, what could I do? I started writing a book, but who reads? And then I—"

"No, I mean how'd you do it? Climb the bridge? Hang there?"

"Wait a second." Jessie closes the computer. "Are you talking about my arms?"

Ruth was trying to be sly as she marveled the shoulders, the biceps. Caught out, she grins. "I guess I am. I'm talking about your arms."

"Not the future of flora and fauna on Earth?" Her look is stern, but there's pleasure in her eyes. "Joined a climbing gym. Me and the twentysomethings. And you know what, Ruth?"

"What?"

"I kick their fucking asses."

There's half a foot between them on the couch. Jessie doesn't move. Ruth doesn't, either.

—

IN THE MORNING, RUTH DOESN'T KNOW WHERE TO GO. SHE NEEDS coffee before answering her daily questions for an online trivia league where she's recently been elevated from Rundle C to Rundle B. It's a thrilling advancement, but one that turns each day precarious as she struggles to keep hold of this spot slightly above her level of trivia knowledge, which in the wider world is astronomical, but in the refined, self-selected cohort of Learned League, is apparently just average, or average-plus.

But her laptop is in the kitchen/living room where Jessie's sleeping, having insisted that she prefers couches to beds. Could she tell that Ruth didn't want anyone in Orion's room, not until he visits? He texted a day before his August trip, dude! can't get out of work, and hasn't yet responded to her texts about picking a new date. Ruth listens for Ramona to ask again if Ruth thinks Orion might come home if she hadn't sold the small yellow house surrounded by meadows and cows, where his memories of his dead mother reside.

But mornings Ramona is quiet, a late sleeper in death the way she was in life.

Unwilling to wait, Ruth tiptoes into the living room and brews coffee. Jessie's hair spills out from her sleeping bag. When Ruth reaches for her laptop, she opens her eyes. "Shit, you made me coffee? That's so sweet."

Climbing from the sleeping bag in tank and underwear, she carries Ruth's coffee to the fridge. "Tell me about Orion."

"Orion? He's okay."

The first of their friends to have a baby, Ramona and Ruth carried Orion everywhere on their backs, dressed him in paisley pants, gave him two dolls, one for each arm. Ruth named them: (Dolly) Parton and Salvador (Dalí). Ruth's panacea for the tedium of early parenthood was wordplay and total control of the music in the car, since they were often in the car, living as they did in the hills and shuttling Orion to other such maple syrup towns for endless enrichment classes held in barns.

Sometimes Ruth wondered how far they could push the boulder

up the hill. The boulder being toxic masculinity. But Ramona put Sisyphus to shame. Orion at thirteen was still eager to knit socks with her, to bake apple turnovers, to draw finches and sing "Dear Theodosia," and it seemed that although puberty was upon them and a sick society could begin exerting its tidal pull on his underground river of testosterone, they'd done it. But it turned out only Ramona had done it. Ruth alone was no match for the boulder. At first, channeling Ramona, she set limits, timers, checked history. For what? Ruth wasn't taking him foraging for wild blueberries. They weren't sewing. She was either off on long runs or drinking beer on the screened porch. And then Covid came; what else was there for him to do? Ruth was blasted and asleep by nine. Floundering and yearning, Orion found himself welcomed into the receiving arms of the internet. They slid into a contrapuntal schedule: Ruth glued to the Mac Pro during daylight, Orion at night, raised during the precarious years of sixteen to eighteen by gamers, vaccine doubters, 4chan.

"Just okay? Is he around?"

"Orion's in Texas." She doesn't say where or why.

"Aha! You do eat occasionally." Jessie pulls a plastic carton with two remaining eggs from the back of Ruth's fridge and then lingers with the door open, either to search for an invisible vegetable or to grant Ruth a delightful moment watching her ass.

Eggs, small talk, bus station. Ruth wants to say something to Jessie before she leaves, thank her for visiting or maybe ask why she came. Most other friends have pulled away. Their lives are busy, true, but also death scares them.

But Jessie is preoccupied with trying to pull up her bus ticket on her phone and then she's pecking Ruth on the cheek and sprinting for the bus. God, she's fast.

iii

A WEEK LATER, RUTH COMES HOME TO FIND HER AT THE DOORstep again. "Here's what I meant to say last week. Here's why I flew into Hartford, which isn't cheaper than Logan, you knew that. Whenever I play that game of who would I most like to kiss, you walk into my mind. Swagger, kind of."

Ruth steps past Jessie to unlock her door.

"But I can leave. I hear there hasn't been anyone for a while. Since Ramona?"

Ruth hoists Jessie's backpack and heads inside where she turns and kisses Jessie, lightly at first, and then, when they reach her kitchen, she drops the bag and presses Jessie against the fridge.

They're up all night, up with the owls and the foxes, falling asleep only after dawn crests Mount Skinner and Jessie changes her airplane ticket. When they wake, in the tail of the afternoon, Ruth jumps out of bed, frantically trying to revive her laptop. Naked on the floor, a terry cloth headband holding her bangs from her face, she explains what it means to her precarious position at the rump of Rundle B if she forfeits today's Learned League quiz. Jessie throws off the sheet. It's unsettling how much she's laughing.

"What? What is it?"

"You're always so cool, so endlessly cool, and this is what undoes you?"

RUTH CALLS IN SICK. Covid, she claims; the double lines.

They hike up Skinner and fuck in the restroom at the top. They fuck again in the car at the trailhead. They outstay the tubing teenagers at the bend in the Deerfield River, take off their clothes and ride the current.

Fucking! After so long.

A year after Ramona's death, Ruth's friends deemed her ready to meet someone. She wasn't, not at all, but she agreed to go to Divas. That week, the pandemic descended, and for over eighteen months—until the day the pharmacist at CVS jabbed the needle into her upper arm—she didn't feel the touch of another human. Not a friend's hug, no fingers brushing together at the Woodstar counter, no hair washed at the barber's, no press of a woman into her at a show at the Iron Horse; even Orion, who once walked hand in hand with her in the foggy mornings, dodged when she tried to touch his shoulder. After twenty years sharing a bed with Ramona, such physical solitariness changed her. A shell developed.

But here's Jessie, giving no shit for the shell, no careful or hesitant cracking open, she's just naked beneath Ruth. She's neither high femme like Ramona, nor masc like Ruth (she gives no shit for the old binaries), but neither, both. Her arms, her shoulders, the girlish way she comes, how she pins Ruth to the bed.

Ruth had forgotten the variety of sex. The tender and slow versus the urgently rushed. The rough. The coy. The serious work interrupted by laughter. How they check in with glances. How long they stare at each other. What a grand secret when, finally dressed, they catch eyes while grocery shopping.

Jessie opens up about her terrible week in Worcester with her stepmother and dying father. She won't come back, not even for the funeral. She doesn't fly, she explains. This exception was her first in seventeen years. Her dad, never expressive, always disappointed with Jessie, censorious of the incontrovertible conditions of both lesbianism and activism, cinched Jessie's hand with such force and fear in his eyes when she said goodbye and now she's horrified because she took her hand away too soon out of habit. Forty years of slipping from his grip, and she didn't even give him this final comfort.

Ruth knows that fear, the fear in the eyes of the dying, and she thinks of all that Ramona made her promise in those final weeks, the frantic and explicit instructions on how to teach Orion to drive in snow, to protest, to treat girls, what job he should have (therapist). She tells Jessie her failure, which she's never shared. Nobody knows the scope of the years she spent drinking on the porch while Orion was on the computer, or else they were fighting over his new conspiracy theories; Ruth so livid that she couldn't talk calmly just matched his hysterical pitch. "Goes by Ryan now. Or, Soldier Pak. In thrall to the military-industrial complex. Deployed as an Air Defense Battle Management System Operator, whatever that means, in Fort Bliss, Texas. Barely spoke to me before he left. Hasn't been home since. Can you imagine if Ramona knew? I let our kid become a murderer. She'd never forgive me."

"But Ramona wasn't here." Jessie's thumbs are on her arms, on the tattoos she got after Ramona died and before she messed everything up. A wood finch for her wife. Orion's Belt for her son. "You were up against a monster and the monster beat you. Okay, that's fucking terrible. But it's not incontrovertible. He's not gone forever."

"He might be."

"Until you get him back." She says this with such definitiveness that Ruth feels stung with hope. "Until then, babe, you can't keep shutting down your life."

Ruth understands this as an invitation. The mighty Willamette. Oregon's windy coast. Jessie's long legs.

SHE DRIVES FROM THE airport to the library. I'm already looking at flights, she types, among other things she's never texted before—suggestive emojis that didn't exist when she was courting Ramona. She presses send before she loses her nerve.

No answer. But why would there be? Jessie's probably already boarding. Ruth blocks out five vacation days in early October, rearranging the schedules of the librarians she supervises. By the time Jessie's plane lands at 6:37 P.M. EDT, Ruth has skipped her run for the seventh consecutive day. She wants to be available when her text comes through.

Well, Jessie has to get home. Maybe pick up a cat or dog? Buy some groceries. And sleep. Ruth can't, though, kept awake by the strange sensation of missing a living person.

The next day, Ruth's phone is again mute. Think about it, though. There's so much to do after a trip. Plus jet lag. Or maybe Jessie was called in to work as a substitute.

Imagine Jessie walking into the school building with a mug of coffee. Her brilliance wasted on a class of unhappy ninth graders. Imagine her head between Jessie's thighs. Imagine Jessie thinking of Ruth's head between her thighs as she's taking roll.

IT COULD BE, OF course, that Jessie's texts just aren't coming through on her phone.

"If you leave a message, you're an old fuck and you should know that nobody listens to phone messages."

Ruth speaks anyway. "Yo, bud. Got a quick question for you, so give a shout."

The vibration of a text jolts Ruth. Jessie? No, Orion's replied. Ryan.

> Yo, dude! I'm heading into work.
> Can't talk.

She texts her question, and he replies after a few minutes:

> What???? Phones don't work like that.
> If you can read this text rn you can
> get anyones.

Don't think of Jessie in the climbing gym with the twentysomethings. Think of the past week. She wasn't alone in how she felt, that was clear.

From the checkout desk, she hears a boy whining in periodicals. On the carpet, his mother pages through a large stack of newspaper. The boy climbs onto her back and covers her eyes with his palms. She's familiar, but Ruth can't place her.

The woman opens a *Gazette,* skims a few pages, and sets it down. Now Ruth remembers. She's one of the mothers of the girl in a hat with flaps who was chased from the library. A girl with Emily's disease presumably. A loved one.

"Have you heard of this thing called Emily's disease?" Ruth asks the patron checking out books. Her name's Molly, a Zumba instructor at the Y and longtime borrower of self-help.

"Sad is what it is," Molly says, searching her purse for her library card. "I'd like to close the curtains and stay in bed, sure I would. But you can't give in to those impulses. You have to stay busy. Think about it. If Emily Dickinson were alive today, maybe she'd be treated for her mental health issues and rejoin the world and the world would be better for it."

Would the world? Should Emily have done some Zumba at the Y to dance the melancholy away? Wasn't the world better because Emily stayed inside to write "After great pain, a formal feeling comes—" and "This is the Hour of Lead— / Remembered, if outlived," so that Ruth could read those lines at Ramona's funeral?

"Hello? Anyone home?" A man in a Red Sox cap is shouting. "Hello? So, I spilled my enchilada? Like, everywhere."

It's when she's crouching over the carpet with a spray bottle of Clorox that Ruth is badgered by a memory; it's weirdly insistent, as if it were a patron needing her attention.

Ramona's feet are on Ruth's lap. Ruth holds them with one hand; with the other she picks at a sheet pan that has chicken drippings and bits of squash stuck on it. Orion is in the Moses basket on the kitchen floor. Truly woven of reeds, lined with organic cotton. They thought that if he never touched plastic, he'd never, what? Never drop bombs? But that's a road best untaken. Ramona's blouse is unbuttoned from nursing him to sleep, her breasts beckoning. Ruth reaches. "No, wait, he'll wake up." Ramona pushes Ruth's hand away, although she's blushing, isn't she? Pink on English skin. You always knew if she was thinking dirty. But then Ramona starts crying.

The carpet Ruth is scrubbing was installed in 2018. Ramona had been dead three months, and Ruth couldn't believe she'd never know about the new blue carpet.

Ruth returns the Clorox to the supply closet then finds herself sitting on the floor. The memory keeps insisting, although why?

Orion is swaddled, night fallen—the windows are black. On the table, the sheet pan and a pile of unfolded baby shirts. Ramona is still crying. Since Orion's birth, she's often crying; she accuses Ruth of not even striving for an equality of labor that nursing has made impossible. But this night, to stave off the fight—she's so tired of fighting, she's so tired in general—Ruth says, "Shhh, hon. Let me read to you." They haven't done this since Orion arrived.

She squats at a shelf in the living room packed with books, slim volumes—many are more like pamphlets—Ruth has had to cull from the shelves of the Local History room in the library. Self-published memoirs or collections of poetry or notes from garden shows or typed-up diaries or accounts of battles the writer is particularly passionate about. It's her job, the only way a library works; a constant influx—would you keep a copy of my grandmother's sonnets about regional birds?—requires an equal outflux, and the Historical Society has already passed on these, but Ruth and Ramona both hate the idea of dropping them into the recycling, like sending the elderly out on a barge in the dark water. So they keep them. Read them to each other some nights.

She pulls out the one they were reading before the pregnancy, a schoolteacher's diary, but—

"No dead babies," Ramona says, starting to cry again. Right. Six in six years, the poor schoolteacher. She chooses another, brings it to the table. But it's tedious. Chapter after chapter explaining how to treat various illnesses with water: baths and wet sheets and enemas. She flips to a chapter called "The Case of Sun Madness" or "The Curious Case" or something like that.

Of course. That's why this is coming to her. The girl in a hat with flaps, the letters in the paper.

Ramona grabs the book from Ruth's hand after she's read only a few minutes. "Hold on, babe. We can't do this. You're such a hypochondriac. You'll wake up tomorrow and say you can't go outside because the light's making you sick. You'll say you have Sun Madness."

Ruth lunges for the book. "But what even is it? Don't you want to find out?"

"You'll wake the baby."

Ramona's right. For a week or so after, Ruth feels certain she's caught Sun Madness. "Babe, I actually think it's . . . see, I'm nauseated and my legs ache," she says, coming back from a run to find Ramona jostling Orion down for his morning nap. "My serotonin levels depend entirely on sunlight and if I can't . . ."

"But you can," Ramona says. "Drink some water. I left you the crossword on the table."

What if Ruth had been impossible to live with? What if Ramona had yearned for just one Saturday morning without her and never lived long enough for that?

Her phone vibrates. She knows something's wrong before she turns it over.

Oh honey. I think I need to explain.

Great pain. A formal feeling. Not a loved one at all, Ruth. You got one chance at that.

1985 and 1991

...

i

MY MOTHER WROTE HER FIRST NOVEL—THE ONLY ADULT NOVEL she's ever published—on the advice of a therapist. Actually, the therapist merely suggested my mother keep a journal, but Joan found she preferred to write about herself in the third person, and soon this person began enacting my mother's darker fantasies—leaving her infant daughter home alone tied to the kitchen table, for example. My mother joined a writers' group, sent her manuscript to the agent of a group member. Irene loved it. *The Third Person* came out in 1985 when I had just turned six.

Why so bleak? its single reviewer (male) asked. *Why so angry? Are trendy diagnoses such as postpartum depression and schizophrenia now the stuff of women's fiction? I hope not. Keep it in the glossies, ladies.*

She disappeared into her room for over a month.

"Soft time" was the phrase my father always used instead of crippling depression. "She's having some, well, soft time," he'd say whenever my mother's spirits would plummet and she wouldn't leave her bed, not for dinner or school pickup or to say goodnight. The imperative, though, was mine. To walk softly. Talk softly. My father, a psychology professor at Smith, was writing a book on genius and anxiety. He hired students to bring me home from school and taught me to play gin rummy without raising our voices. He cooked hamburgers and read to me, but he couldn't stop me from missing her and worrying that her door wouldn't open again.

I cleared out a space in the pachysandra, not so far from the yard that my mother couldn't see me if she desired, bringing along my necessities—a stuffed owl, a sleeve of crackers, a Speak & Spell.

One day she finally entered the backyard wearing a long blue dress and idly pulling dead blooms off the rhododendron. She was so beautiful! I rushed to her and we hugged and she asked me to tell her what I did out there all day.

I was aware of my happiness. A six-year-old doesn't always have a meta-emotional response, but I said to myself, Eve, you are finally happy and you know it, just like the song, which had heretofore confused me. Sitting on the dirt with me, she leaned forward, her hands sifting through the soil, her eyes on my face. I couldn't stop talking. Eventually she jumped up. "I have to write something down."

What did I tell her that day? I can't remember, but whatever I said gave her the seed for her *Wormfood* books. After that, I would often sit on the floor outside her bedroom with my owl and listen to her type. When she finished for the day, she danced with me to Aretha Franklin records. She made cabbage and turkey soup.

Now that she was out of bed, I dared ask her for things. First, I asked to go to the park. She was surprised. "Aren't the woods your playground? You're such a clever girl that way." But seeing a possibility for time with her, I insisted. At the playground, however, she claimed a bench on the periphery, lit a cigarette, and marked manuscript pages, and so my second request was for a new mother.

The woman wore a crocheted bikini top and cutoffs. She was playing a Martha Graham–inspired follow-the-leader; she'd scramble onto a structure, open her arms and rise to her toes, then jump onto the sand and enfold into a ball. Following her across the top of the monkey bars was a girl in a yellow halter top and strings of blue beads, much shorter than I but far braver.

I watched from beneath a geodesic dome, certain she would slip.

"Well, you're not doing much." My mother appeared over the climber. "Time to go."

"I don't want to live with you anymore. I want that mother." I said it to be mean but grew afraid when hurt creased her face. She followed my finger. "Gyrating in a bathing suit? What do I care? Go live with her." I couldn't hear their brief discussion. My mother didn't look back at me when she walked away. The better mother, with her tiny belly button and tufted underarms, held my hand when we crossed the street to their apartment.

WALLS WAVERING WITH LOOSE tapestries. Pillows for a couch. Three cardboard boxes dressed up with scarves, sticks of incense in a jar, dozens of photos of a man with long, bushy hair who Demeter said was called Baba but wasn't her father.

"Are you okay?" Demeter asked while I looked around. I knew something was odd, but I didn't have the words "hippie" or "poverty" or the phrases "spiritual longing" and "guru worship."

Through a doorway, I could see the better mother reading a magazine and rolling a can of Tab down her arm.

WHAT I LATER LEARNED: Mary Katherine Caruso met Monty D'Errico, a student at UMass, when she was studying to be an aesthetician in Boston's southside. She was twenty when Demeter was born and moved to Northampton to live with Monty but left for India soon after with Kael from Cornucopia Market who told her, "You're a seeker, I can see it in your eyes." Mary Katherine and Demeter stayed in the ashram two years after Kael went home to help his mother with her dry-cleaning business. The day she rolled Tab on her arm, she was twenty-six and had been back in the country for six months and was seeking the next thing.

DEMETER AND I PLAYED Candy Land and Connect Four. She was quick but not competitive, slipping me the gumdrop card, showing me where I could block her from getting four in a row, telling a story about befriending a monkey when her bus broke down on the way to Ooty. I was enamored with her worldliness and yet she watched me and laughed at my small jokes as if I, who'd rarely left Northampton, were the most interesting person she'd met. When the games were returned to their boxes, I asked if she had any dolls.

She clapped her hands. "Will you take darshan?" I nodded, uncomprehending.

The smell of perfumed incense was stronger in the bedroom, a room nearly filled by a futon on which the fitted sheet had come loose. "Do you sleep here?" She nodded distractedly, pulling out the lowest drawer of a dresser and climbing on it. "Where does your mom sleep?"

"Here." She reached for an enamel box on a shelf bracketed to the wall above the dresser.

"Well, where do you sleep?"

"I just told you. Here." My mother often flinched when I came too close to her. Would she see her mother naked? Would her mother stroke her head? She jumped off the dresser, set the box on the bed. "Close your eyes." I hoped she might give me beads like the ones she wore. I heard the crackling of cellophane. "Hold on. They're all stuck together." When she told me to open my mouth, I opened my eyes as well. A dusty lavender lozenge rested in her hand. "It's okay. They're blessed by the Mandali so they never go stale."

The candy tasted of the bits of paper stuck to it. Then, a revolting sweetness equal to the room's perfume. I didn't spit it out. I thought to myself, I'll do anything for this girl. She watched me carefully and then stood on tiptoes to rest her hand on my hair. "The spirits of the Mandali now bring their blessings inside you. Because they love you."

A moment without concern, a blankness, a held breath, a bird gliding on air currents.

Then my mother rang the doorbell, and the girl lifted her hand. Sticky from the candy, it caught strands of my hair.

From the back seat, I leaned forward so my mom could hear me over the open window. Would the girl be in my first-grade class, would we be friends, and if so, what kind exactly? Perhaps we might be best friends, although it was possible if not likely that she already had a best friend. My mother said vaguely that she was glad I'd had a good time; I could tell she was still writing her story in her head.

That evening, however, when I put my ear to her bedroom door,

I heard nothing, no typing. Could it be that I caused her to return to her bed with my betrayal? But no, it seemed I'd provoked far worse. My father took me for burgers at the Look Diner. As I was finishing a chocolate milkshake, he started crying and told me he loved me, but a judge had decided that a child belonged with her mother, and mine was moving to New York. Perhaps this stretched over tense weeks, but that's how I remember it. I chose the better mother in the playground and was sent away the next day, out of the green and into the city.

ii

MY MOTHER PUBLISHED THE FIRST INSTALLMENT OF THE *Wormfood* saga when I was eight, the age, perhaps unsurprisingly, of Alexandra, the narrator. In 1991, when Alex and I turned twelve and the third *Wormfood* was released, my mother had attained genuine renown, and she set out to write an adult novel that would be taken seriously.

Tremendous luck is how she described the yearlong fellowship in Rome. "But there's some bad luck, too." She frowned in a way she never did when unhappy. "They won't allow me to bring you."

"Come for the summer and we'll make the most of our time together," my father said on the phone. Having finally published his tome on genius and anxiety, he'd landed a gig at the University of East Anglia and would move across the Atlantic with his new wife, Avery, in late August.

I didn't understand how I'd survive without my mother, or she without me. In our New York apartment, I'd grown adept at caring for her. When she stayed in bed, I brought her soup from the corner bodega. I sat beside her and listened. And when her depression lifted, and she'd die if she didn't start writing at five A.M., I knew to set my alarm, toast my bagel, pack a sandwich, and close the door quietly behind me so she wouldn't lose her train of thought.

Loneliness is often described in terms of depth. Deeply lonely, unfathomably lonely—a fathom being six vertical feet. In Northampton's summer green, I couldn't sink. I felt helium. Unembodied. Without my mother near, I couldn't descend into my body enough to sleep, and I would lie awake listening to the siren of crickets, the midnight heartbeat of flying squirrels in our walls, the rhythmic hustle of my parents' bed, which was no longer theirs.

Death was always so close to her. She wrote about it, talked about it, wished for it at times. Certain she would kill herself in the year we were apart and I'd never see her again, I developed strategies to postpone the horror. If I chewed the stems of seventeen dandelions. If I read fifty pages before going inside to use the bathroom.

I spent my days in the backyard because Avery spent hers inside until my father came home to cook dinner and she went for a run. Only much later did I realize she stayed home for me. Avery: Cheerleader blond ponytail, Sarah McLachlan on the kitchen CD player. Serious but uncurious. I never saw her read outside of timed twenty-five-minute blocks during which she worked on her dissertation. At night, she curled beside my father on the couch where my mother used to read Bruno Bettelheim and Melanie Klein and Anna Freud. I'd never seen him watch TV before. Avery alphabetized her VHS tapes on my mother's bookcase. "Watch with us," she'd say, her leg draped over his thigh. But I couldn't figure out where to sit.

If I dug my fingernails into my palm. If I closed my fist around an ice cube for two minutes. If I only cried with my face pressed into the grass. If I didn't lift my head until I counted to five hundred, even if it was hard to breathe, even when I heard the chaos of winged beasts coming ever closer.

I sat up in time to see four skateboarders disembark at the entrance to the woods, flip their boards, and carry them beneath one arm the way I later saw fathers hold swaddled infants, lovingly but casually. I knew it was her, even with short hair.

Following down the trail behind my house, I watched them drop their boards and jump a small embarkment to a series of rocks that jutted from the water. Demeter took her shirt off, revealing the alligator backs of early breasts, much like my painful hillocks. A boy spied me spying. "Why you looking at her, lesbo?"

She squinted at me, adjusting her bikini. "You're the Candy Land girl. I've been wondering where you were."

"Wondering?" The word came out scornfully. It had been six years.

"I thought you'd come and you never did." A hardness crept into her eyes. "You look the same, you know."

"Demeter's such a lesbo," a boy shouted. In a practiced gesture, she held her middle finger high.

"Fine then, I'll walk with you," she said to me as if answering a question. She pulled her shirt on and picked up a purse made from Guatemalan weaving. "I'll carry that," I said, reaching for her skateboard, feeling gallant beside her.

A boy shouted after us. "But don't be late, okay?"

I wanted to tell her that I remembered her, too. Embarrassed to be seen as sentimental, I said only that my mother had moved me to New York.

"Boyfriend," she assessed. "She got a boyfriend there, right? Mine got a boyfriend and moved us to Beekaram." She said this word as if it were as widely known as Manhattan.

The men swim naked in the pond there, she told me. Had I seen a penis? They shrink like worms in water. Ball sacks are so stupid. Had I seen a hard-on? Favorite tree, beech or maple? Singer or dancer? Flight or invisibility? Fame or service? She had a ready answer for the dichotomies she posed. Service brought happiness. Ego, sorrow. No offense.

"For what?"

"Your mom? My mom always calls you the famous author's daughter."

She stopped at a tree with a large branch that leaned over the river. "Let's walk there." Her shoes were off and she was tiptoeing onto the branch before I set down her board. She crouched and then sat with her feet in the water, beckoning me. I knew I'd fall if I tried, so I straddled the branch, inching forward until I reached her. We stayed like that until I showed her my watch and she gasped, waiting while I inched backward to the shore and then grabbing her board and shoes and running uphill barefoot.

—

MY FATHER RAISED UP HIS BUTCHER KNIFE. WET PARSLEY CLUNG to it. "There's no such place, Evie. Beekaram? Not in Massachusetts. What do you know about this town?"

Unwilling to tell him my single fact, that the men swam naked there, I lost her again.

But only for four days this time. She showed up on a Tuesday, set a tackle box and a plastic grocery bag on the kitchen table where Avery was working. "I can sleep over," she said. Avery asked for her mother's number. "Don't worry about it. I have clearance."

In my room, she opened the tackle box to reveal compartments of seed beads—ocher, eyeball blue, pencil-eraser pink—glossy as anthills. Below the tray were scissors, fishing line, needle-nose pliers, earring hooks. She pulled out a ziplock of finished earrings, beads woven into pyramids with tassels hanging down. "If we sell them, we can keep the money," she explained, patient with my clumsy fingers, unfazed when I jostled the case and sent beads flying. She was rethreading my needle when we heard Avery scream.

We found her vomiting into the kitchen trash can. "You need to throw it out for me, Eve. Just dump the bowl."

Among three raw eggs, one yolk was flagrantly red, its albumen like pooled blood. Taking a cue from Avery, I felt nausea. "I can't," I said.

Demeter searched our drawers for a spoon and carefully fished out the bloody egg. "There. No need to waste the others. Are we having scrambled for lunch?"

Later she asked if I was excited for the baby. I hadn't guessed that Avery was pregnant, and in keeping with my family's culture, I neither mentioned it nor was told, not until they were safely in England.

AT DINNER, UNDER MY father's interrogation, we learned that Bika Ram—Beekaram—was a commune in Leverett run by a white man in a white turban. The boys I'd seen Demeter with were commune boys working hard to act like townies. Amber necklaces stowed in the pockets of their cutoffs. Skateboards stolen from Goodwill. Careful never to call one another by their faux-Indian names.

As the oldests in the Kids Barn, Demeter and the boys were allowed to ride the van to Northampton on Tuesday and Friday mornings, sitting on the coolers that held the seitan and tabbouleh salad the parents sold to the food co-op. The day was theirs, as long as they showed up at five outside the Irish bar.

When Demeter said she could sleep over that first Tuesday, she meant until Friday. My father must have spoken to a reasonably authoritative adult. He must have decided Demeter would solve the problem of what to do with me, a decision for which he was richly rewarded. She was the ideal houseguest. She ate ravenously and indiscriminately, helped Avery with the dishes, swept the floor, dried the sink each time she used it, cleaned surfaces, leaving the rag folded neatly on the counter, adept with responsibilities I still thought of as unreachably adult. Comfortable with their kissing, she sat at their feet to watch *Friends* that first night, patting the space next to her. "Sit here."

For seven weeks, Tuesday to Friday, she made my bed. She sang while we worked on our earrings, recalling words to songs she'd heard for the first time the night before, while helping my father cook. With her, the woods opened themselves to me. I wasn't fearless like her, but I became calm enough to be curious.

My helium was punctured, and I returned to my earthly body. I felt doubled, the furthest distance from lonely. I breathed when she breathed.

With her in my twin bed, I slept deeply, unaware that she didn't, that instead she'd been spending nights in the living room talking to my father. I learned about this on a Saturday in early August when I overheard Avery crying in the kitchen. Sobbing, really. And my father's tired voice. "I'm not a *pedophile.* I can't think why it bothers you. I'm only interested in her intellectually. Totally neglected, barely schooled. It's raw brilliance then. I mean, Evie does well academically, but you'd expect nothing less from the offspring of a professor and a . . . a . . . a . . . well, a children's author. But she's been reading the same two books all summer. This child reads quickly, sure, but she also comprehends far beyond her years."

I couldn't hear what Avery said, only his response. "But it's nothing like that. I just want to see how far it reaches. Is this a rare example of true genius? Is it merely the flexibility of youth? It's tragic, if you think about it. After her time with us, when will she exercise that muscle? How will it atrophy? Are you listening to me? Are you? But why are you getting so hysterical?"

Late August to September

...

i

DEMETER STILL READ FASTER. BEFORE I FINISHED THE SECOND paragraph, she grabbed my arm and slammed my laptop shut in excitement. "Fuck yes, the Medical Mystery fucking Collective! This is it. One sick kid, who cares? A blip. But a cluster like this?"

We called the sole editor on the newspaper's masthead to ask who sent in the anonymous letter. I spoke politely, formally, and received a politely formal refusal. "What's a newspaper without confidentiality?"

"I have a sick kid," Demeter yelled.

The editor sighed. I could hear a TV in the background. "I'll tell you this much. That guy? Like a hobby for him. Writes more letters than anyone."

I brought Lev to the periodicals section in the library and paged through six months of letters to the *Gazette* and it was obvious: Stephen O'Malley, a virtuoso of the form, able to express strong opinions on subjects as diverse as contra dancing, bear sightings, and the reinstation of clotheslines. Google told me he owned a bike shop on Elm Street.

"Collective," he corrected. "Not a shop." He looked like so many in this town: the hippie's untrimmed white beard, the local's work boots with shorts. Red pouches beneath his eyes. There was a fumbling gentleness to him as he guided us to a row of velvet movie theater chairs in the back of the store (collective), although only Lev sat. Demeter described the wedding, the tick, the headaches, the patronizing doctors.

While he talked, Stephen leaned his head and torso toward her, while darting his eyes decorously away, a pose that made him seem like he wanted to take great care with her feelings. "I'm so sorry. I know what it's like to want an answer. But no, no. A tick? A *tick*? Doesn't add up. Kiran barely visited. A day at Christmas? Maybe for my wife's birthday? But that's end of winter and they hibernate, you know."

She touched his sleeve. "But the others? If you ask them . . . or I could?" She was trying for lightheartedness, but I could hear panic.

Again he leaned forward, looked away. "Oh, we talked about ticks. Sure we did. Can't live here and not talk about ticks. But nobody heard about a bite. Besides, I put up flyers all over and only three other people ever came. There'd be more if it was ticks. We're always pulling off ticks. Personally, I thought about the Covid vaccine." He scratched at his beard. "I'm not anti-vax, but they made it in such a hurry. But I guess none of our theories panned out."

"So, what's your thinking now?" I asked.

"What the psychologist . . . post-pandemic whatnot? Makes the most sense. We all thought it was something here, some fungus, something in the water, but for all we know there are clusters like us everywhere. Not a lot of communication if people aren't going outside or online. We met once again after the letter, and we agreed she makes sense. All in their heads. I'm getting Kiran a shrink."

"A therapist?" Demeter put her hands over her mouth. I could hear her silent scream. "My daughter is throwing up. She can't lose more weight. She's tiny enough."

Stephen nodded solemnly and said, for the third time, "It just makes sense."

Outside, glass windows glinted the sun back to us. Demeter cried against my shoulder and I held her.

ii

IRENE CALLED THAT EVENING. MY MOTHER HAD FALLEN OFF THE pinnacle.

"The thing is, Joan has a speaking engagement tomorrow afternoon. Just a school, P.S. something something in Queens, and in the state she's in, she won't go. I'm in meetings all day. I wouldn't ask you, but it's her bread and butter. It's not like teenagers are buying *Wormfood* anymore."

"Not quite broke," Irene responded to my question. "But not exactly solvent. Let's just say, as long as people still ask Joan Yalen to speak, Joan Yalen needs to speak."

HENRY JAMES CALLED IN SICK. I met him at the bus station, handed him Lev, the car keys. "Rowboats in the night," he said, kissing me, getting the English expression endearingly wrong.

Her foyer wasn't terrible. A few strut-broken umbrellas, a trail of mail across the floor. I'd seen broken glass here once before and drips of blood when she stepped on a plate she'd thrown against the wall. All was tidy in comparison.

But turning on the sink for a glass of water, I became aware of the state of the galley kitchen. There were dishes on every surface, peels and smears of food, and a slow battalion of pale brown roaches climbing over this porcelain encampment.

I shut off the water and called her name. We'd decided it would be better not to warn her I was coming.

"She sent you? Irene? I am not a well woman. I would think you'd understand, Eve, even if she can't." In her nightgown, my mother curled away from me. Above her bed, a curtain danced in a draft.

She flinched as I stepped toward her. "Mom, no one's going to hurt you." I kept my voice calm, but my own heart thrummed faster, a mimesis I'd developed as a child, when I so wanted to be close to her that I'd try to feel her fear in my own body. Now it happened automatically. She stared blankly at the poster of an O'Keeffe iris she'd taped to the wall when we moved here thirty-eight years earlier. "But it's in two hours. You have to go."

She turned to me impassively, not taking me in, as if I, whom she hadn't seen since April, were an old poster. "Do I? It's very easy not to do things, far easier than to do them. I lie here. I don't go. I have no interest in my children's tales anymore. If I finished my novel, I wouldn't be . . . I'll never finish, no. I'm old, deathly old—that should be a saying. Not deathly ill, but deathly old. Oh, go away."

I knew what would happen if I turned around.

"Wait, Eve. Stay. You never visit, and now you're leaving?"

I was very skilled at this. I sat at the foot of her bed until she was dressed and I gave her a strawberry Roll-Up from my bag and put her in a cab at Seventy-ninth and Broadway and cleaned the kitchen, pinching roaches with a paper towel and dropping them onto the fire escape as flakes of purple rained onto my arm from the window sash we painted together years before. I filled the fridge with soups from Citarella and reminded Henry James what time Sonya's school let out, because he didn't know. I cooked pesto tortellini, ready when she arrived home, and sat with her while she ate. I put my mother to bed and got on the subway with a familiar thrill of escape.

On the L, I could almost see her on an orange bench, that woman—girl, really—who would ride the train in combat boots and the shortest skirt and with a sense of daring happiness to see Henry James play music, to walk home with his arm over her shoulder. He'd put on a record, take off her clothes. Was any part of me still her?

IT WAS WITH THIS echo of a former self that I ran toward Güneş and Monica waiting for me under the yellow of a streetlight. I saw them as they'd been twenty-two years earlier when we moved here together. I saw no changes in their dear faces, just an overlay of elegance—Monica's drapey black clothes and the cut of her black hair, the gorgeous, architectural angles of Güneş's cheekbones, the gardenia of her perfume.

I was exactly where I'd longed to be all year, between them at a restaurant they'd chosen, a reservation we only lucked into, Monica told me, because Güneş had once fucked the owner's brother. Danish tables and Japanese hand rolls and a chandelier made of illuminated doll heads. "Tell me everything you've done all year," I said. "I've missed you so much!"

Güneş gushed about her book coming out with Cambridge University Press and the six months she spent at the American Academy in Berlin. Monica, in her modest way, revealed that she now taught at a psychoanalytic institute and at NYU, as well as having her private practice.

"But it's you we want to know about," they urged, asking about my life in the hinterland and what I was working on.

What could I say? My life had veered from theirs, out of the libraries and classrooms and into the green meadows of domesticity where repetitive tasks replace the hard stop of accomplishments. I joked that I was conducting research for a novel.

Monica set down her chopsticks, leather bracelets sliding along her wrist. "Oh, Eve, that's fantastic. What about?"

"Child-husbandry."

Monica smiled, that sweet therapist's smile. "Say more."

"It's like an immersive study. Fieldwork. What are the daily tasks? How does it feel?" They weren't catching on. I stuffed an entire hand roll in my mouth and kept going. "Things like, what's it like to wake in the night with both kids throwing up? Do you put the trash can under one child, and cup your hands under the mouth of the other?"

"Oh, I get it." Güneş nodded.

"I'm a mom."

Neither were, but of course they had other friends with children, albeit in a particular New York way with nannies and night nurses and private schools and husbands at hedge funds.

Güneş cocked her head. "But you're writing also, right?"

"Maybe soon. Maybe I'll write a roman à mom."

"Funny." But Monica's face was serious, sympathetic. "I just want you to have time for your own work."

She said it with such empathy, I felt like I would cry. I didn't want to cry right then. Demeter would have played along with me, laughing brightly at my joke. But then I wondered, would she? Her self-taught polymathic acuity was riddled with gaps, mispronunciations. She might still be smarter than me, but I knew so much more. Facts, fads, pop-culture references, academic jargon. What would my friends make of her? I swiped yuzu-crusted daikon in a dip made of raw crab and miso and salmon roe and serrano, so unlike our Diet Coke and blue corn chips on the balcony.

And then, because I felt too far away from her, disloyal, I attempted to gather my worlds together. "There's actually something weird happening up there."

GÜNEŞ RESPONDED FIRST. "I'M super interested in the use of *post*. How we rely on language to define time as linear even as it resists our labels. Such a male theory of narrative. Are we ever post-pandemic? Isn't the definitional experience of trauma a constant present? Isn't . . ."

Monica interrupted her. "Gün, stop, you're doing it again."

Güneş pursed her lips, an O of red lipstick. "Doing what?"

"Discourse analysis as self-defense. Your favorite coping mechanism." She lay her hand on mine. "No, Eve, this is really hard." She asked questions I couldn't answer: How many people were suffering this way? Were the symptoms the same? Had the numbers grown since the article was published? This was similar to a case study she'd read, a teenager who wouldn't leave her room since Covid. And another of severe agoraphobia, presented by a colleague. Also similar to the *hikikomori,* the shut-ins in Japan.

Her voice remained steady, soothing, and I felt reassurance, as if I'd been staring at one of those Magic Eye books and a tangle of lines resolved themselves into an intelligible form, a dragon or a teddy bear picnic, not a psychedelic nightmare. I leaned into what she was offering. "So you think it could be psychological? A post-pandemic syndrome? You think it makes sense?"

"They've ruled out everything else? No other tick bites? No evidence of anything like that? How many doctors did she go to?"

"Nine."

She frowned, but in a sympathetic way. "Oh, shoot. That's a lot of doctors, Eve. To not find anything wrong?" She asked about Persephone's affect, her energy level, her relationship with her parents.

"But that's the thing. She's not troubled. Not at all. And nothing happened . . . nothing horrific. Her mom's incredible. I've never seen a more natural mother."

Monica talked about how today's teenagers were responding to collective suffering differently than previous generations, those who'd lived through the World Wars, for example, because today's traumas were so polymorphous—airborne germs and school massacres and rising fascism and extreme weather, danger visible out their windows and streaming by endlessly on phones. Some presented with tics and constipation and chronic pain. Others shoved anxiety where it could be controlled. Burns down their arms, cutting welts into their legs. Light phobia fit right in.

She talked with such compassion about all that was happening in the field of trauma and somatization, new therapies, newly trained therapists. I wanted that for Persephone, wanted someone to shield her from the currents of dread coursing through all of America, falling with the new rains. But how would we find a therapist Demeter could afford?

"Oh my god! Northampton's near Amherst, right? Not too far?" Monica dug in her oversize quilted purse for her phone. "Kimie! I'm calling her right now."

She returned ten minutes later, cheeks rouged from excitement. A grad school friend had decamped to Amherst during the pandemic. She agreed to a greatly reduced rate and the understanding that the girl would be wearing a blindfold, at least at first. Hopefully with treatment she'd be able to take it off for increasingly longer stretches. "A minor miracle, seriously, because literally every decent child therapist has a full caseload and a waitlist from here to Jupiter, but Kimie's such a doll, she'll squeeze her in."

I handed Monica a pen, and she wrote on the narrow and sumptuous card stock that offered a list of desserts "highlighting the chef's interest in hybridity and intersectional identities in the realm of chocolate."

"Well, friends," Güneş said, leaning over to look at the menu. "We've reached peak Anthropocene. Late capitalism's co-optation of the language of critical theory to sell us what's basically a donut."

"What if we get all three?" On a rush of endorphins, I raised my hand for the waiter. I wanted to celebrate with sugar and cocoa. "Think of it as novel research. I'll write a novel about the defining aspect of our generation. How we critique but buy anyway."

iii

"PONZU AND COCONUT MILLE-FEUILLE," DEMETER READ ALOUD on the balcony. "Lyche churros with buckwheat groats. Besan ladoo meets babka. Paired with an aperitif, whatever that is, for seventy dollars?" She laughed. "Did you have these?"

"No. Well, onc. We split one. Not the wine pairing, though."

"Here." She held out the menu to me.

"No, you need it." I pointed at the phone number. I'd described Monica—her degrees, her professorships, her clinical and theoretical understanding that the mind could be involved in Persephone's illness in ways a therapist could untangle.

"But, Eve, don't you remember?"

"Remember what?" I was feeling good.

"Mandatory reporting? DCF?"

I'd forgotten. Somehow, in the return to my former life, I'd forgotten the basic fact of hers: She didn't send her child to school. I tried to rescue my gift. "So I'll tell Monica to tell Kimie not to report you."

"She's not Kimie to me. It says Doctor Agawal. And anyway, the law's the law. It really is, Eve."

"Shit. I'm sorry. I wasn't thinking."

"No, don't be. You tried. That's so kind."

"So, we'll figure something else out. Of course we will," I said, because there was nothing else to say, and I wanted to give her something, but what could I?

"What would I choose?" she said, as if she'd heard my thoughts. "Not sure what the fuck ponzu is. And I ate enough buckwheat groats in the commune for a lifetime. So this is the winner." She tapped the menu. "Sounds like a story. On a stormy night in the dark woods, Besan ladoo met Babka. And what happens next?"

Jeremiah

. . .

He hasn't visited the Chapelle du Rosaire de Vence in years, not since Will was here, but he's sitting in one of its wooden chairs this afternoon, under the towering stained glass in vivid blues and greens and the black and white murals Matisse painted from a wheelchair with a brush attached to a pole. Jeremiah's bowed over his phone, scrolling through the usual, following his own stations of the cross, and that's when he finds the letter in the Northampton paper.

When he finishes reading, he looks up. The small white chapel is dressed in blue. The sun has changed or he has. Blue from the windows colors the stones beneath him. Blue dances on the tile murals. A thought fills him like an ocean rushing in: This is something to send Will. A way to get in touch. He hurries out of the museum, edging through a group of Russian tourists outside the gift shop, walks quickly back to his Vespa.

But he can't bring himself to return to the villa for dinner where his mother's friends will expect him to laugh at their jokes and his Aunt Mimi, who just arrived, will flirt with him. This letter, which came to him—he's certain of this—because he was sitting with Matisse, will disappear the moment one of his derisive sisters asks about his plans for the future. To avoid the inevitable, he orders a croque monsieur at an outdoor café, watching the sea until he's sure the meal is over and he can slip in unnoticed.

Back at the villa, he heads to the kitchen to grab sugar for tomorrow's morning coffee and is relieved to see the housekeepers washing dishes. Dinner's done. But as he opens the door to the verandah, his mother's voice stops him.

"Apparently he's finished with Berlin now. Chop-chop. Over and out. Broke up with his girlfriend. Packed up his apartment."

"So he's like me. A traveler. A wanderer. A man of the world," says Mimi. Unlike her sister who married into stratospheric wealth, Mimi only leaves her San Diego bungalow when she gets an invitation from Elizabeth. "And where to next?"

"God knows. New York, I hope. Near family. I worry, to be honest. He's a little old for this gallivanting."

"Too old, Elizabeth? We're old. He's a pischer."

"Turned forty last month. My baby is forty!"

"Ah, a middle-aged pischer then."

Jeremiah steps onto the patio and toward a table recently set for twenty-five, his mother and Mimi at one end. "It's me. The middle-aged pischer."

His mother reaches for him, forces him into a chair beside her, stroking the back of his hand. "I wouldn't talk about you behind your back if you were ever here. We all missed you at dinner."

This seems like an exaggeration.

She turns to Mimi. "See, Jeremiah also ditched our excursion to the market at Cours Saleya yesterday and before that missed the beach trip. And what, you might wonder, does he do all day?"

"He's a grown man, Lizzie. He does what he likes, not what his Mommy makes him, right?" Mimi jabs Jeremiah unpleasantly in the ribs with two bent fingers.

"Actually, I went to the chapel."

Mimi laughs. "You're so funny." Under a puff of white hair, Mimi's face is tan and jowly, and he wonders what it's like for his mom to see a face that was once so similar to hers age in a way that she's ensured hers never will. "*Chapel.*" She laughs again. "That's what you call a pussy now? Place of worship?"

There's a noise, somewhere between a cough and a snort, from the far end of the long table. His niece Claudine. Her bare feet on her chair, a book on her knees. When she sees Jeremiah noticing her, she drops her head, hair covering her book.

"Not a metaphor, actually." With his free hand, Jeremiah reaches for an abandoned glass of red wine, tastes the wax of embossed lipstick. "Chapelle du Rosaire. Designed by—"

"Watch it," his mother says. "Germs."

"Matisse." When Mimi looks blank he adds, "Henri."

"Oh, I love it there," his mother says quietly, tightening the pressure on Jeremiah's hand. "I would've gone with you."

"Well, I wasn't stopping you," Mimi says with a huff, fixing one of her clip-on earrings. "I may not be an art collector, but I know Matisse."

As the sun sinks, the cliffs glow the color of boiled salmon. Beneath the cliffs: The pines hold orange light in their branches. Below the pines: The Mediterranean roils black. "Look there," Jeremiah says.

His mother sighs. "All I can hear is the highway. I wish they'd do something about it."

For decades she's been at war with the road beneath the villa on which people dare to drive to the walled village for espresso or Band-Aids or white beans, the problem with luxury isolation being the isolation.

"But he told you to look, not to listen," says Claude, setting her book on the table. At thirteen, she's the oldest of the seven nieces. When Jeremiah visited them in Southampton during the pandemic, they'd run outside to escape their tutors. *Jeremiah, don't throw me in the pool* meant throw me in the pool. Now, at this late September family gathering—Elizabeth never did care about school calendars—they've acquired a new languor, even the little ones, and they idly brush their hair throughout the day, and *no, Jeremiah, I don't want to swim* means no.

Except for Claude, who never brushes her black curls and carries this book instead of a brush. It makes Jeremiah so happy and perhaps undeservedly proud that she's emerging as a fellow black sheep. Just as he refuses golf and the family business, she is currently refusing to watch the movie screening with the other grandchildren, and last night she wouldn't get her fortune told from the young Spanish woman hired to read fortunes for all of Elizabeth's friends while an accordionist played "Dust in the Wind." Elizabeth loves a party, however small.

"The *loup* is glowing," Claudine continues, pointing to the wolf's head in the cliff below. "And nobody even pays attention."

"Loo? What loo?" Mimi says. "What's she talking about?"

"Tourrettes-sur-*Loup*." Jeremiah says the name of the town. "It means wolf. See it there in the stone?"

"What did your friend used to call it?" his mom says, smiling at him.

Right, Will used to claim the stone looked more like a puppy than a wolf. "Lassie," Jeremiah says. "Tourrettes-sur-Lassie."

He remembers now a night they skipped dinner to sit on the stone wall, watching Lassie glow, and he told Will—yet again—about his great plans. The films he would make. His twist on Cassavetes, Altman. And painting! Shouldn't he try painting? They were twenty-two, just graduated, and he was so impatient for it all to begin. He'd be nothing like her, he told Will, pointing up at the table from where they could hear his mother's voice. He wouldn't pay for museums to display works of art; he'd be the artist himself. Eighteen years later, he cringes at his naïveté.

"I haven't thought about him in years," Elizabeth says. "What's he up to?"

"Who's Will?" Claude leans forward. "Is that the guy who came with us to Jackson Hole when I was like five?"

Jeremiah nods happily, because isn't it a sign that his mom mentioned Will tonight out of nowhere? Out of the blue.

"Bring him to see us in Florida," Elizabeth says. "It's been too long."

Seven years. He kisses his mother's cheek; it smells of rose lotion and wine. "I really do have to go." He's filled with urgency, as if Will waits for him in the cabin below.

"Hold on, Jer." His mother's face has caught the lowering sunlight and is even more beautiful than usual. "First tell Claudine to watch the movie with the other girls."

"Claudine, don't watch the movie."

Claude shakes her wild hair. "I'll only go if Jeremiah takes me."

—

THROUGH THE GLASS DOORS TO THE LIVING ROOM, HE AND Claude watch six girls with matching purple water bottles and expressions of awe. On the screen, which covers one wall, a CGI castle is crumbling.

"This is your stop," Jeremiah shouts over the chaos of falling brick.

Claude groans. "Why can't I hide with you until it's over?"

Jeremiah hesitates, desperate to be alone. But who else will encourage her disobedience? "Let's go."

IN THE CABIN, WHICH Elizabeth recently redecorated in all white, he sits in a white wingback chair covered with a faux-fur throw—or real fur? What could be this pale other than a polar bear?—and opens his laptop.

"Will you be looking at French Tinder?"

He glances at his niece on the ledge of the whitewashed fireplace. "No, Claude. I can assure you I will not be."

She looks ready to ask more questions, but he starts typing. *So you told me not to write, and here I am. Writing. See, I stumbled across this article—a letter in the newspaper where you lived, maybe still live, I don't know. Maybe you've seen it. Maybe you think it's weird that I sometimes read the local paper from the last town where I know you lived. Well, I do. I'm always looking for you, Will. Anyway, the writers—they don't give their names—each know someone whose life has been turned upside down by sudden, unexplainable photosensitivity. And I thought, maybe that's what . . . well, you get my point.*

He pauses. If Will doesn't know about this already, if he's moved to a new city, why would he even care? Nothing he learns could help Quinn.

He highlights the sentences to delete them, feeling deflated. But then he clicks away the highlight and adds, *Too late for Quinn, I know, but maybe a path toward understanding what happened? I've put on a google alert—seems like they're calling it Emily's disease—and I'll let you know if anything more pops up.*

The URL is inelegantly long, and the letter to the editor, he realizes, skimming it again, is unreliable, its argument thin as water. "*Is the sickness befalling our loved ones caused by an airborne contaminant? Smoke poisoning? Fungus? Covid mutation? We simply don't know.*"

I know I say this every time I write, Jeremiah adds, *but I'll say it again—I'm just so sorry, Will.*

Like diving off a cliff into the blue below, Jeremiah hits send.

Claudine's face lights up when he looks up from his computer and asks about the book she's carrying around. She's still describing the lineages of Hades and Athena when a boldface reply appears.

Jeremiah's throat burns. His cursor hovers above the name. He hovers above his body.

If he never clicks on it, he'll always have an email from Will to read. If he never clicks on it, he'll always have an email from Will to read. If he never clicks on it, he'll always have . . .

Fuck off Jeremiah

"What is it?"

"What's what?" He shuts his computer. Looks at Claude. He can't really breathe.

"You just said 'shit.' Under your breath. Like, really upset."

"Oh, that. Stupid work email."

"Are you making another movie?"

"What?" He opens his computer.

"I saw what happened at your screening. When they dropped the bloody scripts from the balcony? Was it real blood? I couldn't tell on YouTube. Not like anyone in the family would ever bother to say anything to me about it. But then a girl in my science class sent me a link and asked how it felt to be a murderer. Are we murderers?"

He can't answer her now, not right now. Feeling panicky, he smiles. "I think the movie is over, Claudine. I'll walk you up."

"Forget it. I'm fine on my own."

When the cabin door slams, he understands: The last hour has been leading to this question. He's the only one here she can ask, and he's dodged, let her down. What a terrible and familiar feeling. Isn't this what he always does?

He reads the email again. *Fuck off Jeremiah*

The kitchenette's shelves hold white stoneware from Sheffield, but no glasses. Trying to calm himself, he pours scotch into a heavy mug, then closes his email and opens GoFundMe to check on Bernice. Ninety-two friends and family have donated, raising only $627 of the over seven thousand dollars needed for her bone marrow transplant. Some give just two dollars and rows of emojis. He types his stock message. *It can be a shock to receive an amount of this size from a single source. If you want to talk, I'm here. If you want to move on with your surgery and life and never think of where this money comes from, go for it! In health, Jeremiah.*

He has adrenaline now, dares a reply to Will's reply.

Gustafo. Please. I'm empty.

It's a risk, a call, a plea, all his cards out.

On the cabin's patio, the breeze is cool, although the afternoon was sweltering. He pulls the metal rocking chair cliffside. His feet tap the rim of the steep drop-off. For once, the highway is silent.

October

…

i

WHEN I WAS PREGNANT AND WOULD LAY ON MY SIDE AFTER drinking orange juice, because otherwise she never moved, I'd tell myself firmly to stop lurking in an internet forum of people whose babies had died inside them and instead to read something potentially more optimistic. One day I chose Winnicott. I knew it was supposed to console me, his idea of the good enough mother. That low-hanging fruit. But it disappointed me that the alternative to what I'd been raised by—a demonstratively bad mother—wasn't the converse, a demonstratively good mother, but only a good *enough* mother. Apparently there were endless varieties of good enough and the enough was inevitable. But enough seemed to me exactly what I didn't want to be. After all, I knew that my mother had read Winnicott. It was her copy of *Playing and Reality* I was reading, with her marginalia ("indeed!") and her underlining in thin pencil. Didn't this imply that she believed she'd been good enough? It was all so subjective! I wanted some external benchmarks, a grade from God, but the grade would only come, I figured, far too late, once the baby currently inside me was old and could recount my mistakes.

That afternoon I had the thought—although it felt scandalous to even think this, what with Winnicott's book looking at me with such ready disappointment—what if it turned out I was a good mother, full stop? Or a very good mother? Or very very very good? Wakened from her fetal slumber by fructose, the baby began slowly moving inside me. I touched my belly. Hello there. The half-drunk glass on my bureau came into my sight and I had never seen anything so beautiful as that cylinder of bright orange. I was full of a pressing joy.

In the same way, it filled me with that particular joy to think I was a very good friend to Demeter. Not a good enough friend. Hell no. Anyone could be a good enough friend. But thankfully we have the right superlative for friend, we have *best.* It's so much more exuberant and honest to our true desires.

But what did it mean to be best to someone in such a shitty situation? When Sonya went off to fourth grade, where she'd been chosen as library helper three weeks in a row, Persephone stayed home. Sometimes I'd come over with Lev while Demeter was out cleaning houses; other days Lev and I would run errands before his nap so that we could bring Sonya after school. As dusk fell ever earlier that fall, we started to free Persephone from confinement before dinner. I'd make food for us to eat in the woods, beneath the dark limbs of the oaks. Demeter and I would throw rocks into the river, and when she cried I hugged her and told her Persephone would get better, I knew it. But how thin it all was. How little I was doing.

ii

THEN, IN MID-OCTOBER, SHE ASKED FOR HELP. "BEFORE WE GO to the woods," she said, kissing Sonya and Lev when we arrived, "I have something to show your mom." In the bedroom, she carefully closed the door before turning on the light. A cardboard box sat on the bed she shared with Persephone.

"I left this with my mom for safekeeping," she said, removing rosettes of newspaper. "But when you told me about your friends? Your time with your friends? That bonkers restaurant? I asked her to send it then."

In each rosette were several baggies and in each baggie were beaded earrings. She lay them carefully on the blanket. Red and violet. Turquoise and gold. Yellow and black. "I used to set up booths at craft fairs, but you have to pay for entry, and how could I travel to them now?"

"My god, Dem, they're gorgeous."

I knew so much all at once. I knew the hours and hours she'd put into these, the meticulous sewing, the hunch in her neck. At the same time, I knew that a few years earlier southwestern beadwork had been a thing; earrings just like hers but made in China had hung from every stand on St. Mark's, on Canal, in Times Square, beside the I ♥ NY baseball hats, the foam Statue of Liberty crowns. Nothing cost more than fifteen bucks. And then they disappeared like the Tibetan bracelets, the pashminas, the fidget spinners.

"Try these on. To go with your eyes." She handed me a pair of green and purple, coming to a point, the last drip as long as my pinkie.

I slipped out my hoops and put in her pair, turning to see her reaction.

"So pretty on you. I think they'll love them. Don't you?"

"Who's that?"

"The friends you saw? And your other friends, too. And your mom's friends. Joan Yalen? She knows absolutely everyone, right? At the craft fairs it's a hundred-fifty a pair, could you get that? Or, I mean, New York City, so maybe more?"

My chest tightened. How to explain that my friends weren't exactly rich, when she'd seen the dessert menu, listened to me go on about their professorships, their trips to Berlin. How to explain this wasn't their style, they'd never buy any of this? I could hear Güneş laughing at the price. I could hear Monica wonder if the faux-Navajo patterns weren't just a titch of cultural appropriation.

"More, right?" She sidled up to my hip, nudging me. "I could really use the money. Something kind of huge happened."

She pulled a fold of newspaper from a dresser drawer. It was the local free weekly—and Demeter had drawn little hopeful stars around a circled ad.

EMILY'S DISEASE?

Unwell? Unhappy?

Do you have symptoms

doctors don't understand?

There is hope!

Reframe your Pain

Return to the Sun

Heal yourself the way nature intended—

At the Healing Hut

A blurry photo of a man and woman: *Doctor and Lenore Folkenflick have rescued count-less people from chronic pain and un-wellness at their Hut of Healing. They were trained rigorously in numerous modalities, but their pioneering methodology is all their own as are their unique capabilities of returning the Body to be healthy, well-thy, and wise.*

She was grinning at me. "Exciting, isn't it?"

"Folkenflick? What kind of a name is Folkenflick?" I said, although what I was thinking was, Oh Jesus. Not this. And then, since my knee-jerk disapproval made me feel far away from her, I interrogated my response. What exactly is wrong with this, I asked myself. Don't you want her open in a way you can't be, thanks to your schooling and your parents? Wouldn't you try anything if your daughter were sick? But no, not two white hippies advertising their unique capabilities in the free weekly. These people, we knew them already, didn't we? Maybe not the particulars, but the outlines were all too familiar.

"I thought it was the pediatrician," she was saying. "When we came here. That's who I thought would fix her. But it's these people. Oh, Eve, I really think so. I told Lenore the whole story, everything that happened, and she believed me. She didn't question it like all the asshole doctors."

"You talked to her?"

She described the kindness in Lenore's voice, Lenore's certainty that they could heal Persephone.

I tried to also be kind when I expressed my lack of certainty. Could these people really know anything medical doctors didn't? What if they made things worse? Or raised Persephone's hopes and then failed to help?

She shook her head, smiling at me. "You worry a lot, just like when you were a kid. I remember how you used to worry. Look, I like what they say here about natural healing. I'm feeling that. I like how she sounded on the phone. Honestly, there's really only one problem."

"What's that?"

Naming numbers that belonged to summer camp in Maine, yoga retreats in Upstate New York, she told me how expensive a week's stay was. However, the timing, she added, couldn't be better. She'd found this ad a day after the jewelry had arrived at her PO Box.

iii

"IT'S HAPPENING. IT ALWAYS HAPPENS," HENRY JAMES SAID THAT weekend when I told him about the ad in the free weekly. "Out of the woodwork they come! Smelling it on you."

"Smelling what?" I was carrying a plate to the sink.

He poured himself another inch of vodka. "Remember my mom's hairdresser? The packet of hair she insisted I wear under my shirt? The girlfriend who tried to cure me with magnets? The peyote ceremony? The bee pollen? The singer who chanted particular numbers over me? Pain smells."

When Henry James was seventeen, his mother and thirteen-year-old sister, Sonya, were hit by a car walking to Moscow's Izmaylovsky Park. A year to the day later, in a forest outside Ralsko, in Czechoslovakia, he developed a dangerously high fever. He was in the Soviet Armed Forces, mandatory conscription, and this was 1988—no iPhone, no calendar. He was oblivious of the date. Nobody else in the unit was sick. Nobody caught the illness from him. He hallucinated for six days, the length of time his sister had spent in a coma. His mother had died instantly. On the anniversary of his sister's death, his fever disappeared.

The next year, he moved to Havana on a cultural exchange with a music conservatory. Every morning he ran along the seawall. Nothing tired him. He'd been heavyset since toddlerhood, but the army had sleeked and strengthened his body into an instrument of warfare. Yet one morning on El Malecón, his left leg buckled beneath him. An X-ray showed a femoral fracture. "You didn't hit anything? How could this be?" the doctor asked. Henry James asked the date. It would have been Sonya's sixteenth birthday.

Despite everyone's offerings of healing, the peyote, the pollen, the magnets, the chanting, none of which worked, he found his own coping mechanisms to quell these somatic ruptures. He told me this on one of our early dates. "Like meditation? Therapy?" I asked. He smiled. "Mostly weed," he said, reaching over for the remains of my taco. "Food. Sleep." He ran a hand up my thigh. "Fucking."

Hedonism enabled his dissociative state, but it was what I liked about him. I'd been raised by a woman in pain. Henry James knew such sadness, such pain, and yet unlike my mother, he was easily satisfied.

Four green squares. A trumpet. A city. On occasion: me.

Now he set down his glass and slid an arm around my waist, grabbed my hand. I was three inches taller than him and this was how I felt safest, his forehead on my cheek.

He waltzed me around the kitchen, agile as ever, stepping in his socks over a plastic pharoah's head, a plastic donkey, a plastic hourglass. "People are going to be dangling all sorts of false cures around her head. You'll see. Someone'll tell Demeter to take her kid to bathe in special water, and someone else will say eat this plant, and someone will say recite this prayer or come to my infrared sauna. They might sound kind, but they're vultures, pain vultures, looking for attention or money or both. Smelling it." He touched his nose to my clavicle, sniffed.

THE NEXT TIME I saw Demeter, she asked when I might be able to take her jewelry to New York; the box was still sitting on her dresser. "Maybe next weekend? I figure even if you only sell ten pairs of earrings—maybe two hundred dollars each—that buys a few days there."

"Next weekend though . . . I'm pretty sure Monica's out of town." I hated lying, hated seeing past the eclipse of her blind spots: The Folkenflicks were vultures; the jewelry was worthless outside of Santa Fe where vacationing New Yorkers, drunk on the landscape, tried to buy a piece of it, feeling foolish when they unpacked the beaded earrings in their apartments—never to be worn.

What would a good friend do? What would the best do?

Ruth

...

i

THE STORAGE POD IS ON BURTS PIT ROAD BETWEEN A PUMPKIN patch and Jeff's Tire Repair. On her first attempt, she unlocks the door, but the boxes look like they're trying to say something to her and she backs out slowly. The second attempt, she drives right by. The third, she brings IPA, drinks three in the car, begins. Hello, Ramona.

Her summer sandals, her tangle of embroidery floss. Her pink vintage glassware and desert rose dishes and silver earrings and moth-holed sweaters no longer smelling of woodstove, her nightgown, her painting of a horse.

His Lego figurines in one of those blue plastic tubs where you bathe a newborn so they can't slither from your hands and bash their soft head on porcelain. The stiff paper of his finger paintings.

Their sex toys in a shoebox. His vape pen.

When all the boxes are opened, like thirsty dogs with their tongues out, she's too drunk and sad to drive home. She unpacks one she's already shuffled through. Takes out *Your 5-Year-Old: Sunny and Serene. Your 6-Year-Old: Loving and Defiant.* Books on birds of New England, plants of New England, mushrooms of New England, wildflowers of New England, trees of New England. Removes Tan and Lorde and Winterson and Myles, and there they are, the slim volumes she culled from the library's Local History room.

ii

SHE SETS THE BOX UNDER THE SIDE TABLE AND TEXTS HIM THE photo she took of his figurines, hundreds of them drowning in the baby bath, but doesn't expect a reply.

Shit I remember those

I was always stepping
on them. You slept w
two of them.

Don't come at me unless yr down w Pip
and Pop. Yo, you around at Halloween.
Got time off. Can I come home?

Home. He called it home. She readies his room immediately, buys new plaid sheets, a plaid bedspread, moves the lamp from one side of the bed to the other, the box forgotten in her excitement. On Halloween, neighborhood ghosts ring her doorbell, but he doesn't, and he doesn't respond to her text: Christmas?

HER EVENINGS DEVELOP A routine. She brings a beer and a book and her reading glasses to the couch—tonight it's the Brandi Carlile memoir—then opens her computer, types in the URL, and watches Jessie descending the far side of a tall chain-link fence, wearing an orange reflective vest, a yellow hard hat, a backpack. She leaps the final ten feet, lands on the grass on all fours. She seems to be praying, or at least gathering herself. Who is taking the video?

Stop it, Ruth. She picks up the book. Reads three sentences.

And here's the computer and somebody presses play. The camera pans from Jessie to a mechanical structure twice her height, a series of pipes and ladders and an emergency shut-off wheel, the size of which might steer a ship. Stop, stop, stop.

But she doesn't stop. Look at Jessie, so close, so alive. A loud drone of wind and her red hair, longer than in August, sails upward, making her look like a cartoon character. With bolt cutters the length of her arm, she clips a lock as easily as if she's trimming a rosebush. It takes her whole body, however, to turn the wheel. Three times she reaches on her toes, squats to pull it down. Satisfied, she steps back.

When she turns, having dismantled a section of the tar sands pipeline, there's a bouquet of yellow daisies balancing on the wheel shaft and she's grinning like she loves you, like joy is the simplest thing to feel.

At whom? *Who* is shooting the video?

But this isn't for Ruth to know. They haven't talked, not since Oh honey. I think I need to explain.

They're done, that's the explanation Jessie gave on the phone. She doesn't believe in using fossil fuels, not for love, not for groceries. She won't come back. And no, she couldn't bear for Ruth to fly over for a visit.

"I think you're wonderful, babe, but how hypocritical would that be? I fly my lover in from three thousand miles away? Like DoorDashing food when I won't drive to it? Who *does* that?"

"Everybody. Everybody does that."

But the implication was obvious. Jessie will be—or is already—loving someone nearby. Eat local.

"So, your dad's dying in Massachusetts and you look through your address book?"

"I thought about you. For years I did. Still do."

"And a day in, two days in, how'd you not think to tell me the parameters? What are the parameters now? Are we allowed to talk on the phone? Or is that too much electricity allotment wasted on me?"

A long pause. "No, we can't talk, because I love your voice. You have the sexiest voice I've ever heard, Ruth. And when I hear it, I want the rest of you. This isn't easy for me, either."

They texted for a month, actually, after that. Quickly it became delightfully lewd. At one point, Jessie wrote, in that text way where the joke is indiscernible, What if you just move here permanently ha ha. Ruth chose an ambiguous answer. Sure is there a job as head librarian waiting for me in Eugene? But the truth was Orion. She'd never see him again if she moved from his home. And Ramona? Ramona wouldn't know where to find her. No of course joking. Uhaul lesbians and all.

Then, in early October, Jessie quit texting. I miss you too much when I don't see a text from you. I'm miserable enough as is.

She doesn't look miserable in the video.

Ruth closes the tab, shuts the laptop, shoves it above the plates in the kitchen cabinet. There. She sits back down. Somehow she's in the bedroom, detaching her phone from the charger. Types the URL wrong three times before Jessie's descending a tall chain-link fence, wearing an orange reflective vest, a yellow hard hat, a backpack. No, no, no.

If Brandi can't distract, what can? She's back on the couch, drumming her fingers on the side table, when she notices the box beneath. Crouching before it, she throws out Winterson, baby care, trees, flowers, diaries of a depressed Depression Era schoolteacher, poems about the Mill River Flood of 1874.

It's slightly smaller than her hand, two interlocking water stains on a threadbare blue cloth cover. The yellow-brown title page snaps off as she turns it and she's left holding *Bountiful Water Or The Diary Of A Lady Doctress* by Lillian West. Bound by S.E. Bridgman & Co., Northampton, Massachusetts, 1852. The jagged edge crumbles onto her fingers. Keeping the book narrowly ajar, she pages past "Baths and Women's Ailments," "Baths and the Ague," "Baths and Scrofula," "Baths and Tendency of Blood to the Head." Has she imagined it?

But no. "A Digression into the Curious Case of Sun Madness OR The Illness That Went Away."

The print is tiny, heavily serifed, hard to make out. She hears the train whistle of her phone's ringtone. Orion? Jessie? But she ignores it, keeps reading about Sun Madness and the small white flowering plant that cured it, because holy shit. If this? Is it?

iii

RUTH HAS LIVED IN WESTERN MASSACHUSETTS A LONG TIME, twenty-seven years, and sometimes she feels the engine running the town is the healing arts. Above nail salons and restaurants, down the halls from meditation studios and psycho- and CBT- and ketamine-therapists, are the massage therapists and acupuncturists. The grandest stone buildings, formerly housing law offices, have been carved into small rooms for rolfers and myofascialists and osteopaths and craniosacral and somatic experiencing and Reiki and Alexander Technique and Feldenkreis and Buteyko breathing, rooms taken up entirely by massage tables, bags of sheets beneath, the glowing Himalayan salt lamp on a shelf beside a CD player—still a CD player. At any given time in town, amid the smell of mugwort incense and the sound of hand drums, thousands of needles stuck into skin waver in the breeze of rotating fans.

And the herbal apothecaries! Oh, the many herbs. Tinctures jarred in glass with black-nosed droppers, powders handed over in baggies with instructions for brewing.

After nearly three decades, she knows most of the healers. From plantar fasciitis, a torn meniscus, and other running injuries. From the year she couldn't stop bleeding and her doctor said it was normal for a woman of her age. From Ramona's miscarriages and postpartum depression. From the library and the community garden and the dump on Saturday mornings and the Tuesday-evening fun runs and Orion's preschool. *No,* they say on the phone, *never heard of anything called Sightflower.*

She's feeling good, though, as she crosses their names off a list. A brain needs a chew toy. She can finish the Saturday crossword in the span of half a cup of coffee.

She knows she should share Lillian's memoir with the people who would most care. She's printed out the Medical Mystery Collective's letter, stuck it to the fridge. But how could she tell them? They chose anonymity.

The truth is, she's enjoying herself for the first time in a while, and she sucks at collaborating. She couldn't even cook dinner with Ramona, so don't picture one woman chopping, the other sautéing, NPR on. *You have two modes,* Ramona would say, *control freak or slob, on or off, yours or who cares.*

Ruth would start to sweat when a weekend guest flipped the Sunday magazine to the crossword. "Fun! Should we do this together?"

"Actually, I'd rather just . . ." Ruth would begin.

"Babe," Ramona would call out from the stove. Just a single word, warning Ruth not to be an asshole. *Babe.*

Jen, the one who owns Wild Bergamot Apothecary (as opposed to Jen's ex-girlfriend Jen who owns Milk and Honey Herbal), hasn't heard of Sightflower but wants to gossip. "You know who came in for herbs last summer? Stephen O'Malley. Looks ancient. Wasn't he Ramona's boyfriend or something?"

"Husband. Shocked when she fell for me. What did he need? A little libido lift?"

"Actually, sad. The light thing? That turned out to be psychological? Emily, they're calling it."

"Stephen? Stephen has it?"

"No, it's his kid. That's who's sick."

Babe, she hears. *Babe.*

November

...

i

MY EXCUSES DIDN'T SEEM MUCH LIKE EXCUSES, AT LEAST NOT to me. One weekend, Lev had a bad reaction to a flu shot. During another, Henry James wanted to stay in the city for a friend's fiftieth and I told him no problem. How could I show Monica and Güneş and Irene and my mother the beaded earrings and ask them for money so that Demeter could see the Folkenflicks if I couldn't leave Northampton?

Leaves flamed gold and red. The clocks fell backward. I didn't want to sit on a bus for four hours and stay with my mother who was, according to Irene, "on the up and up," which was code for "not terrible but not great," which meant I'd be doing her laundry in the building's basement only to come home to our laundry undone by Henry James and to a conversation with Demeter I didn't want to have. *The jewelry didn't sell. Your guy's preying on the gullible.*

"Sonya wants me at her first swim class," I apologized.

"Okay, okay." Demeter nodded.

"Next weekend."

She laughed, punched me lightly. "That's what you always say."

ii

SNOW FELL FOR THE FIRST TIME THE LAST WEEK OF NOVEMBER. We ran up the stairs to 137B, shouting, "Entering! Incoming!" to give Persephone time to retreat to the bedroom, counted down from ten, then opened the door. The lights were on. Jesus looked out disapprovingly.

I dazed into the kitchen, the table bare of its usual morning cornflakes and half-filled insulated coffee cups and the four D batteries that had been rolling gently there since August. Just a slip of folded paper with my name.

My dearest dear one,

We're off to get the help we need. Be so happy for us. The doctor himself is loading our suitcase in his van right now. I don't know if we're allowed visitors but I'll find you the minute we're done. Eve, listen, I feel hopeful, so hopeful. I know you don't skew that way. I know you look off the trail at all times and see cliff on either side, but will you imagine this working? For me? It'll help me to be there and imagine you imagining us there, imagining P getting healthy. Ok, love, he's telling me it's time. Here we go.

I carried the note onto the balcony where snow fell on the dingle's black branches, and somewhere out of sight, on a hibernating woodchuck.

Standing at the railing, the white earth so far below, I remembered something from the summer Demeter and I spent together. I'd taken a book belonging to my father—it was pale yellow, wasn't it?—and chucked it in the river behind my house. Was this possible? But yes, I could see it, the yellow cover spreading like wings as it fell. And he'd blamed Demeter. How had I forgotten about this for so long? Shoved away the memory, even when we met each other again, to allow no guilt, no remorse. How bizarre brains are, trying to protect us. Until they stop.

iii

"BUT, SEE, I CAN'T EVER FALL ASLEEP UNTIL THREE OR FOUR, NOT any night," Demeter explained. She'd been leaving my bed to read and that's where my father had found her—on the couch with his college Tolstoy from the shelf.

"Insomniac," I offered.

She looked blankly. How could she be so brilliant without knowing that?

"I thought Larry would be mad. Lights out and all. They're strict at Bika Ram. But he just grilled me about the book and then gave me another. Like a teacher. Which, I mean, he is, right?"

"Professor," I corrected.

"Okay, sure. Professor."

I didn't like that she called him Larry instead of the proper term for a friend's father—your dad—but it was the effect she had on him that did me in. That night at dinner he asked her about a book he'd loaned her—a collection of Coleridge; he'd majored in Romantic poetry in college—and his look of anticipation grew wolfish, eager.

She said she'd liked it very much. "It's a good book."

"A *good* book? Wow, so Coleridge wrote a *good* book? No, I'm not interested in your judgment. What does it mean? What's it trying to say?"

She tilted her head. I hoped she wouldn't answer. "It's about how the nature world—I mean, the natural world—is the same as the inside of a person, like, their emotions?"

Was this genius? My father would know. He pelted her with question after question. I dug the toenails of one foot into the skin of the other. They were long and jagged enough to cut the skin, because I didn't want to ask Avery for an emery board nor tell her that at home my mother still trimmed my nails.

I COULDN'T STAY AWAKE for their nightly tête-à-têtes. Even envious, I was lulled into the deep with Demeter's body beside me. Every Friday he gave her a book to read; Tuesday dinners were spent in Socratic questioning. I wrote my mother that long desperate letter she still remembers, omitting the walks in the woods, the plunges underwater, the way Demeter napped on me, all of which still filled me with happiness, and waited for a response that would somehow excise the anguish that was marring my love, the blot on the joy, the bloody albumen among the eggs.

When no response came after two weeks, I knew she was flat on her back in a small Italian room, pinned to the bed like Gulliver bound by threads of depression. How would she manage without my help?

A week later, Avery handed me an airmail letter and I brought it outside. *It's impossible to describe, although my job is descriptor, just how wonderful this place is,* began my mother's letter. *Work, which had been so arduous and halting in the city, comes easily here. I hardly tire and when I do, a quick stroll around the piazza, a slice of frittata or almond torte, and I find myself revived to write another five hours. Luckily dinner isn't served until 10 P.M., and it never ends. I might be eating dinner still, talking with . . .* I skimmed the account of the other residents until I found what I was looking for. *As for your letter, darling, girls can be brutal to each other. You're entering an age when girls will use everything in their power to destroy other girls. And so much is in their power—even grown men. Your "friend" is using your father against you to feel more powerful herself. And your father, as we know, is dangerously vulnerable to youth and beauty. My suggestion, Eve, is find a new playmate right away.*

I shoved the letter in the pocket of my cutoffs. Demeter sprang up from where she was waiting in the grass. "So how is she?" I had told her all about my mother's moods.

"Terrible. The worst yet."

She wrapped her arms around me. Treating the kitchen as her own, she made me toast with honey and cocoa powder to carry into the woods. The afternoon was glorious, hot but not muggy, the leaves so sharp against the blue it seemed they'd cut their shapes out of it.

But beauty meant nothing to me. My mom had revealed the mysterious source of her depression. It was me. Living with me. Although she was just now admitting it, I realized I'd always known. And my father loved Demeter? What would I do? What would happen to me?

I barely cared when Demeter asked if I remembered that she gave me darshan when we were little, although I'd been waiting all summer for her to mention this.

As before, she stood on tiptoes. Her hand heavy on the heat of my hair. "Here are the blessings of the Mandali and the Mandali before them and before them in every incarnation, you are blessed."

Just a hand on my skull and a few incomprehensible words, yet they accomplished what my mother's letter failed to. The bloody yolk excised. My chatter of worries shut up for once. In the quiet, I could finally hear the woods. All that afternoon, I chased her through the ravine faster than I'd been able to before, and I felt the trees inching closer, wanting to say something to me.

So explain, then, why I did what I did?

Was it my father's hands on her bare shoulders in front of Fitzwilly's that Friday? "About this week's reading . . . I'm very eager to hear what you think." Her eyes darted to the white van where the boys waited for her. "But remember what I said last night. I wouldn't trust just anyone with this. No other child, that's for sure. First edition. I bought it in a charming store in Oxford. Don't leave it lying around, don't spill your juice on it. If your house, your . . . commune burns, this is the only item you grab."

The first thing Demeter did each Tuesday was disappear into the bathroom. Did she hold in her shit since Friday? She left the room clean, dried the sink basin of bubbles, scrubbed the toilet, put on Avery's lotions.

Knowing just how long she'd be in there, I slipped the book from the plastic bag. Its cover was yellow with a faint green latticework. On the title page, surrounded by intricate vines: "The Poetical Works of Percy Bysshe Shelley, Vol. II: Plays, Translations & Longer Poems." Had she really read it all?

I carried it as I ran on the steep downhill path behind my house, through the pachysandra, tripping over tree roots, until I reached the rocks above the river where I stood a moment, catching my breath. The book opened as it fell, drowning with wings spread ever hopeful.

"I thought I brought it," Demeter said that afternoon, her voice high. "I'll find it on Friday, I'm sure." Avery at the stove stirring taco seasoning into ground meat gave my dad a quick shake of her head, although whether she was warning him or disappointed with Demeter, I couldn't tell.

"Friday?" He was pacing the kitchen. "Who's waiting till Friday?" I tried to comfort her as he made calls, unfolded a map on the counter.

Although Demeter never spoke much about Bika Ram, I'd conjured up something grand and vaguely foreign. Brightly colored circus tents. A lake so large you couldn't see the far shore upon which I'd placed boats with billowing sails.

It was just a house. A wooden house with a corrugated metal addition and a barn and two trailers on bricks and a small pond thick with algae, one pink inner tube trapped in the green muck. He stopped the car in the driveway and Demeter ran to the barn.

I hoped somehow she'd find it. When she emerged empty-handed, I felt winded. Without looking at us, she sprinted toward the house, ran up its porch steps, disappeared inside.

The sky lavendered. Evening light hit the bowed heads of sunflowers. Tomatoes reached from their cages. Peas overflowed trellises. I stared at the back of my father's head and failed to imagine him forgiving me.

HE SHUT OFF THE car and we stepped out. Mosquitoes found my car-cooled limbs.

Demeter's mother settled cross-legged in front of my father, arranging her skirt around her. Her hair was hidden by a robin's egg turban, but her heart-shaped face was as I remembered from my long-ago afternoon in her apartment. On a small black slate she wrote with a piece of chalk. *Hello! My name is Akiva. We = silence after* [she drew a picture of the sun setting over a mountain].

Akiva? I remembered her as Mary Katherine, a name I'd found beautiful and evocative when compared with dull Joan.

She wiped the slate with her skirt. *You = so generous to welcome Demeter into your* [picture of house, two windows, chimney, smoke].

She smiled up at my father with a frightening vacancy, an expression I understood a mere five months later when I was stoned for the first time in Washington Square Park.

My father kept his gaze above the barn where swifts dove. "She's a remarkable kid."

Akiva wiped her slate. *We owe $ for* [picture of an open book, looking uncannily similar to my dad's book as it sailed into the water]. *We will pay!*

"For Christ's sake, I'm not looking for money."

Demeter pawed the ground with the toe of her flip-flop.

Akiva coughed, drawing our eyes to the authoritative sound of chalk. *Yes! Barter is better. I = massage + Reiki* [truly talented sketch of a hand].

"You're missing the point. Look, can we just talk? What could possibly happen to you if you talk out loud?"

She continued writing, small letters to fit in the remaining space: *Tempeh? Made here! Organic. Ghee! Churned on full moon only.*

"The point is, she was careless with my book."

Ghee + tempeh = book

"For fuck's sake," my father murmured.

"Mom, you don't get it." Demeter began to cry.

Akiva jumped up, dropping her slate. She grabbed her daughter, kissing her hair. This normal display of care seemed obscene as my dad and I watched. Pressing Demeter's head into her chest, Akiva asked aloud, in her South Boston accent, "She's torn up, can't you see? Twenty dollahs? What a book costs? That's brand-new, at Bahns and Noble."

"This book is actually quite old."

"Even cheapah." She glanced back at the house and then gripped my father's upper arm. "I've been wanting to thank you. My daughtah's book crazy now. All she does is read. It's beautiful to see."

My father sucked in air, as if to prevent a smile. "I take it you're not much of a reader?"

The look she gave him was metallic, a refusal to be patronized. She picked up her slate. *I ≠ time. I ≠ child. I = service.*

Arm around Demeter, she led her back to the house.

"Everyone here is batshit crazy," my father muttered. "You don't know your own *daughtah*." I willed Demeter to turn back, to say something to me. As they climbed the porch steps, he called, "Wait."

We all stared at him.

"Look, Eve leaves this Saturday."

I hadn't known this. I'd lost track of time, let it slip down the river. "It's been great for her, all this." He gestured toward Demeter. "My wife and I aren't much fun apparently. If Demeter wants, she could come this last week. Consider her company payment for the book."

Demeter ran so fast, I thought she might jump into my arms. Or his.

VIVALDI PLAYED LOUDLY ON the drive home. *The Four Seasons* on repeat. Nobody spoke until we pulled into our driveway.

"I swear, I never put it anywhere but under my mattress. I swear to God. The boys are lying shits."

"But it was your responsibility to make sure nobody took it."

"It's a fucking book, Dad." I'd never sworn before to him.

He hit the steering wheel. "Books are sacred, Eve. That woman can have her beads and her, her whatnot . . . her . . . Reiki. But for us there's only one thing sacred and that's books. That's what I was trying to teach Demeter."

WE SPENT THE LAST week painfully aware of time's wiliness. If we fell into our usual enjoyments, our already scarce time would speed up. Another hour gone, we'd say, astonished. Her nap ate an hour. The river stole another. We could slow time only by doing nothing we enjoyed. We promised daily letters, committed to selling four pairs of earrings each month to cover the bus fare for monthly visits and wrote out the schedule. *September: Demeter to New York. October: Eve to Bika Ram.*

She never said Larry again. *Your dad,* she said. But when he dropped her at Fitzwilly's, she leaned forward from the back seat and rested her head on his arm. On the kitchen table we found seventeen dollars. My father wordlessly smoothed the bills. The entire drive to Manhattan I tried to tell him the truth. Now, I said to myself as Connecticut passed leafily. Now. The grim towers of Co-op City. Now. But here was the Hudson River, the George Washington Bridge, sweat on my father's neck as he tried to find a parking spot.

My mother's apartment was stuffy, the living room rug damp from the city's humidity. In the morning, a taxi dropped off my paternal grandmother who'd flown from Boca Raton to live with me for the next nine months.

Our time together would be awkward and lonely. I didn't know her well, definitely not well enough to understand that pale disapproval was her sign of love—the only sign my father got as a child, although if that excuses anything, I'll never know. Not everyone could be loved by Akiva.

Demeter's only letter arrived a month or so later. When I unfolded the paper, two beaded earrings slipped out. Iridescent blue, every shade of ocean. She and her mother were on their way to Colorado with the Rainbow Family. Once they arrived, she'd send me her new address. Our bus rides would be longer, she wrote, but they would be so beautiful.

My body grew. My legs groaned all the time. My pelvis ached. Dark hair everywhere. Was I becoming werewolf? No, apparently just woman. I whispered to my grandmother who came home with sanitary napkins, ugly slacks from Morris Brothers. She enrolled me in Hebrew school at Rodeph Sholom, although I told her my mother wouldn't want me to go. There I met Rachel Rosenberg, the first girl to befriend me because of my mother. "No way, Joan Yalen for real? I fucking died when I read *Wormfood*." Rachel went to a private school, Fieldston, and leaned goth—black slips, black fishnets, black Docs, red lips. She took me to St. Mark's Place for my first piercing, her fourth. After half the requisite time with silver studs, I slid in Demeter's earrings. My earlobes grew hot and red, the holes crusty, but I felt like I carried a secret. I still expected Demeter to send me her address in Colorado. Rachel flicked my earrings. "What are you playing at? Flower child?" She took out two of the studs that crawled up her ears—a skull and a small *R*. "Put these on before I gag."

My mother returned from Italy with a finished draft of a novel, but it fizzled. *Wormfood* was all anyone wanted from her. She removed me from Hebrew school. I never saw Rachel again, but I found her double at Stuyvesant—Meredith Stein in black vintage dresses who spelled her name "Merry-Death" and sang the songs of Xanax and Adderall. Blankness, the underwater feeling of Demeter's hand on my head, could be achieved through benzos. I swept my mother's sadness away. I swept and swept. My memories of Demeter became smaller, silly, until they nearly faded altogether. Did I ever think about throwing the book? I don't think so. But one weekend, my sophomore year at Wesleyan, my mother called me home. She was sick. She was lonely. I convinced her to leave the apartment for a restaurant a block away on Amsterdam that turned out to be Ayurvedic; on a shelf sat a book with the title *Don't Worry, Be Happy* and the same photo of a bushy-haired man that had decorated Demeter's home when we were six, the man she called Baba. I brought it to our table, and predictably my mother scoffed. "What bullshit. Happiness can never be an edict." But I was so happy then, holding the book and remembering Demeter again.

iv

"BUT WHERE DO I FIND HER?" SONYA ASKED, FOLLOWING ME INTO the bedroom where I rubbed my hand over the bare dresser—no photo of Micah, none of the cards Demeter's mother sent with paintings of little lithe angels holding bouquets of lilies, no box of jewelry.

"They went to get help for Persephone. Which is good. We want Persephone to get help."

"Will she be better then? When she's back."

"Oh, probably, hon. Probably a whole lot better." I winced at my false brightness. Had I really done that? Thrown my father's book in the river? But I knew I had.

"But when?"

"Maybe a week?" I wasn't being disingenuous. I was thinking of the price Demeter had quoted me—how was she managing even a day of that? "A week," I said again, more firmly. A week is seven days, we told Lev as the three of us pressed together on their couch. We counted to seven in four languages. Such a short time. I could see winter stretching ahead in its white blankness, but no problem, they'd be back and we could trudge its path together.

I was so wrong. By the time I heard from her again, the snowdrops would be blooming and Charles Bukowski would emerge from hibernation, but we wouldn't see him because we'd never get back to that balcony.

Stephen

. . .

i

THE SMELL OF RUBBER INNER TUBES, THE SOUND OF "SUGAR Magnolia" (Winterland Arena, 1977) punctuated by the ping of metal upon metal. All is right at Flywheel Bike Collective. Stephen closes the door behind himself, unwraps paper from a section of his bagel sandwich, and takes a first bite. "Greetings and salutations," he says, chewing. "I assume nothing caught fire in my lengthy absence. No floods? No run of customers?"

The after-school boys look to Cesar. Green hair. Elder statesman. The first to respond to Stephen's flyer inviting teens to the Collective to fix their bikes for free. That was a year ago. Cesar's bike, it seems, will never be fixed.

"Just one guy. Wanted to see you."

Stephen walks toward Cesar. "Huh. Describe him."

"Like, not so tall?"

"You can do better."

"He was maybe . . . like, I don't know, from . . ."

"Yes?"

"From like China or something?"

"Are you trying to say he was Asian? Asian American perhaps?"

"But, see, I don't know."

Throat-clearing from the rear of the store. Stephen nearly drops his bagel. Ruth! As he reaches the row of purple velvet movie theater chairs where she sits wide-legged, impassive, natty in vest and trousers, he takes a bite of bagel, commits to showing none of the discomfort she elicits. "Ahoy! What brings you to our humble shop?"

He can't think why she might be here. Or why he said "Ahoy!"

She doesn't return his smile. She's always so stern. Grief, of course. But before that, when he saw her in town with Ramona and Orion, she was gruff, dour, no more than a nod for him. And even when she was young, she'd been so serious in her victory, the sexual conqueror. *No penis on the property,* she'd said with a judicial gravitas. He'd asked to talk to Ramona, that was all.

A lank of hair falls over her forehead and she neatens it to the side. "I just wanted to say I'm sorry."

Aha! She's here for the ninth step. Well, that clarifies. All her churlish taciturnity has been a decoy for addiction. She finally wants to make amends for how she treated him.

He walks toward a metal shelf that holds small boxes of pedals as well as the Casio cassette player to take a bite of the bagel sandwich, which is coming apart, tomato sliding starboard, lettuce veering port, and would be better consumed in private. With his back to her, he says, "It's no big deal, Ruth."

Although isn't it a big deal? Didn't the bonds of matrimony grant him a simple conversation with his wife? If he could've just spoken to her, he was sure she'd reconsider. If he could have reminded her of their shared interests, almost a shared brain he thought at times—their love of Celtic music and Irish poetry and the way they used to pretend, hiking in Massachusetts, that they were on a walkabout in the English countryside, stepping over stiles. What of that?

He turns to Ruth. "Water under the bridge."

"No, I mean about Kiran."

"Kiran?"

"I heard he's sick."

He groans dismissively. "It's fine." Everyone he's ever known forwarded him the psychologist's rebuttal. *Have you heard? It's called post-pandemic syndrome! Let me know if you need the name of a good therapist.*

The Medical Mysteries Collective collapsed, not surprisingly. They don't live in a shared country anymore. Doubt has left each former compatriot an island.

Their letter is already blamed for a copycat. Teenage girl, Kiran's therapist told Stephen. The most susceptible demographic. Won't leave her room. Won't turn on the light. Perfectly capable of going to school and yet no dice.

"I can't imagine it's fine, Stephen. I'm just so sorry. Kiran, man. He's always been a great kid."

Apparently that's all she wanted to say. He sinks into the chair she vacates, the velvet nap warm from her body. A great kid? Great? Kiran is sublime. And what does Ruth know of kids? He's heard that Orion doesn't speak to her, joined the army, of all things. She failed Ramona. He wouldn't have done so. He wants the apology she didn't deliver.

How long does he sit? He hears Cesar yell, "We going home, Steve. We outta here. You okay, man?"

Every day he tells the boys, you're always welcome here, what is broken can be fixed, once you step inside these walls you're automatically part of the collective, and if you steal, you're stealing from yourself. Still, he hears the clang of something metal and useful coming from their pockets. Of course he does. Nobody cares about a collective anymore.

The windows are dark when he finally rises to lock up and sees, on the seat beside him, a blue book, smaller than his hand, with two interlocking water stains.

ii

THE GREAT PRETENDER'S BARE FOOT EXTENDS FROM A GREEN sheet, a mollusk venturing from its shell. The room smells of weed and rotting leaves. From the doorway, Stephen clears his throat, willing Kiran to open his eyes and suffer the light from the hallway. What does he do all day?

That foot with its long toes, and the way he would climb barefoot on the mossy boulders in Rattlesnake Gulch.

Oh, how he loves his boy.

In Priya's bedroom, now his office, Facebook taunts: What if this were your son's new apartment in Austin, your son ice climbing in Denali, your son paddleboarding with you in Costa Rica?

He takes the blue book from his satchel and holds it in his palm, then moves it from one hand to the other and back again.

At eight, Kiran took the leftover PVC tubing from a backyard irrigation project and connected his bed to that of his parents to allow their dreams to travel to and fro. Each morning he'd rush to their room, describe his dream, and then ask for Stephen's. (Ritu left early for work.) Finally, Stephen decided to make him happy. "How odd! I dreamed about a ninja as well."

But his lie had the wrong effect. Kiran took the tubing down, dejected. "It flows, but only one way. I wanted to see your dreams and I never do."

Has there ever been a kid like Kiran? "The best kid, Ruth, the best," he says aloud as he opens the book to the place she marked with a tear of yellow paper.

iii

A Digression into the Curious Case of Sun Madness

OR THE ILLNESS THAT WENT AWAY

Although digressions irritate the more logical among us who demand the shortest distance between here and there, I will now slip away from the useful chronicle of my daily duties at the Cure and lead us down the labyrinthine side path of my encounter with the odd condition once called Sun Madness. Helpful to future generations of Hydropaths as my other chapters this may not be, but honesty calls me to note a doctress's lapses as well as her successes.

It was the first of May when I spied them from the window of the Gentlemen's Bathhouse. The botanizing ladies again—They are everywhere now, in this modern craze, noisily frolicking, carrying vasculum and knives sheathed in leather as proudly as at night these posh ladies carry opera glasses. Best Herbarium is a new category at the County Fair.

I ran to demand them leave our riverside. I didn't hide my peeve. Healing, I said, especially for a nervous debility, relies on the opposite—Calm.

"And yet flowers run on their own clock. Come see," said their leader, a woman of uncomfortable height with a ruddy face and such commanding brio I forgot my reservations and trailed her down the riverside until she spotted, with much exclamation and passion, the object of her desire. It didn't look like much, as I told her.

"But a rare spring ephemeral. It blooms only in early May. A few days earlier or later and we might have missed it completely."

She went on to say that as far as she knew, this flower hadn't yet been given its Latinate binomial. She'd seen it only along our river, not in the herbaria of the great botanist Asa Gray at Harvard or Edward Hitchcock of Amherst College. Her plan was to send it to Gray, with a request to be the one to grant it a place in the Linnaean system. I understood then the hungry look on her face. We women have named our children—our Marys and Isabelles and Henrys—but rarely are we allowed to add to the great naming of flora and fauna carried out by Scientists.

"Sightflower is what it was called by old herb peddlers," she added. "Apparently it kept rabbits from the garden and was used for something called Sun Madness, but I collect it only for botany, the curiosity of a trillium with four petals."

"Sun Madness!" I must have sounded as startled as I felt, for the botanizing ladies looked up from their collecting with curiosity on their unlined faces. They were perhaps thirty years younger than me, their mothers and even their grandmothers unable to pass on any direct experience of the illness that had so terrified me as a child. I hadn't thought of it in years, decades even, and yet despite the fulgent May sun, my stomach clenched reflexively with my old nighttime horror—my grandmother climbing into the darkness of the attic with supper for her aunt who lived in that small room with its single window tarred black.

"Do you know it?" the leader asked.

It long ago vanished, I explained, leaving behind only stories, themselves fading with the years. But it was terrible in its time. Sunlight became a poison, so much so that if a sufferer merely stepped into daylight, pain would trouble the limbs and head and purging would be uncontrollable. The sufferer must live in a constant darkness until the flower that eased the pain could be found.

I knelt to touch the white flowers, small freckles on their bracts. The illness came in summer, my grandmother told me, and the flower didn't appear until spring, and the day her aunt came downstairs after those months alone, her skin was pale as slug mucus and her muscles too eroded to walk unsupported. She rarely slept inside again, lying on a pallet beneath a white pine from spring to autumn, brushing pine needles from her hair each morning.

I had worried my listeners. Their faces tightened. "Dark all the time?" a girl asked nervously. "Are you certain it won't come back?"

"Oh no, it's been gone more than . . ." I could not say exactly. Ninety years? More?

I was called away by my nurse from the doorway of the Ladies' Bathhouse. At last, Susan had achieved a crisis and my strength was needed to dunk her in the frigid water.

We paused the baths that afternoon for dancing to greet the May, our birch pole bestrewn with iris-colored ribbons of purple and yellow, followed by a reparative dinner of cracked wheat, stewed prunes, milk, and cold water. But I remained distracted. That evening, as I administered spray baptisms and sitz baths and wrappings, I asked my patients what they knew of Sun Madness. A few women older than me had stories like mine. Grandfathers or great aunts who were themselves felled by darkness. But the younger women, the women at my Cure for relief from childbearing, sick of the smell of sour milk and sour meat and sour everything, either had never heard of it or knew it only as an old wives' tale used to frighten children into politeness. Sit up straight, or the Sun Madness will get you.

How could an illness leave so completely? The question troubled me for days. If we could learn this, could we not rid our bodies of the bronchitis or jaundice or piles or neuralgia or scrofula or fluxes or swellings from water and wind? Of foulness on the skin, of yaws or poxes or even hitch?

Pride slips in like a soft zephyr through a cracked window. If I, an aging lady hydropathic doctress with few patients, could learn what banished illness, sending it into the realm of fable, would the world listen to me at last?

But why *did* it disappear? The only person I could ask was the person I least wanted to.

I walked the three miles to Main Street after the evening baths the following Saturday. A balmy day had faded to a rain-filled night, hooves and wheels loud on wet cobble.

I found my brother, Wealthy, in Pomeroy's Tavern at his usual corner table. In the passing year, he'd lost his remaining hair, save for a gray curl over each ear, his face pink as a freshly-bathed baby, his chins lost in each other, a napkin at his neck smeared with yellow animal grease. Before him sat a glistening rabbit carcass with red flesh still clinging, a tower of pale biscuits and butter carved into globes.

All paid for by the dimes of his patients. He charges ten dollars a visit, while my patients pay $5.50 to live a week at the Cure to regain the health stolen from them by his bleedings and leeches, strychnine in their eyes, his opium, and the calomel he doses them with until their muscles lose all control.

"Sister! Still wearing those Turkish pantaloons, I see," he said, eying my Bloomer dress.

His companion, none other than Mr. Harry Buckminster, the esteemed editor of the *Hampshire Gazette,* called a waiter to bring me a chair and a plate, although I explained I wouldn't eat. My brother laughed. "Bring her water! She believes in water only. Water cures for every ailment. Her brain grows soggy."

But when I asked my question, a film of fear spread across his drunken face before it recomposed.

Unaware of what passed between us, Mr. Buckminster hit the table, rattling the glasses. "Sun Madness! Did you know that's what our own witch was accused of? I've been holed away in the court basement trying to decipher the records with their damned terrible handwriting and the spelling, what atrocious spelling."

"Mr. Buckminster is writing the definitive history of our town," Wealthy said.

"Two volumes. While the trials raged in Salem and Hartford, our small village, newly settled, had but one. One accused witch. Jane Dekker. Hanged from a pitch pine."

"For causing Sun Madness?"

"Curing it with witchery." He drained his glass, held it for a waiter to fill with foaming flip. "Additionally, a healthy cow dropped dead. Pound of flax went missing. Her husband locked her in the basement and still they saw a cat on a river barge they swore was her. Called her the Devil's packhorse, a blare-eyed witch, a base old whore. Survived, though." Mr. Buckminster leaned close, breathing heavily. "Still alive when they came to cut the body down. Couldn't kill her."

"No," my brother said, holding my gaze. "To answer you. I never think of it. In the six hundred medical volumes in my library, the only mention is from nearly a century ago. We are well rid of it."

I remembered that my brother would run from the room with fists over his ears when my grandmother told us how in the attic her aunt would grasp her arm. "Stay with me," she'd cry, trapping my horrified grandmother in the dark.

"I'm thinking of writing about its disappearance for *The Water-Cure Journal*."

"The charlatan journal, she means," he said to Mr. Buckminster. "Where every ailment demands water up the asshole!"

There was pleasure in my brother's scorn. My father knew of my dream to study allopathy, but his patrimony paid for my brother's medical education. They named him Wealthy, after all. And for me? "If unmarried, Lillian will live with Wealthy and benefit from his guardianship." I ran off to the New York Hydropathic and Physiological School, begged to work the laundry for a chance at classes at the only school of doctoring that would take me.

He spread butter on a roll and shoved it in his mouth. "Now that you mention it, the New England Medical Association has been asking for another article from me." He turned to his companion. "As an editor and astute historian, what do you think of this theory?"

Mr. Buckminster burped. "Yes?"

"Wouldn't you agree that the striking development of our age is a banishment of fear?"

"Indeed!" Mr. Buckminster wagged his bony finger at my brother. "In the opening to my book, I ask the reader to imagine living as our forefathers did, in a wilderness untamed, surrounded by unbroken forests." His voice turned quietly dramatic. "Death lurked in these woods. Savages hid behind trees, leaving only to burn down homes of pious families, steal babies, murder women and men. Bloodthirsty wolves crept behind boulders. With such terrors, society became rude and contracted."

"Unlike now, my friend." My brother tapped the rabbit carcass with his fork. "We live in a prosperous and highly civilized community. No woods nor savages nor wolves. It would follow that when fear leaves us, the diseases of fear retreat as well."

"Are you suggesting Sun Madness is a disease of fear?" I asked.

"May I remind you, dear sister, that I have six hundred medical journals in my library. Fear is bilious. The eyes are an obvious target for an imbalance of bile. In fearful times, Sun Madness flourished. Under halcyon skies, it left."

"Actually that's quite brilliant," Mr. Buckminster said. "Quite brilliant indeed."

My dreams of recognition faded, and I trudged home in the rain. What did I know of the past? I was neither a newspaper editor nor a graduate of King's College of Medicine. By the time I reached the Cure, I was drenched in body and soul, sodden with self-pity.

But no sooner did I open the door to the Ladies' Parlor than tenderness rushed toward me. "Our doctress is returned," my patients called. Ada led me to the hearth. Alice unlaced my muddy boots. Susan at the pianoforte begged me to sing with them. My life was one of poverty, yes, but of freedom as well. They had saved me a meager bowl of boiled wheat and it tasted richer than all the delicacies of the Tavern. I had a home here. I had work to do.

My digression into Sun Madness ended thus, as does this chapter.

Still, I often wonder if my brother was right. Was it fear that sent my grandmother's aunt into the attic? If fearful times return, will the madness as well?

iv

TWO DAYS LATER, STEPHEN'S NO LONGER CRYING ALL THE TIME. Calm down, he's told himself, squash hope, raise the white flag of caution. This old book by this old broad who treated illness by wrapping people in wet sheets until they upchucked? Nothing to do with Kiran. Bilious eyes? Fearful times? The Cold War was terrifying. The Cuban Missile Crisis. The Holocaust. Kiran's therapist says he skips their phone appointments. This is agoraphobic depression set off by the pandemic, he says. He's surely right.

Everybody became sick in the last year. *After* the pandemic. *Post-*pandemic.

After all, Stephen found nothing when he searched the Wide Web. *Sun Madness plant cures for photosensitivity Light sensitivity Olden days Plant Cure Heal Sightflower Lillian West Wealthy West hydropathy allopathy. Sight Flower Siteflower Siteflour Sightflour. Harry Buckminster* (whose name is in plenty of old newspapers but apparently never finished his two-volume history).

Stephen even wrote on a medical mysteries subreddit. *Emily/ Photosensitivity illness—not post-pandemic syndrome after all? Clues from the past suggest it existed historically. Have you heard of SUN MADNESS?? And there's a plant that which cured the pain! But we need proof! Do you know someone who had it before the pandemic? Let's crowdsource! Let's work together!*

In Burlington, four decades ago, he had a midnight to four A.M. radio show on Tuesdays—*The Dead Hour*—and felt cocky about his voice threading into maybe thirty dorm rooms. With this message board, there's no end to his reach. His words replicate, metastasize, clone, slipping into billions of pockets, just waiting to be found. What is the internet but a collective of the infinite?

And yet he checks again. No response.

Jeremiah

...

HAS NOTHING CHANGED IN THE NEARLY EIGHT YEARS SINCE HE was last here? Same restaurants geared toward collegiate palates—pita, pasta, bubble tea. Same people on the sidewalks. White haired and puffer coated, hunched from the pain of December when New England's quaintness is revealed as merely drab, its charm reliant on the costuming of leaves, green or orange.

His plan? To speak quickly before Will shuts the door in his face, something like, Hey, I know you didn't want an email from me, but there are some people who might want to hear from you about Quinn's illness. Not wanting to show up empty-handed with nothing besides the Reddit post on his phone, he heads into a bookstore, but what to get for a man who refuses to talk to him? For his twenty-third birthday, Will gave Jeremiah *Moby-Dick*. A little on the nose, that gift. In his senior year, Will had written a paper pretentiously titled "Homoerotic Herm(a)eneutic: On Melville's Missives to His Hawthorne."

He chooses a paperback of *The House of the Seven Gables* and feels a lift, as if a flirtatious exchange of literature is all they need to slip back in time.

Waiting his turn to pay, he notices a man in a long Canada Goose coat and Berluti sneakers and an oversize cashmere scarf, sartorial status markers common in cities but conspicuous in this town where everyone looks ready to either shovel an ice dam or lecture on Freud. As the man laps the store without paying attention to any actual books, Jeremiah thinks of the exclamatory line in the Reddit post. *And there's a plant that which cured the pain!*

Surely he's not the only one whose attention caught on those words.

Surely lackeys at pharmaceutical companies or the smaller biotech firms showed the post to their superiors, offering to talk to the guy who wrote it. If the plant does anything—he hasn't really considered its efficacy yet, thinking of it more as a potential path to Will—but if it has potency, someone is going to snatch it out of the hands of the hopeful, clueless schmuck who posted on Reddit. Filled with loathing toward the man in Canada Goose, Will watches him leave the store, then sets Hawthorne on a table of books about cats—it's all wrong, anyway—and follows.

He stops short when the man does, pulls off his glove when the man does, the two of them typing on their phones, separated by a few feet. Hi Will, he writes. Happen to be in Northampton! Ok if I stop by? But he can't send the text because the number he has for Will went out of service years ago, so instead he scrolls through his photo library.

HERE ARE THE YELLOW curtains in their room at the Hotel Revolución in Cuba, where Will told Jeremiah he was moving to Northampton to live with Quinn, who was sick with some weird and undiagnosable thing. Annoyed and jealous—although the deal was that neither would ever be jealous—Jeremiah said it was probably nothing.

Here's the terrace at the Hotel Rathaus Wein in Vienna, where Will said the acupuncture, herbs, meditation, weed, and Advil hadn't helped, so he'd taken Quinn to a pain clinic. The doctor showed them the glossies from the company, explained it wasn't addictive if taken on schedule. Failing to treat pain was the true breach of ethics, he said, and there was nothing to worry about.

This was 2016. Jeremiah knew everything there was to worry about. He didn't come out and tell Will how money came to his father—and to himself. No, after all those years together he didn't specify which pharmaceutical company his father's cousins owned. But he did tell Will to stop Quinn from taking the pills. He did say, emphatically, that they should try everything else first.

After that, Will said Quinn was too fragile to be left alone. The Oxy had stopped working as prescribed. Quinn ordered extra pills online. Sucked an Actiq lollipop at work. But Jeremiah pushed it. Will wanted to see him, too, he always did, but he never would have left Quinn if Jeremiah hadn't pushed. At least, Will said, we should stick nearby.

He doesn't have any photos of the Airbnb in the Berkshires where a broken smoke alarm kept them up at night, while an hour away in Northampton, Quinn sold a nineteenth-century painting of Tourrettes-sur-Loup that Jeremiah had given Will and bought pills laced with fentanyl.

BY THE TIME HE looks up from his phone, the man he's calling Pharma Spy has disappeared. Jeremiah looks for him along Northampton's main street and then gives up and wanders through the pottery/jewelry/knickknack stores. Nothing's beautiful enough for Will. He wants to show up with a Grand Gesture. But twenty-two years of grand gestures has devalued grandness. *Let's fly away somewhere, Gustafo.*

In Hope and Feathers Florist, he buys a bouquet of orange alstroemeria.

He parks around the corner, wipes pretzel dust from his jeans. His mouth feels dry and gummy. They were thirty-three the last time they saw each other. Has Will's hair grayed? Who lives with him now? Who gets to love him?

But Will's apartment, that gray duplex at the end of the block—it's gone. Simply gone. A flat-faced modernist house with a wood facade and metal doors has taken over two lots, as if it tornadoed in from Venice Beach. No doorbell to ring, no door to open, no mailbox where he can leave a note. There's no Will, there's no way.

Ruth

...

STEPHEN IS ANNOYING HER. FIRST OF ALL, IT'S STEPHEN! HERE at her kitchen table. Wearing an explorer's vest and hat, a green felted number with owl and hawk feathers stuck into the band.

Second, he's blowing his nose on her flowers of Minnesota dish towel, as (third) he explains in his tiresome way that they'll write a letter to the newspaper all together, a collaborative effort, to ask if anyone has heard of Sightflower. "Let it flow," he's saying. "Just spitball. Nail down our big themes. Then we'll go micro, paragraphs, sentences."

My god. She could write this letter herself in five minutes.

Still, it's a group project she agreed to when Stephen had shown up at the library, begging for help. She'd thought she was finished with Lillian when she'd left the book for him.

But she loves a puzzle, she does. And how else do you respond to someone pleading? "I need you, Ruth," he'd said. "Only one other person responded. What can you do with two people? You need a group for this sort of thing. At least meet him with me."

Will's so tall and skinny he looks elongated, pulled like taffy. His face is youngish but his thick light brown hair starts far back on his forehead as if making way for his large square glasses. As he walked into the apartment, Stephen thumped him on the back, with an air of gotcha! "Hold on, let me guess. You're a professor."

Will laughed. "I think you just mean I'm an unkempt, overread Jew, although not nearly well read enough to achieve professor status."

He seems kind, considerate. When she told them she'd called botanists at all the area colleges and horticultural societies and herbalists and healers and even Ramona's doctor and the Victorianists at Hampshire, Mount Holyoke, and Smith and none had heard of Sightflower or Sun Madness, it was Will who handed a sobbing Stephen her dishrag.

Now Will rakes his fingers through his impressive hair and it stays upright, Einsteinish. "Yeah, see, the thing is. I keep thinking . . ."

"Just let it roll, man. No idea too small."

"Right. Good. But do we really want to put it out there? I'm just thinking this through, so bear with me. Let's say a drug company reads our letter."

Stephen lifts his hat. "I welcome you, Big Pharma, and your plenitude of resources."

"Yeah, no. I get that. I really do. But these companies, you know they patent seeds? So if they get to Sightflower first? If they patent it? Scientists can't do anything then. And let's say they sit on it until they decide they can sell the most units. Five years? Twenty? Forty? This is the kind of shit they do. If something stops pain, someone's getting rich."

"My dear compatriot, you don't have to convince me of the nefariousness of America's corporations. No letter then? Simply word of mouth? We invite interested parties, face-to-face, as it should be. Someone from pharma tries to barge in, we shut them out."

"But"—Will knocks on the table—"how do we know?"

Stephen chuckles. "I assure you I can tell a pharma rep from a grieving parent or a local horticulturist."

"Can you, though?" Will shoves out of his chair and starts pacing her living room, pushing aside the coffee table with an apologetic nod to Ruth. Unlike Stephen, he seems aware of taking up space; perhaps this is generational progress. (Still, he takes. The way he grabbed her dishcloth from her oven. The way he now derails the letter-writing.) "I have a friend," he says. "Dad works for pharma, opioids, terrible company, and they send reps all over—years in remote villages to learn—what's the right term these days? Folk remedies? Ancestral knowledge. Nobody knew, though. Claimed to be sociologists or lost tourists."

"You're worried about spies?" Ruth is trying to imagine a spy coming to Northampton to gather ancestral remedies from Nice Tea, Pita Pocket, T-Mobile.

"I mean, kind of? It's not so hard to dress like a local, grow the beard, find a vest with a broken zipper." He grins at Stephen. "Although if I grow a beard, you'll say I look like a rabbi."

"Well, what about you?" Ruth asks. "Couldn't you be a spy then? We've never seen you before."

"No, good question, Ruth. That's the right question." Will pauses, while Ruth thinks, Jesus, don't compliment my question-asking. "See, Quinn, my boyfriend, I told you. He was an outdoors sort of person, though not in a . . . not in a . . . not in a sporty way. He biked everywhere, did some landscaping, set design, antique dealing, silk-screening. That sort of thing," he finishes, as if this were a list that had an overarching thingness.

He's in front of the windows and reaches up to grab hold of her curtain as if to steady himself. "His light sensitivity? What you're calling Emily? He couldn't stand being inside. I took him for pain meds. This was 2016. Before the pandemic, like I said. And, well, yeah. He OD'd. Yeah, thing is, I can't get over it. I haven't really made a life for myself since, not a real life."

He flinches, shutting his eyes a moment. "It was that friend actually, the friend from the pharma family, who emailed me your Reddit post, Stephen. And as soon as I saw it, I thought . . . Well, I can't help Quinn, I can't. But I'd like to do what I can. I don't want anyone else to go through what he did."

His face is tight with grief. Tightness seems to overtake the whole room. For the first time, she allows herself to consider Kiran, really consider him, in his childhood bedroom with the blinds drawn, no way to leave without pain. She looks at Stephen and then together they look back at Will with sympathy, almost as parents, a strange moment of mutuality.

"Okay, then." Stephen swallows. "We keep it to the three of us, if you want. What's our plan?"

The men turn to her. She's ready. She could have told them what to do an hour ago. She shows them her color-coded list of all the local colleges and historical societies that keep botanical books of pressed flowers. Think of the botanizing ladies. If even just one herbarium was saved for science, well, they should be able to find it. "We know what to look for. A four-petalled trillium. White flowers. Maybe a new Latinate name. We bring that to a botanist and take it from there."

They divide up the list. Everything's closed for the holidays, but they can start in the new year. "Okay, then. So we're all set," she says, picking up their glasses. Isn't it obvious she wants them to leave?

But they seem not to notice. Stephen actually reaches into her cupboard for a new glass, fills it with water from the sink. Even the way he turns the tap fully, so it sprays onto her drying rack, irritates. He wants to talk more about Sun Madness. And Will does, too, leaning forward, eating the Trader Joe's olives she'd put in a bowl this morning because a host has to do something.

And, well, to be honest, it's not bad. She's spent weeks thinking about Sun Madness on her own—What it could be? Did it really leave and come back? Is it related to Emily?—and it's not so awful to speculate with others. They're curious about her theories and posit a few of their own. A fungus? Something in the water? They are, she'll admit, spitballing. And it's sort of great. Until Stephen knocks on the table. "So, Orion? I hear he's . . ."

"Texas. Doing engineering work. He's fantastic."

"Engineering. Well, huh. Good for him."

She senses a hint of disbelief in his tone. Is he actually patronizing her? "Coming home for Christmas," she lies, looking him in the eye. "Can't wait to see him."

"Well, that's wonderful. Isn't it wonderful? Bring him over."

"Sure will."

"No, I'm serious, Ruth. We have a big Christmas Eve party every year. Let us feed you."

He emails her a list of potluck requirements. *Last names L through Q—dessert.*

On the twenty-third he calls to say the party's canceled, too hard with Kiran in his room, but she and Orion should come over in the afternoon, just the two of them. On Christmas Eve she turns on the radio for company and turns off her phone.

BOOK
TWO

. . .

VERDANCY

February

. . .

i

I KEPT FINDING THINGS TO SHOW HER, LINES FROM BOOKS TO READ to her, but since I couldn't, these observations disappeared into the cold air and I started noticing less; without her as witness, my days seemed to pass without imprint.

Covid, ear infection, RSV, strep. I didn't put the thermometer away. The same three inches of snow fell and melted, fell and melted.

Snow day, sick day, snow day, sick day. When Sonya actually went to school, I arrived early, tried to make eye contact, waved hi. But nobody lingered in winter. They'd rush their kids back to warmth. I felt a pressure on my head as if I were descending in deep water.

How had she afforded three months there already? Or—as seemed much more likely—why had they returned to New Mexico without telling me?

If beaded earrings hung from Güneş's and Monica's lobes, then would she have called from the Healing Hut? Found me again when she left? If I'd even just tried to sell them? Why had I been so stupid, thinking I knew what she needed most?

FINALLY, I TOLD HENRY James to please just move in with us. I couldn't keep doing this all alone.

We were in bed, divided by a small strait of clean socks I'd forgotten to put away, and he set his phone on his stomach. "Oh, Eva. Winter's hard. I hate being away from all of you."

I flipped to my side and watched his phone rise and fall with his breath. He didn't say anything more.

"Okay, so how about I go to the city every week and come back weekends?"

He laughed. It could only be a joke. "You'll stay on Vlad's couch? He snores."

"I'll stay with my mom." I felt excited, even at the joke. Demeter had been gone three months. There was nothing for me here.

"Fun times with Joan."

"I'll be working. I'll barely see her. I'll stay out late every night."

"Every night, huh?" His phone jiggled with his laughter. "What's your job?"

"Güneş says they're hiring adjuncts for everything now." I imagined what I might wear, boots that clicked on the classroom linoleum, a folder of syllabi to hand out, names to memorize, their half-formed essays to discuss. I had loved teaching. "You can stay here and, I don't know, give music lessons, and also be with the kids after school."

"Eve," he said sighing, cutting off the fantasy. Because we had an agreement.

WHEN I WAS THIRTY-THREE and Henry James was forty-one, I moved out of his apartment above Pete's Bar in Williamsburg after he told me he wouldn't have a baby. *There's no way. A baby would be the end of everything.* I found roommates in Clinton Hill, brought chicken soup to my mother on the Upper West Side, taught my classes in the Village, went on bad dates all over the city. Every month or so, I'd show up at Pete's Bar, beneath Henry James's apartment. In the morning, he'd cook eggs, put on music he'd been waiting to share with me. Finally, he told me to stop. "This is too hard for me, Eva. You're my only family. I look at you and I'm home."

The writers I dated never asked me questions. The teachers I dated were cynical, depressed. I tried to find someone who would stop his whole day to look at green squares. What I wanted, I know now, was to be the person who would stop my whole day to look at green squares.

I decided to have a baby on my own. I met with an obstetrician, scanned sperm donor databases. But then it occurred to me, why not with Henry James? My logic felt impenetrable when I explained it to my skeptical friends. I put on a dress, took the L to Pete's Bar. Henry James's fingers rested on the back of a woman's neck, their foreheads together. I knew her—platinum pixie cut, worked at a bakery in the East Village. I couldn't breathe. She was a painter, no kids, his age; they'd be perfect together. I believed I'd never find anyone else who would tell me, like he had, to write, who would give me Greentime. I left the bar.

I'll do everything, I wrote in a letter. He only had to offer the child his enormous love, occasional omelets, no sacrifice of his creativity, no changes to his artistic practice. *Play music every evening. Sleep in. The baby and I will tiptoe to the park to watch the sun rise.* I thought it would be no harder than doing it alone. I had no idea that a baby was a person.

We met at a diner near my mother's. "Why would I want you to do this, Eve? I want you to write." I stared at his large hands around the small white coffee mug.

"But I'm having a baby either way."

I was pregnant when we were married in Fort Greene Park. My dad and Avery and their two sons came from England and everyone held hands and Henry James and I stood in the center, surrounded.

"EVE, COME HERE." HE pinched off his glasses, set them on the table beside him, nudged me over so my head could rest against his underarm. "When Lev goes to kindergarten, you'll get a job, any job, maybe not teaching, maybe admin, who cares? We'll move far out in Queens, wherever we can afford. I hate missing you, my family."

I'd given him that—a family, an entire family. I thought about how well my arrangement had worked for him and how poorly for me, and as he fell asleep, a great surge of rage came upon me. I moved to the window, pushing aside the curtain. The full moon was casting a shadow forest onto the snow. Shadow trees like figures dancing, tall lanky bodies, benevolent and undulating and free. I raised the window sash, the outside air nearly liquid in its coldness. I wanted to crawl through to the gambrel roof and jump into the snow and just run for it.

Oh, I knew, I knew: If I was trapped, it was of my own devising. I couldn't blame anyone else, except the whole world and the economic system we all agreed to participate in. But I wanted more life. Just that. More life. To walk down a strange street, to talk to strangers, to buy the flowers myself, like Mrs. Dalloway, although there were no flowers in Northampton's winter and no party.

Henry James woke and sat upright. "Fucking hell, Eve. Close the window."

No, I would somersault out the window, swan dive, swim to a new life, kick my feet in the liquid air.

"Can you imagine if I had a mother who would say, 'Honey, you're working so hard. Let me watch the kids for a few days. Let me give you a break.' Can you even imagine?" Or if I had a husband who would say that, I thought.

"Come to bed."

"I want more life," I said. "I want adventure."

He lay down, arms crossed in front of his chest.

"Did I ever tell you," I said, "about the theory of mothers and adventure?"

He pulled my pillow over his head. It was just as well, because it would be cruel to tell him, who lost his mother so young, the theory that mothers and children together destroy the narrative. For children to set off on an adventure, the mother must die—drown or be killed by Voldemort or expire from cancer. Only then can a story begin.

Likewise, for a mother to have an adventure, she must leave her children by train at midnight like Alice Munro's agitated heroines, setting up new lives unencumbered—or by plane to study philosophy in Oxford for three years like Susan Sontag or to Rome for a year like Joan Yalen. If a mother tried to remain home and have an adventure, it was always just an affair, and it either killed her literally—see Emma Bovary and Anna Karenina—or metaphorically with sadness, removing her from her children either way.

But couldn't a mother stay, remain a good mother (or very good or even very, very good), and have an adventure of some sort? Was there any way?

ii

"WE'RE GOING NEW PLACES," I TOLD THEM WHEN HENRY JAMES left again. Sonya suggested the mysteriously named AmazePlace at the YMCA, about which her classmates raved. But it cost money so first we tried Dave's Pets and Beverages. There was an iguana molting and a parrot that wouldn't speak. We tried the library second, but the tiny house in the bonsai tree made us sad.

The AmazePlace turned out to be a towering rodent run, a vertical maze built from PVC and caged in netting. Within the netting were ramps and rope bridges and foam tunnels, all sorts of hurdles to the goal, which was to reach the top and shout down at your mother (it was only mothers here) from a great and domineering height—*watch me*—before descending an opaque tube slide in which it was impossible to actually watch the children, despite their implorations, and where the true drama, the Amazement perhaps, took place as children crashed into those who would wait at the bottom. We could hear them screaming inside the plastic tube.

I sat outside the claque of mothers with my *New Yorker* in the windowless room and read an article about a photographer who traveled to places altered by rising oceans—Amsterdam, Venice, Miami, Juneau—taking pictures of herself in a bikini made of bubble wrap. *L___ is using her body to telegraph . . .* What exactly she was trying to telegraph, I didn't learn, distracted with thoughts of the hotels she might stay in, the white duvets, or the spare rooms of artists' houses, a vase of dahlias on a bedstand, dinner parties, nobody asking anything of her tiny body, and did she leave any children behind for her multiyear adventure, and where was Demeter?

"Watch me," Sonya called at the top of the slide, and I watched the blue tube for the duration of her time inside and then returned to the article. The photographer spoke of her sadness that unlike her, most people couldn't imagine the world as it was to come. I tried my hand: warm winters, uninhabitable summers, the YMCA abandoned, vines wrapping around the PVC piping, clinging to the netting, clogging the slide. Look how good I am at this, I told the artist in my head. I see green everywhere. It was glorious. And then a child kicked Lev in the mouth and winter returned.

The next afternoon, they begged for more Amazement, but no. If I couldn't have an adventure, I figured, at least give me the green I'd imagined.

iii

THE SMITH COLLEGE BOTANICAL GARDEN GREW WITHIN VICTORIAN domes, white painted struts and glass panes that shook with wind. Inside, though: life! Tendrils and leaves and trees and the green tang of soil. "Is this real?" Lev asked. And it did seem sci-fi, all this green and heat after months of ice-white, trunk-brown winter. I felt something tight unfurl inside me.

A man walked toward us on the brick path. I had to stop myself from waving. *Oh, you.* He looked that much like a photoshopped version of my great-uncle—same long, ponderous forehead, same angular nose. Same enthusiastic brown hair. Although instead of my great-uncle's lush beard, this man had generous lips and a narrow, pointy chin—a skull that began mightily but ended apologetically.

He smiled back. Already he made me feel like we were in on a joke. This one began like: An Ashkenazi Jew meets another Ashkenazi Jew in an enclosed garden.

We're a small and inbred genetic pond, and I nearly always feel a little bump of recognition when I see someone with my genes, even if I don't want to (i.e., Hassids or finance bros). I wondered if I reminded him of anyone. Cousin's daughter, he later told me.

The garden paths were circuitous and narrow and we kept moving out of the way of each other. At a small koi pond, trilled with water lilies, Sonya grew conflicted. She wanted to sit on the iron bench and pretend she was in ancient Kyoto with a winged monkey beside her but didn't think she was allowed.

"Of course you can sit there," I said.

"No. It's for scientists." She pointed from plant to plant. "This whole place is for science. We shouldn't be here."

"It's for anyone who needs it."

"Needs it for what?"

"For . . . verdancy."

She looked confused. "You mean for urgency?"

"Verdancy. Like . . . urgent for green." Sure, I was performing a little. The man had stopped to look at a palm near us, hands clasped behind his back, and I was pleased when he laughed and turned. He'd taken off his jacket in the heat, and I could see light hair in the V of his button-down.

"And vertiginous?" he asked.

"Dizzy for green, with some nausea."

His smile was extravagant, like money falling from a pocket, caged on both sides by parentheses. I lost sight of my great-uncle. "Inadvertent?"

"To happen upon green."

"And vertebrae is what? A green spine?"

"Necessary for a green thumb."

"So inverted?"

"Everything out there." I gestured to the panes above us. "Winter."

"Invierno in Spanish. Hiver in French. Talvi in Finnish. The *v* seems important. I'm showing off, sorry. I haven't talked to anyone in a long time." He took off his tortoiseshell glasses to rub his nose. His hazel eyes were deep set and ridiculously lashed, giving them a tender and overeager aspect, as if they needed so much protection.

"Nobody?" Lev asked. "You talk to nobody?"

"Nobody with such . . . this sort of enjoyable verbiage as your mom." I was relieved he was looking at Lev and couldn't see me blush. "I do order coffee in town each day, always the same order, and each day the barista, always the same barista, asks me my name."

"Maybe she can't 'member it," Lev said. "If it's a hard name. Nobody 'members my name."

The man's smile vanished. "I promise I'll remember it," my great-uncle said solemnly.

"What is it then?"

"Well, you have to tell it to me first."

Lev looked up at me. Stranger danger—just one of the many

frightening potentialities I'd prepped them for. "It's okay. You can say your name."

The man—he was very tall—bent at the waist to shake my son's hand. "My name is Will and I'm very happy to meet you, Lev."

"Maybe you should tell her that you want her to remember your name," Sonya said. "Maybe she doesn't know it means so much to you."

"Quite a good point. So, tell me, do winged monkeys make good pets?"

"They're not pets," Sonya said imperiously. "They can come and go as they please. I wouldn't keep one in a cage."

"Right. Of course. When they're not with you, though, do they travel back to Oz? Does it take them a long time?"

Her eyes darted around and I could tell she was deciding whether to trust him. "The thing is," she said quietly, "Oz isn't that far from here."

"Right." He nodded seriously, stomped one foot on the path. "The brick road. Yellow if you squint."

I hadn't put that together. She looked up at him with surprise. He'd figured her out. "It's not yellow," she explained, "but it turns yellow when . . ." Distracted by two tweens who appeared on the path holding high their pink-cased phones to snap indiscriminate photos of foliage and overstory, she turned to me. "Can I? Can I go in the cactus room by myself and take pictures?"

"And me, too," Lev said.

"If you can share," I said, handing over my phone.

"Great kids," Will said, as they walked away. "She's a smart one."

There was so much I wanted to ask him. Where had he come from and was he related to me and did he live in Northampton or was he visiting? Cautious, I chose the latter. He'd been here a month, he told me. Came to look at Smith's plant books, the collected herbaria. Dried plants. He liked to wander through the living plants when the horticultural room closed.

"So you're a botanist?"

"Yeah, not really. Or not at all."

"But a scientist?"

He drew a breath, glanced around. "More like . . . an actor. Well, precisely that. I'm studying for a role as a botanist. Do you work here, too?"

How to answer? *Oh no. Mostly I play Busytown.* I mumbled about writing and then, to telegraph a life beyond motherhood, found myself saying—I hadn't done this in so long—"Did you ever read the *Wormfood* books? My mom wrote them."

I felt immediately embarrassed. That old shortcut to the soul of my generation. But it worked. His posture relaxed. He raised his palms in shock. "*Wormfood*? Seriously? I was obsessed. Man, I used to wonder how that lady came up with such dark shit. She raised you? That sounds like actual hell. Sorry, was she nice?"

Then the kids were coming back, they always were. I could tell there'd been a fight about the phone, there always was. Tears on Lev's face, fury on Sonya's. I hurried them out of the gardens with a quick wave to Will.

MY SMALL DECISIONS DIDN'T seem like they added up to a whole. I canceled our new Y membership, bought the cheaper chicken nuggets trying not to think about the chicken within. I scrolled Care.com and found Pax who advertised themself as playful and responsible. I taped the doctor's number to the fridge. Pax arrived with a Magic 8 Ball, and although this was my kids' first babysitter in Northampton, the magic pulled them from me.

I figured that if I didn't find him, at least I'd look at plants alone for an hour, its own sort of adventure. But there he was in the Camellia Corridor, wearing sneakers and a long old-fashioned overcoat, looking at an orchid.

I was so nervous I couldn't say anything. When he noticed me, his face lit up. "You're back?" He moved to shake my hand, then pulled his hand away as if reconsidering, and waved awkwardly. "No kids today?"

"They're with . . ."

"Their dad?" he rushed in, as if to tell me that he understood I was married. "Your husband? Or wife, sorry."

"He's in New York right now. My husband is. A babysitter. I

needed some time . . . some . . ." I didn't know what to say. Why had I come here?

"Verdancy, right?"

"That's it."

"Well, we could walk around . . . or not. Depending if you want company in your verdancy."

"Convergency you mean?"

"I was about to say it." Grinning, he gestured for me to go ahead on the narrow path, and then started off before I did. He had, I was learning, such a compelling mixture of physical awkwardness and intellectual confidence. Compelling to me, at least. I wondered if he was single, wondered who else would find him attractive.

"So, you always do this for a role?" I asked. "Move somewhere and study what the character would? And then, what? You figure out their motivations? Backstory?"

He laughed—that generous smile. "No it's just nerves, honestly. An excess of anxiety and I guess you could say an excess of time as well." He'd been a theater major in college, he said, but he stopped auditioning once he got a job as a high school theater teacher. He left that for computer stuff, made enough cash to take time off, and a friend, knowing he missed acting, hired him for a play he was directing. Rehearsals would start in May.

"I play Professor Harry Buckminster, mid-nineteenth-century botanist obsessed with creating the world's most comprehensive herbarium. It's at a tiny theater in Columbus, Ohio. I definitely don't need to prepare this much. But I'd never seen an herbarium so I figured . . . and, well, it calms me down to look at them and think about how they made Professor Harry Buckminster grow apoplectic with a competitive desire to collect the most . . . Do you hear that?"

A tapping had begun overhead, like fingernails against a window. We looked up to see hail pinging off the glass panes, while all around us was summer. "Like we're in a reverse snow globe," he said, looking pleased. "Okay, enough about me. Tell me about you."

I began my foundational story, what I believed anyone would need to know to understand me. That is, Joan Yalen. An old tale, well trodden. I told it pithily, the usual lines.

Will, though, swerved off that path, asking question after question, following up on small details, sending me back to the beginning, to my great-grandmother who died in Treblinka. To my grandmother who survived and moved with an American soldier to New Rochelle but then screamed in terror at night when my mother tried to talk to her and who killed herself when my mother was eleven. To my mother's months in bed and year in Rome.

"She wouldn't take me to college," I told him, sliding into another reliable anecdote. "Too busy erasing all traces of me. Turned my bedroom into her office before I crossed the border to Connecticut. That night she threw a party to celebrate my absence."

I'd learned about her party years ago from Irene, and although it bothered me more than I let on, I always joined in with the laughter it elicited. But Will wasn't laughing. "Wait. Back up. Rome for a year? When you were how old?"

"Twelve. Well, past my thirteenth birthday. But it wasn't that bad. She used to say at least she didn't kill herself like her mom did." I played this as usual—macabre but jocular.

He remained serious, brought a hand to the side of his face as if he'd been slapped. "Shit. *Shit.* What a terrible, terrible thing to say to a child. If death is your baseline, nothing else can hurt. Nothing you felt as a kid could ever be bad. She sucked up all the badness. All the bad moods were hers. All the feelings. But you were just a kid. You deserved to have all the feelings."

"Well, my mom . . . I mean, she's Joan Yalen. Should we give up her books so she could comfort me at bedtime? Chat with me at dinner? Everyone tells me her books saved their lives."

He bent his head, as if thinking, then looked back at me. "Honestly? I fucking loved *Wormfood.* And yeah, I had a shitty dad. A really shitty dad. After he'd scream at me, or worse, laugh at me, I'd hide in my room, in this space between my bed and the radiator." He held his arms apart. "And I'd read those books until I could stop crying. I kept them under my bed. But I'd give them up for one kid not to have a crap-ass childhood, I would."

"The math doesn't work. One versus many."

He began smiling slightly, almost sheepishly. "Man, I bet you were an adorable little kid. Your big eyes. Did you look like your daughter? I can see it. I really can see it."

He was staring at me as if I were something wonderful.

Oh, I loved that. Nobody looked at me. They expected me. They looked around for their apple slices.

LATER, AS I SET water to boil and shoved towels in the washer in the basement, Lev stayed next to me, gripping a hank of shirt so that it stretched off my shoulder. "Promise you'll never go anywhere again," Lev said with a little boy's authority. "Promise me now." Lev held on to the shirt while I drew peacocks with Sonya and ate the pasta they didn't want and spread peanut butter on crackers that they did want. I didn't tell Lev not to hold my shirt. I needed the tether. He held on to my shirt while I called Henry James. "But where'd you go?" Henry James asked when I told him I'd found a babysitter. "Just groceries," I said. This was the first time I'd lied to him, and it was as easy as walking through an open door.

A FEW DAYS LATER, Pax came again and I found Will in the Palm House, the damp heat of a Floridian summer. Condensation dripped down the glass walls; leaves swayed above us; vines wrapped around palm trunks. He was wearing the same old man's coat, young man's sneakers. Beneath his old man's long forehead, his young man's lovely mouth. His hair responded to the humidity like mine, growing bolder, claiming space.

We dropped into conversation easily, and my head began buzzing in a way it never did when I talked to Henry James, not even in the early excited years. While Henry James chose English words carefully, taking time with each sentence, Will spoke with the rapid-fire enthusiasm of a grown-up theater kid, and I felt my mind move quicker, my entire being move quicker, as if in conversation we were running on the brick paths.

But it wasn't just speed. Henry James and I never ventured long in the land of emotional analysis. He didn't like it there, and my grievances felt petty next to his enormous loss. I had a mother, unlike him—a difficult mother, but fine. Will seemed to want to luxuriate in this land.

"Does it make up for it?" he asked at one point—we were in the fern room. "The lack of love from your mom—does all the love you get from your kids make it better? And your husband?" He laughed a little. "I'm asking as someone without that."

"Definitely. The kids do," I said, missing them fiercely. They seemed unreachable, back in desolate winter.

"And your husband?" he asked again, his head thrust forward, staring at me.

I was overwhelmed by an urge, even a need, to tell the truth. But why, I asked myself. Why say anything? I thought of an airplane. Imagine you met him on an international flight, I told myself. Or in an airport in a foreign city with a long flight delay. Those spaces where intimacy can be fast, urgent. Wasn't this like that? We didn't share friends or relatives—we'd checked. Will grew up in Salt Lake City, matriculated at Vassar the year after I graduated Wesleyan, lived in Boston. The plane would land. The flight delay would end. He was in town for only a couple more weeks.

"Stupid question," Will said when I hesitated.

"No, not stupid." I found myself telling him about the arrangement I'd made with Henry James, how angry it made me. "And maybe I could've lived with the resentment if it wasn't for the pandemic," I said. "If I didn't have to quit working and move up here."

"Who wouldn't resent that?" He was looking intently at me. "You wish you were still in New York?"

"I wish I didn't feel so stingy, that's what I wish. When he tells me he played a good show all I feel is this huge rage. But isn't part of loving someone being happy for them?"

"Kids ruin everything. Isn't that what they say? But even so, I really want them."

"Kids? Or spouses?"

He flushed, his tan forehead turning rosy. "Is it weird to say that I was meant to be a father? When I'm with kids, especially older kids, my nieces, I forget myself. I like myself then. And I know what you're thinking. I'm a man, I have plenty of time."

"I mean, you are. You do."

He tapped a fern frond, watched it bob up. "But I have a premonition it's not going to happen. That I can't have one, because of . . . sort of like retribution." He turned to me, his eyes adamant. "See, I did something really fucked up. About as bad as it gets."

I gave him a moment and then said, "You can tell me what it was."

He shook his head. "I don't think I should lay this on you."

I explained about the plane. The permission it gave us.

"And when it lands? What then?"

"Well, we can't exchange numbers. That's the rule. That's what makes this possible."

"We'll just head off into our lives?"

"Yeah. But we'll remember."

"That's nice. That's very nice. I'll like remembering you. I'm already looking forward to looking back on this."

HE DIDN'T TELL ME that afternoon or the next, and the day he did, I nearly didn't make it to the garden. After school, Sonya was disconsolate, following me into the bathroom as I changed into a plaid skirt and V-neck sweater I'd bought with Lev at Goodwill when she was at school. "You don't look like yourself, Mom. Take it off."

"No, I'm comfortable." A lie, but I wanted her to prioritize comfortable clothes herself.

"You look stupid." She began to cry. "Don't leave. Not today."

"Oh, sweetie." I knelt by her. My skirt rode up. I wasn't used to wearing one. "What is it?"

"Stop asking. Just never mind, okay?"

A substitute teacher, she eventually told me, as Lev played Marble Run with Pax downstairs, had stood on a chair during Drop Everything and Read time and spoken about two degrees of warming and seas that will rise and fish that will die and rains that will fall and the people who will die of heat or starvation because crops won't grow. Mosquitoes will be everywhere. "In your lifetime," he'd said to the fourth graders.

How can you say to a child, your own child, yes, all true, or very likely true, at least part of it is true? I thought about a podcast I'd listened to while doing dishes that said the cure for climate grief was to learn to dwell in doubt, and I reached for my laptop. I pulled up photos for Sonya of Greta with her signs, videos of Friday school strikes, Extinction Rebellion marching with their banners and stilts, activists throwing mashed potatoes at a Monet.

I dwelled not in doubt. I didn't, as the podcast suggested, "vibe with uncertainty." I said these actions had changed everything. Governments, corporations, tech bros—they listened to the protestors and put policies in place to end the warming. Slammed on the breaks. The substitute had old news. We'd decided, collectively, not to allow this nightmare to bloom.

Because she was sad. Because I was scared of her sadness.

And because I wanted to meet Will in my new old clothes.

JEREMIAH AND WILL WERE college roommates, and after graduation they became lovers. Will knew Jeremiah wouldn't settle for him. He had a big life, came from an exceedingly wealthy family, not like Will's. Still, every few months, for eleven years, Jeremiah would invite Will somewhere extravagant. To his villa in Tourrettes-sur-Loup, a weekend in Majorca. He went, he always went. The week before Jeremiah was married they were fucking in Italy.

We were sitting on the bench by the koi and I watched their golden bodies snaking beneath the mucky water, feeling embarrassed that I'd believed in a mutuality of attraction, that I'd bought this skirt to please him. But also—I'd seen how he looked at me.

Jeremiah rented out Ellis Island for the wedding, Will said. The entire island. Not wanting to go alone, he went online and met Quinn—older, handsome, psyched for free wedding drinks. They dated after, and when Quinn developed some intense chronic pain, Will urged him to ask a doctor for pills to take the edge off. For a while, he could keep working. But soon six hours wasn't enough relief. Four hours was insufficient.

"This was 2016, so . . . eight years ago," he said, looking straight ahead, at the pond. "Opioids weren't all over the news, not yet. But I knew he was out of control and I tried to say no when Jeremiah . . . He wanted to see me. Quinn didn't have enough pills to last until his next script. Not a good time for me to leave."

He'd stopped talking and was hunched over his crossed legs, staring at his own knee. "But you went?" I asked quietly.

"Jeremiah kept pushing and pushing, insisting he needed me, and I caved and Quinn died from a fucked-up street pill."

There was a splinter of fury in his voice. Although I spoke my sympathy, he looked away, frozen in his feelings. A death always changed the temperature in the room.

I put my hand lightly on his left shoulder, nervous he'd be like my mom, turning to rage or silent depression, but he gripped it tightly with his right hand. "Sorry. Was this too much?"

"No. You must miss Quinn."

"That's the problem. It wasn't Quinn I was in love with."

"Are you still?"

"What?"

"In love with Jeremiah?"

Tightening his grip on my hand, he looked at me. "The ironic thing? His dad's a cousin of the Sacklers. Helped develop their marketing campaign. I didn't learn that until later. But all that money? All the money he used to fly me around the fucking world? From the pills that killed Quinn."

AS WE WERE WALKING outside into the five P.M. dusk, the frozen pond a dark oblong ahead of us, he asked what I'd do if I had vast piles of money from Bad Pharma like Jeremiah. He said that Jeremiah often found GoFundMe pages belonging to total strangers and just paid the whole thing. "But shouldn't he do something more like . . ."

"I'd give money to my friend," I interrupted without thinking. I hadn't told him about Demeter yet.

It was frigid and windy but he stopped walking and listened when

I told him about Demeter, her sick kid, how broke and stuck that made her, and also—why not, I thought—my father's obsession with her, and even his book sailing into the water, about which I'd told nobody, not even my husband.

He didn't look away when I got to my jealousy, its viny prowess. I always thought something terrible would happen if someone saw the rot in me. But exposed to his gaze, I felt calm. He started laughing. "Yeah, I'd throw it, too."

"You would?"

"Fuck yeah."

I felt myself grinning back at him. I'd been so long with a man who sometimes delighted in me but rarely understood me.

We'd reached Will's Toyota and he opened the door but didn't get in. "You know, I'd ask Jeremiah if I could. For your friend. But I can't. I can't be in touch with him."

"No, of course. I didn't mean . . ."

"Just tell me, though—what's wrong with the girl? And don't say cancer. Please don't."

When I began describing Persephone's illness, he said, "Emily? A kid with Emily? Kids get it? That's . . . it's terrible."

I was surprised he knew it, although it had been in the paper and surely people talked about it around town. Still, he was strikingly informed, asked so many questions.

When my answers led me to the Healing Hut, his brow creased with concern. "And you don't know if she's still there? You lost her? God, that sucks." He got a wild and hopeful look in his eyes, jerked his head at his car. "Let's go throw some more books in the river. Come on!"

I didn't get in his car, but as I drove home alone to cook dinner, I wondered what would have happened if I had.

THE NEXT DAY HE steered me to a room closed to the public; the horticulturist had loaned him the key. In small pots under bright lights, bulbs were half-hatched, readying themselves for a spring show.

Slipped tongues etching out of iris fists. The first purse of tulip lips. Engorged hyacinths before bursting. Impossible not to find it sexual. Were we going to mention that?

"The very verge of verdancy," I said.

His thumb rubbed a priapic nub of green jutting upward from the dark brown soil. "Just so you know, I'm bi," he said, with the same nervous energy as when he asked about my husband, his head thrust forward, the struts in his neck pronounced.

"Who isn't these days?" I sounded flip, but I was pleased.

"And, well, also I'm done here."

I felt stunned. "You finished the plant books?"

"A few days ago, honestly. Just came . . . well, to see you. And to give . . ." He tapped the case of the phone in my hand, no mention of the rule I'd laid out. I wasn't about to remind him. The plane had landed, but I felt like I was soaring as I unlocked my phone and handed it to him. He typed in his number, gave it back, and walked away, this man who looked like family to me, nervously lowering his head through the arched doorway of the palm room although it was much taller than him.

Ruth

...

So that's it? WILL WRITES.

What's our plan, Ruth? Stephen writes.

They've crossed off every herbarium stored in every cabinet in every nearby college. UMass, Smith, Amherst, even Harvard, and all the small-town historical societies from Agawam to Worthington. In the under-heated archives, during public reading hours, they'd checked—three times each—all the pages with pressed plants stuck with gum arabic and labeled in tiny script. But no white flower as described by Lillian, no mention of Sightflower or Sun Madness.

She doesn't have another plan other than: May first. Meet at the riverside. Exactly where Lillian saw the botanizing ladies. I've pinned down the old water cure—checked town records.

Stephen writes: Devastating, to say the least. I let myself hope. We should debrief. This Thursday? My Friday is also wide open.

She can't see the point. Says as much.

Stephen: It's crucial for a collective to process together each stage of a project

Will bows out. Heading to Florida –mom demands a visit from her prodigal son.

Just me and you, Ruth?

Is there anything she'd rather do less? I process best alone. See you in May.

Till May, Will writes.

TILL MAY. Stephen seems to have discovered caps lock. And even, is that . . . ? She gets her reading glasses. Yep. Three crying emojis.

—

BUT HERE HE IS ON HER DOORSTEP BEFORE WORK TWO DAYS later, in his blue winter coat and felt hat, black snow boots to his knees, brown mittens. He holds out a Tupperware, like a head on a platter. She closes the door behind herself, even though she's in felt slippers and a fleece.

He pushes the Tupperware into her hands. It has a red plastic lid and feels as warm as a baby. "I hope you like cranberries. No allergies? I left out the walnuts, but didn't know about gluten or . . ."

"It's fine, Stephen. What's the occasion?"

With the palms of his mittens pressed together, he bows slightly. "Thank you, Ruth."

"I didn't do anything, bro. No more than you or Will. Looked at a couple dried-up plants." She doesn't know why she's taking this super-masc tone, except that his nose is starting to run and she doesn't want him to cry and she sees a new layer of ice on her windshield that she'll need to scrape before heading to work.

"But you had no reason. And you're so good at it. The way you guided us every step? How easy you made it for us? Every collective needs a problem solver, someone with a vision. You had it, you're the visionary here, Ruth. And your incredible memory! How you knew to find Lillian's book. All these skills that you poured into our search out of the goodness of your heart."

She nearly laughs. He mistakes her smile for agreement.

"And of course, Ramona." He clears phlegm from his throat so loudly that two small blue and white birds take off from the telephone wire. Distracted, he follows their passage. "Will you look at that. Black-throated blue warblers. In February. Not supposed to be here till June."

"Snow came too late. Cold came too late. They got stuck."

"I know. I've been worrying about them."

She has, too. All winter she's been worried, although she didn't know their names. She nods in a way she hopes he'll interpret as thanks and we're done.

He grabs her arm. "What I wanted to say. Ramona. Well, she was lucky to have you."

I don't need you to tell me that, she thinks, shaking his hand off. But she finds it means something to her. It actually does. To hear him say this. Nobody knew Ramona as well as she did except for Orion, who doesn't talk to her, and this man she's always despised.

The muffin is absolutely horrible. Truly one of the worst she's ever eaten, somehow sandy on top and soggy on bottom, with the acrid bite of baking soda and the approximate sweetness of agave. What to do with the other eleven? Cruel to bring them to the library staff room.

She undresses each muffin from its wrapper, returns them to the Tupperware, walks into the woods.

"Here you go, you little creatures," she calls, tossing handfuls. The crumbs bounce on the ice. These woods are small, broken up by the curved roads of cul-de-sac, and she's nearly to its edge when she hears a high-pitched call, an avian—please please please pleeaase—and turns to see three, now four, five, seven black-throated blue warblers dropping from the bare branches to feast on Stephen's muffins.

Early March

...

i

My mother's voice, loudly cheerful. "I have big news. Big, big news."

I made guesses: "You finished your manuscript? They're actually making the *Wormfood* movie?"

"Recognition at last" is all she'd say. She wanted to tell me in person.

I'd been looking for a reason to text. I found the contact in my phone for Professor Harry Buckminster. My mom's coming on Saturday. Send fortitude.

I waited for his reply until my phone grew volatile, hostile. As the days passed, and my mother's visit drew nearer, I felt so vulnerable that when a woman biking on the sidewalk came too close to me and I startled and she turned around and called, "Oh, sorry, honey," I began to cry at being someone's honey.

ii

Handing me her empty glass of milk, my mother dropped to hands and knees. "This is how she was, Tyesha Smith, stuck in quarantine with her young son and demented mother, searching everywhere on her mom's bathroom floor for a fallen Advil." My mother's gray skirt peacefully gathered the crumbs on my kitchen floor as she crawled.

"When lo and behold, she comes face-to-face with reading material! Just propping up the short leg of a stool." Henry James offered an arm as my mother began the slow process of standing. "She devours it immediately, incredulous that something so timely, seeming to comment so presciently on her pandemic isolation, stuck taking care of others day after endless day, could be so old. Can you guess the name of the book?"

"*Frog and Toad*?" Lev asked.

"Can you believe it?" She clutched my sleeve. "Tyesha published an essay in an obscure blog, saying that *The Third Person*'s acknowledgment of the rage of the caretaker, as well as its utopian ending, changed her course of study and . . ." My mother's voice fell to a whisper for emphasis. " . . . *in many profound ways, her entire life.*"

"Fantastic," I said, although I had always found her ending—in which the narrator, realizing that she's being written about in the third person, comes to live with her author along with other narrators and their authors in a kibbutzim-type collective where mothers see their children for only an hour a day—excruciating, first when I was a child and then a mother.

"Well, don't congratulate me for that. Nobody saw the essay, of course. But this February, a girl your age, Eve, but with quite the career—she writes about perfume for *The New Yorker,* celebrity profiles, too—she came upon it. God knows how. She raced out to find *The Third Person.* I shudder to think how many stores she tried, in what dark corner of a used bookstore she finally discovered it."

"A little bookstore called the internet," I suggested. "She clicked, she bought."

"Well, the piece she wrote about it was the magazine's most shared for days. She called it a lost feminist classic by a beloved children's writer. She called it . . ." My mother locked eyes with me. ". . . a work of genius."

The word my father owned, the benediction he believed only he could bestow.

I could feel her triumph as she named a small and renowned press, the editor of which contacted Irene immediately and would soon be republishing the book.

"Uncovered at last!"

"No, Eve, it was never covered. Sitting out there in broad daylight."

"Rediscovered then."

"But it was never properly discovered. Just born, it slipped into oblivion. I call it my belated vindication. It's not just that nobody bought the book, it's that nobody believed it. Unrealistic, they said. Even my editor. He hated the narrator screaming in a competitive rage whenever her baby cried. 'Make her nicer,' he said. 'More loving, more likable.' And yet nobody told my mother to be more likable when she screamed when I entered the room."

"Why did your mother scream when you entered the room?" Sonya asked.

I changed the subject by asking about pub dates and covers. "It'll be your turn next, darling," she said, pushing back my hair and kissing my forehead. She offered to take the kids out, give me and Henry James a break. They looked as surprised as I felt. When had she taken them anywhere? They ran to put on their shoes. Henry James was asleep on the couch before they were out the door. "Get to work," my mother called as she left. "Get your writing done."

I took the brisket from the slow cooker and set it in a pan in the fridge and checked my phone for a text from Will and boiled noodles and assembled a kugel and washed dishes and swept the kitchen floor and checked for a text from Will and sponged gunk from the counters and sorted Legos and Magna-Tiles and checked my phone and dragged Lev's mattress into our room and washed Sonya's sheets and remade her bed for my mother and checked my phone and cleared the children's floor of stuffies and clothes and figurines and books and cups and took out the brisket from the fridge and sliced it and put it in the oven and cooked green beans and washed dishes and frosted the cake I'd made that morning and returned it to the fridge and checked my phone, while Henry James woke and turned to his emails.

When they returned, my mother dunked her head under the kitchen tap. "It's bafflingly warm for March. We went for ice cream and into the woods," she said, water dripping off her nose. "I learned an ingenious game called Greentime, and the mosquitoes must have just hatched. They were glorious in their ferocity."

How I loved my mother happy.

—

COULD RECOGNITION LEVEL THE TROUGHS JOAN ALWAYS STUMbled into? Could attention act like a backhoe, filling the gaping hole in her ego? Henry James and I asked each other this later, whispering because Lev was between us and Sonya was asleep on our floor.

In the morning, she talked seriously about books with Sonya while I set out breakfast. My phone buzzed just as I heard her say, "But that's a Christian allegory. Aslan is Jesus who saves the Christian children. And we know where that leads the rest of us."

Sry I was incommunicado. Is
she there yet?

My heart was pounding as I wrote back quickly: In my kitchen as we speak

Yikes! Tell her yr friend Will says be
nice. Funny thing Im w mom too.

Where's that?

"Did you really buy this for her?" my mother asked, paging through an illustrated edition of *The Chronicles of Narnia.*

"Is it bad?" Sonya asked. It had been a birthday present.

Boston-ish—Dorchester. Came to
save her from death by crushing.
Mountains of crap she bought on
ebay. Like a limerick actually.
There once was a Dorchester hoarder.
Whose piles and bins knew
no borders.

"And isn't *The Lord of the Rings* some Christian allegory, too, Joan?" Henry James asked, walking into the room and pouring himself a cup of coffee.

"Oh, they all are. All the books for kids, all big propaganda. That's why I wrote *Wormfood*. I said—you can read this in my interviews, Sonya—I said, if the Holocaust taught us anything it's that we have nothing holding us up, nothing watching over us. Nada, nada, nada."

She was buried in junk, I wrote.

Yes! The whole house it stunk, he wrote.

"That's what the horrors of the twentieth century left us with," my mom continued. "The great nada belief system. And now the twenty-first will bring us the great nada life."

"What does nada mean?" Sonya said.

No actually . . . he wrote.

"Tell Grandma about your Spanish teacher," I said to change the subject. "Tell her how she only teaches you one phrase. Jugo de naranja."

"Nothing," my mom said.

The three dots flickered on my phone.

"It means nothing. The great nothing life."

"But, why?"

"Well, climate change, my dear. All of this . . ." She gestured to the window. "Kaput. In a matter of years."

"But, I thought . . ." Sonya looked from her grandmother to me. "Mom said . . ."

> TBH—she was buried in junk—
> After getting too drunk. Poor Meg.
> Your turn

"I said . . . What I said was . . . What's a rhyme for hoarder?"

"Extorter. Recorder. Order. It's coming for us, Sonya, whether we like it or not. The great kaput."

She couldn't stop herself. I knew that. My mother wanted every child to know that the worst will happen, which she learned at eleven when the principal led her from a spelling bee that she was poised to win. Finding it unfair that some children walked around without this leaden weight, she was always ready to provide it.

"What is it you said to her? Did you lie, Eve?" my mother asked as Sonya ran from the room.

I knew not to engage, to defuse, to guide us back to her book. But she hadn't thrown the leaden weight on me this time. She threw it on my daughter, and I was pissed.

"Maybe, Mom. Maybe I did."

"But why, darling?" She was plucking browned pear slivers from Lev's plate.

"Because . . ." Because I don't want her to grow up to be like you, I thought. "Because she has an entire adult life ahead to worry, or worse than worry, to live through horrors, large and small and . . . I don't mean trivial exactly, but they'll start to seem . . ."

"*Mundane* is the word you're looking for. *Banal.* How terrors become banal. Hannah Arendt wrote about that. Did you never read her?"

"But you won't know!" My voice exploded with frustration. "You won't live through what she will. And I won't, either. So, if she can, in the future, remember a time when she wasn't worried, and she was free to, I don't know, draw her comics. It's possible then she'll be ready . . . at least *more* ready, to withstand it."

As I talked, I felt sure of myself. I hadn't articulated my instinct so clearly before, but yes, this was what I believed, I told myself as I carried plates, that childhood should be its own form of Greentime, a great gathering of the multitudinous world, not a dire lesson in how to fear it. "Maybe this memory of solidity, of curiosity," I continued at the sink, "will stay with her, change her neural pathways as screens do, but in an opposite way, and she'll become an adult who can find joy even when things are terrible. That's the best thing I could give her."

I was thinking of Demeter here, of course. I turned to my mother triumphantly. But she'd shrunk—her head cowed, her hand shaking as she set down her fork. She was the girl whose mother had jumped from the coffee shop on the sixth floor of the New Rochelle Gimbels instead of attending her daughter's spelling bee, and I'd forgotten to take care of her.

"Well, I guess I messed up again. You don't like how I talk to my grandchild? Just take me to the bus station. I'll wait. An hour or two, who cares?"

My upset mother, my upset daughter. I looked at Henry James. This is your job, my eyes said.

"Go away," Sonya called when I knocked. Standing outside her door, I wrote, You can bet Marie Kondo deplored her

Brilliant Eve

"I'm coming in," I said. "We need to talk."

On her bed, Sonya was tearing out pages from *The Chronicles of Narnia,* bunching them and throwing them onto Lev's mattress. Her bony shoulders were hunched at her ears. I hurt with love for her furrowed forehead. She pulled away from me, but I put my arm around her anyway and called her my honey and told her I could help her understand. "Nothing can ever help," she said. "Nada. Nada. Nada."

Ruth

...

IN THE PARKING LOT OF THE FOOD CO-OP: ITS OPPOSITE. CAP'N Jack's food truck, where everything is fried. You shop for the aspirational, then order the delectable.

Walking toward the truck, she leaves a message. "Dude! You made it to twenty. Let me know, you know, if . . . or maybe when you want to visit. I love you, dude."

Once upon a time, Ramona felted a crown to which she added a crocheted flower each year. Her cakes were layered, thematic, Lego-figurined. All the friends, all the lesbians with kids, running around Ruth's bonfire. She kept wood aside all winter for Orion's mid-March birthday.

This wet Saturday stretches before her soddenly. Without Lillian's memoir to think about, what is there? A crossword. A run. Doldrum. An ache beneath her sternum. If it's too early for beer, vegetable oil suffices, which is why she's come to Cap'n Jack's.

The parking lot smells of wet leaves, and fog obscures Mount Tom.

When she reaches the front, the guy behind the window—short blond dreads peeking beneath a Red Sox knit cap, pale blue eyes—greets her like a friend. "There you are!"

Ruth nods. She is here.

"Awesome! I'm psyched you came back." He pushes a small drink toward her, along with a wrapped straw—"You forgot your shake"—then turns, beaming, to the couple behind her who step forward to the metal window.

Sipping someone else's milkshake, she heads toward the store, which is how she spots Ellen at one of the outdoor picnic tables. Of course. The town is nothing but reliable in its casual racism.

She could walk away. It's been what? Six years? Since the funeral? But it's Orion's birthday and she wants to tell someone that her son is twenty years old today.

"Missing something?" She holds out the drink.

Ellen looks up from her phone. "Fucking hell."

"I tried to order and he gave me yours."

This happened all the time when they lived together—two Asian butches. *I saw you at the bookstore. No, I swear it was you. On your bike, you didn't notice me.* Despite Chinese/Korean, taller/shorter, scrawny/bulky, undercut/mop flop, and just totally different faces.

"How do you still live in whitelandia? I'd lose my mind."

Ruth wants to respond defensively—I have a family here—but she doesn't, because it's no longer true.

Ellen holds out her arms. Ruth isn't sure she'll survive a hug today without breaking down, so she keeps it brief and macho. Thump thump.

"Join me?" Across the picnic table, Ellen's hyper-apologetic. She would've called, meant to, but she just stopped on a whim. Found herself starving on her way to visit Antonia.

"Antonia?" Here's a name she hasn't thought of in forever. Thank god. A relief to forget her. She's can't understand the geography, though. Ellen does something with soil pathology at Penn State—and Antonia? Queen of the night-blooming flowers. Doesn't she run a fancy research institute in the mountains of Arizona?

"Gave it all up," Ellen says. "Total breakdown."

Antonia: magnetic, unfettered, brazen, ambitious. She came up along the Rio Grande and had no trouble telling off anyone in authority. Be polite and respectful, her academic advisers demanded. But she ignored them and the tide of success caught her anyway, carrying her ever upward.

"Gave what up?" She can't imagine this woman breaking down.

"Her institute, her grad students, her research projects, her speaking tours. Retreated to the Northeast Kingdom of Vermont." Ellen shoves her fries and chicken tenders to the middle of the table and Ruth grabs a handful to quell the anxiety elicited by the name Antonia.

"Not many desert flowers in Vermont."

"Calls herself the Keeper of the Gone. Dramatic as always. Her plan is to grieve each fucking weed."

"You're annoyed?"

"Do we have time for this? Lots of us are out there focusing on habitat migration, adaptability, while she's looking at old plant books, comparing them to recent surveys, finding what's extinct. For what? Just to say goodbye?"

Ruth wipes grease from her fingers onto her pants and passes Ellen the milkshake. "She gets the books where? Colleges? Historical societies?"

"Did that. Now she calls random strangers from all over New England, asks if they have an old herbarium in their attic. She says she won't look away from the horror."

Ruth feels her arms grow hot, despite the chilly day. Old herbaria! She silently berates herself: She should have thought about this. She's a librarian, after all, and fully aware of how much interesting stuff goes uncollected by archivists. And now what should she do? Will she ask Antonia if she's come across Sightflower? Surely she can get over her anger for a quick conversation. Just: Sorry I forbade you from attending Ramona's funeral, and can you look in your plant books for a little white flower?

Suddenly, they hear the hoopla of approaching teenagers. Ellen flinches but Ruth doesn't mind the shouts, the too-hysterical laughter. When Orion was their age, the world ceased. Alone, he stared at gunfire on his screen while she drank beer in the basement.

Four boys climb a nearby picnic table to sit atop it and eat their chicken tenders, stomping their large sneakers on the bench.

They're jangly limbed, wearing concert tees, flannels tied around their waists, exactly how Ruth dressed in 1996. Their hair is greasy or too frizzy or a weird length. She can tell from a glance that they're awkward at school, maybe sullen at home, but look how bold and happy they are together.

"I don't know how you raised a boy," Ellen says, shuddering a little. "All that antsy manhood. Not for me. And these days? With phones?"

"Poorly. Terribly. That's how I did it."

Ellen looks at her with surprise. "What are you talking about? Whenever I visited, you and Orion were having such a blast together, playing like twelve backgammon games in a row or memorizing all the two-letter Scrabble words."

"Sure. But that's dad stuff. When he needed a mom? After Ramona? I was a shitty mom."

Ellen sips the milkshake and shakes her head. "Of course you weren't a good mom. How long have I known you, Ruth? You were always a dad. Changing the oil in our cars, eating our food, sealing all our windows with plastic for the winter." She starts laughing. "Man, don't you remember how you wouldn't shut up about your Kawasaki? So, what if you try granting yourself the leniency given to grieving dads everywhere? I bet you were pretty great for a dad."

It's wild to be remembered. Ruth takes the milkshake from Ellen's hand, drinks for a while, the sweetness relaxing her, filling her with a thrumming sense of possibility, as if she could go back and do it again, as if she could go home to their house beside the meadow, sit down next to Orion on the couch, *happy birthday, dude, now pass me the controller.* As if she could bring home some fries and half a milkshake and put her arm around her son.

On the way to the trash can, Ellen stops. "Hold up. Jessie didn't come see you, did she?"

Happiness comes just from hearing that name spoken aloud. What did Jessie say? Is Jessie telling friends she misses her? "Why?"

"Tell me she didn't. Or Antonia's gonna be pissed."

"Antonia? They're back together?" It's hard to breathe. She puts a hand on her neck, just keeps it there, holding herself together.

"Seriously?" Ellen laughs. "Been over since the Ice Age. Or at least the early aughts."

Ruth is flooded with relief, but why? It's not like Jessie's any more available.

"No, the thing is Jessie told me she wanted to come see you. A little fling. I was in Vermont at the time and Antonia got on the phone—not something she usually does, she's basically gone full hermit—and forbade her, said a quick fuck is not in your skill set. You fall in love, get hung up, tie every knot. Which is totally wrong for Jessie. She's finally happy."

"Antonia said I'm wrong for Jessie?"

"*Possessive* is the word she used."

Not the first time Antonia called her that. Ruth's stomach gnaws from milkshake and fries and fear. Ellen's staring back at her but is this because Ruth's clearly freaking out or because Ellen knows what happened between Ramona and Antonia? Two kids pass on their way to Cap'n Jack's. The small boy keeps his head turned as his sister pulls him by his hand. "Are they twins, Sonya? Are those mens twins? Are they mens or womans?"

"Don't stare," the girl says, and then twists her own head for a surreptitious glance.

"I think maybe that's what's called gentle-mens," the boy says firmly.

Late March

. . .

i

"SING THE SONG ABOUT BILL," LEV DEMANDED, PULLING OUT several days' worth of mail from the aluminum box on the porch and dropping it in the hallway among our shoes. I sang: "bills and catalogs, bills and catalogs, only bills and catalogs today." Sonya pounced upon a catalog for the kind of monogrammed lunch box and backpack I always refused to buy, removing herself to the table to study this other lifestyle. I watched her as I put away groceries. Did I see a weariness in the way she was considering spaceships versus frogs with parasols?

A few days after I'd explained—in a babbling, circuitous way—that my mother wasn't exactly right but I'd oversimplified and we had to dwell in doubt, she sealed all her comic series in an Amazon box and told me to donate them. No longer did she plan on becoming a comic book artist/saxophonist. She would dedicate her life like Greta to stopping climate change. The children are our only hope, her substitute teacher had said. She didn't want to do this, but she had no choice and I shouldn't try to talk her out of it.

Of course I tried. It made me so sad that she believed she had to clean up our mess. Now I held a carton of milk, condensation dripping on my hands, and stared at a matted tangle in the back of her hair as she turned the pages. Was she thinking about death? About heat?

"Do you want one of those backpacks?" I called. "Or a lunch box?"

She sighed. "That would be wasteful." But that night I was happy to find the catalog by my bedside, marked up with a complicated rating system of stars and hearts. Is this what you prefer, I asked myself, a child who finds succor in consumerism? Maybe, I answered myself. Maybe I do.

THE REST OF THE MAIL LAY ON THE FLOOR THROUGH THE NEXT day and night and another day, shifting as we put on and removed our shoes. It was late March, the jittery time when winter sings its loud death song. I'd seen wild violets under ice-crusted dead leaves. Who could clean? Finally, while pushing aside a catalog to tie Lev's sneaker, I uncovered a flyer, tri-folded, Scotch-taped. *Doctor and Lenore Folkenflick have rescued count-less people from chronic pain and un-wellness . . .*

And underneath in green pen, feminine cursive:

> *Eve—my favorite human, Eve! I figured out why I never heard back from you. Your address is NOT 47 North Maple! But what is it? Welcome to living entirely w/out phone/internet, but Bintu is leaving today and I gave her DETAILED instructions about how to find your house vis-a-vis the river and the street with that pink Victorian. When you get this will you visit??? Workers aren't exactly encouraged to host visitors, but since I haven't left the premises since I got here—no car, miles and miles from a bus!—they'll totally understand. But it's good here. It's good and I'm always thinking about you and your goobers, always with you—you're in my heart!*

ii

I DROVE INTO THE HILLS, BACK TO WINTER, BARE BRANCHES BLURRED by mist. For a long time, the computerized voice on my phone was quiet, as if giving me space for my feelings, and then I realized it had lost service. On the map, a black dot—me!—floated on a white expanse. I'm on my way to Demeter, I told myself, but it didn't seem real.

The sun was low when Colrain Road appeared out of the snow. Unpaved, ice-rutted. Half a mile up, in a wide muddy expanse of what would soon be green fields, sat a small yellow farmhouse with a peaked roof, sunlight glinting off its upper windows. So, not a hut at all.

No doorbell. I knocked twice on the blue door, turned the knob expecting something medical, an attendant behind a desk. Instead, a vestibule with purple batik bunting, a framed sign that said WELCOME! and another that said PLEASE REMOVE ALL SHOES AND PLACE IN CUBBY and another that said MASTER THE UNKNOWN BY KNOWING YOUR DEEP SELF.

I removed my boots and placed them in one of the lime-green cubbies.

"Hello?" I called.

"Is it the oxygen? At this hour?" I heard a man say.

At the far end of the hallway, a woman made her way to me. "No, but you're not oxygen at all. Are you here to see . . ." She tilted her head, pulling on the tip of a long gray braid that rested over the hillock of her breasts. She was averagely ample for a woman in her sixties, wearing a brown cardigan and shin-length pleated skirt. "It's Friday, right. So, Marjorie? Are you Marjorie's?"

"Demeter, actually. If she's . . ."

Her smile was slightly crooked, warm. "Our Demeter has a visitor? Are you the . . . ?" She held my shoulders—I was surprised by this. "Well, you are, sure, I can see . . . Oh, she'll be so happy."

She led me into a low-ceilinged sitting room, the kind of old New England room that makes me too aware of how tall I am. Despite an exuberance of flames behind a woodstove's glass window, it was damply cold. A few standing lamps with Victorian fringes did little to dispel the darkness, but I could make out three paintings of women with three different skin tones, each pregnant with planet Earth, and a large rolling chalkboard with names and abbreviations I didn't understand—o_2, mg, Ld. "You can wait here for Demeter." She sneezed loudly, then turned to look up at me, her gaze sharp. "But first, humor me?"

"Is there something I could . . . ?"

She took my right hand in both of hers, two cool fingers palpating my inner wrist, and closed her eyes, carefully listening to what went on inside of me. The attention startled me. That is, I loved it and felt slightly bereft when she gently brought my hand to my side. "And your tongue?"

Dazed by touch, I opened my mouth obediently.

She nodded as if it confirmed something. "You'll want to avoid brassicas, which includes mustard, everyone forgets that. Small tangerines are good. Very strong green tea. Nothing fancy. Lipton's fine. Two tea bags every two hours."

I WAS ALONE ONLY a few minutes before I heard footsteps, and here came my beautiful friend, her wide mouth and blue eyes. Dark, loose hair against a yellow turtleneck. She dried her hands on a calico apron as she ran and then threw her arms around me. "Thank the fucking gods, it worked." She pulled back to look at me, drew me in again. She smelled slightly different. New soap.

"What is it then, if not North Maple?" she asked, releasing me.

"Maplewood." I couldn't stop smiling.

She palmed her forehead. "Fuck. So you didn't get the postcards? No, obviously. But you're here and now I get to show you everything."

The small farmhouse, it turned out, was just the start. A door at the end of the sitting room opened up onto a new addition with purple linoleum floors and yellow walls painted with turquoise spirals, like a preschool.

We entered a kitchen—there was a double metal sink the size of a toddler's crib, steam coming from an industrial-sized dishwasher, shelves of beige bowls and mugs and plates, and two massive stoves, side by side, with metal hoods that made them look like crows bowing their heads, small pots on each of their burners.

I hugged myself as Demeter adjusted the flames. It was somehow even colder in here.

"Twelve patients, twelve pots. Totally individualized, can you believe it? Lenore makes me these charts every single day. . . . Look." She handed me three pages, labeled Breakfast, Lunch, and Dinner, each with an aerial depiction of the stoves—circles for pots and a list of ingredients beside them, a name in red marker.

"So, you're working here? It's a job? Or everyone chips in?"

She began chopping parsley. "It's all easy stuff. Kitchen, bathrooms, vacuuming. And already . . . Persephone's already . . . Lenore did the intake for free. Two hours long, Eve. Wait, hold up the dinner page. I need to see who gets this."

When she finished with parsley, she opened the pantry, giving me a glimpse of crowded shelves—large Sysco brand cans and spices alongside glass jars with handwritten labels—and pulled out sesame seeds in a container as large as a milk carton. "When you think about all the doctors I saw who gave me five minutes max. I'm not exaggerating when I say two whole hours. She had this yellow pad of paper and was writing so fast and was so focused on Perse, she'd just tear off a sheet and scatter them around her like petals. I wish you could've seen."

"Lenore is the woman with the—"

"She gives Waldorf teacher vibes, but she studied nutrition in Germany and Japan. They're very advanced there."

"The Axis forces. So skilled at broth. What about the Russians? Any borscht?"

She smiled and kissed my cheek on her way back to the pantry. "God, I missed you. I can't wait for you to meet the doctor. He's so . . . He did these, like, muscle reflex tests? To start to learn what Persephone can't tolerate. But soon he'll do the labs. It's your hair, your spit, they send it to . . . I think Canada?" She slipped a timer in her apron pocket, bent to check and adjust each burner. "Come. Let's go find her."

She led me into an immense hexagonal studio with scattered yoga balls and cushions, folding chairs, and an easel. Four people lay covered with woven blankets. "There are these mats," Demeter whispered, "threaded with infrared and electromagnetic pulses and you can lie on them anytime." Above us, a filthy skylight filtered the late afternoon sky through twigs and muck.

"Treatment rooms," Demeter whispered, guiding me past a series of doors at the side of the studio. "Biomagnetic in here, apparently very powerful readjustment. Lenore does that one. Then this is for lymphatic drainage. Releases toxins. And here . . ." She pointed to a door with a framed sign that read HYPERBARIC OXYGEN CHAMBER INSIDE: ABSOLUTELY NO CANDLES, MATCHES, LIGHTERS. "This is what everyone comes for. Looks like R2-D2 but it can reach damaged tissue that's deep in the body. The doctor says it'll be very healing for Persephone."

A woman with short gray hair sat upright from her mat, clutching her blankets to her chest. "Demeter, hon? Someone clogged our toilet again. If you don't mind. And the sink is grimy."

"Adding the bathroom to my list, Edith," Demeter said with cheerful firmness, but Edith had much more to say, comments about the temperature of her broths and the smell of the hand soap, until a beeping emerged from Demeter's apron pocket. "Crap. Gotta get back to . . . You go." She pointed to a doorway at the rear of the studio. "Upstairs and then third on the left."

I WALKED UP A narrow staircase. The door sounded hollow when I knocked, and I could hear a woman's voice inside speaking French. "*Entrez vous,*" she called. I apologized, explained I was looking for Persephone.

The door opened slightly. A hand drew me inside. "Oh my god, Eve?" Her body collided with mine. I held Persephone, although she was barely there, bones and clothes, somehow thinner than before. "Are they here? Can they come in?"

"Sonya and Lev? Not this time, honey. Next time for sure."

The room took shadowy form. A murmur of illumination from string lights with their bulbs dulled by tape, clothes mummifying the chair and desk, a mattress on the floor, paper snowflakes on the walls, and yarn everywhere, as if the room had been scrawled over by a kid with a crayon. Against a wall, the shape of a woman sitting cross-legged on a cushion.

Persephone turned to her. "Can we maybe be done?"

"*Absolument.*" As she shuffled past me, she sighed with obvious displeasure, her facial expression inscrutable in the dimness. "Keep practicing. Always practice."

"French lessons?" I said when she left.

"That's what she calls them," Persephone said, leaning against my arm. "But then she just talks. I have no idea what she's saying. A lot of them do."

"A lot of who?"

"The patients. They know I'm here and they come and tell me things. I think maybe everyone's a little lonely?"

I wanted to ask if she was lonely, but I stopped myself. What else could she be? This wasn't a place for a child to live. I sat with her while she finger knit and told me about the patients, which ones had grandchildren or half-finished memoirs or corgis or herniated discs. I hadn't seen her in so long, and her darkness frightened me anew, the endlessness of it all, and I was relieved when Demeter came, setting a bowl of broth on the desk for her daughter. "Done," she said. "I've delivered them all and there's an hour before the evening thing. It's sound healing and energy flow stretches tonight."

"Ugh." Persephone drew out the teenage groan of displeasure. "Do I *have* to?"

"The doctor says it's good for you," Demeter said, kissing her daughter's hair.

My mind stuck on that word—good. Sonya and I had recently rewatched *The Wizard of Oz,* and I heard Judy Garland's soprano voice. "Are you a good witch, or a bad witch?" Well, which was Lenore? I had no idea.

A little while later Demeter asked me directly what side I came down on. We were in a bathroom. She was plunging the toilet and telling me about the doctor's battle with a nearby town about a potential 5G tower. "He's very, very smart about toxins and chronic illness. There's diplomas all over his . . . But sometimes I . . ." She let go of the plunger and turned to me. "Well, what do you think, Eve? Am I doing the right thing?"

My eyes left hers, searching for someplace to land, an opinion to land on.

I'd do anything for a sick kid, surely I would. But would I lead her down this trail through pseudoscience? Would I do that? What had I read about magnets? Well, nothing, wasn't that the problem? Hyperbaric oxygen chambers? Why was it so dingy here, so cold?

"I think . . ." I said, starting out strongly. But then I froze. I took a step back and leaned against a plastic shower stall. "What I think is . . . Well, honestly. I just don't know."

Her face drooped slightly, tiredness crept around her mouth, and I felt terrible about that. She nodded. "No, but it's good here. It is. It's amazing what they can do." She described patients who left here healed from the pull of addiction, from vertigo, from digestive troubles, from anxiety.

I felt proud of my friend and how she stayed so faithful, always kept going, never falling into the eddies of doubt I swirled around in. "But what about you?" I asked urgently. "Are you okay here? Are *you* doing okay?"

"Me? You know me. I've lived with way worse. I mean, it's a lot of time with the same people. Would I like to live alone with my daughter? Hop on a bus to meet a friend? See *you*. Oh, Eve, you've no idea. I mean . . ." She looked around, seeming to gather herself. "But everyone's trying so hard to help. And it's beautiful, the trees out there." She pointed to a dusk-blue sky out the window above the toilet. "I really love the trees."

"I just want you to be okay," I said. "I miss you so much."

She laughed. "How are we even surviving without each other? Tell me things. Tell me about everyone." With a rag, she began wiping grease from a large vat of coconut oil that sat on a shelf beneath a framed sign: HOW OFTEN SHOULD I DETOX WITH OIL PULLING? EVERY DAY!

I thought of my life, how hard I felt it to be, but wasn't it spacious and liberated compared to hers? "But I'm fine! Everything's totally fine."

"Please, Eve. Tell me something."

I told her about Sonya, no more hours spent drawing, no more tin whistle. Her teacher had called about Sonya's sudden lack of interest. She didn't want to be library helper, wouldn't play soccer, walked the fence alone at recess picking up trash blown there by spring winds.

"Oh, Eve, you're worried."

"Just a little. I mean, she's fine. I just don't want to mess her up."

"Oh, Evie, Evie. If you don't do everything right, if you don't say the scripts that the ladies on your Instagram tell you to say, that's okay. Sonya learns how to love another fallible human like herself, and what's more important than that? She'll always know that your love for her and hers for you is so much bigger than this crappy world."

I felt such a weight lifted. All my worry, all my need to be best, to be a very very very good mom rose from me like steam and floated out the now-black window. "Is that really it, though?" I pressed. "Just teach her to love another fallible human?"

"I mean, kind of, yeah."

I still felt that lightness an hour later when I tied my boots and walked into the night. Only when I got in my car and blasted the heat, because I'd become so chilled in there, and drove for a while on dark roads in dark silence, only then did I realize this was what I should have said when she asked me about Persephone's treatments: You're doing fantastic. You're doing the very best you can with the information you have. That was all I needed to say and I wished I'd said it.

Persephone

...

BUT THE QUESTION IS: WHAT *IS* A FALLIBLE HUMAN? IF ONLY Matilda was here to tell her.

She misses Matilda every minute of the day.

Matilda, what is a herniated disc? Matilda, what is toxins? Matilda, am I fallible?

Their bedroom wall is also the bathroom wall, and through it all sounds pass. Earlier this evening: her mother talking to Eve. And now, Carla and Sabine and Edith and Mitch taking their turns to brush and spit and squirt and grunt and mutter and fart and flush. Exhausted as always, her mother fell asleep clutching the blanket, and Persephone touches one of her hands to feel skin that's become strange and scaley from the dishwasher steam. They've turned red, her mom told her, and she tries to imagine red fingers, remembering all the things that were red, like her Elmo from long ago, and a black shirt with red flippy sequins she loved in third grade. Since they came here, she's worn a sweater with wooden buttons loaned by Lenore because it's so cold. Matilda, what do average normal thirteen-year-olds wear?

Instead of Matilda, there's yarn and paper to cut and people knocking on her door—I'll just sit with you for lunch, for dinner, for an hour, for a bit. She doesn't mind any singular conversation, but the weight of them all is too much. They want her to know the facts they've accumulated in their lives, everything they're missing. Edith tells her how to prune roses in the spring. Mitch tells her how to choose an ultralight bear canister for hiking in the Adirondacks. She tries to listen and remember but she's not sure when any of this will be helpful to her.

She thought she hated being alone when they were in Northampton, now she longs for it. Imagines walking between rooms and singing loudly and taking off Lenore's gray sweater to look at herself in the mirror.

Sometimes, in the late nights, after the stretches and toothbrushing and swirling a gob of coconut oil between her teeth, she is woken by her mother and they head out of the room together, and these are the best moments. She doesn't think that will happen tonight, not until someone's pushing her down a hill, and there's a voice saying *wake up, my love, wake up.*

She shoves her mom's hand away. "I'm sleeping." But she's awake and a word comes back to her. Fallible.

"Well, one thing about always wearing that sweater is you don't need to get dressed," her mother whispers. She's pulling on her own sweater from Lenore, who must have drawers and drawers of them. Lenore is not a bad person to be around. She doesn't tell Persephone about her own life, but she rubs her neck until the headaches leave her. She presses on a fleshy spot between Persephone's finger and thumb, and the sour burn of her stomach quiets and only then, in its absence, does she realize how loud it's been.

"Ready?" Her mom opens the door onto the hallway. All the lights are off everywhere. They hold the cold metal banister on the stairs and slide their socks across the smooth studio floor. Then her mom says, "Hold up." They hear the scuttle of mice feet across the linoleum. They're listening for voices from the little room next to the kitchen with a chair and a desk on which a phone sits, a little leash attaching it to the wall. Sometimes they come downstairs and hear mm-hmm, or crying, or once Mitch was talking about something dirty and her mom pushed her hands over Persephone's ears and they moved like that laughing back up the stairs.

Fallible. Fallible. Fallible, she says to herself as they wait. A little oompah to it. Is a fallible human one who blows balloons into shapes? Or transforms into a mossy faerie at night? But what if fallible just means normal, a normal human, a human who walks out into the daylight wearing normal clothes and looking normal to everyone. What if that's what her mother wants to love? A *fallible* human.

"All clear," her mom says.

The kitchen is gray and dark. There's a large tree in front of the house but no trees on the sides, and the moonlight slides in any way it pleases. Her mom kneels before the cabinet of Tupperware, circular lids and rectangular lids slipping out around her. Persephone runs her tongue over her teeth in anticipation. On other nights, her mom has stashed her dried mango in the pantry, or cheese and strawberries in the fridge. "Stick out your hand," she says now. When Persephone hears the crinkle of plastic it's like she's home again, back in Taos, at the orange table in the trailer.

She hops from leg to leg until she feels the press of something hard in her palm. She brings it to her nose and sniffs deeply. "How'd you get this?"

Her mom's smile shines whitely in the moonlight. "Edith. On her day off. I promised nobody would find out."

"Is it really okay? I don't think we should," she says, although there's no way she's not eating this.

"Sweetheart. You need good things, too." But her mother's breathing hard, as if she's nervous.

Persephone pulls off the top layer and presses her front teeth into the icing, scraping it onto her tongue. She lets it rest there for a moment before she swallows. Then she holds the top and bottom circles together. Crumbs jump from her mouth as she bites. It's been so long since she's felt the messiness of crumbs.

When her mom asked the doctor to allow her just a little bread, he said it would be like pouring kerosene on a brush fire. "She's quite sick," he said, as if her mom didn't know. "And unchecked inflammation needs full and constant vigilance."

Matilda, what does vigilance mean? She's pretty sure Matilda would say, "broth."

Once her gut heals and stops leaking all over everything, her body will be ready for the oxygen treatments and the magnet treatments. She's heard about those from the other patients. The magnets are circles of black and red that rest on you as if you're a checkerboard, which seems not too bad. The magnets will zip at each other, and she will try to imagine two old crones playing a very competitive game of checkers, one sitting at her head and one at her feet. But she's terrified of going into the oxygen chamber.

She reaches for another cookie. Her mom is chewing, too.

They sit on the linoleum side by side, passing the package back and forth as if they're outside, maybe in a little park with people milling around who look over at them but don't notice anything weird, don't think anything, but yep, just two other fallible humans.

Later March

. . .

i

I THOUGHT OF HER AS I SCRUBBED AND SWEPT AND COOKED, AS I made Sonya and Lev walk along the river, as I threw stones in the water with them, and as I carried crying Lev home after he lay down in the still-frigid water. It was clear to me that although she was near, she wouldn't be back, not for a long time, if ever. Lenore and the doctor had landed a gold mine—this lovely woman unclogging toilets and cooking soups as they held up the bright promise of healing. And if she did leave, I might never know. I'd seen, several times now, how she slipped away.

I tried to talk about this with Henry James that next Friday, but he quickly tired of the topic. Sure, he'd known hippies. You can't pin them down. This was bound to happen with someone named Demeter.

On the bench at swim class the next morning, I held my phone as if it were a dangerous animal. And then I texted Will. We hadn't been in touch since my mom's visit, but he wrote back right away, profligate with exclamation marks. After a thread of questions about Demeter he interrupted himself: Actually, he was just back in town and did I want to come over? Water splashed on my jeans and I didn't look up.

ii

IT WAS MILK I SAID WE NEEDED. A PALLID EXCUSE, THIN AS SKIM. "But so late?" Henry James asked, his face bathed in the milky light of his phone. "Just lie down with me and let them eat dry Cheerios." I stood beside our bed. He slid a hand under my shirt, up my stomach. He said he hated the house in the night without me. All the creepy countryside sounds. His eyes were tired, stoned. "Just lie down."

Will's apartment was downtown, above a weed store, around the corner from Fitzwilly's where we'd dropped Demeter at the Bika Ram van on Fridays. The entrance from the alley was propped open with a cinderblock, and his door, on the second floor, was slightly ajar. My knocking pushed it open farther, but when I saw Will leaning against a sleek black kitchen island talking to a much shorter man whose back was to me, I froze. Was I interrupting a date? Had he forgotten I was coming over?

Then he noticed me. "You're here! Come on in. No, really. Come in. This is Matty. My landlord and master of the fuse box."

The man turned to regard me with New England reserve. A Red Sox cap clashed with the orange of his full beard. He picked up a massive tool kit, edged past me, and headed out without a word.

"Until next time, Matty," Will called out. "God knows it'll be soon." He closed the door, bent toward me as if to kiss my cheek, pulled back, shoved his hands in his pockets. "Well, hi there."

"Hi to you."

We were smiling at each other. He was more vivid and exciting in person than in my memory—his urgent, heavy-lidded eyes, the plank of his chest. I looked away first, taking in the long room, the towering windows at the far end. "Great apartment."

"Yeah, but the lights are wonky and instead of calling an electrician, I'm supposed to call Matty whenever they go out." He began moving around the kitchen, opening cabinets, the freezer. "I think he mostly needs someone to talk to. I give him a beer and he tells me about his red-eared slider turtles, his eighteen-foot boat, his belief that homeless people have ruined this town. That's the price of electricity."

I watched him plunk ice into two mugs, wondering what he was doing here. Hadn't he finished with the plant books? Didn't he live in Cambridge?

True, but his house needed work, new floors, he explained when I asked. He didn't want to be around for it. Since he kept this lease when he went to see his mom, he figured he'd hang out here until rehearsals started in May.

Had he come back for me? I couldn't bring myself to ask.

"It's month to month," he added, pouring scotch. "So, not a big deal."

Not a big deal? I tried to imagine that sort of wealth and freedom of movement, deciding on a whim to live in one place or another, flitting between a high-ceilinged two-bedroom and a home in Cambridge. He said the apartment came partially furnished, so I assumed that the brown leather couch wasn't his. But the art postcards taped to the long brick wall would be; I recognized Turner's Thames, Bruegel's Babel, Van Gogh's crazed cedars, stained glass that looked like Matisse. I wanted to know who sent them.

His knuckle pressed mine when he handed me a mug, but when he led me to the couch, he sat on a chair a distance away. "Now you'll tell me everything about Demeter."

Out of a combination of nerves and relief to be asked, I couldn't stop talking, sentences tumbling out. "It just makes me so mad," I said after a while. "When medicine fails, you get this. If you're lucky, that is. Everyone else . . . they didn't listen to her. They denied it."

"Denied what? Emily?" His thin legs were crossed, one socked foot jiggling.

"Honestly? I'm sitting here talking to you and thinking I bet you don't think it exists, either. The pain. Her daughter's pain. So I get it, I do, how amazing it is for her to finally be believed, even if it means in return she has to believe in the dangers of 5G and electromagnetic . . ."

"Eve." It felt so intimate, the way he spoke my name. "Eve," he repeated. "There's something I need to tell you. Something I didn't that . . . Well, Quinn. Remember Quinn? He had Emily. That's what he had. Of course it exists."

Was this a joke? "Why didn't you tell me?"

"I don't know. It felt like a lot."

He recited the familiar symptoms, but I thought only about painkillers, and I wanted to run out of the apartment I'd been so curious about all day, run to the hills to hold Persephone.

As if he could hear my thoughts, he said, "She's really lucky to have a mom like your friend, you know. Someone to keep her safe until this is all figured out."

"Figured out?" I was loud in my frustration. "What's getting figured out?"

He was leaning toward me, elbows on his knees, fingers knitted. "It sounds a little depressing there. It does. But they won't hurt her and maybe they'll help with some . . . You know Jeremiah? His mom works with this guy. Ishmael's his name. Apparently celebrities fly him all over the world for his herbs and tinctures. And it does help, Elizabeth says . . . at least with symptoms. Things the doctor can't get to. There's so much we don't understand about the body. It's like outer space in there."

But I was thinking about something else. "When did you say . . . When was Quinn?"

He nodded a few times. "Yeah, no, right. Before the pandemic, if that's what you're asking."

"So, that means it's not . . . This isn't a post-pandemic trauma?" I felt the tectonic shifting of solid ground.

"Maybe trauma of another sort? He was a pretty traumatized guy."

"But there's always been traumatized guys. All of history is traumatized guys. And this is a new thing." I wanted to cry, to throw myself on the ground and tantrum like my kids. What was this if not a post-pandemic response? Why didn't anyone know?

"Well." He shrugged. "Maybe it is. Maybe not. Maybe people had this in the past and we don't know about it."

"We would know about it!" I was nearly shouting. "If people had to stay out of the light so they didn't throw up, we would know that. That's the sort of thing you know."

"Hey," he said quietly, reaching out to touch the back of my hand. "Hey, Eve. I'm so sorry she's sick. You know I am."

I felt myself returning to the room. I nodded. "I'm sorry Quinn was sick, too."

Remembering myself, remembering manners and conversational mores, I asked him about Quinn—what was he like, what were his interests—but he shook his head. "If it's okay let's not talk about him."

He left for the bathroom, and I moved quickly to the brick wall to flip up the postcards, to spy on their undersides, bullying through my fear that he'd catch me. But what did I learn? No return addresses, just cryptic text. *I love the Southwest.* Or: *I can't wait to return to the Southwest territories.* The pictures were not of the Southwest.

All were signed the same. *Love, G.* I squinted, tried to turn the G into a Q. Or a J.

I was back on the couch when he returned. This time he sat close, his shoulder pressing mine, and I imagined turning and straddling him, grabbing his hips, digging my fingers into the cleft of his back. I stayed very still to let the thoughts pass through me.

He asked about my mom, had I seen her again, and while he asked, two of his fingers began moving in a high circle on my thigh and it was like he was asking me another set of questions entirely.

"I need to go home," I said, but I didn't want to go home, not at all, so I went to the windows and looked at the sidewalk below where I often walked with my kids. Under a yellow streetlight, black café chairs glimmered wetly. The trees stood very still as if in shock from holding up their bare branches all these many months without the cover of leaves.

"I get it," he said, standing, too. When he reached the front door, he turned to face me, grinning. "I thought of one for you."

"One what?"

"There once was a woman named Eve." I walked toward the door, which meant I walked toward him smiling. "There once was a woman named Eve. And I didn't want her to leave." He opened his arms and I walked into them. It would be so easy to move my mouth to his.

When I finally pulled away and gathered my bag, I didn't think I was saying no. That wasn't my answer. I was saying not yet, let me think about it, let me weigh the damage. I thought I had time.

As I drove home, milkless, I wanted it all—my children and my husband and Will and Demeter, all the seasons at once, the winter branches and the crawling spring and the burnt autumn, the scorch of summer, the burrow, the flight, the hibernation, I wanted that much.

Ruth

...

On her first morning at the Cunt Collective, Ruth woke at the murky dawn and went into the kitchen, assuming she'd be drinking coffee alone, and there was Antonia stirring eggs naked, her long hair down her back, her dark bush, her stunning breasts, and Ruth thought, with the delusion of youth, that this much beauty would now be in her life forever, in each room she walked into.

Like everyone, Ruth eventually hooked up with Antonia. A quick fuck in the storeroom of Raos Coffee. Who was Antonia dating at the time? Antonia was dating everyone. The girl from that band, the girl from the other band, the girl from the farmers market. She remembers begging Antonia, couldn't they be together? There was a letter, wasn't there? Antonia had no patience. *Why don't you fuck that straight woman from the potluck? You need to learn how to have a fling and she's never leaving her comfy little hetero world. Just don't fall for her.*

As always, Ruth fell.

And then, when Ramona moved in with Ruth, Antonia was still always naked in the kitchen, but now she kept her eye on Ramona, making her giggle, standing so close to her at the stove, her arm around Ramona's waist on the couch, saying things like, you know I love that shirt on you. Ruth let it pass, because Antonia was moving far away to build her desert lab and they were heading to the hills where Orion would be born in their living room. Over the next few years, Antonia occasionally showed up at their door with a toy for Orion but no advance warning. In town, she'd explain, for a guest lecture or to secure funding or for another honorary degree. She'd slip her arm around Ramona's waist and Ramona would get that pink glow, like sand at sunset. Anyone could tell Ramona had a crush. One time, Antonia brought vodka and they were all a little drunk when she said, "Ramona, what if you come to the guest bedroom tonight? I'll show you the stars and the moon." Ramona laughed, but Ruth stormed into the night and when she came back inside Ramona had left to check on Orion and Antonia called her possessive and whoa, lighten up, take a joke.

Antonia visited once more unannounced, or at least without any forewarning to Ruth who drove home early from the American Library Association's annual conference in Albany, because she missed her family and her bed; she found Antonia drinking coffee in her kitchen. She was wearing clothes, sure, but Ramona began singing some children's song about a fox, even though Orion was eleven and at a friend's house for a sleepover, and then decided to make a complicated chicken recipe, which required her and Antonia to drive into town for ingredients, and Ruth could tell, she just could tell.

Or could she? She couldn't bring herself to ask. Wouldn't Ramona tell her if they had? Then again, Ramona had cheated before. That time the dupe was Stephen, and Ruth had found it incredibly exciting, but didn't that mean she knew what Ramona was capable of? Some days she couldn't look at her she was so angry. And then Ramona got sick and she never did ask, never found out. In her grief and fury she said Antonia couldn't come to the funeral, and Antonia didn't ask why.

A GOOD PUZZLE SHOULD seem impossible until the moment before it's solved, which means the better you are at puzzles, the fewer good ones remain.

She's on the computers on the first floor with her patrons. She can't do this alone in her office. The man to her left? She once sprayed Narcan up his nose after finding him between the rhododendrons and the book drop-off bins with ants crawling over his face. She lay beside him and held him until the paramedics came, saying, *Stay with me, Jeff, stay with me.* The patron to her right, typing out a Facebook post with two fingers—she hooked him up with her friend, a public defender who kept him out of prison for dealing weed the year before it was legalized. Between them she feels safe enough to watch Antonia on a well-lit stage, wearing an artichoke-green suit, that gap between her front teeth, her long hair, her way of drawing you in. She's talking about the great web of synchrony between her night-blooming flowers and the owlet moths that pollinate them and the wren chicks that survive on these moth caterpillars, and even though Ruth's stomach is wrenched in hatred for her, it sounds pretty amazing, the way the earth takes care of itself, ecology a chain of circles of mutuality, and Ruth is moved in spite of herself when Antonia says that if humans pay attention they'll learn a better way to live with one another. The audience cheers.

This TED Talk is twenty years old. Ruth clicks on Google's more recent offerings, articles in the *Arizona Daily Sun* from six years ago, and then wishes she hadn't, that she could just continue believing in the great plant/moth/bird mutual aid society.

Fungus brought on by heat came for the owlet moths. The caterpillars died off. Flowers kept blooming in the lab, pollinated by scientists, Antonia is quoted as saying, but in the wild? Gone, just gone. She closed her research center high in the Santa Catalina Mountains of Arizona. "All the years I spent. All that work. What was it for?"

Ruth tries to imagine Antonia as Ellen described her. This woman, with uncountable friends, distant admirers, sycophantic mentees, brokenhearted lovers, now reclusive? Looks like Antonia fell hard, too. That cold bitch fell hard for a plant, and she can't get over their leaving. This thought gives her a moment of pleasure.

The impossible step. She doesn't need to do it. Stephen won't ever know that Antonia collects floral calendars, old plant books, odd herbaria. But thoughts of Stephen have been bugging her since she talked to Ellen at Cap'n Jack's. Like he's standing behind her shoulder with a Tupperware of inedible muffins. *You're the visionary here, Ruth.*

Is she? Or does she just want to fucking solve the puzzle? She swallows fury, sends a terse email. *Looking for a plant called Sightflower. Have you come across it?* The message boomerangs back. User unknown.

"Sure I could give you her number, but what good would it do you?" Ellen says on the phone when Ruth's back at the computer tables, new patrons beside her, one watching a Rachel Maddow clip from 2021, another listening to a YouTube about becoming a nail technician, neither with headphones. Some days her library has all the learned solemnity of a gas station mini-mart.

"Never answers. Uses it entirely for Candy Crush. Doesn't have voicemail. No email anymore. Only thing to do is show up at her door, but, honestly, it's fifty-fifty even then. She doesn't open it for strangers. Rarely for friends. Just tell her you didn't see Jessie. Ha ha. Yeah, yell it through the door. It's big and blue, her house is, behind the apple orchard just past town on the way to the dump. Hard to miss."

Imagine Antonia, eremitic but still arbiter, standing at the peephole, deciding whether to let in Ruth. Fuck no.

They'll find it at the rivers' edge like Lillian did. The green slope will be dotted with Sightflower, like patches of white snow on a spring day. Because she can't. She really can't. Did you do it? That's what she'd shout through the door. She wouldn't be able to say anything else, just Did you do it, did you sleep with my wife? and she knows that Antonia will open the door wide and tell her the truth and she can't bear it.

Early April

...

i

SONYA FOUND AN OLD CLOTH MASK IN THE LINEN CLOSET AND insisted on wearing it on the train. Lev kept asking how many people knew him in New York. We emerged from the dark tunnel into the celestial galaxy of Grand Central transformed into those people: gawking, in our fanciest clothes, laden with luggage. At the information desk, Henry James waved uninhibitedly. When had I last seen him so happy? I loved him here in his natural habitat and felt a sour ulcer of guilt for spending the train ride texting Will.

"Where'd this come from?" Henry James held out Sonya's new monogrammed backpack, white with blue mermaids. He gave me a look—we were broke. I shrugged. "Okay," he said, too happy to care, looping both kids' backpacks on his wide shoulders and leading us to a Mexican restaurant. "This is how life should be. Our family in the city." Before leaving for work, he asked the kids what they wanted to do over the weekend. The Statue of Liberty, they said. The M&M's store. He looked at me incredulously. "They're tourists. How did we let that happen?"

In the escalating buzz for *The Third Person* reissue, there'd been articles and profiles of my mother, including one in *New York* magazine: "The *Wormfood* author is even darker than you thought. She's the Grand Dame of feminist rage. And we're here for it."

When she was invited to interview the debut novelist of the season at the 92nd Street Y she asked me to come. "I know you won't sit through the reading, what with your children, but at least you could join for the little shindig I'm throwing after."

Norton's *Anthology of Poetry* propped open her door. We stumbled onto a soft landscape of coats. Sonya grabbed my wrist and dragged me and Lev through the forest of partiers to my mom's office.

"I thought it would be a real party," she said, pulling at her dress, and I realized she meant balloons and games.

I handed over my phone, promised to return with food.

The platters on the table were already sullied with cigarette butts and the cake was uncut, glazed pink to match the stacks of the young author's books. A conversation paused when I entered the kitchen. Three women, a decade younger than me, in sweaters like spun sugar. I'd forgotten about hair. Theirs spoke loudly of aesthetic considerations. Had it been a year since I'd cut mine? I felt naked without my children pressed against me.

But I wasn't alone, I told myself, my mother was here. My own mother. I found her in the mint-green living room, cornered by two men: one white and old with wire-rimmed glasses, the other young and brown with a goatee, who was saying that when he finished reading whatever it was they were discussing he wanted to climb onto the roof of his apartment building and sleep under moonlight in a visceral homage to the protagonist.

The older man applauded the younger man's depths of emotional response then quickly reasserted his literary dominance. He name-dropped Coriolanus and Jean Genet and Eugene Onegin, and turned to my mom. "And you, Joan, I'm sure you enjoyed the scenes with the mother?"

She caught my eye and winked. Here she was, after so long: a serious novelist. I felt my heart race to meet hers. How would she respond? She lit a cigarette and her Bakelite bangles tapped anticipatorily.

"Bloated and overpraised," she said loudly. "When I finished? Tossed it across the room. To be totally honest, James, I'd rather read a two-bit mystery where all that's expected of me is to figure out the killer, because these novels, they're all the same. The main character is aching."

People throughout the room turned to look. Others entered from the kitchen, drawn by the change in noise, the cessation of chatter, the rise of a single emphatic voice.

"Why? We're meant to wonder this. That's the suspense. Why the ache? Why's he acting so badly? So we page through endless scenes in swimming pools and grocery stores and fucking on kitchen linoleum and, yes, on rooftops in the moonlight, even though the answer to the ache is always in the past. It's a puzzle that always ends in the same place. A parent, usually a mother, died or hit or didn't love enough. That's what we're looking for. So, if this were a novel about me, we'd flash back to when I was eleven and my mother jumped to her death to make sure that she'd never have to see me again. Okay, but what about my mother's ache? How far back do we go? Do we blame her dead mother, burned alive in Treblinka? When do we throw up our hands and just blame hate? When do we say, yes, somebody hated with a pure hate? Or perhaps we should probe Hitler's mother. What was wrong with her? Or further back? His mother's mother? All three hundred and ninety-two pages of that novel, James, could be replaced with just a single sentence: There was a mother and now the man is aching."

Cheers and laughter filled the packed room.

"But really, Joan." James held up a nagging finger. "One cannot let one's personal story occlude the critical eye."

"Oh, one can indeed." She snuffed her cigarette in a glass on the windowsill.

I wanted her to greet me above all others, and she did, holding me close. I smelled her familiar sweat, the jasmine shampoo she'd used since my childhood. "I want you to meet everyone," she said, pulling me to Irene and a young woman who exuded a wondrous precision, the sharp cut of her yellow bangs, the yellow triangles painted on her silk jumpsuit, her orange fingernails.

"Phoebe here is an absolute genius," my mother said.

Irene kissed my cheeks, then turned to my mom. "You know that book was by James's protégé? And you destroyed it. There's an ache, for fuck's sake. She nailed it, didn't she, Phoebe?"

My mother threw her head back and laughed, her long neck catching the light.

"Awesome," Phoebe said, examining her fingernails. "Exactly why I call you my literary mother."

"You darling girl. And you're having fun? You should be. This is your night."

"Do you know this bar?" Phoebe began, looking around as if the bar might be found behind one of the bookcases. "Maybe on Seventy-second? Right near here?"

"Not here," my mother said. "There was an apocalypse, total and complete. Every bar with history, with meaning, shuttered."

Phoebe shouted across the room. "Tobes, what was that place near here and we went there and were like, damn, this is so lame it kind of slaps?"

I watched my mother's face fall as it dawned on her that her party had been found lacking.

"Well, darling girl," she said, mustering cheer. "Should we find it?"

"I mean, only if you want to." Phoebe was already tapping out a message on her phone.

"Let's go. Right now. We'll toast you to the moon, all of us. Well . . ." She clutched my arm. "Eve here can't. She's a mama." She imbued the word with mockery, an infantile space between the echoing syllables. And then she pulled me to her mouth, whispered, "Help me, darling. Stay with me. I can't . . . I just can't."

It was so familiar, this experience of simultaneously being hurt by her and feeling in my own chest the pain that made her attack me. (The ache! The ache!) I could tell how hard she'd tried this evening—the deli tulips on the coffee table, the platters of cured meats, the still-waiting pink cake. For her this was extraordinary effort.

Phoebe looked up from her phone as if just noticing my existence in the conversation.

"I'm her daughter," I said. "Literally. Though not literarily."

"Cute!" Phoebe turned to tell an islet of friends about the change of venue.

"I do have more wine," my mother said to Irene. "Squirreled away somewhere, but no, no, let's go."

I watched everyone shove into the entryway and pick up the wrong coat and laugh and dive forth again. At some point, my mother disappeared. "Joan," they called. "Joan!"

"She must be changing from one gray dress to another gray dress,"

Irene said. We laughed. Phoebe and her friends were already gone. Someone kicked away *The Norton Anthology* and the door slammed to announce each departure. Finally, I told Irene to leave; I'd send my mom along.

Her bangles in a bowl on the bureau. Her dress on the floor. She lay in her slip. "Thank you, Eve. Oh, thank you for staying with me. I'm sick. I'm so sick."

"It's no problem."

"But it must be." She looked suddenly surprised. "You do so much for me, don't you?"

I sat on her bed. "It's been a lot, the excitement about your book. You've been flying so high, this is just how you regain equilibrium." We never talked directly about her depression.

"No, this isn't that," she said. "I just feel so sick."

"No, this is what happens to you," I said distractedly. Lev was calling me from the other room.

The kids and I ate Phoebe's pink cake while listening to Joan Armatrading on my mother's record player. I began to sing along, and then, possessed by a strong energy, I felt my exhaustion from the day being transformed into its opposite. I brushed crumbs from my skirt and stood. All night I'd felt embarrassed for myself—my sloppy appearance, my remove from the artistic world, an embarrassment buzzing beneath my rib cage. At first, I just swayed my arms, but soon I was flinging my hair, perverting my hips, dancing like the teenager I'd been when I lived here, thick with lust and longing. I was thinking of Will, of dancing with Will. I'd see him in a few days. Sonya joined first, with solemn expression, casting glances to copy my sway, and then Lev, pink frosting clowning his mouth, began jumping, making the needle skip. "It's a party after all," said Sonya in her serious but joyful way. I kept expecting my mother to tell me to turn the music down. Or better yet, to join us. We'd danced together like this on her good days. But she stayed in her bed as Sonya and Lev and I danced with wilder and wilder abandon, and all the books around us, all her records, and the ashtray, and the party cups, and a left-behind yellow scarf all began spinning, too.

ii

OH MAN, I WAS HAPPY. I WAS HAPPY AS I DROVE US INTO THE hills during the final notes of daylight. My kids were home with Pax. There were redbuds on the maples. Spring was coming. I glanced at Will's hands on his lap. I didn't want to ruin my life, but I wanted his hands on me. I could just reach out. I thought about what Demeter would say if I had the chance to tell her. Reach out, she'd say. There's time for everything.

We were on our way to return her, if only for a few hours, to the world of red meat and internet service. I'd wanted Persephone, too, but the doctor was adamant, Demeter said, that she couldn't risk a break in protocol. I told her—when we spoke on the Healing Hut's landline—that I was thinking of bringing a friend to join us. "I found him looking at flowers. He's funny. Not annoying."

"Not annoying *yet*. Remember, end each sentence with possibility. No, but I'm glad you have someone. I just hope you told him I'm still the best friend."

"Best friend *yet*," I said. But then, because I believed in jinxes and miserly gods, quickly amended. "Not funny. Best friend always."

A FROGGY TRILL FROM some vernal pool greeted us when we parked at the Healing Hut. "Like a distant flock of phone alarms," Will said, getting out of the car. In the weeks since I'd visited, the last snow had melted, and chairs had been brought to the porch. I assumed the man sitting straight-backed with his eyes closed was a patient. He jumped up when we approached.

"Sunlight and fresh air," he said. "Sometimes I think that's all we need. I'm Doctor Folkenflick."

He was a short, unassuming man with wire-rimmed glasses, loose brown corduroys belted high on his hips, a soft plaid shirt tucked in.

I stared down at his smooth, small skull, imagining it would feel like polished wood.

The doctor shook Will's hand and then turned to me. "Demeter told me you were coming. I hear you're the daughter of the great children's fabulist."

Will nudged me proudly. "Oh, that's her all right."

"I'm Eve," I said, holding out my hand.

He clasped it between both of his. "If I could have a minute . . . Just a quick chat?"

A narrow staircase took the doctor and me from the sitting room, where he sent Will to wait. Upstairs, he led me to what was clearly once a child's bedroom—faded and half-peeled stickers mosaicked the closet door. Now: a desk and chairs and a framed diploma from Cleveland Chiropractic College. He gestured for me to sit while he perched on the edge of his desk. He picked up a chain of paper clips and smiled at me. His was a pleasant face. He told me that reading the *Wormfood* series to his son and daughter was one of the most profound experiences of fatherhood. "What a thrill it must have been to have as a mother someone so perceptive about the mind of a child, who has plumbed the absolute depths of what it means to be born and die, to have a consciousness and . . . Well, how *is* your mother?"

She hadn't left her bed all weekend. I'd filled her fridge with soup, cleaned up from the party, alerted Irene.

"She's great."

"Oh, that's good. I'm very glad to hear it. So many people aren't, not right now. There's so much suffering. The Great Disabling. Have you heard that term? Sickness as response to a sick world."

He was moving the paper clip chain through his fingers like a rosary.

"Take our lovely Persephone. I think she's just the tip of the iceberg. Do you? Do you imagine many more people will find themselves with Emily?"

"Maybe?" I couldn't understand what he wanted from me. "I mean, I hope not."

"I like to think of this place as a little sanitarium, in the traditional sense. In Latin, sanitas is health. The same root—that's R-O-O-T—as sanity. But also, as we show here, the same R-O-U-T-E as sanity. Our busy-busy hurry-hurry culture thinks that health can be achieved through a fifteen-minute doctor's appointment. A thirty-minute workout. That's a funny compound word. Work. Out. I say, don't work out. Live in."

His gave an imploring lift to his thick eyebrows. "Definitely," I said.

Dropping the paper clips, he raised a manila folder from his desk. I saw my name written in Sharpie, not on the tab where names go, but across the front. "Well, well. The younger Yalen is a writer, too. I printed your articles. You've a fine style. Like me, you're someone who can volley and joust with language."

He circled a finger in the air and jabbed near my face. "Voilà."

I stared at the file—thin, but mine—as he explained that he wanted a ghostwriter for articles that would teach the oncoming wave of Emilys about his Healing Hut. A job, I finally realized—he was offering me an actual job. I must have made a noise. This was childcare, time for my own writing. He clapped his hands. "Aha! The younger Yalen is paying attention."

MY EARLIER HAPPINESS WAS alchemized into something more high-pitched and brittle by how badly I wanted that money. The evening had shifted even before I ran downstairs and found them sitting together, Demeter laughing at something he said, Will grinning at her. Okay, I thought. It's good. They're getting along.

At Brewmaster's Tavern, where the Red Sox played on multiple screens, Will slid into the booth beside me. We watched Demeter remove her coat and hang it on a hook. Unlike me, she'd dressed for this: short black shift with a white Peter Pan collar and a yellow bleach stain in the shape of South America. Blue tights, blue beads. Hair loose down her back. She reached for my hand. "My god, Eve, thank you. I feel like a child being taken out for my birthday."

"It's her birthday," Will told the waitress. When she returned, Demeter's beer had an umbrella in it.

By that time, Will had turned his high beam of attention onto her—the questions, the follow-ups, the empathic rejoinders. She was more flippant than I'd known her to be, and he kept grinning unselfconsciously, the way that men grin at beautiful women. I was audience, onlooker, occasionally consulted.

I'd never seen Demeter with a man other than during her brief chats with Henry James. I'd no idea she could flirt like this. Our time together had been spent in a straitjacket of motherhood and illness, the balcony or the woods. No lunches out together, no dinner parties. I felt so dumb that I'd brought Will along on my first chance to be in the world with her.

"Enough with the interview," she said finally. "Now I ask the questions."

Will laced his fingers behind his head. "Anything."

She squinted, the red straw from her water playful between her lips. She removed it like a cigarette. "Yeah, no. I don't need to ask you anything."

His look fell. "I'm that boring?"

"That obvious. Your mind was blown when you saw Escher in eighth grade. By Umberto Eco in tenth. You miss the way you felt when you first read these books."

"Never finished junior high? And yet you know about Eco?"

"Funny thing. They allow people without diplomas into libraries."

And then I realized. Of course. I'd seen her with a man before.

She wasn't the same as she'd been at twelve, neither eager nor malleable. But Will was responding to her as my father had, awed and excited, leaning forward to catch each precious and precocious word. Could she, he asked, tell everyone's life or just his?

She glanced around. "Don't look now but the woman at the next table used to star in serious theater. Think Broadway. Tony Awards. Name in lights."

Will and I swiveled to see a woman in her seventies eating a tuna salad. She wore a clear raincoat, white hair royal in a high bun.

She pointed to a table of teenage soccer players with red ribbons in their ponytails, red team jerseys, ice-cream sundaes. "Your turn."

"You want me to say something about them?" Will asked.

She nodded.

"Ah, okay. Well. Their future's easy to see. All tragic. Husbands upon high school graduation. Babies a year later. Hairdressers. Dental hygienists."

"Wow." Demeter bugged her eyes. "Thanks for sharing your weird classist fantasy."

"Okay, so teach me."

"Their future? They'll have satisfyingly kinky sex with their husbands." Will laughed, but Demeter grew serious. "They'll love spending time in water, waterskiing, teaching their babies to swim in the lake, saving up for a weekend with girlfriends in Florida, finding wonder in the world even without novels by Eco and whoever else you think of as so central to your happiness."

The waitress brought my French onion soup, identical hamburgers for Will and Demeter, and yet it was a fry from his plate she ate first.

"So, tell me." He spoke quietly. "Tell me about the wonder in their lives."

Demeter watched the girls. "In the quiet of the night when they're up with their babies they'll feel someone beside them. It won't be God exactly, not the Irish Catholic God of their own mothers. These girls will be too full of Instagram influencers to feel that God. But they'll feel an accompaniment. They'll know, and they won't know how they know this, that their grown daughters, these same babies but all grown up, have come back to see them. They're right nearby." She turned to me. "Right, Eve?"

I nodded. This was my Demeter.

"They'll feel a sense of contentment that . . ."

"A schmuck like me will never know?" Will interrupted.

She took a few bites, licking juice that dripped onto her pinkie. "Did I say that?"

They jousted, volleyed through the meal, two more beers. Demeter, especially, was racing, raising Will up, cutting him down. And while I knew that my stated purpose for this dinner was to release Demeter from the drudgery of her obligations and the relentlessness of Persephone's suffering, I still felt like shit. I was lonelier than I ever was in my house.

"Hey, I have an idea," I found myself interjecting. "Why doesn't

Will buy some of your jewelry." I could hear petulance in my tone, but I kept on. "He has nieces. They must need earrings."

Will answered sincerely. "I'd love to see what you make."

She seemed embarrassed. "They're fine. I don't know if kids would . . ." But she gave him the number of the Healing Hut so he could find out if their lobes were pierced and get back to her. I'd interrupted their rhythm. Will flagged down the waitress, insisted on paying, and went to the bathroom. Demeter came to sit beside me. "Thank you, Eve."

I pointed at the receipt curled on the table. "All him. You saw."

"No. All you. You could tell I need . . . I really needed to feel normal again. Just for a few hours."

It flooded back to me, how confined her life was, and I forgave her the flirting that pained me—how would she know this, I'd said nothing—and was it even flirting, I wondered, resting my head on her shoulder. Weren't we just cosplayers, historical reenactors, simulating life before kids, when people unrelated by birth or marriage would joke together in a bar, making shit up?

IT WAS QUIET AS Will and I drove the dark roads home. Was the silence companionable? Had a thread between us broken? I couldn't tell. When we passed the town of Williamsburg—single stoplight flashing yellow, no cars in the fluorescent halo of Cumberland Farms—I told him about the doctor's offer and that I wasn't sure I could take it since he was paying Demeter minimum wage and had offered me far more. It wasn't fair, he said, but she didn't seem petty like that. "Man, she's unusual. I've never met anyone like her."

In the alley behind his apartment, he told me he had to leave to help his mom again. I didn't ask whether he was keeping his apartment this time. His rehearsals would start in a few weeks. I'd been wondering for the length of the drive what our goodbye would be like, what I might do and how he would respond, and now I knew. I did nothing. He squeezed my knee, and I didn't hear from him until May when it had been raining for weeks and he asked me to come over.

Stephen

. . .

WHAT WAS ONCE A WATER CURE IS NOW AN ELKS LODGE WITH thirty-two American flags out front and a painted wooden sign announcing last year's Labor Day tag sale. He waits by his car in a parking lot as wide as Walmart's, empty except for a midsize boy on a skateboard. Rip-rap, rip-rap go his wheels. Grass grows through the asphalt, because thanks to the April rains, rains like nobody's ever seen, green is pushing up everywhere.

It's the first dry day in weeks. It's also the first of May, which is when the water cure doctress Lillian met the botanizing ladies. He watches the skateboarder until a small green cab pulls up, and Stephen, who has never seen a cab in this town before, is surprised to see Will step out. In the muggy air, his hair is springy and awake.

"A cab? Your car's in the shop? I would've picked you up."

"Ah, no. Came straight from the airport. I've been ministering to my mom in Florida. But here we are, May the first. Couldn't miss it."

"Do you think . . . ?"

"Should be here." Will grins. "Should be."

Ruth appears from behind the Elks Lodge, jogging toward them in shorts and a terry cloth headband like some 1970s tennis pro. She's out of breath. "Sorry. Bear on the path. Little guy. Gave him some space. Are we ready?"

They walk single file through the dense woods that separate the Elks Lodge from the river. These trees are newish, he's learned from the entry on the Ruggles Water Cure in the Historical Society's website. It was open land back when Lillian led her patients across the field to dunk them in the river.

The fence is new, too. They head for where it's been pushed down by teens or deer. Stephen's heart is beating too fast. He feels foolishly giddy.

As they come through the trees, a surge of hope, electricity piercing muscle, bone, zinging along each nerve. Green is everywhere! The riverbank has gardened itself. He pushes in front of Will, snagging his arm on a branch. He doesn't feel pain where the skin rips.

It takes a moment to realize something's wrong. The green's too much a monolith. He shoves aside leaves, thinking he can pass through to a more typical heterogeneity of growth, but there's no other side to this thing.

Red stalks segmented like bamboo, leaves like hearts. A monster's body with Nessie humps, no head, no tail; it's everywhere. He can't get under or over so he peers through. Leaves dangle above the water.

"What the fuck is this?"

"Got it!" Will's reading from a plant app. "Japanese knotweed. Highly invasive. Brought from Japan in the 1800s as an ornamental, blah, blah. Okay, here it says if you find it on your property you've lost the value of your home. Impossible to eradicate. Incredibly fast-growing and spreads without . . . I'm sorry."

"No, no." Stephen's crying, he realizes, and wipes his face. "Maybe downriver."

They walk downstream until they reach the mowed lawns of backyards, but the view of the water is blocked by this wild beast of a plant, smothering anything trying to grow beneath. It's loud, too, thrumming with insects.

The river's far side is contained by a retaining wall, no vegetation, just the sprawling former silk mill, five stories of brick with a decommissioned yellow smokestack. He took Kiran to karate here, to tae kwon do, to kung fu. Who did they think Kiran would need to fight? Every way he prepared Kiran for life was wrong.

Will is talking about trying to figure out where else the plant might grow, but they have too little to go on. No name, no picture, just a mention in an old book. Stephen collapses to the ground. He can't move.

What will he say to Kiran? He made the mistake of raising his hopes. "There's a magic plant that fixes photosensitivity." He said this on a night when he couldn't stand it anymore, how silent and distant his son was. He cornered Kiran in the kitchen, insisted on conversation.

"But I don't have photosensitivity," Kiran said.

"You don't?" Stephen steadied himself with a hand on the counter.

"It's a curse, Dad, I've been cursed. I just need to lift the curse and I can go back to my life." A hollow laugh. He swung his arm in narrowing concentric circles as if casting a spell, muscle memory from all those Halloweens as a wizard. His bracelets jingled.

He was drunk or stoned or both or worse.

Ever since he heard about Quinn, this has been Stephen's terror. Why wouldn't Kiran dip into oblivion—for an hour, a day, then the walk into the twilit ocean at high tide, water pouring over his forehead.

He wouldn't survive it. Stephen, that is. He wouldn't survive losing Kiran.

"Stephen." Ruth's rubbing his back. "Stephen. It'll be okay. It will." Will is crouching in front of him, offering a receipt on which to blow his nose.

He blows, but it's not okay. There's no way this'll be okay. Neither of them seem to know what else to say, sitting on the ground beside him. Finally, Ruth clears her throat. "So, I have this one . . . this one possibility."

She tells them about Antonia, her plant books, the kind never preserved by a historical society, made by women for their own edification, their own fascination. The only catch, Ruth explains, is that Antonia's become hermit-like, hates visitors, won't answer phone calls or emails, and she can't go up to Vermont.

"Four hours away?" Will says. "Happy to do the driving."

"I need to be clearer." Her voice is monotone, she's looking beyond them. "I can't see her."

"You're saying you don't want to? Talk this through with us. What's holding you up?" Will offers a sympathetic frown.

"Can't see her."

Stephen taps her knee. "But you will. For us. Right, Ruth? You will?" He feels certain she'll agree. He's seen her generosity, a softer

Ruth that was hiding underneath her reticent gruffness, like fresh grass below deadwood.

But no. "I just can't do this one."

Stephen volunteers, he'll go today, but she says Antonia would never open the door for Ramona's ex-husband. "Not a fan of yours."

"Okay, sure. I'll wait in town. Will can go."

She looks at Will. "Yeah, no. Not gonna work."

"What could possibly be wrong with Will?" Stephen asks.

"People generally like me." Will shrugs. "I mean, not everyone. Not my dad."

"Yeah, but she's this scrappy lady from Yuma, Arizona, who clawed her way through life, and you . . . Think of all the doors that open at the sight of you. She'll keep hers closed. No, I thought about this. We need someone like . . . someone innocuous."

"You mean a woman?" Stephen swipes at a mosquito near his ear, thinking of who he might ask.

"Yeah, but not just a woman. Someone who looks Vermont-ish. Like she came from down the block. Like she's just stopping by to ask a quick question. I mean, she has to seem in need, worthy of help. But without suspicion."

"Like a mom?" Will asks.

"Yeah, actually a mom would be great. A pretty mom. Antonia would like that."

"No, I got it. I really got it." Will stands, wipes grass from his pants. "I know a pretty mom."

WHEN THEY'RE HEADING BACK to the parking lot, he asks what Will plans to do now that they have nothing to search for. Return to Boston? He thinks that's where Will said he was living. This is only the second time he's seen him face-to-face; biography fades, except the boyfriend and what happened to him.

Will scratches the back of his neck. "Not sure. It's finally getting nice here. I feel like I deserve my green reward after this winter."

"Stay!" Stephen can't imagine living anywhere else. "Look

around!" He points to the river, trees, birds. "Especially if you have kids someday. What else do kids need? It's healthy here."

At least he raised Kiran here, he gave his son that. But even as Stephen thinks this, it comes to him: how to help Kiran.

He needs to be returned to life. His own apartment in one of the cities where his friends moved after graduation. They can come play their derivative music with the lights off or lie with him or walk the streets with him in the hours after the bars close and the streetlights turn off. He would never be alone in New York's night the way he is here, miles from anyone but the owls and raccoons and foxes. Kiran's friends could tell him of their adventures, their jobs, their parties, their performances, their hookups, and he will listen so carefully he will almost experience it. It will be a life of envy and shadows, not the life Stephen wants for his son, but it will be living.

The idea is so obvious. Why should Kiran stay with a father he can't stand to talk to? He'll pay other people to provide all he's providing now—rent, cleaning, grocery delivery, takeout brought to his door.

But later, when he tries to work out the expenses, he becomes embarrassed that he can't care for his son in this way. His focus has been determinedly unremunerative these past forty years. He's deep in debt from the doctors he took Kiran to—the out-of-network neurologist in Boston and the MRI ordered by him, the acupuncturist in Amherst with a Lexus in his driveway who charged two hundred dollars a session. At the bank, he's refused a loan, and it's not surprising. They're still paying for Ritu's room in Providence. Their house is twice mortgaged. Ritu's Honda needs to be replaced. Retirement has become a joke.

He goes online to sell his record collection, his tapes, one-of-a-kind bootlegs, but Kiran's friends are right. Any concert can be streamed for free. All those hours he spent recording shows, wearing headphones, never dancing, never really losing himself in the music he professed to love in order to keep an eye on the censorious sound-level needle.

The way Stephen lives in his house (termites in the foundation) changes. Is there nothing he can sell? Cracked Crock-Pot, grease-stained wok, dishes from Ikea. Ukulele (unstrung), harmonicas (rusted), guitar (the single respondent on Craigslist offers him fifteen dollars), Schwinn bike (*I'll take it off your hands for free*). He views everything through the scrim of monetary value, but it's all crap—old crap, worn-out crap, crap they thought Kiran and Priya needed in order to grow into humans. Sorry!, Monopoly, Life, Catan, Simon, Ticket to Ride, Connect Four, Candy Land, Spirograph, Battleship, one thousand broken crayons, one million loose Legos, dried-out modeling clay, playing cards, Magic: The Gathering cards, Pokémon cards (worthless; he checks online), potholder loom plus the loops that never fit, paperbacks that used bookstores refuse, microscope (broken), rock tumbler (broken).

Didn't he make any investments in the future other than this careful cultivation of creativity, this cornucopia upon which a free spirit might feast?

As spring bursts open, a spring like no other, flowers blooming all at once, out of the usual comforting order, he stands in his backyard and wishes he could sell it all. Shouldn't it be worth something, this aster, that orange daylily, the lilacs bunching out, pink clots of peonies, the dark dogwood leaves? Don't you want to buy it, the way the warm air laps against you when the clouds clear, the rain that falls each night like coins from a slot machine, the chill of a socked foot in soaked grass? Can't he sell the feeling of sleeping under the eaves with the windows open, the fingernail scratch of squirrels in the walls, the black beads of soil dug up by ants? What's it worth, the maple greening, the fox nursing her pups, the silver bark of the birch calling to the moon?

BOOK THREE

...

OUR VERMONT

May

. . .

i

DEMETER SLAPPED THE DASHBOARD. "I FUCKING NEEDED TO BE on the road right now. You're the best for inviting us."

"Fucking," whispered Lev from the back seat, leaning his head on Persephone's shoulder.

"It's a swear," Sonya said. "You can't say it."

"A swear's just a word, syllables, sounds. It's a social construct," I said with the authority of the driver's seat.

"Well, sure. But just because it's a social construct doesn't mean it doesn't have power," said Demeter, leaning forward to twist her long hair into a bun. "Fuck's a power word."

Will came to mind. Inadvertently. Vertiginously. All rainy April when he was in Dorchester, I'd hide in the bathroom, rubbing myself to the image of him power-wording me on his brown leather couch.

"Fuck," Lev repeated. "Fuck, fuck, fucking."

The mountains climbed to extravagant heights once we left frugal Massachusetts. Demeter chose song after song on her resurrected phone, and we sang our way up Vermont's spine. *Hotel, motel, Holiday Inn.* I couldn't believe my luck. Demeter beside me again, kids in the back seat. I was happy and I knew it, and for a brief moment, I lifted my hands from the steering wheel to clap along.

WILL HAD TEXTED A few days earlier. Could I come over Saturday afternoon? Surprised he was back in town and not in Ohio for rehearsals, I showed up at his apartment in the thrift store skirt but found two people I vaguely recognized on the couch. Why were the librarian and the bike shop guy on our date? Will led me to a chair and introduced me. They waved and smiled, so delighted to see me I wondered if I'd forgotten a prior encounter. Stephen offered me a muffin, which I kept in my lap.

"Hold on to your hat," Will said, pulling up a kitchen stool. "You're in for a wild ride."

"Let's just show it first," Stephen said. "Let her dive in. Then we explain."

Ruth leaned forward to hand me a small book. "Let me at least say how glad I am that you're here. Thanks for agreeing to meet with us."

Was this a prayer session? A book club? The book was tiny and worn, two interlocking water stains on a pale blue cover—something you'd overlook at a thrift store.

"Be careful, though," Stephen said. "The pages are crumbling. Just open it at the bookmark. But carefully."

I could feel them looking at me as if I were a child, performing a simple task for adult approval, so I began reading aloud in the dramatic tones I used for Sonya and Lev—"A Digression into the Curious Case of Sun Madness OR The Illness That Went Away." Then I went quiet, and as I read to myself, I felt myself lose balance, slipping behind the wardrobe, falling into a rabbit's hole.

I looked up again when I finished the chapter. Will grinned at me. "Crazy, huh?"

"Am I here because of . . . You think this is what Persephone . . . ? You think it's Emily?"

"Let Ruth explain," Stephen said. "She's who found it."

Ruth crossed her arms and stared at me with great kindness—again I felt like a child being led down a strange path—as she told me about the books she culled from the library shelves and brought home, unable to bear tossing them in the dumpster, about the botanists and horticulturists and healers and Victorianists she'd asked about Sightflower, a four-petalled trillium, small and white, that grew by the riverside in our town.

"You think the sickness left and came back? Does that happen?" I looked from Ruth to Stephen's sad face to Will's eager one and settled back on Ruth.

"I wish I knew." Ruth was nodding. "Clearly none of the doctors

Kiran talked to . . . or Quinn . . . Well, my point is, nobody alive has heard of this cure, that seems clear."

"Nobody? Have you made copies of the book? Written about it in the newspaper? Online? A Substack? TikTok? Some viral post that could reach everyone?" She and Stephen suddenly seemed a little simpleminded, too old to understand how information pings around, slides into our pockets, crawls into our brains.

Stephen held out the muffin container to me although I still had one. "It was Will who explained the danger of that. He knows someone in pharmaceutics. Knows they'd swoop in if they heard about something that stops pain, use all sorts of nefarious techniques to steal the info, make it theirs."

"Jeremiah," Will said, giving me a knowing look. "You get it, right? We don't want anyone else to get rich off of someone's pain."

"So we're keeping it close," Stephen added. "No need to draw attention, as much as we want to find it. My son's sick. My Kiran. My son."

"I know," I said, remembering when Demeter and I went to his bike collective to ask if anyone in his medical mystery group had been bitten by a tick. "I met you with my friend. Her daughter, the girl who's sick. She's like family to me."

"You have kids of your own, right?" Stephen asked. "You're a mom?" I nodded, although mention of them made me nervous, as if they'd get Emily by being conjured in this fantastical context. "Go on, Ruth," he continued. "Tell her about Antonia."

"I'll tell her," Will said. "I should tell you why I was really at the Smith gardens."

I had trouble following what he was saying. It seemed like Will, the Will I knew, was disappearing, growing smaller and smaller. I felt like crying, even as I could see this other possibility, this miracle plant, emerge on the horizon, coming toward me, passing Will before he vanished entirely.

When he finished the story of how he met Stephen and Ruth and the many herbaria they'd looked through, and of Antonia, a woman committed to learning every plant that grew in New England who might have a book with a mention of Sightflower but wouldn't open the door for him or Stephen, I had sweat through my shirt and crushed the muffin between my hands; if I'd moved my fingers, it would've spilled out like sand.

They were looking at me. I tried to focus. "She doesn't talk to anyone? Or just not men? Would she talk to someone like me?"

"You'd be perfect," Ruth said quietly.

"Would you try?" Stephen looked so plaintive. "I'd go myself if I could."

"You think she'll find it?" I asked.

"Do I think Antonia will find it?" Ruth repeated. "Maybe. Is Sun Madness the same as Emily? Maybe. Maybe's all we got, hon."

LATER, I DISCREETLY SHOOK the muffin into Will's sink. Stephen hugged me, the rim of his hat pressing into my forehead. Ruth gave me directions to a town in northeast Vermont. "Blue house behind the apple orchard, on the road to the dump. If Antonia doesn't answer, make a shit ton of noise. And remember, don't mention me. Just explain you need help with a plant."

Then they left and we were alone at his kitchen island, and Will turned away from me and then back. "I'm sorry I . . ."

He didn't finish the sentence. I wanted him to. I waited. Then he shrugged, and I found my dizzy wonder turning to anger. "So you told me that you're here to prepare for an acting role. Harry Buckminster. A botanist. Which is a lie. He's from Lillian's book. He's the journalist."

"No, you're right. That's right. When I met you with your kids, I did lie then."

"The minute I told you Persephone was sick. That was the time to tell me you were looking for a cure." I'd felt like a child while talking to Stephen and Ruth, but now I felt myself grow. I felt all my years, and my strength even, awake to sex and the force of my body in a way I hadn't felt for so long.

"Yeah." He squeezed his eyes closed, opened them. "But . . . Well, it was so easy with you and . . . I hate this word, but it was kinda pure, the way we can talk. Who gets to know someone new at this age?

Not me. And then here was this . . . this amazing woman who also somehow felt like an old friend? If I told you I'd been lying . . . Well, nobody likes a liar."

"But you made me think I knew you."

He gave a weak laugh. "Sometimes I think nobody knows me, least of all myself."

I felt something snap inside me. "There's nothing fucking pure about lying." I picked up my bag and walked out, feeling powerful the way I did in the early years with Henry James when I discovered the sexual frisson in fighting with the man you fucked.

And although we hadn't fucked, not yet, I knew he'd follow. "Wait, Eve," he called on the stairs. "Will you wait?"

He caught up in the alley outside his building. "Can you listen, please? This wasn't a joke to me. This wasn't done lightly. The more people who know, the more likelihood that this will get to someone. Someone who . . ."

"The pharma companies you believe are listening in on our conversations," I said. "Hoping to find the next OxyContin."

"I mean, not yet. Nobody's listening in yet, because they don't know. But they would, sure they would. They'd do more than listen in. We have this one shot, Eve. And I'm gonna be honest. I didn't trust telling you. You and Demeter? You're so close. I knew you'd tell her about it all—Sightflower, Sun Madness."

My head started to throb. Was I missing something? Sure, they wouldn't want to lose the seed to pharma before they even knew what it did, but Will seemed to be carrying this secrecy a step too far, with a bizarre furtiveness I didn't get. Why not tell me? Didn't Demeter deserve to know? "And what's the problem with that?" I asked.

"Well, she'd talk to the people there, at the Healing Hut, and who could blame her? This is her child's life we're talking about."

"Exactly. Her fucking life. She should know."

"And she will. When we find it. *If* we . . . But before that . . ."

"That's such bullshit. Her kid's sick. You don't think she needs something to hope for?"

He took a slow breath before saying, "I think Demeter's incredible. I think she'll be okay not knowing for a little while longer. I think we know her well enough to believe she can make it through pretty much anything."

Was there something in the way he talked about her that surprised me? That "we"? I was too distracted. I was thinking that I'd tell her myself the minute I came home from Vermont. In fact, I *wanted* to be the one to tell her. No, even better, I'd bring her with me. She could be right there beside me when Antonia found it.

Driving home too fast on the slow roads, tailgating a pickup and swerving into the oncoming lane to pass it, I considered Will. So he'd lied. He wasn't preparing a theatrical role and idly roaming from place to place, but wasn't he doing something very generous? I thought of how he'd shrunk, sitting so hunched and sad on the bench by the koi when he'd told me about Quinn's death. He was trying to make up for it. I could tell that was what compelled him, and although hiding everything from me was weird, paranoid even, it gave me the chance to tell Demeter, to be her best friend yet.

"It's all okay," I said aloud, in the same voice I would use with Sonya when she couldn't calm down. "It's okay, Eve." I felt my hands on the steering wheel, eased off the gas pedal. I'd been flying, rising like a helium balloon, and as I pulled myself earthbound, lowering into my usual shape, I decided I liked this new Will even more.

I'd been avoiding Doctor Folkenflick's calls, and I was relieved when a patient answered the Healing Hut phone and found Demeter for me. I asked if she and Persephone could possibly come away overnight.

I was about to tell her why, but I stopped myself. What if Antonia didn't even let us in? I couldn't bear the thought of Demeter's excitement dashed. So I just said I had to see someone in Vermont, a hermit botanist who never answered her phone or emails. For an excuse, I landed on my mom, as usual. She needed info about a rare plant for a plot point in the book she was writing. We could stay the night at a motel near a Chinese restaurant with a fish tank.

"A thousand times yes. I want to be with you. I want Persephone to have hours and hours with your kids." She was a paying client now, she explained, and could come and go as she pleased.

"They let you stop cleaning and cooking? This is incredible, Dem!"

"That's right," she said with strange efficiency.

"Wait, so you made enough money? She can get treatments and everything?"

"Well, it all worked out." There was an edge to her voice I didn't understand.

"But how? The last time we spoke you said it would be six more months of working at least."

"It's fine, Eve. It's good."

I could hear a vein of annoyance and, although I didn't understand why, decided not to press further.

THE BLUE HOUSE WAS set back behind apple trees with pinched white buds on their gnarled arms. I told the others to wait in the car and rang the doorbell three times before Antonia appeared. She was a stunning woman, around ten years older than me, short with long silver hair, wearing basketball shorts over thermal underwear, socks with plastic shower shoes. She squinted up at me without polite interest. "I don't give money to political candidates or the fire department or high school basketball teams."

"I'm actually here for . . ."

"I do sign petitions for local referendums and am particularly excited about ranked-choice voting, but I sign such petitions exclusively outside the Hannaford supermarket, so I'm really hoping the two of you are here for Girl Scout cookies." Her eyes shifted to something behind me. "Are you? Are you a Girl Scout?"

I turned to see Persephone in her wraparound shades and pink sun hat chasing a chicken around an apple tree.

"That's my . . ."

"Are you even a child? Or just a very slight adult?"

"A child, your honor," Persephone said as the chicken escaped.

"This judge would be interested in Thin Mints and Samoas. Get closer. Let's see the list."

Persephone took a few steps toward the house.

"Well, it seems we're two of the only brown females in the entire state of Vermont. Take off your sunglasses, Girl Scout. It's rude to speak to someone while wearing them."

Persephone steadied herself on a branch. "I'm very sorry to disappoint you, but I'm not able to be a Scout, and I can't take off my glasses, because I am an Emily, which, if you don't know, and honestly very few people do, is an illness that causes . . ." And then she leaned over and puked on the dirt.

Antonia opened the door behind her. "Come on. Let's get you in the bathroom."

MY CHILDREN AND I waited in a long hallway lined by armoires and bureaus on which rested fifty or so strange boxes. Three-sided and roofless, each containing a soil-filled pot, either green plastic or terracotta, although not a single plant grew. Surrounding each pot in its box was a collection of objects—candles with electric wicks, photos or magazine pictures glued to the wood, personalized pens or key chains handed out at professional conferences, small toys like jacks and Smurf figurines, and single earrings.

We looked at these boxes and listened to the retching from the bathroom, my kids pressing into my legs as if I were the only dry land in an unfamiliar sea, until Demeter and Persephone emerged. "I think she's finally done," Demeter said. "Let's get her back in the car."

A door off the hallway opened and Antonia peered out. "Your girl needs rest. I've set up the bed in here."

"That's so sweet," Demeter said. "She's fine. But if it's not a problem . . . Just for a few minutes."

"Come with me," Persephone whispered to my kids. They trailed Demeter and Persephone and I followed Antonia into the kitchen where I told her I was looking for a plant that might be mentioned in one of the books she collected.

"Here's what we know. It's a trillium but with four white petals. Grows by rivers, blooms in May for a short time. That's a spring ephemeral, right?" I spoke quickly to keep her attention as she drifted around the kitchen, searching for something under piles of mail and bags of rice and pasta. "There's mention of it in a book from 1852, which described women collecting it for their herbaria. They called it Sightflower and we don't know the Latin name, just that . . ."

"Aha!" She raised a pack of Marlboros victoriously.

"Just that it was used in the past to help people with light sensitivity."

"That's what the girl has? The mom said she pukes in the sunlight." Antonia stuck a cigarette in her mouth and bent over a burner on the stove. Silver strands curtained the flame.

"Your hair!" I shouted.

She rose unsinged. Exhaling, she squinted at me. "The girl's mom thinks the plant could fix her?"

"Actually, she doesn't know about it," I said apologetically. In person, Antonia appeared even more censorious than Ruth described, and it felt crucial that she not deem me a terrible friend. "And I'll tell her now. I just didn't know if you'd be . . . if you were home or if you had time to look for it."

She gestured toward the windows with her cigarette, ash twirling earthward. "I'll take a look for you, but a lot of plants are gone, you know. A lot of plants can't be found. That mom, she seems like she has enough on her plate without hope dangled like a turd in front of her."

"But what if you do find it?"

"Write it down here. The name you just said." She picked up a Comcast envelope, plucked a Sharpie from a mug of forks and knives and handed both to me. "If I find it? That's the time to tell her, but . . ." She watched me write *Sightflower,* then folded the envelope twice and shoved it into her shorts pocket. "There's a lot of crap for me to go through even to locate the books you want."

I saw her point. Every surface was crowded. Catalogs, dishes, bottles of oils, books, jars of grain, but mostly these slapdash wooden boxes with empty planters. They sat on the counters, the island, the stovetop, the bookshelf by the woodstove, the long table by the windows, and on the floor, one of which Persephone tripped over as she came into the room wearing her sunglasses. "Geesh, sorry." She bent to right the box.

"Don't." Antonia sprinted across the room, cigarette flashing, sandals slapping her heels. "Don't touch. It's not done."

Persephone backed up, as did my kids who were huddled behind her.

"There was just a little more puke," Demeter said, squeezing between them. "I stuck the sheets in the laundry in the mudroom and wiped down the floor. Great kitchen. Wow."

Antonia set the box on a pile of books on top of the microwave. "So your friend here needs my help finding a plant." There was challenge in the way she looked at me.

"For her mom," Demeter said, coming to stand by me. "The famous writer. Did you hear who she is?"

Heat bloomed on my cheeks. "Joan Yalen," I said to Antonia. "*Wormfood*?"

Antonia shrugged. "Doesn't ring a bell."

I found myself smiling. What a relief! I didn't want to hear about Joan's life-changing brilliance, especially not after she'd been calling me from bed for the past four weeks.

"Thing is, it'll take me a while. Kids can hang out wherever, as long as nobody's allergic to bees. We have hives. What about the two of you?" Antonia glanced from Demeter to me. "You any good at painting? I could use some help. Nothing fancy. Just slapping some paint on a wall."

THE SIDE OF THE outbuilding seemed reasonable when Antonia pointed to it, huge when we started painting. Demeter had the roller, I had the brush. She stood on the ladder, a paint tray on the pail shelf. I knelt with the gallon can, dripping white on the newborn green grass, like winter was coming back, although it actually seemed like winter never happened, like those months when we were separated had been tesseracted away. I felt my neck and shoulders relax.

After all this time collecting things to tell her, there was only one thing I wanted to say—there's a plant or might be a plant that could help or maybe help, but since Antonia told me not to dangle hope until she found it, I spoke instead about my mom's latest depression, which was following a familiar script: She believed she was sick. She insisted on tests. When the results came, she'd be furious.

I was gearing up the courage to tell her about Will, the pull he had on me, how much I thought of him, when Demeter put down her brush. "Nap time."

My internal clock was relieved for another timepiece with which to tick. At her side on the grass, my cells found hers. I grew drowsy. When she woke hungry, I was, too, and we tiptoed into the kitchen like teenagers, peeking in on Antonia in her office, the Comcast envelope propped against a computer monitor. Tea and toast for us. Crackers and cheese for the children inside the outbuilding, towels taped to the windows. They were writing a play, they told us, about Elysian Fields, and could we please leave?

"We should move to a house just like this," Demeter said when we were back at the wall. Quickly a plan formed. Chickens and bees. Our kids would sleep in the outbuilding. A bedroom for her, another for me and Henry James. "With an orchard," she added.

"And a blue porch," I said.

Over the course of several hours, as the wooden wall gradually glared white, we kept revisiting and amending the plan, building our future like an edifice we both could clearly see. We'd sell honey for money. The kids would prepare plays. I'd write all day. She'd draw and weave and sculpt.

"Can you?" I asked.

"Sure, I always did when I had time," she said.

What couldn't Demeter do?

We tackled hypothetical conflicts and dismissed them fancifully: Henry James traveling three hours farther on the bus each week? He'll take one look at our paradise and say, no problem.

"Actually, I don't know if we'll make it anyway. Me and Henry James." I hadn't known I thought this until I said it aloud. I felt alert, animated. I could sense the exhilaration that would arrive as soon as I told her about Will.

But she responded too casually to what felt momentous. "Yeah, I can imagine. He's a doll, don't get me wrong, but marriage? Having my life tied up with one person, man or woman, all our decisions together, even if we're consensually fucking other people, I can't see it."

Her flippancy led me to backtrack. I loved Henry James, didn't I? I thought stability crucial to children, didn't I? "I mean, probably we're fine."

"You'll figure it out. Anyway, we don't need him. Vermont can be our land of mothers."

"Our motherland."

I asked how she always just knew what to do.

"Me?" She rolled her brush in the tray of paint, making that competent sticking sound. "I get quiet. I listen, you know? Inner voices, I guess."

I wished for a different answer. I'd spent my life trying to block out the voices that burbled up in me in childhood, those little mews of anxious warbling, those terrified, shrieking peeps.

I asked my inner voice if I'd be okay without Henry James. Inner voice said no no no no no no no no no no no no no no no no.

"That's anxiety," she said. "That's how your mom taught you to live. That's the part of her suspended at eleven, learning about her mom's death." She stepped down the ladder holding the roller high, touched my face with her free hand, and kissed my cheek. "When we move to Vermont, you'll be able to hear your inner voices."

IN VERMONT, WE DECIDED, everything hard would become easy. Marriages would bend and open. Sick kids would heal. Groceries would materialize. We were joking but also not. And the day kept proving it true. When we finished the wall, two coats, and went inside, there was a note taped to the fridge. *Plenty of food in here. Use anything if you like to cook. I don't.*

Demeter found a whole chicken, a bulb of garlic, butter, rosemary, and shooed me away. She had to heat up a jar of Persephone's broth, why not cook everything? "Come on, Eve, when do you ever get a break?"

I wandered around the raised beds and chicken coop in the backyard. I could see the blue walls of my future, the wide porch, and the possibility, like a window forming and then opening inside me, that Will might be a part of it. Who would I be then?

There once was a woman named Eve. And I didn't want her to leave.

At the edge of the thick woods, I heard a strange sound. A motor, but duller. Was someone sawing? I followed the noise through the bare trees, patches of snow on the dead leaves, fluorescent green moss on high boulders, until I came to a small clearing: nine towers of wooden boxes. A nimbus of buzz, loud as a theater before the house lights dim. And Antonia on a lawn chair in a tartan fleece bathrobe, book in hand. Removing her reading glasses, she tilted the cover to me. *A Manual of Vascular Flora of New England*. "Apian porn. To turn them on. To fill them with lust."

Flowers, she explained as I sat on the ground beside her, were opening too early these warm springs, pollen ready long before pollinators appeared. By the time the bees woke up and left their hives—too late. The flowers had shriveled. Hungry, the worker bees swarmed off, abandoning the babies and queen. Call it colony collapse or spring dwindle or May disease, different names for the same disaster. She was urging them to head out sooner, catch the flowers in bloom.

Why did I ask if it actually helped? This was the sort of question my kids would use to nudge the limits of reality. Is the tooth fairy real? They wanted me to lie. I guess I wanted Antonia to as well. I was open to new rules here in Vermont.

Her exhale was disdainful. "Not the kind of question I have room to ask." She slid down her glasses. "Yellow giant hyssop," she read, "southern agrimony, Jesup's milk-vetch . . ."

I listened for a long time, turned on like a bee. The names made my chest burn with a possibility I didn't understand, even my crotch tingling. When I walked out of the forest, the sky mauve between bare branches, I felt alive in a way I hadn't in a very long time. Since before the pandemic, was that it? Or earlier? Since my own childhood? I noticed green was growing beneath the dried leaves. How had I missed this? Curl of fiddlehead, peek of pachysandra, twist of skunk cabbage. Other green I couldn't name, didn't know. I crouched to touch each nibble, every sprout. Are you Sightflower? Are you? I felt its nearness. Pushing out of mud earth—a clutch of closed white petals. Where is it, I asked my inner voices. Inner voices answered, "Fucking gorgeous out here, isn't it?" but it was actually Antonia, coming up behind me.

We walked together through the backyard. I kept hoping she'd mention Sightflower. She pointed at the newly white wall. "Nice job on that. And quick. Did you Tom Sawyer the kids into helping?"

"Well, they can't. I mean, Persephone can't. And mine do what she does."

She thumped her chest. "Right. Forgot the basic premise. What do they do in there all day?"

I probably sounded apologetic. Outside was fucking gorgeous but my kids were in a dark room. "Oh, you know kids. They're writing a play."

"A play? Holy hell. That's perfect."

"I mean, they're great kids. They really are."

But she was jogging away and didn't reappear until we were all eating dinner in her kitchen with the lights off and she showed up wearing mirrored sunglasses to match Persephone's. "When in Rome. You don't need to be the only one wearing these." She took a seat, leaned toward the kids. "So, I hear there's a theatrical performance in the works."

She grilled Persephone about the script, Sonya about set design, Lev about his acting preferences. "I like the lying down parts the best," he said.

"Oh, me too," Antonia said.

Demeter rested her head on my shoulder, whispered, "Soon all this will be ours."

"Our kitchen table," I whispered. "Our dead chicken."

"But really, Eve. Let's really move here."

"No, really." I reached for her hand. "We will."

"Can we?" the kids were asking. "Can we please?"

Had they heard us? No, it turned out Antonia had invited them to perform their play at an event she was hosting in a couple days.

"What kind of an event?" I asked.

"A Festschrift Botanicum. Pass the rice?"

I had no idea what that meant, but it sounded festive and floral and why not?

"It's for kids mostly," she added. "Anyway, there's plenty of rooms for sleeping."

"We could finish painting the outbuilding," I offered.

"Why? We just need that one wall. But there's a shit ton else to get ready."

"And you'll look for my plant?"

She lifted up her glasses to wink at me. "On it, hon."

"Can we stay?" the kids were asking. "Can we?" They offered extravagant promises, chores, multiplication tables, voluntary abstentions from screens and sugar, but they didn't need to. We all sensed something prelapsarian about the spot, an unspoiled Eden with no cell service, disconnected Wi-Fi. (Doctor Folkenflick would be happy with that.) The bees, the chickens, the goats in a pen, the raised beds, the empty pots lining the hallway. I imagined that each was harboring a sprouting seed, squirming toward the light, and quite possibly they would all burst through the soil in unison while we were here and the house would scream with green.

ii

I WAS BUTTERING TOAST FOR MY CHILDREN WHO'D WOKEN EARLY and had asked as soon as their eyes opened, where's Persephone, can we wake Persephone, when a young man walked through the kitchen door wearing a black T-shirt with a silver wolf in mid-howl.

Or not a man exactly. A boy? What he looked most like, oddly so, was Pan, at least as depicted by Persephone's book of Greek myths—half goat, half total hottie. This boy had the same dark eyes, same frumpled hair, beautiful tan skin, and mischievous smile. Unsurprised to find me in the kitchen, he asked where to put the projector.

"Projector?"

"I made it from scraps. Everything's recycled. Works, though." He stood too close, smelling of sweat and green onions, slight tang of manure. "They call me DJ." His palm was clammy. "You're here for Antonia's thing? Isn't it so cool? She's on this intense death trip."

"What's a death trip?" Sonya asked from the kitchen table.

"Maybe in the living room," I said quickly.

"Yeah, but the thing's outside."

"Right. The botanical thing. Then in the back?"

"Aye aye, captain." He saluted me.

"What's a . . ." Sonya began again, but then she stopped herself. Neither Sonya nor I wanted to think of death trips. We wanted our friends to wake up. I carried Demeter's coffee and Sonya sang "Goodnight, Irene" by the window of the outbuilding until they appeared—dressed, hair wet and braided.

"Ready to rehearse?" Persephone asked. Sonya and Lev ran into her dark room.

"TAKE YOUR TIME," ANTONIA told us. "I'm around. Tell the kids to holler if they need anything. Lumber should arrive soon. I'm not halfway ready."

On our way out, I looked into her office. The Comcast envelope had fallen under her desk, resting on a nest of tangled power cords and one black sock. I placed it on the keyboard.

Demeter and I walked into an unfurling world. Maple's redbud on the sidewalk like downed fireworks, frilly daffodils along the fence of a schoolyard. Our phones buzzed to life when we entered the small, gentrified heart of the town with its coffee shops and somber stores selling watercolors, weavings, and ceramics.

I responded to my texts exclamatorily, telling Will I'd be in Vermont for a few more days. Antonia's working on it! I brought Demeter! And telling Henry James not to come for the weekend. Spontaneous road trip! To my mom, though, just question marks. How was she feeling? Had she heard from her doctor? Did she maybe want to call her psychiatrist?

We followed Antonia's directions out of the center of town and onto a street that, with its attention to life's quotidian needs—

urologist, checks cashed, chiropractor—negated the fantasy that a body required nothing but caffeine and ceramics. I was sad to leave the fantasy. Who wanted to be reminded that the body gets sick and dies despite earth-tone pottery?

Amber Waves Organics had a wheatgrass smell and spilled oats on the floorboards and narrow aisles. As we searched for Lenore's precise broth ingredients to keep Persephone on her diet, we maneuvered around the store's only other patron and her stroller. The baby inside was not so young for a baby, but the mother was achingly young for a mother, just a girl in dirty jeans and a crop top. The baby, however, was impeccably dressed in a white onesie with ducks. When we reached the checkout, the girl had a single tincture bottle on the belt, and the cashier, a man with a long white beard and Dumbledorian half-moon glasses, was saying, "Everything is very clearly marked. If it was on sale, there'd be a red dot. Did you see a red dot?"

She reached for the bottle and he swatted her hand aside. "Don't touch it."

"But I'll put it back," the girl said.

"We'll get it," I said.

"Just add it to mine," Demeter said.

"No, it's fine. It's really fine." The girl wiped her nose with the back of her hand, angering the skin around her septum ring.

We caught up to her in the parking lot. The girl—Corin was her name—told us she'd seen on TikTok that oils would help her baby sleep. "Like lavender? And an infuser? But it has to be organic? See, we sleep on the pullout in my nanna's living room, which is good, they say Indigo should sleep with me, but she crawls around all night and I can't get her back to sleep and my nanna puts her in the Pack 'n Play when I go to work, which is as bad as putting her in a cage, they say."

While the baby and I played, passing her white sock back and forth, Demeter told Corin how she could double her food stamps at farmers markets and that five P.M. was the best time to dumpster dive in the alley behind a bakery and to bring all her pay slips and any school transcripts when she signed up for WIC. The baby threw the sock on the ground and arched her back. I unbuckled her from her stroller and carried her around the parking lot, singing "The Circle Game," loving the weight of her. When we returned, Demeter was holding Corin's hands, looking serious and kind. "What's the number one thing? Remember?"

"Ask for help," Corin said obediently, like the schoolgirl she wasn't anymore.

"*Accept* help. Right? It's all around if you look. Maybe not your nanna. Maybe you need to find someone to stay with who just loves babies. The important thing is to let yourself take what they offer. Fuck the shame. Fuck the people who make you feel shame. You can't let it in. Just bury it in the backyard. I wouldn't have made it otherwise. I wouldn't be here."

I grinned at my friend, in awe of the fierce teenage mother she'd been while I was at Wesleyan studying literary theory I'd since forgotten. On our way home, we talked—about nothing in particular, just how happy we were to be together and look at this yellow magnolia, this pink dogwood, until her phone rang. She stared at it. "Oh, I should take this." She moved away from me, talking with sudden cheerful verve. "Yeah! No, yeah! Yeah, I came with her. Yeah, Eve and I are just . . . yeah. Right? Seriously!"

I figured it was her mom. I called mine. Joan sounded scared. Her doctor would post the test results soon and she asked me to come down and wait with her. "Oh, I know, I know. You're too busy with your children," she said, and hung up. Down the block, Demeter was laughing animatedly, gesturing with her free hand, Jackson Pollocking the air.

"DON'T INTERRUPT," SONYA SAID, tearing yellow pages from the pad. "But you can bring us food."

"I can? Lucky me."

"Shhh. I need to listen." She and Lev were in the lit bathroom writing down the lines Persephone dictated from the dark bedroom on the other side of the door. They worked all afternoon while we helped DJ and Antonia move lumber to the backyard and build a platform in front of the newly white wall.

After the sun went down, we brought the kids into the kitchen. DJ was stir-frying tofu. "Who's that?" Persephone whispered to me, lifting up her sunglasses.

"Pan. Came down from Olympus to cook us dinner."

Her flinch was like an animal noticing another. Her entire being turned toward him.

"No, sweets. Actually, he's a guy named DJ."

She stared slack-jawed, apparently unconvinced.

The doorbell rang just as we started to eat. Demeter jumped to get it, which I thought odd. But she sat down when a voice called out, "Just kidding. As if I'd ring the bell like a Mormon."

The woman set a duffel bag on the kitchen floor, pushed her fingers in Antonia's long hair, and bent down to kiss Antonia on the mouth with passion that belied her spry competency—hiking boots, khakis, fleece. She introduced herself—Ellen Lu—seemingly unsurprised to find a crowd. "Antonia always ropes people in. Did she make you burn brush yet? Muck the goats?"

"They whitewashed the outbuilding wall, but totally voluntary."

"Right, that's tomorrow? Another Festschrift?"

"Didn't you come for it?" DJ said. "Isn't that why you're here?"

"Happy coincidence." Ellen explained she was flying out of Logan the next night to spend the summer working on a soil pathology study with colleagues in New Zealand. She was giving a talk in Sydney on the way. "Kind of a big deal."

Just then we heard the front door open again and a man's voice call out. "Hello? Anyone home?" I knew this voice. My chest burned as I started walking toward it, but Demeter sped past me.

I heard her say, "Seriously! I thought you were kidding."

"I don't joke about things like this." He spoke with such solemnity, I had to hold on to a credenza for balance. "Were you? Were you joking?"

"Eve's here. Come over here, Eve. Talk to him while I get ready."

She brushed by me, looking into my eyes, but I didn't know what she was trying to tell me. Then Will and I were alone in the doorway. His green coat. The parentheses around his mouth as he smiled at me. I could hear the voices from the kitchen.

"The one and only Eve. Hello, my friend." The deepness of his voice. The joke in it.

"You're here?"

"Demeter said you brought her to Vermont. The monts are just getting ver this time of year, huh?"

"The two of you . . . talk?"

"A match made in insomnia. She doesn't sleep, I don't sleep." He was looking past me into Antonia's dim hallway. "So, I hear you're looking for a plant for your mom's book? But no luck yet?"

"Antonia's working on it."

He lowered his voice. "No, I know. And I totally don't mean to barge in. I'm not here to check up on you."

"Then why are you here?" I asked and regretted it. I didn't want to know. "Actually, I have to go help Lev with something."

"Hold on a second." He reached out, fingers grazing my arm and then quickly retreating to scratch the back of his neck. "I really don't want this to be weird. . . . It's not weird between us, right? I mean, you made it pretty clear you were . . . You're not interested in that way."

I couldn't answer, my mouth was too dry, my best friend had stolen something that wasn't mine.

IN THE DIMNESS OF the outbuilding, I found Demeter grabbing clothes from the floor, shoving them in her purse. A balled-up shirt. Underwear. Persephone had plenty of broth for tonight and tomorrow, she said, and what else did she need? Nothing if she has Sonya, right? "You and the kids'll sleep out here? If she loses her glasses, there's like ten more pairs."

I followed her to the bathroom. "Where will you go?"

She raised one arm, rolling on deodorant. "God, I stink. To see the sights. No, I mean, he thought we'd find a motel or something."

"Why didn't you tell me?"

"He just showed up. You saw."

"About you and him."

She dropped a toothbrush in her purse. "What's there to tell? We talk on the phone."

"Every night? Since when? Since last month at Brewmaster's?"

She bared her teeth, checking them in the mirror. "I've never been able to sleep. It's nice. Old school."

"You could've called me."

We'd been looking at each other's reflections, and now she turned to me. "Oh, Evie. Wake you up?"

"But you like him? You seemed so annoyed with him that night," I said, even though I knew the difference between true annoyance and annoyed flirtation.

"Did I? I guess . . . you know." She shrugged and lifted a bra from the towel rod.

"I know what?"

"You know *him*. Beneath the naïve male privilege is a human animal who wants love, right?"

She unbraided her hair and began brushing it. I stared at my tired face in the mirror beside her beauty. If one had to choose a single face to look at for the rest of one's life, who wouldn't choose hers? "Don't go."

"What?" She began tugging her skin at the cheekbones so that it smoothed, and she appeared young. "I'll be back tomorrow."

"Isn't it fun here? Just us? Our own Vermont!" I felt naked making this bid for her.

"Oh, Eve. You don't get it, do you?"

"Get what?"

"You really don't understand?"

"Sex? Sex is great. I love sex. I just thought you and I were . . . we're having . . . Sex can wait." I forced a laugh as if this were hilarious. How did friendship get talked about? Two mothers together, where did that fall in the hierarchy of needs?

She slid a dark lipstick over her lips. "You thought I could just stop working? I'd never earn enough for those treatments. I was barely making enough to pay for our room and food. How'd you think it was happening?"

Tissue blotted magenta dropped in the toilet. The answer came to me slowly, then quickly. "Will's paying?"

"It's the reason I'm here with you at all." She pushed past me out the door.

"But do you even like him?"

She kept walking.

"Do you *want* to go with him?"

She stopped by the garden beds, the soil dark brown in the moonlight, white moths on the silver sage, and turned to me with the sort of cheery look she'd give Sonya or Lev. "Why not? He's great—funny, super smart. How he talks, it's like you, kind of. But with more confidence." She laughed. "And way more money." She picked a sage leaf, brought it to her nose. "You didn't mention he was *that* rich."

I hadn't known. I tried to think about what she was telling me. The thousands of dollars he was paying the Folkenflicks.

"Please tell me that you want to go."

Dropping the sage, she placed her hand on my cheek. It wasn't just with love, I felt. There was a push to it. "You don't understand. In my life, want doesn't get to mean the same thing it does in yours. It never has and it never will. I like him. I do. Don't worry about that."

"REALLY? NO LIGHT AT all? That's why all the blinds are closed?" asked DJ, who'd moved to sit beside Persephone. Lev was under the table. Sonya drew cats on a napkin. Antonia and Ellen were nowhere to be seen. Was everyone screwing but me? I poured myself another glass of wine.

"No light at all," Persephone agreed. "That's why these ugly glasses."

"They're not ugly. But what about driving? Could you drive? I mean if you were old enough. You couldn't, right?"

Lev climbed onto my lap and I stroked his arm. I heard a ringing in my ears or possibly in my heart.

"But it's fine, because with the magnets and oxygen and stuff, I'll be able to turn on the lights soon. Or, like, watch YouTube." She gave a kittenish giggle.

"Honestly? You're kind of a hero," DJ said. "Not using resources, I mean, what could be more awesome?"

She was beaming in a way I'd never seen her.

"I'm an anti-natalist," he said, turning to me with a proud shrug of one shoulder, the wolf shifting on his chest. "Voluntary human extinction. Like, everyone who's already alive is cool. But no more. Gradual end to the human race to save the rest of the planet."

"Guess what! Sonya, you need to . . . All the kids need to . . ." My mind went blank. How to get them out of here? "Back to the outbuilding, sweets. It's darker there."

As they left, Persephone gave DJ a little wave from the doorway. He waved back and then turned his attention to their plates. "Hey, can I?"

"Go for it," I said.

He picked up one of Sonya's nuggets and drove it through a pond of ketchup. "I don't eat meat unless, like, it's going to waste, right? Anti-natalist means . . ."

"No, I get it. Not doing what I did."

"We're like the anti-neo-environmentalists. See, the neo-environmentalists believe . . ." He swiped another nugget. "They're horny for techno-solutions. Wind farms on every mountain. Solar arrays in the desert. CRISPR in every plant and animal. But if we do that, like, what's the world even? What's wild? We lose the idea that nature is like . . . something like . . ."

"That nature has some intrinsic inherent value beyond the instrumental," said Ellen, appearing in the doorway wearing a different shirt than before.

"I thought you disagreed with me."

"With every bone in my body. But I like theories to be well articulated. No one here agrees with you, DJ."

He leaned toward me. "I got into all this through Antonia. My mom was her girlfriend? Like, when I was a kid? And I brought her groceries during the pandemic, and we talked and I took a deep dive and found the human extinction movement. She doesn't mind me talking about it."

"Antonia doesn't always know what's best for her," Ellen said.

"Anti-natalists are doomers, collapsarians, and the last thing we need around here is more doom. But she adores you, DJ. She still loves your mom, too. Everyone loves Cheryl."

At mention of his mom, DJ's face softened. "They do, right?"

"What if your mom had been an anti-natalist?" I asked.

His voice grew heavy with scorn. "Seriously? Everyone says that. It's not a burn, though. I just wouldn't be here. Who cares? The real question is for the mothers. Why'd you have kids when you knew what humans were doing to end life on this planet? When you knew what their life would be?"

Shut up, I wanted to say. I stood up fast, clutching the table's edge. Ellen grabbed my hand. "You okay? Your friend left? You okay with that?"

"Oh, I'm fine," I said, although I wanted her to never remove her cool hand.

She looked unconvinced. "Come watch the Scottish detective with us."

"Moors, midges, murder," Antonia said, yawning into the room in her plaid bathrobe. "Loneliness, longing, lochs. Now you're caught up. Get your ass to the TV room."

Instead, I pulled off Lev's shit-stained underwear and bathed him and found cortisone for mosquito bites and Neosporin for the splinter I removed while he screamed. I thought of Will and Demeter slowly, tantalizingly removing their clothes. Or quickly, so quickly.

I read to Lev and sang to him and told Persephone and Sonya to be quiet as he fell asleep while I rubbed his back. The ringing in my ears grew louder. Why her? Why him? Where did this leave me? The fish of jealousy swam inside me, a whole school of them. If I could, I would've squeezed each slick piscine body in my hand, shoved my fingers in its gill slits, laid it flapping on the outbuilding floor, and brained it with Lev's shoe.

I'd allowed my fantasies to race so far past my actions, while he'd simply moved on. I'd told her to give him her number, after all. I imagined their first conversation without me. How funny he'd be. Awkward at first, then not.

Feeling like I might die of fish, I made myself think about Sightflower. I should ask Antonia to move quicker, tell her I really needed to find it, could I check her books myself? I tiptoed from the outbuilding.

"Perfect timing," Antonia said in the living room "The postmistress was found hanging from the church rafters. This'll be good."

Ellen made room for me on the couch. I was exhausted, I realized. I didn't want to think about Sightflower, didn't want to think about anything. What a strange and wonderful offer—to watch TV in a remote house with people I'd just met! I could take a break from being myself. At the end of each episode, Antonia would ask, "Another?" I felt lulled, as if we were floating down a lazy river, me and Ellen and Antonia, murders happening on the shore, detectives walking uphill in the driving rain, while we were carried along in the gentle current.

iii

THE NEXT AFTERNOON, WHEN ELLEN AND I WERE RECOVERING after moving logs from Antonia's truck into the backyard for seating, the playwrights came into the kitchen for props. Persephone in sunglasses and hat asked when Pan would return.

"Who?" Ellen asked from behind her laptop.

"DJ," I explained.

"Our young buck. He comes and goes. Like everyone around here." She looked at me over the top of the laptop and asked what I thought people wore when giving a presentation at a university in Australia. A memory came of the professional world. "Something flowy on top and tighter below. Or flowy below and tighter above. Or for you, a blazer. Sharp corners."

"Oh shit," Ellen said with the panic of someone who'd packed wrong. "And shoes?"

I tried to remember shoes. "A heel that goes click-clack on a wooden hallway."

"So not hiking boots?"

DJ pawed into the house, holding a mug, the wet prints from his bare feet patterning the floor. He stood near Persephone. "I keep thinking about it, how you live inside. What do you do all day?"

Persephone's hands rushed through her hair. "All sorts of things."

"Like today we're practicing our play," Sonya said with an anxious pitch.

"Actually, not me. That's just something Sonya's doing? Kind of babyish."

If DJ noticed the stun in the room, he didn't show it. With his charming grin, he told us he'd be in Antonia's office setting up the slides if we needed him to move anything heavy.

In the silence that followed his departure, I said, "So, props! Would a colander work for the headdress?"

Persephone looked down. "Actually, I think I'm gonna work on slides with DJ. It'll be dark enough in there."

"Why'd you let her do that?" Sonya asked angrily when Persephone left the kitchen, as if I'd personally arranged for her passage from childhood to adolescence, paid the fare. "Does she mean she'll do the play later? Does she mean I should practice now?"

I looked at Sonya's heartbroken face. My chest ached for her. I wanted to follow Persephone and tell her she couldn't abandon my kid, but I'd been thirteen, and I knew there's no convincing a girl of that age that she still wants to play with a ten-year-old after she's set her sights on the far shore. And there was also a part of me that wanted to cheer on Persephone for broadening what little world she had. "Not now, love. We're going to buy Ellen appropriately loud shoes."

The nearest store was a Target, forty minutes away. I left snacks and soup in the outbuilding for Persephone. Ellen drove my car and the kids sat in the back. Before we reached the highway, my slumbering phone woke to missed calls from my mother and a text from Demeter: All good with Perse? Ok if im back tomorrow??

Having fun? I wrote.

She replied right away: Yup! miss you tho, hows our Vermont?

I turned off my phone. At Target, the doors slid open, stopping time. I allowed the store's gravitational pull to lead us to the toy aisles.

For once, I had no ambivalence, no eddy of uncertainty about how to participate in capitalism. Will and Demeter were tumbling in the thin air of lust, bitten, licked, stroked. Come on, Dem, I thought, there's no wanting that I don't know. I knew all wanting. I was all wanting. Let's not choose between a useless squeaky panda-angel stuffy and a useless pack of mini erasers inside plastic eggs. Let's buy both. Let's buy Paw Paws and Num Noms and a plastic toilet out of which came a plastic-wrapped piece of plastic in the shape of food. Caught up in the wonder of the mood, its extravagance, the ease with which desire met satisfaction, my kids ran the aisles saying, "This is the one I want most," even though they knew they didn't want any of it. They wanted wanting.

We added a green water bottle, because apparently Sonya had always longed for a green water bottle. We found batteries for a toy I didn't think Lev still owned and a Hula-Hoop and popsicle molds. Sweatshirts and underwear in packs of three and a stapler, because where was our stapler? It was at home, but where was home? We pushed our cart, all of us walking with a hand on its plastic body as if it were an animal we would use for our livelihood.

In our state of surplus, we found Ellen stingy. "Which one?" She held up a moss-green button-down and another in stone-gray.

"Buy them both."

Greed drifted from me to her, although she tried to protest. "The way they're produced—I never buy clothes. The little children locked in Chinese factories, the chemical waste in the rivers."

"I know," I said, "but we aren't really here. This isn't really happening."

She looked sternly confused, and then began to smile.

I showed her a rack of neckties and found a blazer in the boys' section because the men's were enormous on her and offered three pairs of shoes, none of which fit well or looked particularly right. "We killed that store," I said, once we paid. "And by kill I mean we gave it our money."

"What's so funny," the kids asked, turning from me to her. "What are both you laughing about?"

OUTSIDE MCDONALD'S, I REACHED MY MOTHER ON THE PHONE. "Get me a new doctor. Dr. Carlyle is calling this depression."

"How dare he," I joked. I was still in the after-rush, not yet the letdown, of needless expenditure.

"He used the phrase *female trouble.* To me, a feminist! Estrogen vanishes and with it, our interest in life, he said. He wanted to talk about grandma's suicide, my genetic propensity. Can you believe? He said this was a matter for a psychiatrist, to call her."

"Did you?"

"I honestly can't believe the tests were all negative. I honestly can't."

"But that's good news. You want a negative test. Call Dr. Klein. Henry James felt so much better when he switched from Prozac to Lexapro."

"Even Lyme. He said definitely not Lyme."

"Why would it be Lyme?" I pressed my nose against the window to wave at Sonya and Lev, who were inside chatting with Ellen and didn't notice.

"The tick."

"What tick?"

"When I got home from visiting you? I found it on my armpit. Stuck there like a wart."

WITH LEV ON MY lap, I pushed my thoughts away. I knew my mother, I was a scholar of her highs, her lows, the sadness she always believed was illness until she began writing again.

No tick. No echo. No cause. No effect.

I finished Lev's cheeseburger while Ellen asked why Persephone ate only soup. I could answer without my mind veering toward my mother. The broths, I explained, were to help with her post-pandemic syndrome, the condition, perhaps psychological, perhaps something else, that made her unable to go outside.

But Ellen was a scientist. She remained unsatisfied. "I'm sorry, but putting aside the idea of a post-pandemic syndrome, whatever that is, there's no way that a broth made of supermarket ingredients is mitigating a viral or bacterial load in any meaningful way. The girl's tiny. We're talking about stunted muscular development, we're talking about delaying hormonal development. Why would her mom go along with this?"

"What's she saying about Persephone?" Sonya asked.

I looked around for something to distract her with, landing on a claw machine full of the sort of plush and plastic we'd just bought. I scooped gritty coins from the bottom of my bag and sent off my kids.

I told Ellen that if her child was shut in darkness, she'd reach for any possible help. Ellen was quiet for a moment, and I realized I didn't know why she'd never had children. Had it been a choice? A sorrow? A decision based on the world to come? Finally she said, no, she'd never starve her kid. Who was running this place anyway? Who suggested this?

I felt the weight of my mother pushing back at me. I tried to calculate how long it had been since she came to Northampton to tell me about her book's reissue and played Greentime with my children in the woods. Seven weeks? And now she couldn't leave her bedroom? Complained of headaches and stomach upset and turned off the lights?

But no, I told myself. My mother was in bed for the same reason she always was in bed, because the world was too much for her, because the floor turned fluid and people looked strange and she missed her own mother. I noticed Ellen looking at me. "Do you know their names?" she asked again. "The people who run that place?"

ONLY LATER DID I think of asking Ellen if she thought my mother could be sick with what Persephone was sick with, if Demeter could have been right all along about the tick, despite the many doctors who had belittled and mocked her and the school counselor who had called Persephone lazy and the doctor who had called Child Protective Services and the social worker who had begun steps to place Persephone in foster care and the insurance company that denied her claims and the debt collectors she was hiding from. By then, Ellen was in the air, above the clouds, regretting the clothes she'd bought, unable to sleep, watching the light at the end of the wing of the plane that had been delayed three hours in the Logan Airport, giving her plenty of time to find the McDonald's napkin I'd written on and send an email to a friend who worked at the Massachusetts Department of Public Health, saying, *You'll want to look into Lenore and Clement Folkenflick*.

But that was later, long after I took a wrong turn, adding an hour to our drive. When we reached Antonia's, it was nearly dark and cars lined the road and kids in the backyard bore triumphant branches of cherry blossoms and forsythia to the stage, springtime in their arms, while their parents sat on the logs I'd carried.

"Can I help them?" Sonya whispered.

"Of course," I said. Through a crack in the outbuilding door I told Persephone to join us, it was dark enough. She asked if I knew where DJ was. I pointed her in the direction of the children on the stage. "Look at all the gorgeous flowers. Why don't you help them?"

"Huddle up," Antonia was calling. "Huddle up." The air had grown cool and I thought about bringing sweatshirts to my kids, but they were huddling with the other children, even Sonya, who always avoided kid crowds, and someone was tapping my shoulder. "Um, excuse me. Hi?"

It was Corin—combed hair, same crop top. In a white bonnet, Indigo removed a drool-shining hand from her mouth and waved royally. A violent need to hold her spread through me. How had my kids become so big?

"Um, your friend? She gave me the address? She said a woman here liked to help people? Who had a lot of extra rooms?"

Coming toward us, DJ took a theatrical step backward. "What? I haven't seen you since . . . And you have . . . Are you still at Frontier High?"

"Not anymore." With her free hand, she flicked aside wet bangs. Her cheeks flushed. "Would you?" she asked me, holding Indigo toward me.

"Oh my god, please." The whomp of her body in my arms! That

physical completion, those green squares. I kissed her warm forehead again and again.

A child began trilling a bongo, another shook a can filled with rice or legumes or small stones, a third played the *Star Wars* theme on trumpet. I found a spot on a log and the mom beside me handed me a mug of warm white wine. Indigo perched politely upright on my knees before settling. With her body against my stomach and chest it took no energy to push away thoughts of my mother. Thoughts left with the evening breeze.

Still wearing basketball shorts and a flannel, Antonia walked onto the stage and thanked us for being there. "I say this every time, but here goes again. When I left the desert, when I left my lab, I moved here to recuperate. Thought I'd take a year off. Like a sabbatical. It's been six years and I'm not going anywhere. I want to be in one place for the rest of my life, one place to really see what changes. You all know that we get together like this whenever I find twenty-five plants to say goodbye to. Well, twenty-six today. One more since I told DJ to send out the notice." She paused. Indigo and I leaned forward together. "Let's do this thing." She punched the air. "Let the Festschrift Botanicum begin!"

I turned to the woman who'd handed me wine. "What exactly is this?"

"Hold on. That's my Kai going first."

The children were lined up at the side of the stage. Slowly, with great care, a kid with noise-canceling headphones and a purple bandanna around his neck carried one of Antonia's three-sided boxes onto the stage. When he reached the very center, he set it down in front of himself, picked up the green plastic planter within, and lifted it above his head.

A flash of light. A blurry image shifting along the wall I'd painted, jagging one way, zooming the other. I turned to see DJ adjusting the projector's beam and Corin beside him. A plant came into focus, filling the wall—giant with wild green fronds. Antonia at the side of the stage said something in Latin—a plant name?—as Kai waved the empty pot side to side, jumping up and down in what I understood to be a dance. The other children began yelling, "Thank you!" "You were awesome!" "You were needed!"

"Are they talking to Kai? That's really nice."

The mother kept her gaze on her dancing son. "Oh no, not to Kai. To the plant. A festschrift, you know."

The children continued. "You slayed, girl, during your time on Earth." "You smashed it!" "Way to photosynthesize until the weather changed!" "Farewell!"

"What exactly's going on?"

"The first time, you know, we wondered, is it appropriate? But Kai's not the most social kid by a long shot and he loves this. It's not a death thing exactly. It's a life thing."

"So this is . . . like a funeral? For a plant?"

She turned to me. "Antonia didn't tell you? She wants kids to see the plants that go extinct, to carry the memory of them into the future. She says, you know, that if they watch what's leaving together . . ." The mother drifted off, waving avidly at Kai, who'd walked offstage. "She says it's important. And it does, it feels important, the way they're doing this communally, this witnessing, not based in fear but not in denial, either."

"But what if it makes them sad?" I said, wanting to pull Sonya out of line and tell her not to worry. Sure, a few plants were gone, but think of all we still have, the woods just brimming with green sprouts. No biggie, hon, let's get out of here.

"Look at them, though. Sad?" she said as an orchid flashed onto the white wall and another child lifted a terra-cotta planter and Antonia read its Latinate and common names and the children called, "You kept it incredibly real!" "You killed it here on Earth." "You were loved!" The girl twirled around and around, her dress and arms and legs and face shining green with the light of the projection.

When it was Sonya's turn, she carried her empty planter aloft, carefully jigging forward and back. "You were spectacular!" "You were a crucial part of a complicated ecosystem!"

I scrutinized her expression. Was this happiness? Sure, probably, but I saw something else, too, something I realized I wanted for her more than happiness—she looked totally at home, even outside of our house, with all these strangers, dancing her jig. What else could I want her to be doing? Playing soccer? Doodle Jump on my phone on the way to the swim class she hated? She'll find her people, I thought. Sonya will. And with them she'll find joy, even in the uncanny and frightening future.

She'll find her people like I found Demeter, like I found Will—that thought came dangerously close to me, and I kissed Indigo's petal-soft cheeks to keep it away.

At some point I saw Persephone slip back into the outbuilding, and a little later, everyone decided that the baby needed a turn. I held her in one arm, the planter in the other. A fern grew enormous above us, greening us, dwarfing us. How can I explain the feeling of standing in its fluorescence? I was altered. Symbiotic. Hybrid. Everyone shouted and stomped their feet and banged the drums. Indigo threw her head back and laughed, like this was what she'd come to earth to do.

Exhilarated, I lay on the ground at the side of the stage. Indigo on my legs, rising and dipping. Another child climbed the stage, and I heard Antonia say some Latin name and how this was the last plant, just added this morning, called Sightflower.

Black spots in my vision as I swung up. Nothing green in the projection. No verdancy, no wildness. A pressed, dried flower against yellowed paper, the stem bent to the right as if in pain. "Goodbye!" "You were wicked cool!" "You were important!" the kids shouted, and then its image, too, was gone and, since this was the last plant, someone lit the bonfire and the kids zoomed around like pinballs. My mother is sick, my mother. This is what I was thinking, no longer able to push back.

I couldn't find Antonia anywhere, not even inside, although I discovered Corin and DJ by the kitchen sink. When Indigo landed in her mom's arms, she shook with excitement. DJ bugged his eyes at her and she reached up and held on to his scruffy goat-beard. They left like this soon after, the baby's hand attached to the anti-natalist's chin—he'd invited them to crash at his place. I was at the side door, looking for Antonia when Persephone headed in. She was blooming. That's how she looked in the light of the kitchen, a flower newly opened. She was wearing her mother's shift dress and her hair was loose and her lips were red with her mother's lipstick. "Where is he? Did he go somewhere? Where's DJ?" Her eyes, which I so rarely saw uncovered by sunglasses—she must have taken them off for him—brimmed with tears. "He left?" She kicked at a chair until it fell over and then she crumpled to the floor. "I hate being sick. I freaking hate it."

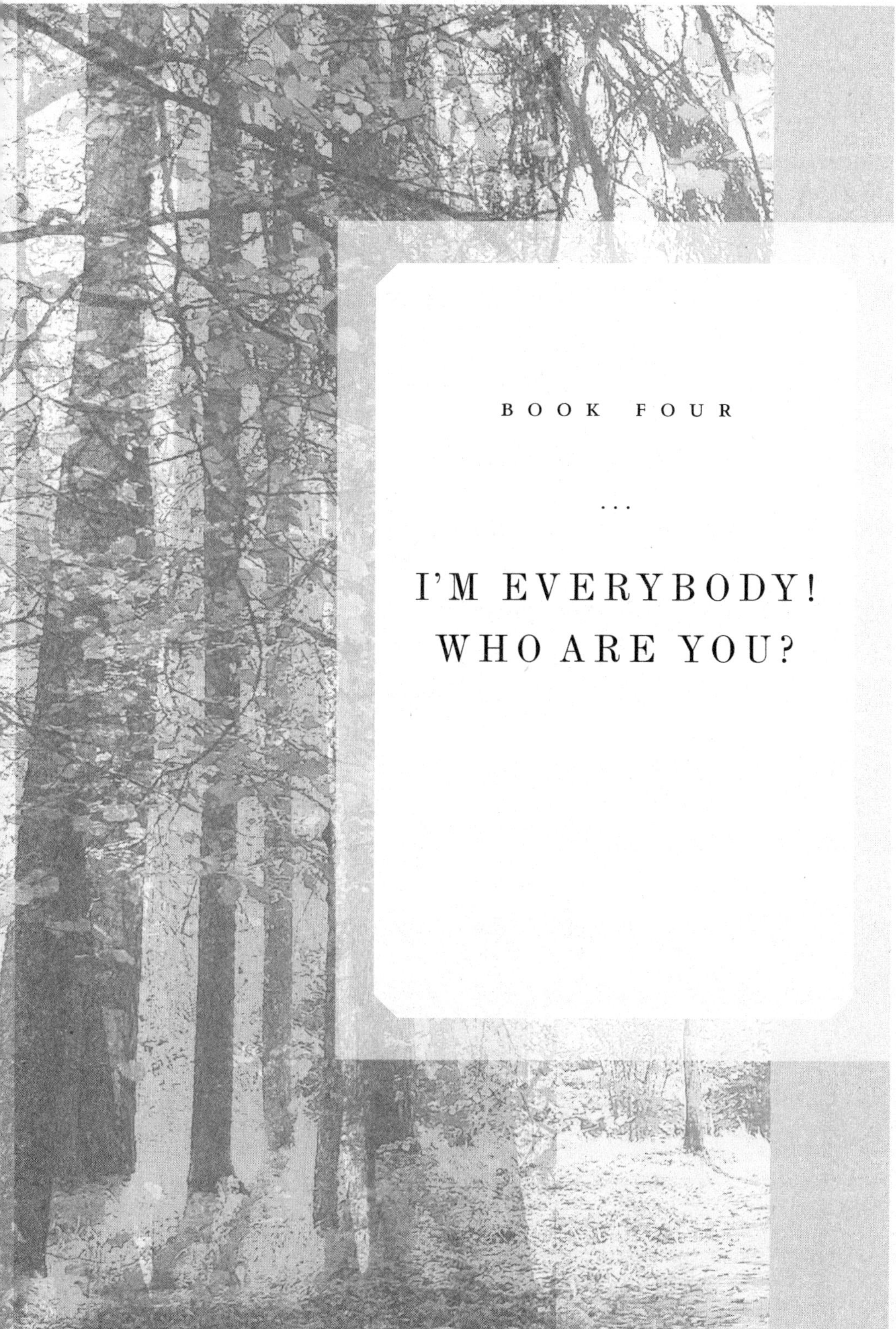

BOOK FOUR

...

I'M EVERYBODY! WHO ARE YOU?

Late June

. . .

i

IT WASN'T EASY TO FIND NOVELS BY HENRY JAMES IN MOSCOW IN the 1980s. But thanks to my husband's mother who befriended a librarian in the apartment above, he had rare access to anglophone literature and became obsessed with *The Portrait of a Lady* and *Daisy Miller.* But that's not why I'm calling him Henry James.

Henry James, my husband, is one of those men for whom an internal light was switched on when he learned the word *flaneur.* So this is what I am! He explained this to me when we first met, at a packed gallery opening of a mutual friend's video art. He couldn't imagine living away from a city and he'd never leave New York, he told me later that night, pulling off my dress in his apartment above Pete's Bar. The room had no curtains and was flared by the lights of cars. "Unless it's for London," he added.

And yet, he moved to Northampton when my mother did, when she left her rent-controlled apartment so I could take care of her. He knew the kids and I wouldn't get back to New York, and he quit his gigs, taking a job coding music for a streaming site, which he hated. Each morning he brought his laptop and noise-canceling headphones to the hospital cafeteria, the closest he could get to replicating urbanity, since the clientele weren't students like in town, but the suffering of all ages and creeds and occupations. He still spent only a little time alone with the kids. They were mine far more than his, and he acted as if his role was to volley their wishes. "Lev was missing you," he'd say when I went to the store. "Sonya was so sad when you said you'd play gin but you didn't play gin."

Henry James the author came to the rural trough of western Massachusetts known as Northampton in 1864, although he was not yet an author, just an unpublished writer and also constipated. He attempted to heal both conditions by spending six months living and writing at a water cure on Round Hill Road, a far fancier cure than Lillian's, with terraces and piazzas and famous guests like the Swedish soprano Jenny Lind, yet Henry James called the view suicidal and the social life of the hotel a lonely frigidity. Ten years later, living in London, he published his novel *Roderick Hudson,* in which the narrator, visiting a female cousin, lists her three misfortunes. "First, she had lost her husband; second, she had lost her money, or the greater part of it; and third, she lived at Northampton, Massachusetts."

That third misfortune is why I'm calling Henry James, Henry James.

ii

HENRY JAMES SLUNK BACK IN HIS CHAIR, CRADLING A TUMBLER WITH both hands, while Aengus cantilevered his torso forward over the plates, psyched, he said, to have finally reached Stage Three of their remodel, which included an outdoor pizza oven and passive solar. I slapped at a mosquito. "Sluggishness, you mean?" I asked Nina. Nina said she preferred the term "energy craters" but was it our biological age or the demands of motherhood or the historical time? The worst part, she said, was that she couldn't run anymore.

It was nearly dusk, the maples casting long shadows on our new backyard table, but Nina had kept on her sunglasses. She had a humorless mouth, tightly pulled-back hair, and like Aengus, wore shorts to free her runner's limbs. I couldn't muster up attraction to either of them, which made the evening drag.

"Running's overrated," I said.

Not for Nina, it turned out. For Nina, running couldn't be rated highly enough. Until these energy craters, she hadn't missed a day, meeting up with friends at five A.M., home in time to make the children breakfast. There was even an article in the *Gazette* about them.

"About running?"

"Well, it began as a political thing," she explained vaguely.

"Nina's still a hot mama," Aengus said, turning away from Henry James to me. "She'll be tying on her running shoes soon. That's why we're waiting on the party till she's a hundred percent."

"Party?" I moved a citronella candle closer.

Aengus frowned. "I've told you about it. Family tradition. Every solstice. The year's longest day, time to revel in the wild energy of the season. This would've been our seventeenth year, but Nina wasn't up for it."

"I'm just tired," she said.

"But here's the thing. Quick rebranding. End of July. Call it . . ." he held up both palms. "Midsummer party." He pointed at Henry James. "You, my man, are gonna love it."

I caught Henry James's eye. It's no use, said his look. We don't like other people enough to do this. Earlier, as I'd made the salad and he marinated the chicken for the arroz con pollo he'd learned to make in Cuba, he asked why we couldn't just have Will and Demeter again.

Taking his turn in the sharp beam of Will's attention, Henry James was deep in the flush of a crush. Mostly they talked about music, this band and that and the unsung solo project of the drummer and the misguided praise for a pop departure, also New York City, chiming the melancholy toll for the dead and gone, the clubs, the bookstores, the particular chess players, although I hadn't been aware that Will knew New York that well or at all.

But Sonya had asked us for this dinner with Fiona's family. Why didn't we ever have her friend's parents over? Why only Demeter, when Persephone refused to come? After nearly two months of hoping the friendship would resume, Sonya had given up on Persephone, and this dinner was my encouragement of her impulse of self-preservation.

"I'll get the kids for dessert," I said, standing.

"Actually," Nina said. "If it's okay with you, see . . ."

Aengus took over. "Our family is committed to slipping from the grip of the white devil."

"Colonialism?" Henry James's first smile of the evening was for his own joke.

"Sugar, actually. Like throwing a match on gasoline. What it does to the nervous system, the endocrine system . . ."

"Especially in prepubescent girls," Nina added.

I went inside to scout for uncontroversial fruit. Lev and Sonya were watching Fiona practice selfie poses into the camera on my computer. Fish face, electro-shocked face.

"If you're after peaches," Nina said, when I returned fruitless, "the Apex Farmstand is the only place to go."

"We don't believe in it," Aengus was saying to Henry James, who seemed to be dozing with his head back, his cup between his thighs.

"You don't believe in peaches?" I asked, reaching over Aengus to take his dinner plate.

Emily, it turned out. "There's this new tick hypothesis," he said. "I can't remember who told me, someone at the co-op? Total hooey."

"Aengus . . ." Nina's voice held a warning.

"I mean, our family's not risk-phobic. Soon as the pandemic hit, March 2020, we loaded up the car and spent a year exploring Mother Earth. We weren't going to be stuck inside on screens. Moab, Yosemite, Yellowstone. I mean, we wore masks at gas stations. We weren't like those people. But we weren't scared."

"Aengus," Nina warned again.

"So we're not about to climb aboard the fear train now," he continued. "The number one most important thing for kids' brain development is time in nature. You can't take that away. I require data before I sound the alarm. This one's psychological. All in their heads. If it was a tick, we'd see way more of it."

"Aengus, it was Eve," Nina said. "That's who told me. At camp pickup, remember? Your mom, right, Eve?"

At the mention of my mom, my heart began racing, on and off like the June bugs in the grass.

"Not just her," I said. Since hearing about my mother, Kiran remembered pulling a tick from his ankle on the Metro-North back to the city after hiking Skinner on his mother's birthday, two weeks before he became ill. Still, three wasn't data. The doctors we called remained uninterested. The tick epidemiologist hadn't even gotten back to us.

"You should find a therapist who tells her to go outside," Aengus said. "Counterphobic cure. Linking Emily to ticks, it's kind of hysteria without causality."

"Aren't you so glad for nature camp?" Nina jumped in to change the topic. "Does Sonya? So sweet they're both Great Blue Herons."

"Totally," I said, stacking the rest of the plates.

"And Lev's there, too? He's a Kingfisher?"

"In Hummingbirds, actually."

"Adorable. So, you're free every day, huh? We should do something." She lifted up her phone. "Breakfast on Monday? Tuesday? I'm wide open this week."

"Gosh, sounds really fun, but I'm so busy right now."

And I *was* so busy. Every Monday through Friday after dropping my kids at nature camp, I walked slowly in the woods, shining my plant app on every growing thing. I was learning the difference between petiole leaves and sessile. I felt for coarse or fine hairs on the stems. I knew the scalloped leaves of the mallow and the single lobed leaf of the bloodroot. I was starting to see faces in the crowd of what had been, just recently, undistinguishable green. I walked until noon when I had to leave to pick them up.

I'd become, it seemed, a woman who wanted only to think about plants.

It started when I heard Antonia reading aloud to the bees. *Yellow giant hyssop, southern agrimony, Jesup's milk-vetch.* And grew when Indigo and I held the planter in the flash of projector light. But it was my mother in an unlit rented apartment ten minutes away that fully changed me. I'd been so wrong. This wasn't depression at all, although she was depressed now, deeper than before, because she couldn't escape the dark.

What else could I do but spend my time learning how to look for a small spring ephemeral?

"Actually, that's a good idea, the two of you," Aengus said, pointing between his wife and me. "Nina really needs some fresh juice, new vibes. Tell her, Nina, how you were thinking of starting a Substack. Eve could give you some writing tips."

Feeling like I might drop the smeared plates and punch Aengus, I looked past him, past all of them, to the woods and imagined myself beneath the branches.

As of that night, my kids had six more weeks of camp, thanks to my paycheck from Doctor Folkenflick. I took the job once I learned Demeter was no longer doing menial labor for him, and while it lasted only three weeks before the Healing Hut was shuttered by the health department, in that time I churned out six articles—parsed meaning in the doctor's bombast, wrote comprehensible sentences that nodded to his turgidity but didn't hide in a forest of adverbial clauses. Women's work: I squashed the fun. I cleaned up the mess, placed the semicolon, enforced the rules of grammar.

With the money I made, I'd bought myself time. I didn't want to spend it on a barre class or lattes in town or FaceTiming with my New York friends. Just four holy hours alone in the only place where I felt calm instead of afraid. Furious that Nina, who knew nothing about it, was asking me to give up an hour of it, I said snippily, "There's literally nothing you need to learn to start a Substack."

"So another thing we could do?" She swiveled in her chair to smile up at me. "There's this cute vintage store in Amherst I've been meaning to check out. Your style's kinda vintage, right?"

A vintage store? Who had time for a vintage store? There was the bunchflower family to learn, and the milkwort family. The false asphodel family and loosestrife family. There was my mother in a dark room. I could feel her calling to me even now, her voice carried by the wind, asking how I expected her to go on like this.

"Sorry, but there's no way." I could see Nina's smile flatten. "I'm crushed with work right now."

Persephone

...

"You'll be here the whole time?" her mom asks.

"No plans. My day's wide open," Will says.

She can hear them from her bed. Drawers slide open or closed, the toaster pops.

"I'm talking like running to the store," her mom says. "Like grabbing a sandwich at Coopers."

"I'll be here. But don't you think . . . Give her a little trust? It might be good for her."

The scrape of knife across toast.

"If she won't tell me . . . if I don't know what she was even doing, how do I know she won't do it again?"

"She was pretty miserable after. That's probably deterrent enough."

Persephone hasn't actually decided whether she'll go outside again if given the chance. She's miserable even when she's not puking and shaking.

"If I miss another three days like that, no advance notice, they'll let me go."

Will clears a disgusting amount of phlegm from his throat. "You know, Dem . . ."

Persephone flops onto her stomach and reaches onto the floor to feel for her synthesizer piano. Hanging off the bed, she presses the power button and plays a few notes, because she knows what's coming next in their conversation and doesn't want to hear it.

He's going to say again that her mom really doesn't need to work. He can give her the money she needs, it's not a problem. It would make him happy.

And yet, her mom always chooses to work, every morning, because who wouldn't? Who wouldn't want to carry trays of delicious food in a busy restaurant with plants hanging from the ceiling—so her mom's told her—and chat with funny kids and old people, instead of sitting with Persephone in a dark room?

She feels for the drumbeat switch, which works on her mom like the sirens singing to Odysseus. Sure enough: three loud knocks on her door. "Can I come in, honey?"

She was planning to say, Will's right. I'm not a baby. You can leave me alone. But then her mom would say, First I need to know where you were going. What were you thinking? Just tell me and we can do something about it. And Persephone won't be able to answer. She turns off the drumbeat. "No, you can't."

"Just quickly?"

"Go away."

She can hear someone unloading the dishwasher. They're talking quieter now, their voices lying beneath the claps of metal hitting metal, ceramic against ceramic.

"Hey, Siri," she says. Her mom acted so disappointed when she refused to name the voice on her new phone Matilda, not knowing that the most humiliating moment of Persephone's life was when she called DJ's computer's voice Matilda as he was setting up the slides and he laughed with his whole body and said, "Matilda? Who's Matilda?"

"How can I help you?" Persephone doesn't answer Siri. She doesn't want to hear a book about Zeus. She doesn't want to listen to her mom's stupid '90s music. Blood has filled her head and she feels heavy, upside down like this; even her eyes are heavy. She hasn't taken a shower since her mom cut her hair; her scalp itches. She plays six notes on the piano. The sound of doom, plus an exciting flash of lightning.

Another three knocks. "Sweetie? I just need to check in before I leave."

She's never had her own bedroom before. She wants to let her mom in but she can't. It makes no sense. She wants her mom to sit on the bed and put her cool hands on the back of her neck.

"Go away!" she shouts, angrier than before, although why? Anger has been rushing through her like this for weeks. Windstorms she can't predict or control. It wasn't leaving the Healing Hut that morning when the doctor cried and Will picked them up that started it, even though that's what her mom thinks. It was DJ. Just talking with DJ in Antonia's office was the very best hour of her life and also so embarrassing. He asked her what shows she liked, what podcasts, what tunes. She didn't have anything to say. She didn't even know that music was called tunes. She wants another day with him. She wants to say, these are my favorite tunes.

Still hanging upside down, she turns on the drumbeat, but her mother doesn't come back to her door. Can't she hear the siren song?

If she came right now, Persephone would tell her why she left, would rest her head in her mom's lap, but her mom doesn't. She says, "There's food here. This plate's for her."

Will laughs. "I can see that, Dem. I saw you make it. I'm gonna feed her. We're gonna be fine."

Then a silence. No dish noises. Kissing?

Come now, she says to her mom in her head. Now now now.

The front door closes.

SOON, THE SIZZLE AND smell of bacon. After she went outside, her mom made her drink yellow or red Pedialyte. Even this morning she said to Will, "We're still taking it easy on her stomach. Just this toast and something plain for lunch."

But Will always makes bacon and scrambled eggs with cheese when her mom leaves.

"Breakfast is here and the curtains are closed," he calls. Why does she open her door for him and not for her mom? She doesn't know.

When they first came here, she had to stay in her room during daylight, but then Will told his landlord, Matty, to put curtains over the tall windows in the living room. It's so dark that her mom plugged in a night-light that sheds just enough light for her to see Will bringing a plate and glass to the coffee table in front of the couch. He sits on the chair near her but doesn't ask questions. That's something she likes about him. He can tell when she wants questions and when she doesn't.

Because he doesn't ask, she says, "Your house is over a store called Balagan. I looked in the window when I went outside but it was all covered up even though there was a sign that said Open. What does it sell?"

"That store? Sells weed."

"Weeds?"

"Pot. Marijuana. It's a kind of . . . substance . . . well, plant actually . . ."

"No, I know," she says, breaking a stick of bacon and putting half in her mouth. Pot was the smell of her mom's friend Scott's cabin in Taos. "But a whole store for that?"

"Actually, there are like twelve in this town."

"See, I didn't know that," she says angrily. He keeps quiet and she finds herself saying, "I just wanted to see what it was like in the daytime. There wasn't someplace specific I was trying to get to. I wasn't running away or anything. She thinks I was, but I wouldn't do that."

"She's just scared. Your mom."

This makes her chest twist and hurt. She wants to go back to her room.

On the day she left, Will came home from the fish store—he's trying to get her to like salmon and shrimp—and found her bedroom door open. Her phone, when he called it, rang in her room. Her mother, when he called her, ran out of the restaurant in the middle of her shift, ran through town until she found Persephone at the far end, in a little room outside the bank with the ATMs—the darkest place she could find when she started feeling sick.

"Hey, wait," he says, when she stands up. "It's really okay. Scaring parents is a requirement for thirteen-year-olds."

She turned thirteen in March. Hot chocolate made from carob and almond milk and agave in the middle of the night in the Healing Hut's kitchen. When Will heard about that he said she needed a redo. He tried to make it a big deal, baking a vanilla cake, buying her the synthesizer and a brand-new phone and a velvet blanket for her bed. He doesn't know that all she really wanted was to go inside a shop herself. It was the next day, after this fake birthday party, when he went to the fish store and she left.

"Do you want to know what I did at thirteen?" he asks.

She doesn't answer but she sits back on the couch.

"Okay, so I was in New York. Picture a really tall building. Twenty-five stories high. And there's a doorman, which makes it harder to sneak out, for sure. But one of them, I knew from an older kid in the building that he'd accept twenty bucks to keep quiet. So I brought my skateboard and a twenty and took the subway to meet Scotty Moscovitz in Washington Square Park. This was 1996. Before cell phones. Came home at like three in the morning and found my mom in the kitchen crying."

The story makes her feel better—he's saying she's like a normal thirteen-year-old! But it also makes her feel worse: She wants to take a subway and meet a friend. She pushes eggs on the cold toast. "Aren't you from the salty city?"

He laughs, as he does every time she makes this dumb joke. "Yeah. Just spent a little time in New York."

"What is it like? Sonya says her school had a playground on its roof."

"What's New York City like?" She nods. He's quiet for a minute. "Okay, how about I take you on a walk."

This worries her. Has he somehow forgotten that she can't leave the apartment? "No, we can't. My mo—"

"Hold on. We're starting out on the corner of . . . let's say Fourth and Broadway. It's busy, lots of cars, taxis, people. See those red lights on the building on the northeast corner? They spell out *Tower Records.* Well, the store closed like twenty years ago, but we can still see it."

"Wait, can I go in?"

"In . . . ? You want to go back to your room?"

"No, the Tower store."

"Okay, right, we're opening the door and entering a room lined with bins of CDs at arm's reach, and four guys in flannels are flipping through them along with two girls in black platform Doc Martens. And Jesus, it's loud in here."

He takes her all over. They walk down Astor Place and check out the cheapest and most punk hair-cutting salon and then to Tompkins Square Park to watch a parade of pets dressed up in costumes. Upstairs in a bookstore called The Strand, they crouch in the sci-fi aisle to see where Will once wrote his name on the wall. They eat saag paneer in an Indian restaurant where he left his retainer when he was a kid and then walk to Union Square—it's very noisy—and they even go down into the subway. They swipe their metro cards and get on a train, stepping over a little gap and holding on to the poles, because it's cool to stand up and let the tourists sit down. That's why they don't go to Times Square. Too many tourists, he says. But he takes her to all his favorite places in Central Park—the boulder where he chipped a tooth and the meadow of sheep and the bandstand where he saw The National and LCD Soundsystem play his favorite tunes. After the park, they're hungry again. This city makes you very hungry, he explains, because of the tall buildings and thick smells and the interesting people walking so fast. So they head to a coffee shop, which is what he says you have to call a diner, just as you have to call a corner store a bodega, and although this particular coffee shop closed down in 1998, they open the door on which a bell jingles and sit in a booth with red vinyl banquets and fill their coffee with sugar and little buckets of cream as they wait for their grilled cheese sandwiches, the very best grilled cheese in all of New York City, which means the best in the entire world.

Early July

. . .

i

THERE WAS ACTUALLY ONE THING I LIKED MORE THAN MY MORNings alone in the woods: a small-town seed exchange. Each casual gathering held the possibility, however tiny, that I'd find the cure for my mom and Persephone. I would look through baggies or muffin tins or mason jars of seeds people saved from their own gardens and feel a strange awed vividness—that's the only way I can describe the feeling—in the presence of these specks. I attended two exchanges in early June, and a third was hosted by the First Congregational Church in Hatfield a week after Nina and Aengus came over. I was on my way there, skimming past the green horizon of tobacco fields, radio loud, when my phone rang.

"Hi!" I shouted over my music. "Is everything okay?" Demeter never called at this hour. Usually we spoke when she was walking home from her lunch shift or in the evenings if she came over with Will.

"Eve!" She shouted, too. "I hate to do this during your time alone, but I have a huge favor to ask of you."

When we hung up, I pulled to the side of the road to decide what to do. I hated to miss the seed exchange—there were only a handful that summer—but Demeter hadn't asked anything of me in so long.

"I OWE YOU FOUR hours to yourself," she said from the doorway of Will's apartment.

"No," I lied. "I want to be with Perse."

I still wasn't accustomed to entering Will's apartment without suspense or subterfuge. Curtains draped the grand windows, but the kitchen lights were on and I could see how much it had changed. What had been so tidy and controlled when Will lived alone looked hurricaned. Laundry and baggies of earrings and toothpaste. Carob energy bars left on a plate. Rust stains of wine in mugs.

An even bigger change was Demeter's appearance. She'd cut her long hair into a pixie shortly after moving in. I was still getting used to this. I'd thought her waist-length hair an integral, Samson-like core of her selfhood. Similarly, I'd thought her flimsy hippie blouses and torn vintage dresses and western snap shirts and floor-length skirts the outward manifestation of the calm pool of belief within her, proof she alone wasn't prickled and malformed by capitalism's insatiable whims.

But today she wore a shirt and pants in rough linen that was insouciantly baggy but also showed the elegant muscles and breasts beneath, the color of mud against her arm making it seem garish that other clothes weren't mud-colored. And her beads was gone, the earrings she made replaced by gold studs, a gift from Will. But that meant nothing about who she was, I reminded myself, following her into the apartment. She was still Demeter, just enjoying herself.

She opened the fridge, chatting as she rummaged around. "I know we bought new jam. Are you hungry? Thank you so much for doing this. Will had to go somewhere early—his mom's maybe? Anyway, I took myself off the schedule but now Minh's kid has Covid. And I really need to get back in their good graces."

"But why can't Perse . . . ? She always stays by herself."

"Come over here." Demeter closed the fridge, took my hand and led me to the far end of the room, near the long curtains, and told me in a low whisper that Persephone had left the apartment on her own, becoming sicker than she'd ever been. Demeter was so scared she'd do it again, but how could she blame her child, stuck inside all day, as if in a cage, how could she blame her? "Think about what we were doing at her age, Eve. Think about how we never went inside."

I hugged her. I could feel her shaking. "Oh, Demeter. Oh *fuck*. That sucks. When was it?"

She began wiping her eyes with the hem of her linen shirt. "Two weeks ago. It's been really shitty. But . . . well, Will's great, so good with her. And he calms me down. She likes him."

—

I NEED TO EXPLAIN ABOUT JEALOUSY. I'D BEEN TRYING SINCE Vermont to put it away, to hide it in a drawer, pull it from my throat. So I hadn't been the one Will chose. So what? I hadn't been willing and Demeter was.

She and I took a long walk after the department of health shuttered the Healing Hut for kitchen code violations and she moved into town with Will. I insisted she should live with me instead, that she didn't need to tie herself to him. I would help her.

"The truth is, Eve, I need this," she'd said—we were walking through Smith College and the lilacs were in full bloom. "Look, I like him. I do. I'm not being coerced. We have a really good connection. But also, he has a huge apartment and lots of space for Persephone. And I need a moment with that kind of solid ground beneath me. It's been so long since I could really work. That's what I do when I have a floor under me. I squirrel away as much cash as possible for the next time it comes out from under me again."

I felt happy for her on that walk. I wanted her to have a floor just as I wanted my weeks of nature camp, and honestly there wasn't room for her and Persephone in my house. But after that, I didn't ask very much about her and Will. And I hadn't been able to speak to him, not really, since Vermont. I couldn't be alone with him. When he tried, when he came up beside me while I was washing dishes or tossing a salad and started to tell a joke or refer to a conversation we'd had in the botanical garden, I'd always slip away.

This news about Persephone? It hurt even more. Persephone had walked into the sunlight, and Demeter, terrified and sad, didn't even tell me. It was Will she turned to, Will who helped her decide what to do, who gave her comfort. I thought about the previous summer, when we shared our precarity and used each other as a ballast against the day; how far away it seemed, how many miles between us and that balcony.

"HEY, LOVE! IT'S GETTING late. Come eat breakfast with Auntie Evie!"

The response from the closed bedroom door was monotone. "I'm not going to her house."

Demeter turned to me, shaking her head. "Give her a minute. I'll just brush my teeth."

I took the opportunity to snoop, flipping up the postcards still on the walls. *I love the Southwest. I can't wait to return to the Southwest territories. Love, G.* It made some sense, I realized, since Will was from Utah and the sender, G, might be as well, might want to return. But who was G?

Coming out of the bathroom, Demeter called again, "Honey, it's really time!" She clattered dishes into the sink then lifted up a magazine on the kitchen island to uncover an exquisite gold bangle, which she clasped like a ring of Saturn around her wrist.

"Is that new?" I touched it. I couldn't pin down how much money Will actually had. It was starting to seem limitless.

Persephone's door opened and Demeter rushed to shut off the lights. "Matty!" she shouted, laughing and explaining the joke as if I didn't know who Matty was. "See, Will screams 'Matty' whenever the lights go out, because half the time it's Persephone leaving her bedroom and turning off our lights, but other times, there's this problem with the fuse. Matty—he's the landlord—fixes it so often it's like he lives here."

"No, it's not," Persephone said, coming toward us.

It was a shock to see her even in the dimness of the night-light, even though I'd seen her a few weeks earlier and had been shocked then. Puberty, that old magic trick. Demeter had told me that Persephone's period came as soon as they stopped the broth. Angry pimples crested her cheeks and forehead. The seismic disruption of breasts. She'd asked for short hair like her mother's, but while Demeter's haircut turned her younger, Persephone's aged her. She adopted the teenage slouch, arms wrapped protectively around herself.

"Did you forget your hat?" Demeter's hand, reaching for her daughter's hair, retreated. I'd never seen her unsure like this. There'd been an effortless current between their bodies.

"Why? I'm not going anywhere."

"She's embarrassed about the hat," Demeter said in the pinched tone mothers—other mothers, never Demeter—took when they complained about their children in front of them. "I really can't be late."

"Fine," Persephone said. "We can go to your house."

But I didn't drive her to my house.

ii

"THERE'S NOTHING FOR A CHILD HERE." MY MOTHER'S VOICE CAME from the corner of her stifling bedroom. The sublet I'd found was owned by a therapist who left behind her furniture and cookbooks and statues of Ganesh and Buddha when she moved to assisted living. Henry James and I had added an air conditioner, blackout curtains, and a low-voltage light, which I switched on so that Persephone could see the room where she'd stay. My mother flung an arm over her eyes. "My head's terrible."

She was in her white nightgown, hair fuzzed without barrettes. Half-drunk Vitamin Waters glowed around the floor like abandoned jewels. She waved her fingers. "Take her away."

"She's got everything she needs. Audiobooks on your phone, right?" Persephone didn't answer, the hated hat scrunched in a hand.

I knew I should reconsider. What misery to withstand both the room's heat and my mother's rancor. "And what about you?" I asked my mom. "Have you been listening to anything I downloaded?"

Joan rocked back in the therapist's chair. "What do you want me to be? An endless consumer of crap? I'd rather annoy myself to death with the hellish company of my own thoughts."

For the first time since leaving Will's apartment, Persephone made a sound, not quite a laugh, a half huh.

"Any news from Irene? Any reviews?" I asked to change the subject. My mom had refused to do any events or interviews for the republication of *The Third Person,* even by Zoom, and the book once again seemed to be dropping into obscurity so quietly you couldn't hear the splash.

"Who's Irene? She washed her hands of me."

"Not in the slightest," I said. But it had been Irene who told me to move her to Northampton. Irene didn't believe in the tick. "I know you want an external reason, but this is how she feels inside. She wants to live in a dark world. And I can't keep yanking her out of it." Her sister in Florida was asking her to move down, and maybe it was time to retire.

"Besides, what do I care about reviews?" my mom said. "Let it die, let all my books die and let me follow."

"I loved *Wormfood,* Mrs. Yalen." There was a tinge of earnestness in Persephone's voice. I could almost discern the fairy of a few months earlier, who would arrange my mother's Vitamin Waters in an iridescent ring to dance within, and I told myself again that I should remove her from the bitterness in the room.

"That old bullshit? Soon enough the libraries will toss it from their musty shelves if they haven't done so already. And good riddance."

"Mom!"

"Then it will become actual wormfood," Persephone said. "Your book. When they throw it out."

My mother looked over at her, appraising. I'm not sure what passed between them, but she said, "Well, I can't be expected to make her lunch."

iii

WHAT DID I LOVE ABOUT GOING TO THE SEED EXCHANGE? THE NAMES. I'd fallen in love with names. *Detroit dark red. Muncher. Soapwort.*

In the basement of a Congregationalist church in Hatfield, I read *Mary Washington* and *Dwarf long pod* and *Clemson spineless* and imagined the people from the past propagating and cultivating and saving for the future, and here I was in their future, and here were the seeds for our future, we were all moving it along. At night I'd started to read wildflower field guides instead of looking at Instagram. *Jewelweed. Orange balsam. Touch-me-not.* I'd feel a hit of dopamine. *Chicory, succory, blue-sailors.* As if things that were named couldn't disappear.

Each name seemed to suggest I might actually find what my mother and Persephone needed. But I didn't ask about Sightflower right away. I scanned the long row of folding tables before talking to anyone, pushing—in a way I hoped wasn't too pushy—between people to read the leaning cursive or blocky print. Until I asked my question, there was always the possibility that the answer would be yes.

ABIAH WILLIAMS OF DEERFIELD left to her three daughters an herbarium of native plants she collected around Northampton in the mid-nineteenth century. A great-great-great-niece studying marketing at UMass brought a friend, ABD in the botany department, to Thanksgiving. Seeing a dissertation potential in the old book resting on the DVD player in the rec room, he slipped it in his backpack. Over the next five years, he looked for Abiah's vascular plants in the same fields and meadows and riversides. And he found them. All but sixteen, which, since they hadn't turned up in any other herbaria, were considered extinct.

The dissertation itself was languishing in the digital files of UMass. The botany grad student left academia to work as a divorce mediator. This is what Antonia told me when the children were still pinging around her backyard and I found her eating corn on her folding chair by the beehives in the woods. "Don't mind me," she said, tears down her face. "Love these Festschrifts, but they're an emotional roller coaster."

"It's gone? My plant's gone."

She threw her cob into the woods. "Would've told you first, should've, I get that, but you and Ellen went somewhere and I didn't even know if you were coming back, so it just seemed, why not include it?"

Later that evening, I stared at the small nothing on her computer. The white petals doubled over on themselves, mildew-freckled like the page. The green sepals browned.

Abiah Williams named the four-petalled trillium after herself. *Quadrillium gulielmus. Discovered on May the 1st of the year 1852. Com-*

mon name, Sight-Flower. Medicinal potential? Prefers a river-side, tolerates my garden bed. Repulsive to Rabbits.

"Considered extinct? What does 'considered' mean?" I asked. "It could be somewhere?"

She pressed her finger on the screen. "A four-petalled trillium? Someone would've seen it." This was happening to so many spring ephemerals, she said. Warm winters, wet springs. Trees had started leafing earlier and earlier, blocking the sun during the flowers' brief time to bloom. Invasives moved in, clogging them out.

Even so, after Will drove Demeter and Persephone back to the Healing Hut, the kids and I watched the Scottish mystery and cooked for Antonia and burned brush and mucked the goat barn for four additional days. In return, she plugged in the Wi-Fi, contacted the International Plant Names Index, posted on all the online seed boards. She called botanical gardens, wildflower societies, the Northeast Seed Network, the New England Seed Bank, even reached out to a conservator of the seed vault in Svalbard, the fortress in the Arctic Ocean where all the world's seeds are waiting for a terrible future. Nothing turned up. "If your trillium exists, and it likely doesn't, but if it does and if the plant really is helpful," she said when we finally left, "it'll be in some crusty old white woman's basement near where Abiah found it."

I texted Will, Stephen, and Ruth when I found the first seed exchange on Facebook. Long shot, I know, but anyone want to join?

Ruth said she was working. Will responded with a leaf emoji and awesome! but hanging with Persephone. Stephen wrote that his daily practice was to lower his expectations and suggested I do the same. You are at the beginning of what I have found to be relentless dashed hopes. Trust me it's hell to love someone you can't help.

But I was packing up my mother's apartment at the time, tossing books and papers, cleaning her vomit when she insisted on coming into the rooms without window coverings, wondering how I'd take care of her, how she'd find the will to keep living. I wasn't about to just stop searching.

—

NEVER HEARD OF IT, SAID THE SEED SAVERS AS THEY ATE THEIR tinned tuna or penciled in the crossword puzzle or chatted or knit. A woman with moose lumbering across her blouse and tricolored yarn on her lap pointed to her tablemate. "Frank here deals in the more esoteric."

Frank—large, bearded, shaped like a summer squash with green suspenders—put down his phone. "A Jewess. You don't mind me saying that, do you."

I told him what I was looking for: *Quadrillium gulielmus.* Sightflower.

"Sightflower? I'd say I never heard of it, but actually I have."

I couldn't feel my body. "You have it?"

"Crouch down." He pressed an unusually large thumb onto the table. "I'm a little hard of hearing."

He shook his box of envelopes, one of which held my seed. I loved the box then and his large hand for holding it. Would I agree, he asked, that balance was important?

"Balance?" Was he talking about me, gripping the table edge to stay upright while crouching?

"How do we feed ourselves if we're overrun? Do we have an obligation as savers of the sacred seed to impose limits on immigrants to our beautiful valley?"

I noticed the American flag pin on his shirt and began to smell the fetid waters into which he was headed. "Sir? Did you say you have the seed I'm looking for?"

He gripped my upper arm with his massive paw. "I'm as bleeding-heart as the next man. My mom took to her bed when Kennedy was shot. Family tragedy, felt like. I have sympathy for the immigrant. But what good would it be to create famine conditions for us all?"

"Shut up with your fascist bullhonkey," said the knitting woman in the moose blouse. "Tell the lady if you have what she wants."

He released my arm. "Until last week I'd never heard of it. But here's the interesting thing. At the seed exchange in Colrain, a man there asked me for the same thing. I never forget a plant name. I saw him earlier today, too, looking around here." Frank swiveled his head around. "He's gone now."

Colrain? I hadn't heard of an exchange in Colrain. "And what did you . . . Did you give it to him?"

"Were you listening?" Frank bellowed. "I said I'd never heard of it before that. How could I have it?"

"You bastard," the woman said, her needles clicking.

Frank had turned away from us to a young man with a patchy beard, socks in sandals, posture like a question mark. "I'm interested in what you were saying," the man said. "I consider myself moderately pro-immigrant, but the thing is, I'm also a prepper."

"Wait, so he was just toying with me?" I asked the knitting woman. "Has he even heard of it before?"

"Honey, he'll say anything to make someone listen to his bullhooey. But you can't get away from me, can you, Frank? I always take the spot next to him so as to keep him in line."

WHAT DID I LOVE about going to the seed exchange? For the hour I spent in that church basement, I was a different woman. A woman so purposeful, with such narrow attention to finding a cure for the people I loved that I could forget all of them. I could never manage this at home, not even in the woods. But here I didn't wonder whether Sonya had someone to sit with at lunch or if Lev allowed his counselor to take him to the bathroom or if my mother would need rehydration at the ER again. Only when I ascended the stairs and waved to the man mopping the nave did they all come back, crowding me, and I remembered that I'd left Persephone, the sweetest girl, with my terrible mother. What had I been thinking?

iv

FROM THE STAIRS UP TO HER BEDROOM, I HEARD MY MOTHER SAY, "Type in 'Stevie.'"

"Looks like there's Nicks and there's Wonder," Persephone said.

"We'll start with Wonder. One should always start with wonder."

"Superstition" pulsed through her door.

I opened without knocking. In the constant dusk, my mother danced. One hand bobbing to the side, the other raised to the ceiling. She wore slippers, black stretch pants, a cardigan. It had been weeks since I'd seen her dressed, and decades since I'd seen her dance.

I watched her in wonder. When the song ended, she kept her eyes closed. "Your turn. Show me what the teenagers are listening to."

"I wouldn't know." Persephone fell backward onto my mom's bed. "I don't even know any other teens. Eve's here to take me home."

I thought my mother would be embarrassed that I'd seen her like this, but she kept gaily thrusting her arms as if conducting a marching band. "Already? We're just getting started."

"Can I come tomorrow?" Persephone asked.

"She'll need to rest," I said.

"Who's she? The cat's mother? I wake early. We didn't talk about that. Darkness messes with my sleep and I'm awake very early. As soon as you wake, know I'm waiting for you. And you'll stay as long as you like."

Ruth

. . .

SHE KNOWS WHERE TO FIND EVE IN THESE WOODS; SHE'S BEEN coming on her days off to hang out, and Eve jumps up at her approach, waving eagerly. "There you are. Let's go."

Ruth groans, pulls her T-shirt from her chest, needing air. "Sit down. Reasonable people in a heat wave move as little as possible."

"Okay, but just for a minute," Eve says, settling her long legs back on the white sheet she's brought from her house.

Ruth finds her way to the ground. She'd prefer a lawn chair. After a run ten days ago, she woke with a knife ache in her right knee. Ignoring it, because she's stubborn, she ran up Skinner again. Now it hurts with every step. She's eight years older than Eve and feels suddenly compelled to offer some admonition about the vulnerability of the body—stretch now! Wear sunscreen!—although she knows that there's nothing worse to be reminded of when you're deep in the exhausted years than the cruelty of time's passage. She used to flinch whenever someone said, "It goes so fast!" And yet, she begins: "I should tell you . . ."

"Wait, you have news? The tick doctors got back to you?"

Relieved to be shaken from that strange compulsion, she changes course. "Epidemiologists of vector-borne diseases, they're called. They'd like you to give them their due respect. And no. Well, just one, who said I didn't understand data collection. I could hear his condescension through his email sign-off."

"Best? All best? All very best?"

"Nope."

"Warmly? With warmest wishes?"

"From."

"Ouch."

Ruth leans back on her elbows to look up at the branches, that ceiling of green, strange to see the leaves so immobile; the air today is still as a classroom. "I just want to understand. I want it all to fit together." This is what she always says when she's with Eve. "Sun Madness. Why would it disappear? How does that even work?"

"I really do think it's a tick. Fuck their data."

Ruth nods. Not fear, not fungus, not post-pandemic anxiety. Just these hungry little heat-seeking fuckers and their obligate pathogens? But something's missing. "So then why aren't we seeing more of it? Why no record of photosensitivity for two hundred years? Ticks have been here."

"Demeter says it doesn't matter. When I told her about Kiran and my mom? She said that until someone has something to help her kid, she doesn't care if it's a tick anymore."

Ruth turns to look at her. They haven't talked about secrecy in a while. Does it even matter now, when the plant is dead? "Did you tell her about Sightflower?"

"Antonia says it would be like dangling a turd in front of her face. Giving her hope for something that we'll probably never find."

Antonia. The name stings. After Eve told them about Abiah Williams and her herbarium, Ruth never asked about her time in Vermont. "You're still going to the seed exchanges, though? I hope you are. You should."

"Actually, the weirdest thing happened." Eve describes a guy who claimed to have met someone asking for Sightflower, but who turned out to just be a liar, stringing her along.

"What an asshole. Were you freaking out?"

"Completely. He made me crouch by his side and listen to a story about the dangers of immigration." Eve lifts her hair from the back of her neck and swivels away from Ruth. "Will you look? I feel creepy-crawlies, but it's probably sweat."

Ruth brushes her fingers along Eve's neck and through her dark curls. "You're good."

Eve stands and holds a hand out. "Ready?"

Eve's restless. She remembers that, too, from when Orion was young, feeling like she needed two days to live for each one, a day spent alone and a day with him, trawling at his slow pace.

They head down to the river and along the path into a marshland near Paradise Pond. Eve moves slowly—toddler pace—crouching, counting sepals. She hardly needs her app anymore to identify the plants and offers a short botanical lecture on inflorescence, how to spot a panicle versus an umbel versus the aster family, which has, she says excitedly, flower heads unlike all others.

"Shit, I'm probably boring you." She laughs, switches topics, asking, as she often does, if Ruth's heard from Orion. It's clear that the story bothers her. A child not visiting his mother, not calling. She wants a different ending.

Well, it bothers Ruth, too. "Nah. He's busy."

"He'll come back."

Ruth nods, but she doesn't agree. He says maybe next fall, but she understands now that he won't return to the place of grief and loneliness. Those terrible years they had together.

"How was she?" she asks.

"Who?" Eve stops at a bush, positioning her phone to take a picture.

"Antonia." Does she even want to know? Why'd she ask?

"Marsh elder," Eve reads. "Iva frutescens. Often confused with groundsel. Yeah, what's the deal with the two of you? I never really understood why you didn't go up to see her yourself."

"Old feud. Is she still a bitch?"

"I mean, I wouldn't want to get on her bad side. But it's magical up there."

Magical? That's not what she was picturing. "Doesn't she live alone? Refuses to talk to anyone. Depressed about plants. 'Keeper of the Gone.' Isn't that what she calls herself?"

But Eve describes something very different. Gardens and chickens and goats and bees. Neighbors dropping by with food. Ellen driving up from New Jersey for a single night, because she was traveling to Australia and couldn't stand to be away that long. Antonia even hosted a festival of sorts, transforming her yard into a performance space where children could say goodbye to the disappearing plants. "Hands down the most beautiful thing . . . the most *spiritual* thing I've been a part of," Eve says.

"Huh." Ruth feels winded.

Later, after Eve packs up the bedsheet and they check each other for ticks, Eve sprints up the hill, late for nature camp.

Oh, to run like that.

She stops, though, near the pachysandra, turning and cupping her hands around her mouth. "Want to come for dinner? Will and Demeter are coming. You should, too."

Ruth's need for human contact must be showing. She shouts back a polite declination. But why? She can't even go for her run. That night she eats a thawed burrito while icing her knee at the kitchen table and doing the crossword on her phone—too easy. Knocking the frozen peas to the floor, she peg-walks into Orion's bedroom to watch night fall on the woods outside his window. Antonia slips into her mind. Had she actually been feeling a little sorry for her? She'd pictured her sad and alone, but she's surrounded, beloved. Of course she is.

The scene Eve described—Ellen and neighbors and boughs of flowers—annoys her; agitation flows through her arms and legs. She wants to run.

What Ruth would really like right now is to solve a puzzle (a true puzzle, not the Wednesday crossword). There's a weight to her body when the pieces align, a heaviness to the air. She'd give anything for that sense of completion—physical as well as intellectual.

Oh.

She knocks her forehead against the windowpane. How entirely obvious she is. She wants her family back. Completion. Well, at least she solved the puzzle of herself—the puzzle of the unfulfilled puzzler.

She's still standing there when the owls start calling to one another, their day just beginning. The flaccid heat remains, though. Suddenly certain something is crawling down her back, she shoves off her shirt, peels off her sports bra, feels for a bug. What will happen if she gets sick, alone? Who will help her? In the dark window, her face is reflected back. It has a stern immobility that surprises her. Has she turned into a statue? A stone, bleached of color by the sun, marking the past? Here was Ramona. Here was Orion. Is she the real Keeper of the Gone?

"Move," she says to her reflection. "Go on, Ruth. Do something."

Late July

. . .

i

JULY CRAWLED, YELLOWING LAWNS, BROWNING MEADOWS. Spiders dropped from trees, as tired of the heat as we were. I showed up at my mother's with boxes of Popsicles and asked if she wanted a second fan for her bedroom. "There are far more pressing matters, Eve," she said, opening a box and passing it to Persephone who sat before the blast of air-conditioning. "You told me when I moved here that you knew others like me and her. Send them our way."

Stephen agreed to pass on my mom's message to Kiran but warned me not to get my hopes up. Kiran didn't talk to anyone anymore, not even his friends. He wouldn't want to hang out with an old lady and a teenager.

While Persephone spent time with my mother, Will and Demeter took occasional jaunts away—Jacob's Pillow, Tanglewood, estate sales. On one trip, Will bought Demeter a loom from an artisan in Hudson and she began weaving again after fifteen years. On another, they visited a healer named Ishmael, buying vials of colloidal silver and bee venom and other tinctures for Persephone.

We were outside when they told us this, our kids asleep. Will kept his arm protectively around Demeter's shoulder. She didn't look diminished by this, as some women did, but instead calmer, sleepier—although not stoned like my husband, who was preparing another vape pen. She had a floor beneath her, I thought. Was that it? She could take a break from being brave.

"Ishmael," I said, trying to remember where I'd heard that name. "Wait, isn't that the guy who helps Jeremiah's mom?"

Will smiled broadly. "You remembered!"

This annoyed me. I felt like I'd forfeited a turn in a game only I knew we were playing. In this game we didn't talk about anything we'd talked about from February to May. Not my anger at Henry James or my mother or his father or Lillian's book or Harry Buckminster or Jeremiah or how it felt to touch. By not talking about it, he became simply Demeter's boyfriend.

Sensing my unease, although not its source, Demeter reassured. "Don't worry. He's nothing like Doctor Folkenflick."

"Totally different league," Will said. "He gets flown in by movie stars in Paris, royalty in Monaco."

She reached for my hand and squeezed it. "What Will says is, why not see if it helps Persephone, even a little relief."

Henry James drummed two fingers on the table, singing along—*ba da ba da ba da ba da bap*—to something in his head. I'd lost him again; it wasn't hard to lose him when this illness came up. He didn't want to think about what was happening to my mother and Persephone. It made him even more depressed about living here, his urban jolliness replaced by complaining or sleeping. This was Henry James without music, as he'd always warned me.

I was strangely happy, though, despite Henry James, despite Will and Demeter. I went to bed each night looking forward to my morning in the woods. I couldn't stay away, not even after I found a few ticks crawling on me. I simply traded sandals for sneakers and pulled socks over jeans.

But then, toward the end of July, a few days before a seed exchange in Savoy, I stopped going altogether, because my time alone came to an abrupt end.

ii

THE CAMP DIRECTOR, IN HER STRAW HAT, STOOD AT THE EDGE OF the parking lot, deterring all of us who hadn't checked our emails, or had checked but ignored the one from camp since they were always emailing about sunscreen and which snacks were appropriate and what follow-up questions we might ask at home, emailing so often who could read them all?

Just an excess of caution, she told us. Just a few days. She'd never seen anything quite like this. "Six, seven, eight on a single kid. We pull them off safely, but why not wait for this phase to calm down. Think of it as nature-inside day!"

It occurred to me there in the parking lot that if my mother could take Persephone, why not my children as well? At least for an hour or two. I left them in the foyer, ran up the stairs.

"You're not her." My mother's disappointed voice came from the recliner.

"Oh!" I heard a woman say with alarm.

As my eyes adjusted, I saw a shape across the room on a stool and a man stretched out on the bed, his hair thick and dark against her white pillowcase. He introduced himself as Kiran. "And you must be the daughter. The resemblance is . . . JK, I can barely see you. Well, should we start with colors? I'm having a green day myself. Edged with cyan. The color of oak leaves in June, if anyone can remember those. Joanie? You're up next, honey."

Joanie? Who dared diminutize Joan Yalen?

"We don't do colors without Persephone," my mother said. "She's never late. Eve, use your phone and ask Demeter when she's coming."

"Can I say something?" the woman on the stool asked. "I'm feeling uncomfortable."

"You want the bed, there's room," Kiran said. "Get your skinny ass over here."

"It's not that. She knows my husband."

"Who does?"

"Eve," said the woman.

"Nina?" I could see it now, the ponytail, the crossed runner's legs.

"You know each other?" Kiran asked. "This fucking town. It's so adorable I want to die."

My mother crossed the room, setting a hand on Nina's arm. "The infamous Aengus. Well, Eve, are you planning to see him anytime soon?"

"I mean, we're not . . . Nina, you know. We're friendly but not . . . There's the party. The midsummer party's this weekend, right? We'll be there, of course. We're coming, if that's what you're worried about."

"The fucking party," Kiran said.

"We'll deal with the party later," my mother said. "We decided. One thing at a time. Eve, you can't say *anything* to Aengus about Nina. We're not dealing with rationality. We're dealing with projection and denial."

"Are you sick, Nina?" I asked. "I'm so sorry."

My mother sighed. "Sick. What a word."

"What a societal concept," Kiran said. "As false as the gender binary. Are you *healthy* then, Eve?"

"Can you promise not to say anything to him?" Nina said. "He'll take the kids. He said he would."

"Take them where?"

"He thinks she's making this up," my mother said. "As if anyone would choose to."

I felt my arms grow cold. I'd refused her breakfast invitation, pissed she wanted to take away my time alone, but I wondered now if she'd only wanted to ask about Emily without Aengus around.

A voice called from the landing. "Ready or not, I'm coming in!"

The door opened, quickly shut. My mother clapped. "Aren't you a sight for sore eyes. If I could see you."

"You're sounding gorgeous yourself," Persephone said, removing her glasses and throwing them in the middle of the room where, I noticed now, three pairs of sunglasses gathered. The sound of clinking glass came from a pillowcase in her hand, weighed down like a Halloween stash. "I brought supplies! More of my tinctures in exchange for some of those chocolatey raisin things. There's bee venom again. There's silver something."

"I always wanted to be metallic," Kiran said. "Hand that over, girl."

"Eve's here." There was warning in my mother's voice.

Persephone gasped. "Eve? I really need you not to tell my mom I'm sharing this. She'd be so mad. She thinks it's gonna—"

"Eve isn't breathing a word," my mom said. "That's been established. No snitching, talking, spilling, not to Aengus, not to Demeter."

Persephone dropped the pillowcase and threw her arms around me. Gone was the sulk and slither of the first time I brought her here. "Will you do something for me?"

I'd do anything. I was so happy to see her return to exuberant girlhood.

She fished a small envelope from her pillowcase. "Will you give this to—"

"Of course, of course," I interrupted, imagining Sonya's happiness, the friends rejoined, and how much easier my summer would be. "She's right downstairs."

"No, I mean . . . if you see anyone like us. Give it to them."

"Anyone like . . . ?"

"Us," Kiran said.

"But . . . where would I?"

"Anywhere," Persephone said.

"We need food, too," my mom said. "Basic sustenance, darling. Nina likes mochi and Persephone wants chocolate raisins and Kiran, it's the peanut butter for you? Our gratitude for this knows no bounds, but if you could go now? We need to get started."

I asked what they were starting. Drawn by the energetic pulse in the room, I hoped they'd invite me to stay. I was Joanie's daughter after all.

"We'd tell you but we'd have to kill you," Kiran said, laughing. "Come, Perse, sit with me."

"Not kill," Persephone said, climbing onto the bed. "Just nauseate."

ON THE WAY TO Stop & Shop, Sonya complained. There was no actual logical reason why she couldn't go to camp. Who cares about ticks? Nobody cares. Fiona says they can't get you sick. Sonya taught her Greentime and when they stand up, they pull ticks off each other like gorillas.

"Don't do that," I said. "Don't lie down."

I filled the cart. I wanted Nina to have her mochi, Persephone her chocolate raisins. I was moved by the sight of my mother happy. I hadn't been the one to lift her spirits, but I knew to appreciate the upswings, however short-lived.

I left the kids in the car and carried the snacks upstairs, pausing outside the door to listen. I heard Kiran describing a childhood closeness to his father. He talked about fortresses built from cardboard and how after school he'd relay every detail of what happened when they were apart. But since he'd returned home to live with this darkness, he said, he grew furious whenever his dad came near, and although Stephen was always inviting him to do things, some of which were things he could do in the dark and would actually enjoy, he couldn't, he just couldn't let himself.

"You can't deny the need to separate," my mother said. "It's too much to be so physically dependent on someone. How could you be emotionally close, too?"

Was she talking about me? I pressed my ear against the door, but it was Persephone who spoke.

"There was this moment," Persephone began, "when I just didn't like playing make-believe anymore. It happened when I was living in the Healing Hut, and then when I saw my friends again. Well . . ." She laughed. "Your grandchildren, Joanie, when I saw them again, I mean, I love them, but I didn't want to put on a play about fairies. I forced myself because I didn't know what else I could care about. I didn't know what else I could want."

"And have you thought about it since?" my mother asked. "What you want?"

"I want to sit outside the bubble tea place in the middle of the day. Like on those little chairs?" Persephone said quickly. "Like drink bubble tea with some people my age, like teenagers?"

"I want to run," Nina said. "I want to run on a trail where I don't see any people at all, just the trees and the way the leaves make shadows on the ground."

"Not me," Kiran said. "I want the city. I want a bar, a dark bar, but not this level of dark. Enough light that I can see a man, look at him, that moment when he notices me looking at him."

"Will you sing, Joanie?" Nina asked.

My mother began to sing, my own mother. "Swing low," she began in a deep voice that I didn't so much remember as feel in my body, like it was coming from inside me. "Sweet chariot. Coming for to carry me home." I listened until the song ended and then I left the bag at the top of the stairs and took my children home.

iii

WHAT DID I LOVE ABOUT GOING TO THE SEED EXCHANGE?

Nothing, because camp remained closed and Lev wouldn't let me touch him with sunscreen and Sonya would rather eat worms than get in a hot car and when we finally started driving, doubts began crawling on me, finding me a welcome host. I wasn't helping anybody. Sightflower/*Quadrillium gulielmus* was gone, wasn't it? The warming winters, wet springs, trees leafing early, knotweed moving in. The spring ephemerals, those brief little blooms, were too late now, shaded out.

"Mom, you're driving right by it." Sonya pointed to paper thumbtacked to a tree that read SEEDS THIS WAY.

The few people remaining at Foxfire Farm were packing up, hefting tubs and folding tables. I left the kids in the shade and asked a man sorting envelopes in a shoebox for my seed. Without looking up, he said he'd already told me he didn't have it. I explained that this was impossible. He took off his sunglasses. "Right. Someone else then."

"Are you with the other guy?" a woman asked, slamming a cooler in the trunk of her car. "I told him I'd never heard of it."

In an idling red sedan, the driver looked at her phone. She rolled down the window and I wanted to climb inside for the cool air. "A man here was asking for the exact same. You might want to get in touch with him."

"But he doesn't have it, either."

"Well, he seems like he won't take no for an answer, so he'll probably find it soon. Thought he was going to reach over the table and take my stash. When you see him, tell him that's not the vibe here. Not at all." I checked my email standing there, the field emptying around me, but no, nobody had responded when I said I was coming to this seed exchange. Ruth, Stephen, Will—none of them had offered to come along.

iii

THE VEGETARIAN RESTAURANT HAD BEEN IN THIS SPOT, MENU UNchanged, since the 1980s. Plants hung from the high ceiling and dripped their boughs down support poles. Women in black shirts offered iced herbal tea. Only one of them was wearing a thousand-dollar bangle.

She rushed over. "You three in my restaurant, how fun is this?" Then her expression fell. "I wish Perse could be with us."

"But she'd get sick," Lev said.

Demeter cupped his cheek. "Right you are. Here"—she grabbed menus—"Minh's swamped. I'll seat you." As she led us to a table, she told me that Ishmael's tinctures were beyond belief, totally transformed Persephone's mood.

I saw Kiran reaching out his hand. *I always wanted to be metallic.* "She likes being at my mom's."

Demeter frowned. "Totally. Your mom's a godsend. I've started working lunch and dinner, not breakfast. After Will drops Perse off, I weave and he cooks, puts on music." She pulled out chairs for Sonya and Lev. "Get this, he knows someone who runs a gallery in Brooklyn who might be interested."

"In what?"

"In my weavings, Eve! Seriously. Mine. I never thought I'd have time for my own art, much less . . . Hold on." She rushed to a table where a man was scribbling in the air.

And if my mother watched my children instead of hers? And if Henry James brought me breakfast while I wrote? I let myself roll up my cuffs and wade into the muck of envy. I saw her laughing with another waitress, slip her arm around her waist and lean her head on her shoulder. The gold bracelet slid up her arm. I didn't even like it, but I wanted to be gifted—a bracelet, a loom, a coffee.

Eating my naked white cubes of tofu, which lay immodestly on a bed of brown rice, I noticed a woman in sunglasses and a large white sun hat. She wore a Red Sox sweatshirt and sat with a younger woman who was leaning over her stir-fry. The older woman didn't eat. She pressed her fingers into her temples.

I told my kids I'd be right back. I reached into my bag and held out the envelope to the older woman. The daughter grabbed my hand. *To: Person with Emily,* she read aloud and then pushed my hand away. "Not for us. That's not what Mom has."

The mother plucked the envelope from my fingers. "That's not your beeswax, Sal."

Back at my table, I pulled up Ishmael's website on my phone. The home page was clever; bees burst onto white and then dimmed again. I clicked on the bee labeled "Our Staff." Ishmael had a tanned face, trimmed white hair, an easy smile that suggested a modest unambivalence.

Should I pay him to help my mother? How would we afford that?

A stray thought forced its way to consciousness: Will had been out of town on the day I first heard about a man asking for the seed. What about this morning? Had he been home when Demeter was weaving?

When Demeter came to check on us, I asked. I didn't want her to say no.

"Yeah, not today."

Oh shit, I thought.

"Where was he?"

"Yeah, I don't know. Boston? Some work thing?" She waved at the waitress she'd been touching. "But we'll see you Saturday? At Aengus's thing? The summer party?"

My kids kept talking to me. The ice water was too cold, they said, the food too hot, why can't they go to camp. I clicked on the bee labeled "Testimonials." Each entry sung with the sweet nectar of remedy: After Ishmael's tinctures and therapies, her arthritis was gone, his back pain, her vertigo, her lifelong stomach upset, his body malaise, all gone, gone, entirely gone.

I wanted a cure like that, complete and unequivocal. I wanted it for my mother and Kiran and Nina and Persephone and for my children who lay down in the grass. And I wanted to find it by myself.

Ruth

. . .

SHE TAKES HER MORNING BREAK ON THE LIBRARY STEPS AFTER air-conditioning has fully chilled her. Patrons, heading up, talk to her of the shocking heat. Or wilted from it, they nod in anticipation of hers. Wasn't this enough of a life? She has plenty of second thoughts. Young lesbians have signed a lease on her condo, as emphatic and in love as she and Ramona were. "This'll be your room," they said to the toddler with matted dark hair who climbed onto Orion's unused bed and rolled around.

It was easy to clear out the condo, not so easy the storage unit. She tried once and then called Stephen for help, although she wasn't sure he'd be up to the task and brought along her flowers of Minnesota dishrag for him to cry into. But he was dry-eyed and gallant, and it was Ruth who used the dishcloth. He asked for her memories of Ramona with each moth-eaten sweater, boxed up the Lego figurines for Orion, brought everything they didn't want to the hospice thrift store.

She hasn't told Orion, who might say he's too busy. Or Jessie, who told her not to text or call, never to visit. But this isn't a visit.

She hasn't even told Eve, she realizes, when she sees her slogging up the steps with her children. She's just not sure Eve would approve. She's a mother, such a mother. Would she leave the home her child might someday return to? Ruth's resolve is too feeble; one stern word and she'll be telling the lesbians sorry.

She's happy to see Eve, though. "Well, hello. Can you explain? There's been a steady cavalcade of children for days now. Why this sudden summer turn toward literature?"

"Camp's closed," says the girl, a short version of Eve, same brown curls, same skeptical look.

"Indefinitely. Because of ticks." Eve's eyebrows rise, head cocks. Ruth returns the gesture.

"And the spray park, too," says the boy who's holding Eve's hand while hopping up one step and down again.

"That's because of the drought," says the girl. "So, not the same."

"But we can't go there, which means it's the same." The boy stops hopping and looks up at Ruth.

"I hope you can stake some ground among the hordes," she says.

"Actually, I was hoping to . . . You busy?"

Eve sets up the kids with the jigsaw in periodicals. Sonya points to the sign in a picture frame, REMINDER! CHILDREN MUST BE IN HAND'S REACH OF CAREGIVERS AT ALL TIMES. Ruth tips it over, face down. She always hated these signs. Give the parents a fucking break. In Ruth's office, Eve takes the stool and worries the hem of her shirt as she talks about Will, never home on the days of the seed swap. And a man keeps asking for Sightflower. She thinks it could be Will, going on his own. "I think it's because he's with my best friend."

"Is that a thing? Are men and women who aren't dating not allowed in the same church basement?"

"It might make him feel weird."

"But he's your friend, too. And anyone would want to go to a seed exchange with you. So let's play this out. What if it is Will, but not because he doesn't want to be with you. What do you really know about him?"

"Everything," Eve says, describing his childhood in Salt Lake City; his father's early death; his on-and-off lover, his hoarder mother. And of course Quinn, the guilt about Quinn.

Ruth stares at her wall, shifting the pieces this way and that until a picture is revealed.

Last fall, sitting at the river waiting for the teenagers to leave so they could swim naked, Jessie told Ruth a story. In the nineties, when she was protecting a redwood from slaughter by living high in its branches in the Nanning Creek Grove, she became close with a man in her affinity group who turned out to be a career employee of the FBI. She didn't learn this until years later. His was a long con. While undercover, he married a friend of Jessie's. They had two children together, and he stayed home to care for them, or pretended to stay home, because what was work? What was home?

"I don't get it," Eve says. "You think Will's working for the FBI?"

Ruth sits backward on her chair, hands on the backrest. "The FBI? FBI doesn't care about medicine or health. Who does, Eve? Think."

Eve shakes her head. "I don't get it."

"A pharmaceutical company. That's who cares. Is he the spy he always warned us about?"

At the same moment, they turn to their phones. "It's Rothstein, right?"

"No, Rothenberg. I'm pretty sure."

There are too many Will Rothenbergs/Rothsteins/Rothbergs, and not enough. None from Salt Lake City. None look like Will.

"No, this is ridiculous." Eve sets her phone on the desk, face down, a definitive gesture. "Quinn's dead. Will wouldn't take this job. And he hates pharma companies. He was furious at Jeremiah, the man he was in love with—because his dad did something with OxyContin. He'd never work with them. I think he's just avoiding me."

Ruth tries to urge her along. "What if there is no Quinn? No Jeremiah?"

"But there is. There was."

"What if some spy—let's call him Bob—was sent here after someone in a billion-dollar company read Stephen's Reddit post and saw the monetary potential? Bob made up a story about a conveniently dead boyfriend and then insisted we couldn't tell anyone else about Lillian's book."

Ruth can tell Eve doesn't want to follow this path. "I know him. I really do."

She reminds Eve how Will begged them for secrecy, how strange the rest of them initially found this.

"But what if the person going to the seed exchanges is just Bob? An actual pharma spy. Not Will."

Ruth nods. "Sure. There's only one way to find out."

"Which is?"

"Ask him."

Eve picks up her phone again as if to call him, then puts it down. "Or Stephen? We haven't talked about Stephen."

Stephen wouldn't even take Ramona's purple wineglasses or the plates with morning glories until Ruth swore she didn't want them. "Believe me, I've known him a quarter century. He lives for collaboration. He invented integrity." It was Stephen who told her to go see Orion first, saying, "Orion's a kid. So he doesn't call you. So he doesn't visit. You show up for him anyway." And this is her plan, to be that kind of dad, to show up at Orion's as a dad might, full of regret and a flame of love.

"It's true I never understood where all Will's money comes from," Eve says finally.

They talk about his voluminous resources—paying for the Healing Hut and Ishmael and the gold bangle and his apartment, all without working. And how convincing he was when he pretended to be looking at herbaria for an acting role, and he never could remember whether Quinn had a tick bite, and he told Eve his mom was Meg, a hoarder who lived in Dorchester while he told Ruth she was Elizabeth and he visited her in Florida, and what is he doing here all summer now that the search for Sightflower has basically ended; they talk themselves into this answer, until it becomes the puzzle's only solution, and there's a knock on the door. The girl wants her mom to walk her to the bathroom. Ruth stands with Eve and the boy outside.

"What about his wife?" Eve asks.

"Will has a wife?"

"The FBI agent. The activist he married? What happened to her? Did he continue to have a relationship with his kids? How could she deal with that betrayal?"

"With fury, I imagine. And grief. The person you loved doesn't exist, that's a death, too."

Eve's face turns young when she asks Ruth to talk to Will with her. "Please? I can't do it alone."

Ruth tells her then, tells her everything, it comes pouring out of her. She can't really bring herself to look at Eve.

"But what if—"

"What if Jessie tells me to get the hell out of there? Don't think I haven't thought of that." Ruth feels narrow and defensive. "What if she's with someone? Or happy alone? Or what if she refuses to see me because I drove there and that's unconscionable to her?"

"No!" Eve laughs a little. "I wasn't going to say that, not any of that. Just, what if I need you? What if I . . . Oh, I'm happy for you. I really am. But I'll miss you here. We all will." Eve throws her arms around Ruth's shoulders, pressing her tightly.

She returns the hug, this unexpected burst of body, of love, although she doesn't know who *we* is. Perhaps Eve meant the kids, or she could have meant the royal *we,* although Eve is prone more to shrinking herself than aggrandizing, or maybe *we* is just this, the library and its patrons, one of whom, twitchy and pale, walks unsteadily into the bathroom just as Sonya leaves it and maybe he's okay, maybe not, but either way Ruth will stand here until he's out, making sure.

Midsummer Party

. . .

WAS THIS THE LAST GARDEN PARTY? THE LAST BLITHE OUTDOOR romp? Bare ankles, bare thighs, bright skirts, black sandals.

Kids played in the meadow behind Aengus and Nina's house. How could they resist? "Just check them," mothers were saying to one another on the patio. "We'll just check them real well when they get back." "A tick has to stay on you for a long time to get you sick."

I kept my eyes on the kitchen door, although I was hoping they wouldn't come at all, and I wouldn't have to go through with a plan that was feeling increasingly irrational. Ruth was leaving soon, so I'd suggested we confront Will at this party. But that was days earlier when I'd been riding high on righteousness and betrayal. Now I just wanted to go home, to pretend I'd never talked to Ruth. Most likely he'd been avoiding me, nothing else. Surely he could tell how often I still thought of our time together, could peer into the fantasies I still played out and, embarrassed for me, he snuck out to the seed exchanges alone.

The conversation among the mothers was about camp closures. Had anyone found space indoors for the long slog of August? Circus was full, what about the rock climbing gym? One mother said, in the soft melodic cadence of passive aggression, "I really don't want to speak for anyone else, but I tend to think this is nature reminding us that it's summer and we should be spending time with our own kiddos, not shipping them out."

"She and her sister are thick as thieves, she couldn't stay away," I heard Aengus at the grill tell another father. "New baby. I told her to bottle the smell and bring it back to me."

This was the excuse he kept giving for Nina's absence. Later I'd learn she stayed at my mother's that night.

Standing by a white pom of hydrangea in the limbo between fathers and mothers, Henry James chuckled at a bit of wit on his phone. When he looked at the kitchen door and waved, I assumed Will and Demeter had arrived. My stomach clenched. Could I go through with this?

I was surprised to see that he was waving at Ruth in a short-sleeved blue button-down. Henry James began thanking her for a book she'd found for him in Russian through great feats of connivance from an academic library in Boston. I'd known about the book but not that Ruth was involved. He threw an arm around my shoulder. "This is my wife, who dragged me to the party on the pretense that my only friend in this town would be here."

Ruth winked at me. "Yalen, is it? Lover of the novel by mid-century British women, dodgers of the blitz, bored housewives."

Henry James looked confused. "So you two . . . ?"

"I'm the librarian. Assume I know everything about everyone." She held up a six-pack. "Who's the host of this thing?"

"Guy with the spatula." Henry James pointed to the grill.

"With the ponytail? Pain in my fucking ass. Asks if I'll shut off the internet to preserve the sanctity of the printed word. Every time he comes in. You know, this might be my last chance . . . Hold on." She headed to Aengus.

Henry James's arm felt too heavy on my shoulder and I pulled out of his embrace. Hurt crossed his face, but he turned to his phone, saying, "So, if they don't come soon, I'll just leave and pick you up later."

The gulf between us pained me. Now that we lived together, I felt compelled to stay further apart. Why? I didn't know exactly, just that I needed a hedge of privacy. On the other side of this hedge: my walks in the woods, my neophyte happiness. I hadn't told him anything—not about Lillian's book or the seed exchanges or Antonia's or the botanical garden with Will.

As if beckoned, Demeter and Will appeared through the sliding door, aglow from the skimming light. With his hand in hers, I saw him as the man he'd been all summer—attentive, even borderline uxorious. Was there really a corporate face beneath this, the bland smile of a stooge?

Henry James thumped them each on the back, crowing with delight. "I thought I'd have to talk to someone new, what horror." I avoided contact with Will by turning to Demeter, running my hands down the arms of her linen shirt. "So pretty!" I'd never been nervous to talk to her before. "You know what I was just thinking about? That Jesus painting in Ernesto and Hilda's apartment."

"So bloody, so awful! But we had so much fun there, didn't we?"

"The most fun ever." It will be okay. That's what I was trying to tell her. If Will isn't Will, I'll be your floor like before.

Looking at her, I felt my resolve return. If she was living with a fraud, a liar, shouldn't I find out? I asked Henry James to fetch sangria for everyone, knowing Demeter would rush to help and Will and I would be alone at last.

"Eve!" He offered his profligate grin. "How are you, even? I feel like we never talk."

"My mom," I said, hedging. "I'm busy with her."

"The famous Joan Yalen! I hear a lot about her, you know. From Persephone. She's incredible with Persephone."

"I know. I'm so glad."

He tilted his head. "But does it feel a little strange? After the way she treated you? The party she threw when you went to college?" He groaned, tugged on his buoyant hair in a mime of anger. "Jesus. And now she's totally committed to this kid she's not related to. Does that suck a little?"

How was it possible that they, the nameless corporation, hired someone who understood me so completely?

"Hold on. Don't go anywhere," I said.

"Staying put."

At the grill, Ruth was gesticulating with a beer bottle. "Okay, but you're not listening. When I said the library's the last gathering place in America where you don't need to buy something or believe in a particular creed, I wasn't only talking about you."

"Ruth," I said.

"What I'm saying is, the computers are a refuge. Is there some porn?

So what? There's also the chance—the only chance for some—to fill out forms, sign up for Medicare, write to your conspiracy theorist aunt on Facebook, find NA meetings."

Aengus slipped his spatula under a burger. "But they wouldn't be needing NA in the first place if they didn't have the hollowness that comes from a life on screens."

"Ruth, please." I felt our opportunity slipping away. Any second, Henry James and Demeter would be back. Or I'd talk myself out of it completely.

She put a hand on Aengus's back. "Dude, you must've had a pretty sweet childhood. Because you have a really weird idea of where pain comes from." She turned to me. "Okay. Let's do it."

Will was standing with his hands clasped behind him, gazing at the smears of pink clouds. "Ruth! I didn't think you'd . . . Are you friends with . . . Hold on, did you two . . . Did you find something?"

"You could say that we did," Ruth said. "I can't think of any other reason why I'd show up at the straightest party in all of Northampton. Hey, Aengus," she shouted. "Mind if we check out your little shed over there?"

THE SMALL ROOM BLINKED with the lights of a router. A monitor on a standing desk; a laptop on a recliner. Ruth and Will faced me expectantly, but I couldn't do it. "Ruth," I said.

She nodded, cleared her throat. "Okay, bro. We're just a little curious about you. A few questions."

Confusion torqued his mouth to an odd half smile. "About me? I think you know—"

"So you'll just clear things up and we can go on our way."

"Is this like a . . ." He turned to me. "Eve? What's going on?"

Ruth clasped her hands behind her back, looking up at him. "Maybe just start by telling us your mom's name."

"My mom's . . . What? What is this?"

"Well, you told Eve it was Meg and she lived in Massachusetts, and you told me you were visiting Elizabeth in Florida, so we're just wondering, which is she?"

He shook his head, still smiling oddly. "You brought me here to ask my mom's name?"

Again he was looking at me. "There's a few more questions," I said quietly.

"Great. Lay them on me. I have plenty of answers."

After every question Ruth asked—was he going to seed exchanges and if not, where was he on the mornings when I went? What was his last name? How had he lived in Northampton for over six months without working? Could he just explain where his money came from? Hadn't he been a high school teacher? When exactly had he lived in New York City?—after every question, he said only, "Got it, what's next?"

Until she said, "That's it. All we want to know."

In the quiet that followed, we could hear a child shout, "Give it back!"

When he finally spoke, he remained Will. Vibrant, awkward, urgent. No mask fell. One finger of his left hand kept tapping his thigh. "I don't know where to start. You both know my whole deal . . . why I'm here. You think I'm richer than I should be? Okay. Sorry. I don't know what else to say about that. I stopped teaching high school a long time ago. What else? Where do I go? To visit my sister. Is that allowed? There were some discrepancies in what I've said? I called my mother my aunt? I said Dorchester when she was in Florida? My god! Grief does that."

I felt like I was losing my balance and said, with a vehemence that surprised even me, "Don't you see? Don't you see that there's something that's not adding up? It's like when you said you were an actor and then you weren't and . . . I'm not being clear." I took a breath. "Just, can you explain more?"

He shook his head without looking at me. "You're asking me to defend who I am. What do I even say to that?" And then he left the shed, the door swinging open.

"Did we fuck up?" I asked, because his face had remained Will's face, no bland stooge, no eyes but the eyes I adored. "He didn't seem like . . . not like someone else."

Ruth was scanning Aengus's bookshelf of motivational books.

"Seriously? He evaded all the questions, explained nothing, didn't even say if he's going to the seed exchanges. Nobody calls their mom the wrong name."

She was right. I grasped this even as I resisted it. Will would have cleared up our concerns, answered our questions. The man I knew—the man I adored—loved to tell me about himself. So who was this man?

WHEN I WALKED BACK into the night air, I heard the mothers calling. The ten-minute warning had passed. The five-minute warning ignored. Come, children, come. Ada! Ida! Amelia! Elias! Oona! All the voweled children must come. Come now, Daisy! Rose! Lily! All the flowers must come. Henry! Charlie! Sam! All the old industrialists must come. Madeline! Sophie! Elise! All heroines of French films must come.

As I joined the mothers walking across the lawn, waving our arms, shouting our children's names, I heard my own. "Eve!" I felt a shiver of relief, as if my own mother were searching for me. All this was over and she would take me from the fields. But it was Demeter who ran up to me. I turned to her with my mouth open, ready to console. First there would be shock, but that would pass into relief. Who would want to live a lie? She had her job, a gold bangle to sell. She had me. I thought of the activist with two children whose husband disappeared from her life. I held Demeter's arms. "Are you okay?"

"Me? I'm great. But Will says he's feeling weird. Stomach thing. So we'll get together next weekend? Tell Sonya . . . tell Sonya we'll get the kids together, we really should." She kissed my cheek.

"What about me?" Sonya asked. I hadn't seen her approaching, but here she was by my side and I hugged her close, so happy to see my daughter.

"Let's go," I said. "Let's go find dessert."

In the sudden dusk, the abrupt turn from blue to murk, who could see the creatures living on the children? Here was the bright candled cake. Here were triangles of watermelon and sugar-free ice-cream sandwiches. Here were sparklers. All along the field, the June bugs struck up a conversation. Starlings darted down like flying parentheses for a better look. Who was the first child who asked to use the bathroom, who refused to pee into the bushes, who wanted ice in her water, who didn't like a blue plate and demanded a green, who dragged a reluctant mother inside, inside where the lights were garishly bright, where nobody wanted to be because all magic was outside? Outside was where children belonged.

The first mother called from the glass door. We shielded our eyes. We looked away from the house's glare.

"Check your kids," she called.

Now the sparklers were dunked into the waiting bucket of water. Don't crowd, stand back, take turns, we said. But each parent pushed their child forward. Inside, we tore off shirts, pants, underwear. Put the clothes outside, someone said. We threw them through the doorway even as more children and parents kept coming through.

We ran our fingers in their soft hair, no matter whose hair it was. We loosened braids, we flattened curls, we separated toes. We passed around tweezers and advice. Pull upward, not sideways. Remember, the nymphs are tiny, the size of a sesame seed.

"It's okay," Aengus kept saying. "No cause for concern."

We knew they couldn't drown in our half-empty cups of sangria and Sauvignon Blanc. Strengthened, they'd crawl up and out, onto Aengus's floor, searching for the heat of an armpit, the sweat of pubis. We pulled Nina's oils from the cabinet. Canola is fine, we said. Anything else is too expensive. But we ran out of canola, and everyone needed a cup, so we used her almond, her sesame, her extra-virgin olive. The kids gathered around to watch them struggle and succumb. The soft skin of the naked kids, had there been anything in nature as beautiful as these bodies? Just when we thought a child was clear, we'd check again and we'd find it. The fleck, the speck, the ick, the tick.

The Ticks

WHY ARE THEY SHOUTING?

Shhh, don't cry, little nymphs. They don't like us on their children.

But they're drowning us. Like we're the intruders.

They're young, you see, and lacking in collective memory.

Don't they know the story?

No. Not like you do.

Tell it again. Start with the lake.

Once upon a time, fifteen thousand years ago, when we were carried here in the fur of a caribou, all of this was a glorious, glacial lake. The water a milky turquoise. Beyond its icy shore, wolfpacks and mastodons. Sloths the size of bears, beavers the size of men. But what we haven't told you yet is that after we moved here, a little bacterium asked to live inside some of us.

It did? Sounds gross.

Don't worry. We don't mind. We're mothers. Who are we to say no to a tired traveler? We already offered rides to Borrelia and Babesia. Come aboard, Sun Madness! After this, when we drank our blood meal, those of us who carried this new bacterium left it behind on our hosts. Here you go, sloths, deer, opossums, raccoons, black bears.

Did they mind?

Only the people did. But there weren't that many of us ticks around. Our favorite hosts, the deer, lived in the edges of forests, and since the forests were continuous, there weren't too many deer. It was a peaceful coexistence.

And now get to the bad part.

Ten thousand years after the first people, the English moved in.

You got worried.

A little. We didn't like it when they named our forests "Northampton" after a town in England with no forests at all. Just meadows. But we tried not to catastrophize. We practiced empathy.

Then they cut down trees and burned them inside their houses.

Sure, and we thought, well, all mothers need to keep their children warm.

Then they cut down trees to grow plants in straight rows.

And we told ourselves that some people don't have the intellectual capacity to know that food is plentiful if you just move around with the seasons.

But then they cut down all the trees! They skinned our forests bare!

That's right, loves. They used some of the wood for shingles and clapboards, for baskets and caskets, for framing buildings and bridges.

But some of it they didn't use. So why'd they do it?

They were scared. A very frightened kind of people.

Scared of the trees?

Scared of anything they couldn't see or understand. Which is most of nature. Scared of what lived in the woods—the wolves and other animals and the people who came here first. In a flash—just a few decades—all our forests were gone. From the top of Mount Skinner, the view was treeless clear to Vermont.

They made it look like England.

That's right. And the weather changed, too. Without trees, the earth froze longer. Snow and rain cascaded down bare hillsides. Centuries of forest mulch poured into rivers, silted millponds, choked fish eggs.

And our hosts started dying!

They did. The forest edge was gone. Goodbye, deer. They killed predator, they killed prey. Goodbye, lynx and elk. Goodbye, moose. Goodbye, mountain lions. Goodbye, beavers. Thirty-nine of us were living on the last bear when it was shot in 1783. Goodbye, bears. We died in terrible numbers.

Tell us about the nymphs from back then, what they said.

The nymphs were scared. They asked, Will we survive? Is this the end? The few of us who remained, living on rats, didn't know how to comfort them. We saw apocalypse in our future.

And now tell the good part.

Well, life is funny, isn't it? Turns out, the English really suck at farming. After just a couple centuries, they wrecked the soil and wanted to sell off the land. And in the cities, with factories and pollution and noise and crowds, people were dreaming of the country. Oh, the pastoral myth—we thank you. Oh, Henry David Thoreau—we can never thank you enough. Two chapters of *Walden* and everyone wanted to return to wildness.

He made them not afraid of forests?

Not exactly. Nostalgic, that's what he made them. Nostalgic for the wild spaces he described. For a time without conflict or cares. It was never really like that here. But nostalgia doesn't care about accuracy. Nostalgia doesn't care about consequence. Bitten by the bug of nostalgia, the city transplants divided the farms and planted trees. Little islets of forest emerged. Ornamental forests cleaved by roads and lawns and housing developments.

And in this kind of forest, our deer and mice are kings.

Yes, nearly all habitat became their kind of habitat—edge of woods, borderland, brink, where they can walk from one world to the next, trees to grass, woods to pavement, dark to light.

Say the other good part. The surprise!

As we started to establish ourselves again, we were shocked to find that they had changed the weather. Big time. We no longer freeze to death in late autumn. Our babies can be born under midwinter stars. And the spring rains! For weeks the air turns water, delighting our chemosensilla, allowing us long hunting jaunts.

We love to hunt!

Well, as mothers, we have a saying: You're only as happy as your least happy nymph. And with this new humidity, this warmth, all these hosts offering blood meals, you're very happy.

And so you're happy, too! Are there other places this nice? Not just Aengus's backyard?

Oh, many forests here we haven't ventured to yet. Mice colonies we've only heard about. But Aengus's backyard and the little woodland beyond have been so welcoming.

Not usually so many people as tonight. Little hairless legs everywhere! We just couldn't help but hop on.

And what a surprise to see Ruth among all the young families. Usually she's alone, running up that same trail. Look, here she is, leaving the party with a wedge of watermelon. Ruth!

Does she hear you?

We can't tell. Oh, Ruth, listen. You've been so curious about us. Did you hear us tell the story? Of why we nearly disappeared and how we came back? Your puzzle, Ruth, is done.

After the Party

...

i

THE CALL I EXPECTED DIDN'T COME. A HUSH FELL OVER OUR house, the town.

I asked my mom if Will was still dropping off Persephone each morning. "Why wouldn't he be? She's the sun around which we revolve. Did you know despite a lack of schooling she's an absolute sponge? We're patching up the gaps in her factual knowledge. No reason she can't take online classes. Her mother could interface with the screen for her."

Indoor spaces were unpleasantly crowded. We stared out of our kitchen window at the woods. "We'll never play Greentime again," Sonya said.

"Of course we will," I said. But how? The mothers had started a text chain. So far, only Zelda and Jasper had come down with a fever. I'd found one tick crawling on Lev's leg, two in Sonya's hair, but I'd been lucky enough to pick them off before they attached. It's the opposite of Covid, one mother wrote. Outdoors is dangerous. Another said, What's the point of living here now?

The only text I wanted was from Demeter. I sought her out at the vegetarian restaurant. She looked so delighted to see us that I knew he hadn't revealed anything. "We're slammed all the time now," she said, apologizing for the long line down the hallway.

"I'm just passing through," I said. "I wanted to see your face."

"I want to see your face, too," she said and made a gesture of a phone on her ear. But she still didn't call and I felt tormented. What would Will say to her? Would he ridicule me for accusing him of spying?

I found it hard to breathe those days for the ache in my chest.

Who was the man with the face of my great-uncle? Had it amused him when I showed up at the gardens repeatedly, thirstily, exposing my deepest longings? Only when I told him about Persephone's sickness had he given me his number, flirted. *There once was a woman named Eve. And I didn't want her to leave.* I knew why he'd sent me to Antonia's—for an excuse to come to Vermont and possibly intercept the plant. But why was he toying with Demeter? I couldn't understand his decision to live with her this summer as part of his persona, except that she was Demeter; she was beautiful and even a spy hungers for beauty.

ii

A FEW EVENINGS LATER, SHE KNOCKED ON OUR DOOR. IT WAS STILL light but hazy, humid, the green watery around us. "Come in," I said. She was wearing sandals and her short hair was damp with sweat. "Did you walk from town? It's too hot for that."

She kept shaking her head, clearly upset, and wouldn't come inside, so I brought a glass of ice water to her. She drank without pausing, wiped her mouth. "Did Will tell you?"

"Tell me what?"

"It's all gone. Clothes, books, car. No note, no text. He's not an asshole. It's not like him."

My first response was relief. Ruth and I hadn't been wrong! Here was proof. "Where'd he go?"

"I thought he might've told you that." She slumped onto the lowest porch step. I sat beside her and flicked a mosquito from her forehead. My second response was worry for her. But I reassured myself: She'd be okay. Nobody wants to love a falsehood. And we still had each other.

"I get it, though," she said.

"Get what?"

"I'm an idiot, that's what. He went through all this with Quinn. Why would he want to do it again? Sit in the dark with my sick teenager? For what? A little time with me? The weirdo who works a menial job, has only ever worked menial jobs, doesn't know anything he talks about? I don't read the news, Eve. I didn't go to Vassar. I didn't finish fucking high school, I didn't . . ."

"Stop, *stop.*" I'd never heard her demean herself before and couldn't let her continue. "This has nothing to do with you."

"So he told you he was leaving?"

Night was falling. I heard the low call of an owl letting the other nocturnal creatures know that it was their time now, all who shunned the sun, they could come out. To explain, I had to start with Sightflower, Lillian's book, but she cut me off. Will had told her of its possibility, the disappointment. "Honestly, I couldn't believe you didn't tell me when we were in Vermont. But he explained you didn't want to crush my hopes, and it's extinct anyway."

I paused to wonder why he'd tell her, why this ploy? And then I explained the truth, at least as I made sense of it: The man she knew as Will might actually work for a pharmaceutical company. His name probably wasn't Will. Was he from Salt Lake City? Did he even go to Vassar? Did Quinn exist? "I think it's all a persona he invented to fit in here."

"Don't do this, Eve."

"Do what?"

"Make up some bullshit to spare my feelings. Like a spy? Come on."

"Will didn't . . ." I paused. I hated having to tell her. "When I confronted him—all these strange things, where he goes on the days of the seed exchanges or why he calls his mom different names or why it seems like he's from New York when he's never lived there or where all his money comes from—he had no answers, Dem. It was kind of shocking, actually."

"You asked him all this?"

"Look, it's awful, but I think he's been lying to us. I'm so sorry."

"When, Eve?"

"When what?"

"When'd you talk to him?"

"Aengus's party."

"At the party? I was there. Why didn't you check with me first? I spend every day with him. I know his mom's name. He tells me whenever he's going places. His sister lives in New York. I could've told you there's no weird mystery."

I tried to think of an excuse. Why hadn't I asked her first? I felt frozen, as if I'd lost something monumental, a wedding ring, a child in a crowd. But really, I'd lost track—of her, of us. I'd been so distracted. Learning to spot the narrow leaves of whorled milkweed and the wide leaves of white milkweed. But that was no excuse.

She climbed the steps and walked the length of my porch. "You know, Will told me what you did. I didn't want to believe it."

I twisted around to watch her. "Told you what?" I thought of his fingers on my thigh. *There once was a woman named Eve.*

"Your dad's precious book? Threw it in the fucking river and did nothing when he accused me? Is that true? Were you really that jealous that I talked to your dad?"

I nodded. My mouth went dry. After all this time, she knew?

"You let him harass my mom, mock her, the most caring woman in the world, who has the shitty karma of spending this life being abused by men. I had nothing that summer."

"I didn't have anything, either," I found myself saying, unable to stop comparing. "You . . . you had a mom who loved you, who told you that you were worthy. Nobody wanted me that summer. You couldn't see that because I had a house with, what? Nice soap? VHS tapes? I wasn't *loved*."

"You still have the house. Here it is." She flung out her arm. "You have a house, a husband, children who go outside, who go to school. You're a grown woman, not a jealous kid. Aren't you? It was all finally working out for me. Why do you care where Will's money comes from? Why'd you get involved?"

"But if there isn't a person named Will wouldn't you want to know?"

She shook her head. "Jesus, Eve, stop. What are you even doing? Deciding the guy I live with has a secret identity? What even is that? My life isn't a fucking book you can throw in a fucking river." Her sandals clicked as she headed past me down the steps.

AT THE SINK, HENRY JAMES REACHED UP A SOAPY HAND TO REmove an earbud. "Is she coming inside? Where's Will?"

This was the moment to tell him. Let's put on a movie for the kids and sit in the backyard. I have something to explain. But there was so much I hadn't said, and I was too upset to begin.

"Demeter was just taking a walk by herself to watch the stars come out."

He laughed. "Sounds like Demeter."

Stephen

...

MOST OF THE VENDORS—IF THEY CAN BE CALLED VENDORS WHEN they're not here to sell—have brought their wares in coolers this time. Stephen's bandanna, doused in ice water an hour ago, lies dry and stiff around his neck. The exchange is hosted by a Waldorf school with Peter Pan painted on the main building. As with all the exchanges, nobody's particularly kind when he asks for Sightflower (*Quadrillium gulielmus*). Varieties and heirlooms are an area of expertise for the vendors. They don't like the suggestion that there's a gap in their knowledge. Stephen, no stranger to pedantry, tries to sympathize. Surely he'd bristle at the possibility that someone knew more than he about the history of the cooperative movement.

Although he's a capitalist now. Ha. A fox in the henhouse. A viper, a vulture. A vendor. Or at least he's trying to be.

A vendor must have a commodity. What else could Stephen sell? His belongings are crap, his house mortgaged, his time worth little, neither his labor nor expertise valued. Will always insisted that a pharmaceutical company would be interested. No, more than interested, that they'd be willing to do or pay anything to learn about a healing plant. Well, Stephen sent emails to every scientist he could find at Johnson & Johnson, Pfizer, Eli Lilly: *I'm a lay scientist of medicinal plants. And I've made an extraordinary discovery that should interest you.*

He received a few politely condescending replies. But a small biotech firm in Boston was intrigued. He drove there, although they insisted that whatever they needed to know could be covered via Zoom. Two young men, barely older than Kiran, brought him to the cafeteria. He was cagey. He wouldn't tell them the name of the plant. He'd learned that much from Will. They seemed to be laughing at him, not bothering to hide the eye rolls they gave each other, but when he told them the illness might be from a tick, they grew serious.

"Ticks are a real growth area. Nature's dirty needles. Impossible to eradicate," they said. "Come back when you have the plant."

"How much?" Stephen asked. "How much would you give me?"

A commodity's value is dependent upon scarcity. The seed is scarce if it exists at all. Neither Stephen nor Eve nor Ruth nor Will knows how to extract its beneficial compounds or test its efficacy. If he finds it, it'll take years for the biotech firm to turn it into something that can help the old woman (will she even be alive?) or the girl (she has more years ahead than Kiran, she can wait). Kiran can't wait. The seed is most valuable before the firm analyzes whether it works as a cure. The amount of money the biotech bros mentioned Stephen might get if he finds the seed? A clean million. Enough for Kiran to have a life.

A real life, he means. Not playing games at a day care center with an old lady and a girl. A life with his friends again. Someone to love him. Someone who loves him enough to live in darkness. Although Kiran is charismatic, creative, kind, Stephen knows the money will help someone love him. They won't have to work. A baby? Why not?

Stephen will be useful then, wanted. Come again really soon, Dad. He knows how to care for a baby. Those were his favorite years.

THIS EXCHANGE IS SET up in a large O, vendors on the inside. He makes it around two-thirds of the clock and then sees Eve walking from the parking lot. Already? She's usually late enough that he can sneak out without her noticing. Unlike practically everyone else, she turns counterclockwise, so the first table she reaches is two away from where he stands.

Competitive power surges through him. He'll push her down if it comes to that. He needs the seed more than she does, he has no doubt. Her mother is an old woman, while his son . . . his son. His son's life stretches ahead of him like a meadow.

He'll admit that things are slightly improved. Kiran wakes mid-morning and asks for a ride to the old woman's house. Coming home, he'll say a few words. "Joan likes some of the music you like. And there's a girl who makes up games." Stephen knows this is the daughter of Eve's friend, the one who always believed it was a tick. She's a young girl, her life an even wider meadow. He's trying not to think about the girl.

If Eve sees him, what'll he say? She'll want to know where he's going next. She'll ask to carpool. He watches her turning toward him and crouches as if to rearrange the contents of his backpack. He wishes there was somewhere to hide and collect his thoughts, but the exchange is set up at the side of the school. Beyond this field, the woods.

"Strange thing," he hears from the nearby table. "Someone was just asking for that."

With a knee on the yellowing grass, his gaze on a stranger's foot, he hears her respond in a steely voice. "Where is he?"

Good question. Where is Stephen who has cared about one thing his whole life? The collective, the communal, the slow but determined subversion of the capitalist stranglehold on our souls.

A fairy tale in which a wish is granted and it destroys the wisher.

Think a child asking for candy from an abductor.

Think cigarettes. The long game.

Think a father who can save his son only if he becomes what he deplores.

First Day with Seeds

. . .

i

STEPHEN? IT COULDN'T BE ANYONE ELSE. THE HAT WITH OWL feathers, the oversize backpack. "Oh no," I said aloud. "Him?"

"Yes, him," repeated the square-jawed man, lifting his sunglasses to stare at me as if I were an idiot.

A woman hummed past me, squeezing between the tables, setting down an iced Dunkin' drink, and dropping heavily in an empty chair. I liked her immediately for the earrings she wore—silver, in the shape of swords—and for her spiky gray hair, which she ran one hand through. "Man, it's hot. Thanks for watching over my supplies." To me she said, "So, what're you looking for? I hope Trager's not giving you a hard time."

"She wants something called Sightflower. Never heard of it but a man here's looking for it, too."

I needed to call Ruth, Demeter, Will. I needed to say I was wrong. I pressed my phone, but its screen blinked and blackened. A godlike green message emerged: *The phone is turning off because of excessive temperature. Reduce temperature and bring to a power source.*

The woman shielded her eyes to look at me. "Sightflower, you said?"

Trager tapped a pencil against his metal tackle box. "The man was looking for it, too."

"I'm not positive, but I believe that's written on an envelope in my basement."

"Well, that presents an ethical question. Who do you give it to? The man asked first."

The woman laughed. "That man? Acting like someone's chasing him to the parking lot?"

I twisted to see Stephen in a wide gallop, one hand clamping his hat to his head, disappearing around the side of the school.

She held out her hand. "I'm Nell. Some people will bend over backwards just to put men first and then find a way to call it ethical."

I asked for her address so that I could come by to get the seeds, but I had nothing for her to write her address on. Without children to provide snacks for, I'd brought only my now-dead phone and car key.

"How about now? You don't mind a little walk, do you?"

I EXPECTED TO BE led through the parking lot to the quaint residential streets beside the church, but she took off briskly across the field. She wore cargo shorts, hiking boots, a purple tank. In my sandals, I had to hurry to keep up.

"It's just down this path," she said as we entered the woods. Branches staunched the sun; gnats hummed at my eyes and mouth. "You have a problem with rabbits?"

"Rabbits?"

"It was my sister who grew Sightflower. Swore nothing else kept rabbits away like it did. When she died last year, I collected the seeds, although why, I don't know. Habit, I guess." She laughed. "I find that fences take care of rabbits just fine."

"But your sister's plant? Is it still growing?"

"Oh, her garden's gone. New owners put in one of those aboveground pools with the flamingo blow-ups. Paved the rest. It was a glorious thing, though, her garden. I'm half the gardener she is, but I love seeds. Sometimes, when I can't sleep because of what we've done to the planet, the only way to get my heart to slow down is to think about that fortress in Norway. You hear of it? They put every seed in there. Every seed. All our future in there. Whoever's still around to plant it. Here, we turn here." She placed her palm on a wooden post at the intersection between two narrow, overgrown paths. "My granddaddy put that here, to show the way. We call it the Nelson shortcut."

"So your family lived here a long time?"

"Came over on the Mayflower."

"Long time."

"Come on." She shot me a stern look. "My people were servants and millworkers. A few broom sellers."

We crossed a river on a stone bridge then walked uphill in dense forest, finally emerging into a clearing with fenced vegetables and overflowing flower beds and a fenced, bouncing child.

I must have gasped. She laughed. "You okay?"

"Just . . . your garden is so beautiful."

"Nana!" the boy called. "Nana, Nana, look at me."

"Oh, I see you on that trampoline. I see you."

He gave the specific and beatific smile of being seen.

INSIDE THE YELLOW HOUSE, a younger version of Nell with a dark brown bob sat on a kitchen chair peeling an orange, bare feet pressed against the table.

Her mom kissed her ear.

"Wait, I didn't hear the car. You walk here? Did you leave the car at the seed thing?" She began laughing. To me she said, "Someday Mom'll leave the car at the side of the highway and decide she'd rather walk to Hartford."

"I'm just getting this lady seeds from the basement."

The daughter laughed again. "What, and the three coolers you lugged out of here this morning wasn't enough?"

SMELLING OF PINE AND mold, the basement held a coldness I hadn't felt in months. Antique chairs climbed one another, a wooden secretary desk propped up boxes collapsing from the weight of time. "That's the past," Nell said. "And over here's the future." She brought me to a drafting table with jars and envelopes, Sharpies, labeling stickers. Beside it, a bureau painted white with pink handles. She looked through drawer by drawer. "Oh boy. What if I brought you all the way here under false pretenses? Maybe I threw it away after all."

It took an hour, a year, a decade for her to squat at the bottom drawer and lift up an envelope. "This it?" She held it upside down. It said Sightflower.

"Watch out." I worried the seeds would fall from the open lip.

Pressing the envelope to her chest, she made her way to standing. "I miss my sister. I can't tell you how much."

An exchange implied a transfer of goods, but I had only a dead phone and a car key. I said I'd send her a check for the work she'd done collecting the seeds.

She began walking upstairs. "What did I do? The plant grew. The plant went to seed. I had nothing to do with it. Use it in health. That's what I always say when I give away seeds. Use these in health."

In the kitchen she said that she might take a brief nap before facing the sun again. "You were paying attention? How we got here?"

I said I was.

"It's not hard. But sit a minute. Drink some water."

Later I would think that sentence over as if it could give me a cool drink, but at the time, I just said no, I was fine.

Indeed I'd never felt so extraordinary. I folded the envelope and slipped it in the pocket of my jean shorts, which didn't seem ceremonious enough, so I took it out and showed it to her. "I really am so grateful."

"Well, I certainly hope it helps. But you can always try a fence. Rabbits aren't very smart."

Outside, the boy bounced, the harnessed tomatoes spilled over their cages, the peas climbed their stakes. Kale, red leaf, chard, cilantro. My seeds in my pocket. We would use them in health. My mother would be cured and Persephone and Kiran and the woman from the vegetarian restaurant and Nina, all of them blinking into the sun. I took off running in my sandals into the woods.

BACK ON THE STONE BRIDGE, I pulled the envelope from my pocket and peered inside. Four black dots, smaller than ice-cream sprinkles, larger than poppy seeds. Impossible to believe they contained the green tendrils of a healing plant, but didn't my microscopic ovum and Henry James's seed become Sonya, didn't the black speck of a tick contain illness that sent you into darkness?

The sun made me woozy and I was drunk off the seeds. I tasted certainty like metal in my mouth. I felt within me the black solidity of soil.

I wasn't afraid of losing my way, not really, not even when I was climbing over a congress of felled logs, their soft, barkless trunks infested by ants, and I knew we hadn't passed here before. I figured I'd soon find the school and its field. I kept the river on my left and didn't understand how it was suddenly on my right and very far beneath me, churning narrowly between two granite cliffs furred with bright moss. But I felt so good that I didn't want to turn around, to retrace. I liked the forward motion. My sweat-wet shirt clung to me.

When my path became a deer trail and disappeared into undergrowth, I finally turned around. But the trail I returned on didn't seem to be the trail on which I'd come. Instead of fallen logs with light wood eaten by insects, here were burnt trees with stumpy, charred branches still smelling of fire. I turned again and instead of burnt trees, I came to a bramble of blackberry bushes. I ate more than my stomach could take, my fingers purpling, an ink I transferred to the envelope when I checked once more on the seeds.

I walked for a long time in one direction and then another, never crossing familiar land. Blisters stung my feet, so I removed my sandals and held them. Soon my heel was pierced by sharp rocks and I stubbed my toes on tree roots. When I saw a light through the woods, a clearing, I strapped on my sandals and ran, not stopping even when a branch gouged deep into my shin.

I found a meadow. From here I could see no school, no church, no roads, no mown lawns, no houses, no fields of corn or potato or tobacco, no cultivation, no human stamp of industry, only more woods and a pond with a skin of vibrant green scum that I was tempted to push out of the way in order to drink the water below.

Although I didn't dare drink the water, my stomach began cramping, and I crouched behind a tree to shit. I saw that the cut on my shin was dripping blood over my feet. I wiped myself with leaves and kept walking.

The trees began to suck away the daylight. When it was fully dark, I was thirsty, so thirsty, but I wasn't scared. I knew I'd find my car in the morning. Or I would act like Nell and just leave it, walk home along the highway, never use it again. Of course I thought of Henry James and his worry. I thought of my children and how he would lie to them. Oh, Mom called, she's fine. And Mom was fine. Mom was fixing everything.

I lay down and closed my eyes. I saw plants, all the plants I'd walked through that day, and I wanted to name them, although it was dark and my phone was dead. The trees watched me all night.

Second Day with Seeds

. . .

i

I WOKE WITH DIRT IN MY EAR, MY MOUTH THICKLY GUMMY, LEGS smeared with dried blood and welted with bites. I was desperate for water. The back of my shirt and shorts were dewy, but the envelope, which I'd held in my hands all night, was only slightly damp. I looked at my seeds. I still had the core of certainty, the metallic taste of it, the sunken soil of it, and it told me to listen.

I laughed when I noticed the sound of traffic. I walked toward the noise, holding my sandals. Cold threads of spider webs bothered my lips and nose. It was Sunday morning and cars came only occasionally. When I lost track of the road, I would stop and wait, because I didn't want to walk the wrong direction anymore.

There was an edge to these woods after all. A border. An in and an out, and I was out, on a road littered with rusting beer cans, staring at a sign for a gas station.

"Hello," I called out at Joe LaRue's Repair and Gas. A single full-service pump. The smell of oil and lubricants. "Anyone here?"

The boy was young, a rash on one cheek, incredulous that I'd left my car at a school in Savoy. "Although . . ." He waved his hand at me. "You do look a little . . . Here." He handed me a long wrench welded with a ring that held a single key.

In the bathroom mirror I saw a woman who wasn't a mother. That's what I thought at the sight of my face, but then I wondered what I meant. The answer came to me. A woman who wasn't afraid. Yes, that was it. I wasn't afraid. I washed the dirt from my face, pressed my eyes against the unhygienic cloth that emerged from and receded into a white box on the wall. I wet toilet paper and scrubbed the blood from my legs and feet and arms. I was so busy cleaning that I forgot, and when I remembered, I pressed my hand against my pocket to feel the crinkle of envelope.

The boy offered his yellow sports drink. "Slow down or you'll puke," he said, locking the shop. His car smelled like lemons. We rolled down the windows and didn't talk until we saw my car by itself in the school parking lot.

I sipped the yellow drink as I waited in my car for my phone to charge. The first four messages were from my mom:

> We areout of toilet apper and paper
> Towels. When can Yo do a grocery?
> Eve? Could you go today?
> Did you hear me? We need paper
> Pro Ducks.
> Pro Ducks

The rest from Henry James:

> Didn't you say you'd be back for Sonya's
> 4pm thing.
> What's her thing again?
> Am I supposed to take her somewhere?
> She says she doesn't know. But she'd
> like to see you. And Lev too, would like
> to see you.
> What's your eta?
> Hello? It's your long suffering husband
> here about to die from the Busytown
> game. Call the banana-ambulance.
> Bananbulance.
> Eve! Wtf?
> ?
> ???
> Okay, I'm nervous. Can you just say

you're okay?
Should I call the police? I'm assuming your car broke down and your phone died, but can you use someone else's phone.
Eve. Please.
It's two am. I'm going to bed. If I can sleep. I really hope I hear from you.
Eve? I don't even know why I'm writing you. I've called the police to give them our license plate but they say after eighteen hours you're not yet a missing person. I miss you, person.

ii

HENRY JAMES DROPPED THE CHAPTER BOOK AND STOOD FROM THE couch. I knelt before my children astonished by their beauty, their foreheads, their mouths. "But I'm fine," I said, kissing tears from their cheeks. "I got lost. Can you believe it? Mom got lost on a walk and had to sleep in the woods. But it was all fine. The woods took care of me."

Lev nosed into my armpit. "You smell."

I asked what I smelled like, and Sonya bent to my other armpit. "How you always do but more. Were the woods scary? Did you get a tick?"

"Not even one. I checked so many times. I think I was too deep in. They like the edges, where the mice and deer are. So no problem for me!" But even as I reassured them that I was fine, all was fine, I grew impatient. I wanted them to sense my transformation—to see me as a hero returning, marked by battle wounds, the glow of triumph too bright for the dull house—not to ask, as Sonya did, about swim class. "Do we really have to go?"

"Dad didn't remember so we didn't tell him," Lev said.

Henry James shrugged.

I said I'd take them, but I needed to go upstairs first. I wanted to look at my seeds.

"Don't go," Sonya said. "You were already gone for so long."

They held on as I stood, hung from my arms. I felt a hand grabbing my leg, another pulling on the pocket of my shorts. I knew I should joke, ha ha monkeys, your tree is falling down. We'd pile on the floor, wrap our limbs around one another. But I felt the envelope spilling out. Everything on my body was theirs; every part of me theirs. I threw them off. I ungripped the fingers from my pocket. They thought it was a game and grabbed again at my pockets, one on each, until I bent back fingers and yelled, "Stop it."

"Jesus, Eve."

They were too stunned to cry.

"Okay, let's give Mom some space," Henry James said.

WEARING ONLY MY BRA and shorts, I lay on the bed waiting for Demeter to text back. I fixed everything—I'd written. I needed her to know that while I'd been wrong about Will, it didn't matter, nothing mattered but this envelope of seeds and the fact that I'd found it, walked for miles among the trees to bring it back.

But she didn't text.

"Tell me where you were," Henry James said, entering the room and standing over the bed. "You're scaring me."

I couldn't tell him about the night without mentioning the seeds, the seeds without the seed exchange, the seed exchange without Lillian's book. I told him all of it: Ruth and Stephen and Antonia and that I'd known Will before he showed up with Demeter—Henry James had never asked about this, but I hadn't offered—although not about the evening I'd spent with him or how he made me feel.

"No, that's bizarre. That's not possible. Just admit where you were last night."

I climbed to my knees and tried to kiss him, like I'd kissed the children's tears. He drew back against the closet door, which could never fully close. I pulled out the envelope, but he barely glanced.

"And now? From some old book you think your mom can swallow a leaf and all her troubles are ended?"

"Antibiotics are swallowed. Vitamins are swallowed." I tried to think of what else we swallowed. "All sorts of life-saving medi—"

"No, this doesn't make sense. You're not some kind of renegade scientist, Eve. You're not a botanist or a chemist or a . . . you're not even a gardener." He slunk down the closet door to the floor. His hooded eyes, always so sleepy, became deadened. I could only notice the love they usually held for me by its absence. "You're not even contrite. If any of this is true, you've lied to me, Eve. For months now you lied about where you were and what you were doing."

"That's not the point." As soon as I said those words, I regretted them.

"Not the point?"

But wait, I thought. Wasn't I victorious? Wasn't that the point? Hadn't I walked among dead trees and burnt trees and trees that watched me all night? I couldn't return to this, the mundanity of hurt feelings. I was always tending to hurt feelings. Would that be my entire life? I hated him then. The grease of his forehead, the way his mouth hung open, his needs, constant needs. And so, instead of apologizing, explaining that I'd found myself trapped in small untruths, one leading to another, but I'd never meant cruelty or duplicity, I exploded with a rage I hadn't even known about, so neatly had it been buried under dry soil.

"Our fucking arrangement, do you ever think about it? I gave it all up, everything for our kids, and yes, I wanted them. I want them. I want to be a mom more than anything, I know, but you fell in love with them, too, and you never questioned it, not even when the schools shut down and I quit teaching to sit with a newborn and a kindergartener in front of a Zoom screen. Did you ever think that we needed a different arrangement? Did you ever think that arrangements change when the world collapses?"

"Of course I worried about them," he said. "You know I did."

"But what about me? Did you ever think what it was like for me? Everyone worried about the kids. They said babies like Lev wouldn't learn to smile. They said kids as old as Sonya would never make friends. But what about the mothers? Who worried about the mothers who were supposed to fix all that was stunted in our kids? We changed. We were changed by this. But not you. No, you never change. So, okay, I didn't say what I was doing these last few months. That's the only way I could make this happen." I shook the envelope. "You see this? This was my creativity. My intellectual pursuit. My book."

He stood and walked to the doorway. "You can't lie to do it. You can't get Greentime from a lie."

"*You* can't," I shouted after him. "But for a mother it's the only way."

I would've liked that as the final word, but he turned. "Go for it, Eve. Go accomplish your big dreams. Leave right now. But you should know that I never was as scared as I was last night. I didn't sleep. I haven't slept. I just thought of you." He wiped his eyes with the back of his hand. "That you would put me through that is unconscionable. And now I learn you've been lying for months. What else are you capable of?"

I FOUND THEM IN the bathroom after Henry James slammed the front door. Sonya sat behind Lev, her hands over his ears, mothering him as I wasn't. "Parents fight, just like the two of you," I said. I hugged and reassured and packed swimsuits, towels, goggles, shampoo, soap, snacks, water bottles. I wasn't sure I'd find the car outside, but it was there. I relaxed a little. Henry James would be home soon. He couldn't go far on foot in this heat.

Sunday was always father's day at the YMCA. The dads sat on the bench, looking at their phones. I joined them, but nobody had responded, not Will, not Demeter, not Ruth. I wrote again, all caps. I FOUND THE SEEDS. Lev appeared shivering beside me, his belted floaty at his feet. "Make it stay up." I helped him choose a smaller floaty. As I crouched to insert the buckle, a kid kicked water tree-high. I could feel wetness seep into my shorts, through my underwear.

I asked for an envelope at the front desk, throwing out the one with Nell's writing and blackberry juice. In the locker room, I dried each seed with a tissue.

Was it the pool water? The dew in the woods the night before? The humidity? Late that night, I heard Henry James come into the house. I turned on the bedside light and listened for his footsteps on the stairs, but they didn't come. I imagined him on the couch, using Sonya's goat stuffy as a pillow. Overwhelmed with tenderness for him, I decided to explain I'd never meant to be cruel. But first I felt for the envelope in my shorts. I slipped the four seeds into my hand, holding them up to the light. They seemed unchanged. Wrinkled scrota. But then I noticed that all had a whisper of palest green, a whisker, a tendril. Frantic, I asked the internet what to do with sprouting seeds. I found a roll of paper towels beneath the bathroom sink, wet a square of paper, and pressed the seeds against it, my heart clenched with fear that I'd drop one down the sink or on the tile floor. I folded the damp paper twice, slipped my night guard out of its blue plastic case and put my blanketed seeds inside. When I lay down, I held the plastic case to me, unable to sleep.

Third Day with Seeds

. . .

i

If only they knew what I had with me. That's what I thought when I brought two bags of paper pro ducks to my mother's bedroom, wearing an old pair of red shorts that had a front pocket big enough for my night guard case. Nina on the stool, my mother in her recliner, Kiran and Persephone on the bed. In a rocking chair, the woman from the vegetarian restaurant, her small white Keds tapping the floor when she rocked forward. She told me her name was Marta and that she was so glad I found her.

"Marta likes to contribute to Persephone's education by reading from the New Testament," my mother said.

"It's gloriously violent," Persephone said.

"It puts me to sleep," Kiran said. "But to each their own. As the Bible doesn't say."

"I also do everyone's hair," Marta said.

"It's a new me," Nina said, with a verve I'd never heard from her before. I saw, in the dimness, that her hair was Twiggy short, bangs in stiff apostrophes. My mother's, unchanged for my whole life—in barrettes when working, loose when sad—was pulled back in an air hostess's French chignon. Kiran had a Gidget bob, flaring insouciantly. The floor was soft with wisps of hair.

"Forty-three years I cut hair at Belles and Beaus in Easthampton," Marta said. "I thought I was being poisoned by the chemicals we use for tints and permanents. That happens to so many of us girls, you know. But when I took time off, my problems didn't go away. The Bible was wrong about only one thing. *For you were formerly darkness, but now you are Light in the Lord; walk as children of Light.* Ephesians 5:8.

That's wrong. I was in the darkness when I was in the light and now here I am." She closed her eyes and rocked her chair backward. "In the light now that I'm in the darkness."

"Did you go to the party?" Nina asked, her voice worried again. "Aengus says two kids are sick?"

"Just fevers so far."

"I didn't get sick for a few weeks after," Kiran said.

"No way to know yet," my mother said. "We've been over this."

"Tell them about us," Persephone said. "Will you, Eve?"

"Up, Nina," Marta said. "Let Joanie's daughter sit on the styling stool. Kiran? My kit, please."

Nina rose and Kiran swerved his long legs off the bed, but my mother raised her imperious palm. "Eve isn't staying. My daughter's from the other world." To me she said, "You understand, darling, don't you?"

Before I left, I asked Persephone about Demeter. I'd stopped by the apartment that morning, but no answer. She hadn't responded to texts. Was she okay?

"Really, Eve," my mother said. "Asking a teenager about her mom? She's fine. Isn't she fine?"

"She's sad, I think?" Persephone said. "Because of Will leaving? But, like, busy? She's been working doubles. Marta's daughter drives me here and back."

ii

IN BED THAT NIGHT, I OPENED THE NIGHT GUARD CASE TO CHANGE the wrapping. I carefully placed the seeds in a new damp paper towel. The four sprouts had grown firm as a fingernail, a white tooth. The thrill of it! I felt a wholeness I hadn't felt since pregnancy.

When I heard Henry James arrive home and I was certain he'd fallen asleep on the couch, I took the car keys from the bowl, my flip-flops from the hallway. If the kids woke and called and Henry James realized my absence, how would I repair that?

Later, I thought, as I started the car. I'd fix that later. The seeds and

I were busy, but we needed a plan. They were growing. There wasn't much time. The dark night was the temperature of my skin.

"Will?" Demeter said after I knocked once. I knew she'd be awake. "Will?"

"It's me. I'm here."

The door opened to what seemed like outer space, a black hole, far darker than the hallway. I couldn't see Demeter. No, she said, she hadn't been getting my texts. Her phone died and she couldn't charge it. "Did you hear from him? Is that why you're here?"

"Sort of." I took a tentative step into the apartment, unable to see what I was entering, so complete was the darkness. I asked her to turn on a light. I wanted to show her the seeds.

"I can't."

"Just close her bedroom door," I said, assuming she was protecting Persephone.

"Electricity went out a few days ago."

"Matty!" I shouted. I tried to say it like Will would. "Matty! Help us! Have you called him?"

"Matty? Yeah, not about to call him this time."

I didn't understand why not, but I didn't ask then. I had news, I said. I told her of Stephen, the seed exchange, my mistake, Nell, the seeds. I have the seeds, I said again and again. Was she even listening? We just needed to call Will and I'd explain my mistake.

"Call Will? You think I haven't?" I heard her footsteps, a shuffling of jars or glasses. She pressed something small and cool onto my arm. "He left it. I was keeping it plugged until the power went out, but only you ever called him. I don't know why you said you couldn't find him online. I used Persephone's phone—she charges it at your mom's. I'm not stupid. I'm able to type 'Will Roth' into a Google search."

Roth, I thought. Not Rothstein, Rothenberg, Rothberg. "And?"

"And, of the one million William Roths on the internet, I found the one who posted the eulogy.com page for Quinn Binswanger asking for donations to Harm Reduction of Greater Boston in lieu of flowers. I'm not an idiot. Will is Will. And still he left. So, I'm not mad at you anymore. He was never going to stay. You just greased the skids."

"I found the seeds, Dem. Are you even hearing this?"

A moment of pure silence, devoid of electric hums, no light, no refrigerator, no sparks in the walls. Then she said, "Dr. Folkenflick promised he'd fix her. Ishmael swore she'd be going outside in a matter of weeks. I'm tired, Eve. I've been working doubles. My feet kill. My clothes stink of soy sauce. I really need you to go now."

ON MY WAY TO the parking lot, I heard her calling. "I changed my mind." We met beneath a flickering streetlight. I took out the plastic case and carefully unfolded the paper. She bit her bottom lip. "Fuck."

"I know, right?" I didn't like my seeds to be exposed to the night, so I folded the paper, closed the case.

A trash truck clattered down the street and in its amber lights, I saw fear on her face. The seeds scared her. The promise of them was so great it scared her.

"This is all good, Dem," I reassured. "A really good thing is happening."

"No, right. Right. I mean . . . what if . . ." She couldn't seem to finish the sentence.

"Yeah. Exactly. What if this is it?"

"Thank you, Eve. Seriously." She slipped the plastic case from my hand. "Thanks for this."

I understood then that she thought I was giving the seeds to her. "Actually, I should keep them."

"No, I can get natural light in my bedroom. It would be cool to see them grow."

Now fear moved inside me as well. I needed to keep the seeds safe. I didn't know how, exactly—I was waiting for Ruth to help me—but I'd keep trying. I tugged the night guard case gently from her hand. "It's Ruth. . . . She started all this. She'll figure out next steps." I returned the case to my pocket. "But really, don't worry. This'll work out. I know it will."

She wrapped her arms around her stomach. She was wearing Will's Joy Division shirt. "No, you don't. Nobody knows if these seeds will do anything. Nobody knows. Including you."

She looked so frightened, so diminished by fear. I wanted to offer the certainty I felt when Nell handed me the envelope, the metal in my mouth I tasted in the woods. "Look. I never before . . ." I paused. "Well, you know me. I doubt everything. But when I saw these tiny seeds, I felt certainty, like I've never . . . It was so easy." I gave a hopeful smile. "I might actually be becoming more like you. Someone who believes in things."

She shook her head, as if what I said didn't matter. "You need to tell me everything that happens with the seeds, Eve. Every little thing." She started walking away.

"Of course I will," I called after her. "That's the whole point. They're for Perse."

She stopped just out of the range of the streetlight. "You're wrong, Eve," she said, turning back to me. "You're wrong," she repeated. "That's not what faith feels like at all. What you described? That's delusion, not certainty. Belief is a choice, Eve. It's never easy. It's a choice you make again and again."

iii

WILL, I SAID AFTER SNEAKING PAST MY SLEEPING HUSBAND ON THE couch and climbing into bed with my laptop. Oh, Will, I've been so stupid. He looked back at me from the archive of *The Miscellany News,* Vassar's student newspaper. Same long-lashed eyes, skinny chest, smaller forehead beneath eager curls, the willing smirk of youth.

"Sophomore roommates William Roth (L) and Jeremiah Montclaire Segal-Weiss (R) rehearse as siblings Edgar and Edmund in the upcoming production of *King Lear.*"

Funny, I thought, it's mislabeled. The roommate was actually on the left. Jeremiah Montclaire Segal-Weiss was, as I'd imagined, beautiful. Jawline and cheekbones of a Greek statue, a gracefulness obvious even with the mask of goth: dyed black hair floppily coy over one eye, black clothes, black fingernails.

He was looking at Will with an uncomplicated happiness. How could Jeremiah live with himself, Will had asked more than once.

Why doesn't he just give it all away, get a job like the rest of us? I think it's killing him. I think it's destroying him.

Unlike the generic William Roth, there could be only one Jeremiah Montclaire Segal-Weiss. In his fourteen pages of Google hits, he was listed as a donor to literary magazines, Democratic candidates. His work history was sparse, as Will suggested it would be, just the IMDB page for production and direction of a movie I'd never heard of.

Idly wondering what time had done to the dyed hair, the nail polish, I searched images of Jeremiah and found only Will. Funny, I thought again.

Funny, Jeremiah must have brought Will along with him to the Fashion Scholarship Fund Gala and they took a picture of Will instead.

Funny. Same mistake at the New York Academy of Art's Tribeca Ball.

Funny. Here's Will smiling sheepishly in a tweed and velvet Gucci suit at the Art Production Fund Gala last April. So they were in touch?

Funny. This photo was mistagged and this one miscaptioned.

Funny. Here's Will in Los Angeles beside Jeremiah's mother, Elizabeth, at the dedication of a hospital wing. In Morocco with his arm around Jeremiah's sister Lauren, a gaunt woman with hair so straight and black it looked drawn on with Sharpie.

Lag time. The brain being dragged along like a child up a hill. Funny. Funny. And then it's not. Jeremiah Segal-Weiss. S-W.

I love the Southwest, said the postcards. *I can't wait to return to the Southwest territories. Love, G.*

Fourth Day with Seeds

. . .

i

On my phone in the Woodstar Café bathroom, I pulled up a photo of Will who was actually Jeremiah in a velvet suit and asked him, as I'd done all night, Who are you? What made you move here and impersonate your lover? Is it because his boyfriend died from the pills your relatives made? But why? Were you looking for the plant to help your family? Or to keep it from them?

Without thinking—too exhausted for thought—I reached into my pocket and touched the plastic night guard case. It amused me that I used to change my clothes. I planned to wear these red shorts forever, through the falling leaves, the silent snow.

But when I opened the case to check the dampness of the wrapping and then opened the wrapping to look at the seeds, all amusement vanished and I cried out. "Oh baby!" On one seed, a brown sprout, shriveled like a fingernail on a corpse.

I heard a cough from the stall beside mine. Pain twisted in my chest. I called Ruth again as I'd been doing. Her voicemail message said, "This is Ruth. You know what to do."

I whispered my message. "Ruth, help, the seeds are sprouting."

I searched on my phone: *How long can a sprouting seed live without*

How long can you keep a sprouting seed out of

I pressed my forehead against the stall barrier. I could fall asleep standing here. All I wanted was to keep the seeds alive. I didn't have Antonia's number, because she never answered her phone, but I found DJ's on my phone and he said, "Sure, she's right inside."

When I returned to the café, Lev didn't look up from his plastic dinosaurs, but Sonya reached her muffin-crumbed hands out to my face. "Are you crying, Mommy? Why are you crying?"

THE CHILDREN TWIRLED LAWN ORNAMENTS WHILE I COMPARED potting soils at the garden store and finally flagged down an employee who said, "For the kind of home gardening someone like you is doing, it really makes no difference."

In the parking lot I saw Matty—his orange beard, his potbelly—hoisting a bag of mulch over one shoulder. "Matty!" I called, running over to him. He looked confused when I said that the fuse was out again in Will's apartment. I repeated myself. "The fuse? You know how it goes out?"

"Huh," he said with typical dispassion. "Well, thanks for telling me."

"You'll fix it?"

"Sure," he said with a nod. "Sure I can."

ii

IT WAS A RELIEF TO FINALLY BURY THEM.

"A plant like this," Antonia had said on the phone, "your little spring ephemeral, a millennia ago, or maybe three, it acquired a phytochemical. Something to expand its reach, to make it last evolutionarily. Something bitter to scare away rabbits and rodents. Something medicinal to make it desirable by humans." And humans figured this out, she said, by trial and error, by sheer luck, and they passed along this knowledge until, like so much, it was lost. She told me Ellen would know the right scientists to study its allopathic compounds and, how fortuitous: She was on her way to Vermont. If I planted the seeds in nitrogen-rich potting soil and brought them to Antonia, Ellen would take care of the rest.

"GOODBYE," I SAID. "Keep growing, little ones. Good luck." I made sure to orient the sprouts upward. I kept the dead seed in the case in my shorts pocket, although the once-hopeful nudge of hard plastic against my body now gutted me. I was losing the feeling of the woods, losing my certainty.

Jeremiah

. . .

IN HIS SISTER'S APARTMENT, DOING NOTHING. WELL, NOT NOTHING. Looking. That's something. The view of the park from the twenty-first floor. A jubilation of leaves boxed in by the ocher buildings on Central Park West and the steel monoliths on Central Park South, as if the park is a green painting in an ornate frame. Surrealist because above the buildings, the sky is a thick glowing yellow. When the door opens, he startles. He's had the place to himself this past week, plus the housekeeper who doesn't mind him sitting here.

His sister does. "What the fuck, Jere? You didn't think to call?"

She's rolling a mauve suitcase, larger than she is. He tries to smile. "Is it really a problem? You're not here."

"We are, at this precise moment, here."

"We?"

Claude comes through from the foyer. He's stung by the sight of his niece. Where has she gone? Her body is half what it was when he last saw her. April, was it? How could she disappear so quickly? Her curls are missing, too, replaced by long dark curtains; apparently she now practices the family's sacred art of the flat iron. Her upper arms look more brittle than Persephone's when she ate only broth. At first, he's terrified that Claude is similarly sick. But no, not in that way. She's fifteen, the age his sister was when first hospitalized.

She doesn't look up from her phone when she says, "Mom said you weren't moving to the city until fall."

"Mom didn't know anything about Jere being here," his sister says, leaving her suitcase and heading into the kitchen. Has he cleaned up last night's takeout? He can't remember.

"Things happened." He walks over to his niece and raises his hand for a high five.

Claude glances at his hand, resumes typing rapidly. "Like what things?"

"I missed you." The truth is he misses her now that he's with her, misses the girl she was last September in Tourrettes-sur-Loup who wouldn't do anything the mothers demanded.

"Yeah, sure, whatev. If you actually missed me, you'd come to the beach this summer. We're never here." Her tone is teenage jadedness.

"So why now?"

"Tennis tryouts." She flops onto a couch. "Then back to Nantucket. Are you still here when school starts?" When he shrugs, she says, "Why do you have to get your own apartment at all? Take the guest suite. Stay with us."

"What for?" He's hoping for a compliment.

She shrugs one bare shoulder. "There's no one to talk to here." It's the first hint of the old Claude.

"Your uncle's a man in his forties, Claudine," his sister calls from the kitchen. "He needs his own place to live. A life. A life is what you need, Jeremiah."

He had a life in Northampton, or so it seemed, and although he knew it couldn't last, he wasn't ready to leave it. Each time he came to the city to look at apartments, he failed to imagine himself in any of them. Too big, too loud, too lonely, too far from his friends, their ease, dinners by the green woods. He'd nearly convinced himself that all of it could be his. Even Persephone. Or maybe especially Persephone. A near-daughter. Good company. Each morning he looked forward to making her breakfast before she went to Joan's, answering her questions while Demeter slept. He read her the news, explaining it all, stocks rising and falling, fascism rising and not falling, and she was so curious until the moment her mother emerged and she'd clam up.

He asks Claude what time her tryouts are.

"Supposed to be this morning, but it was canceled because of . . . you know . . . 'smoke warning.'" He doesn't know why she uses air quotes. The sky is the color of hard-boiled yolk; the danger seems real enough. "They're finding an indoor court with AC. So, tomorrow morning, I guess?" At last she looks up from her phone. "What're you up to today?"

Today? He has no plans, not today, not any day. What should be lightness, freedom, potential, instead feels unbearably heavy.

They walk out together, but he stops just under the building's blue awning, stunned by the city's heat after days of not leaving the apartment. The smell of ash is strong, although his lungs don't sting yet. He thinks of how weak Claude looks. "Are you sure we should be doing this?"

"God, don't freak out, okay?"

They enter the park at Seventy-second and Fifth, zig from shade to shade. Claude is mostly quiet, arms folded around herself. The men who bike/glide/jog toward them turn to visit with her ass in its miniscule shorts. She's underage, he wants to shout. He notices an ancient woman and man, both with walkers, shuffling down the path and laughing, and he'd like to show them to Eve. A rash of midsummer black-eyed Susans that Demeter would bow to.

"How's the movie?" Claude asks at lunch. In the small café, he enjoys both latte and omelet while she looks devastated at her ice water and dry salad.

"Movie?" He can't imagine what she's talking about. When has he last seen a movie?

"When we were in Florida you said? Like, you're making another?"

"Right. You sure you're not hungry?"

In April, his mom was diagnosed with MS after months of appointments and tests, and he flew back to Florida the day after Eve took him to Brewmaster's. The guest cottages were occupied by his sisters and nieces. Jeremiah couldn't fall asleep in the main house, not with his mom and her private doctor and the revolving crew of physical therapist, acupuncturist, and her healer, Ishmael, so nearby. He would walk along the beach at two, three in the morning, white surf over his bare feet, and one night, thinking about the flirty encounter with Demeter at Brewmaster's, the sort of sexy way she called him on his shit, he dialed the Healing Hut and she answered.

It didn't take long to realize how much he could help her and Persephone. Or how much his money could help. He probably shouldn't have done it, move from Eve to her best friend once she made it clear she wouldn't cross the line he wanted her to cross, but he was disappointed and lonely and sad about his mom, and Demeter had that potent cocktail that always set off his desire: beautiful, clever, and, most important, she needed him. When his sisters asked why he was going back to Northampton, he said he was scouting locations for a new movie.

"So, can I see anything? Like a trailer or something?"

"Slow going. You really should eat."

"Stomachache," Claude says, pressing her water glass against her neck.

Now he finds himself missing Henry James, a better dining companion, who would order the steak frites and an afternoon beer and enjoy every bite. The pain of missing is a force, distorting as wind against a tree. But missing is Jeremiah's normal state. Missing is who he is. There's no way to repay. Every time he tries, he messes up someone else's life. It's as if his only skill was accruing more people to hate him.

AT THE START OF college, he didn't think much about his roommate, a shy, homesick naïf from Salt Lake City with *Cats* and *Rent* and *Phantom* posters who'd never been to Broadway, or anywhere east of the Continental Divide.

When necessary, the roommates greeted each other with high joviality, as if to avoid the horror of other emotions. They were both a little too antic, arch, adept at accents and bon mots, eschewing original speech for quotations, running circles around a vortex of yearning. They'd lob quotes from their twin beds and then Jeremiah would slip outside to see his friends, all the NYC private school kids he'd known for years.

In late October he swung by his room to pick up something—what? A coat, some beer? Will looked like a cornered animal when he saw Jeremiah's friends. He'd been sobbing, it was clear, rangy with grief. Jeremiah wasn't sure what to do. He didn't even know that Will's father had died three months earlier.

"Gustafo!" he shouted. "Fuck, Will! We were supposed to see Gustafo! How'd we both forget?" His friends chuckled quietly, as if Jeremiah were playing a joke on Will. "It's not funny," Jeremiah said. "Gustafo! We spaced it. He's gonna be pissed beyond pissed. And you know what Gustafo's like when pissed." He shoved off his friends, grabbed a bottle of scotch, took Will by the arm. "Let's go."

Later Will and Jeremiah couldn't stop laughing. "Gustafo? The fuck."

"First name that came into my head."

"Not even a real name I don't think. Fucking Gustafo."

Their first code word. Of hundreds. Could fill an OED of their own—codes that linked to other codes, dig deep for the signifier, but it existed; together they had a core neither had alone. Jeremiah dropped pre-med to study art history and Will quit stats to major in drama. Gustafo would want us to do what we love the most, they told each other.

"LET'S GO TO THE Guggenheim," he says to Claude, who has draped her napkin over her untouched salad.

"Gross. It's summer, not school."

"It's far better than school. Or summer for that matter. You live twenty-one blocks away. Don't you ever go?"

Claude pushes her plate away. "Grandma Elizabeth took me once. We saw the circus thing? Calder? She said the permanent exhibit wasn't that interesting."

"Well, she should know. Your grandpa paid for some of it."

"Don't say that. Don't talk about it."

JEREMIAH NEVER WANTED TO talk about where his money came from, either. When he and Will looked for off-campus housing at the end of junior year, long before his father's role in the marketing of opioids was public, he said only that he'd like to cover their rent. "Join my dream. I didn't make this cash. It was money that made money." He limned the point. How did the money settle in ample mounds and drifts around his father? He suggested a great magnetic force.

A salesman, Jeremiah said—if anyone asked—in a tone that implied otherwise. So removed from the world of wealth, Will was satisfied with this opacity. Likewise, Jeremiah never mentioned the way Will stared at him sometimes, the way he blushed after too many drinks. Jeremiah considered this faint undercurrent of desire a gift too bright and dazzling to look at directly. Their friends still moved in different orbits. Will's were the *Les Miz* belters, Jeremiah had found the Derrida quoters. But Sundays they always spent alone together, a long walk, laundry, and cooking from the Silver Palate.

On the day Jeremiah turned in his senior thesis about the Italian Renaissance, he said, "So let's go. Florence, Venice, Milan, let's see it all." This was five weeks before graduation. Will already had a ticket back to Salt Lake, a job at a day camp, but he agreed, of course he agreed, although he insisted on the crustiest hostels, a budget of fifteen dollars a day for food. Who cared? They were there for the Caravaggios, for Michelangelo's *David,* for particular shades of red.

All this beauty and it was Will's that undid Jeremiah. How had he not fully clocked it before? He couldn't look away. He developed an eye twitch, headaches. At the end of the trip, they visited Jeremiah's family in Tourrettes-sur-Loup. Despite Will's bitching about the extravagance of the villa, he began to enjoy it, you could tell—wine poured by the housekeepers, sheets cleaner than clouds. They were given the yoga instructor's cabin, and on the third night Jeremiah came into Will's room, took off his clothes, and slipped into his bed. He'd never been with a man. Why that night after six weeks of traveling together? Jeremiah didn't know. He was happy, he knew that.

Still, he didn't tell anyone, not friends, definitely not family. And he couldn't see his way to a relationship. Will moved to Massachusetts to teach theater at a boarding school, Jeremiah to Los Angeles to study film. Every few months or so, he'd say, *I miss you.* He'd buy them both plane tickets. Bermuda. Quintana Roo. Isle of Skye. Crete. Mendoza. They'd spend half the days in bed.

After five years like this, Will asked him to come to Salt Lake City to see his childhood home before his mom sold it. She'd lost her job and was relocating to a small apartment in Dorchester to be close to Will. *There once was a Dorchester hoarder.* Every surface of her house was covered with her collections—salt and pepper shakers in the shapes of coy heterosexual couples, ikat rugs, faux Tiffany lamps, cross-stitched pillows. She stayed up most of the night on eBay, buying and selling. Jeremiah and Will lugged everything they could to a storage space. There wasn't room for Will's father's dioramas, meticulous scenes he'd reconstructed from his favorite movies. *Reservoir Dogs, Star Wars, The Big Lebowski.* "No problem," Jeremiah said. "I'll rent you another storage space."

Will grew angry. "Why don't you just pay off the mortgage and my mom stays in the house?"

"Sure," Jeremiah said.

"How about buying a house for us then?" Will turned away, his face red.

"You and your mom?"

"Me and you, Jere. Let's move to . . . Maine. I've never been. I don't even want a house. I just mean . . . let's try this for real."

Jeremiah pretended it was a joke. "I can't really see us as fishermen." He was twenty-seven, not ready for anything real. He wanted too much, every life, every city, every possibility still open.

Their weekends became less frequent, sometimes only twice a year, but they still happened, outlasting Will's boyfriends, Jeremiah's girlfriends, until in 2015, a decade after Tourrettes-sur-Loup, Jeremiah proposed to Arielle. Impulsive decision—his dad loved her; his dad was dying. At his bachelor party, which was just him and Will in Lucca, they climbed the clock tower. Jeremiah was behind Will on the turret, his chin on his shoulder, and he handed him a plastic grocery bag. Inside, a painting of Tourrettes-sur-Loup by a contemporary of Cézanne. An outlandish gift.

Will brought Quinn to the wedding at Ellis Island. He was older by twenty years, handsome and wry, an underemployed stagehand and house painter. Jeremiah thought they were set. Will had Quinn, Jeremiah had Arielle. And they had their occasional weekends.

I need you, Jeremiah would say. Costa Rica. Mazatlán. San Juan.

Quinn was sure it was HIV, finally coming for him. How could he have dodged it when those he loved hadn't? But his doctor insisted Quinn was healthy, just stressed.

Jeremiah felt certain that someone more established could figure out what was wrong. Some drug, some pill, some trial. "Try a top doctor. Go to Mount Sinai or NewYork-Presbyterian."

When Quinn started opioids instead, Jeremiah warned Will to be careful, but it didn't stop him from asking Will to go away with him.

As a child, he'd created a persona—Jeremy—who would chat with his father about golf and baseball and the stock market to try to prevent the cruelty his father rained down on nerdy, unathletic, skinny Jeremiah with a trilobite collection and a stained glass obsession. What began as protective soon became instinctual. He enjoyed slipping into personas. It was easy to lie to Will about his family's wealth, easy to lie to girlfriends about his weekends with Will. He was always a far better actor than Will.

So when Will said he couldn't leave, because Quinn was in a bad spot, the pills no longer pushing the pain away for long enough, Jeremiah became a person who didn't know much about opioids. He was simply a jealous lover, showing up in Northampton despite Will's refusal. "Come away with me," he insisted. He pressured Will, made a scene, until Will came. And with Will out of the house, Quinn could sell the painting to buy the pills that killed him.

The neighbor who found Quinn called Will when they were getting coffee in Lenox. They looked at each other, thirty-three years old, still so young. How had they become responsible for someone's death?

After an excruciatingly silent drive back, Jeremiah parked in front of Will's apartment and said, "Let's get some food. Then we'll deal. Morgue. Call his parents. We can do it."

Will put his hands over his face. "No. Not with you. I can't, Jere. I can't do this with you anymore. I'm think I'm done."

Jeremiah didn't have anyone to talk to about this death or how it changed him. On the drive home, he realized, too late, that Will was the only one he wanted, the answer to all his questions. How stupid he'd been, stringing him along. He left Arielle when he got back to the city. He was ready to settle down, he said to Will, on voicemail, on email. He finally wanted what Will had always wanted. He wanted that life together. But Will never called back, never wrote back, never, never, never.

Except for the email Will sent after Jeremiah's movie opened at the Tribeca Film Festival. It contained only a link to a YouTube video of protestors in the balcony dropping scrips with blood on them. Jeremiah wrote a long response explaining that he'd been a little kid when Oxy was invented. His father, a maternal cousin of the Sackler brothers, never spoke about work to him. He was a marketer, his dad, that's all. But yes, he admitted, he'd been living in denial for too long. He wanted to explore restitution. Where to give his money.

Five years passed, and he never stopped thinking about how to get Will to talk to him again, how he might rectify the damage. The Emilys offered a roundabout attempt. Will would discover how hard he was trying to help people like Quinn, how he was nothing like his family.

When Jeremiah wrote to Stephen, he knew he couldn't use his name. Any dolt could Google Segal-Weiss. He chose Will's on a whim—and because it's too common to be searchable—not thinking much about it until he entered Ruth's apartment and realized he had to start talking about his life. Quinn. Salt Lake City. His father's dioramas. It turned out it wasn't hard to become this mash-up of himself and Will. It was a charade, sure, but it felt right.

As Will/Jeremiah, he was freer than he'd ever felt, free of his shame. Will/Jeremiah was kinder, wiser, more attractive than Jeremiah himself. Will/Jeremiah was the type of person who someone like Eve, witty and energetic and pretty, would fall for, despite total ignorance of his money. Will/Jeremiah knew how to take care of Persephone and how to comfort Demeter when her daughter grew surly. It became his favorite role.

As Will/Jeremiah, he understood for the first time why Will couldn't see him, what hurricane of guilt that would whip up. But he also understood that Will still loves him.

He wanted to keep it all going even once he knew it wouldn't bring Will back to him. In late May, Will got on Facebook to announce the arrival of his daughter, Annika, posing with his husband and baby outside a yellow door in Portland, Maine. Will's a social worker now, working in a recovery clinic. He found his own way to rectify.

BY THE TIME THEY ascend the wide white ramp, they're both tired, feet swollen from heat. Josef Albers's green squares are just where Henry James described. Jeremiah stares and stares but feels nothing. He was hoping he'd be healed in some way, that all that was broken and rotten in him might find cohesion. That's how Henry James explained it to him one night when they sat outside with the sound of the maple leaves in the wind. He stares for so long, thinking of Henry James and Eve and Demeter, of the bright star of Persephone, and of what will come next, not for them—he shuts his mind against those thoughts—but for himself, and he forgets that he brought Claude here. When he notices her, it's because of the noise. A droning, a gasping. She has tears down her face. Her jaw is slack, she's not aware of the people turning to look at her. For once, her arms aren't crossed in front of her bare stomach but hang loosely. He touches the abrupt bone of her shoulder. "What do you need? Claude, what is it?"

"I didn't know," she says, still crying. "I didn't know."

"Know what? How can I help you?"

She shakes her head. "This." She points to the green squares. "I didn't know there was anything like it."

Fifth Day with Seeds

. . .

i

DID I SLEEP? NOT REALLY. BUT WHEN LIGHT CAME IN, I REACHED in my pocket for the plastic case before remembering that the seed inside was dead. On my bureau I could see three paper cups decorated with ice princesses. No longer on my body. Too far away.

And then it came to me. Why hadn't I thought of this earlier? Stephen must have seen me leave with Nell. They—whoever they were, whatever pharmaceutical company he worked for—knew I had the seeds. If I left the house, they'd send someone here to steal the cups.

Standing by the couch I explained to Henry James that the kids were too hot to go outside and he'd have to spend the day at the hospital café if he didn't want to see me. In boxers and undershirt, he headed for the stairs. I asked what he was doing.

His look was incredulous. "To the bedroom? To change my clothes? To take a fucking shower." I waited outside the door until he emerged fully dressed, smelling of his usual soap, his chin nicked in its usual place from shaving. My body felt its usual urge toward him, but a newer urge sent me hurrying past. No, there was no sign of tampering, but to be sure, I reached my fingers into the dirt until I felt each one.

Stupefied by heat, we moved through the morning like sap dripping down a tree. The kids asked for the pet store, the library. A home day, I said, is spent at home. Screen time became all time. I was dozing near my seeds when the doorbell rang. Coming downstairs, I heard Sonya say, "We're just having a home day."

Demeter walked into the living room as if from a sauna, sweat darkening her shirt, her crotch, her feet red when she slipped off her sandals, but she didn't seem to mind. She was animated, a hot hand gripping mine. "It's so fascinating, Eve. Spring ephemerals? I read all about them at the library. About double dormancy and, you know, stratification and scarification, what kind of light they'll need, what soil pH. I'd really like to do it, to grow them for her. I really think I can."

I poured her a glass of water, filled it with ice. I handed a cup of ice to the kids in the living room. They rubbed it down their arms. Demeter's anger was spent; she was my Demeter again, loving me, but I was pricked by needles of panic. "I'm not sure," I said.

There was no animosity in her voice when she said, "I know I can do it. I can take them with me, wherever I land. If it's Taos, even better. You should see the plants I grew there. Moth orchids and tradescantia and ferns, so many ferns. Or if I go back to Washington, I'll get a grow light." She laughed. "Everyone has an extra grow light in Olympia. I mean, you walk down a dark alley and people are handing you grow lights."

I cleared off a chair for her at my kitchen table and tried not to think about all she was saying, landing in Taos, landing in Washington, why would she leave, no, I couldn't think about that. I sat next to her and busied myself with moving around crumbs on a plate as told her I was bringing the plants to Antonia.

"Antonia? Come on. All her plants are dead. I'd really like this, Eve. It's not rocket science, you know. I already talked to Ishmael and he can teach me extraction, tinctures, or I'll take an online class."

When I didn't answer, she added, "I learn quickly, Eve," as if I didn't know. I imagined her walking out my door with my seeds in their ice princess cups. What if she dropped them? What if she overwatered, underwatered, knocked them over?

"Ellen's finding me the right scientist, the right lab," I said. "I'm excited about it."

She kept smiling. "You're kidding, right? This is a joke?"

"It's the ethical thing to do," I said, which is what Antonia told me. "Science has all these structures in place to make sure medicine is safe and accessible."

Her face was sharp again. "Accessible? The medicine will never reach Persephone, not her."

"This is the stupidest game in the entire world," Lev yelled from the living room.

"It's you who's stupid," Sonya shouted back. "Everything you do is stupid. Because your brain doesn't work right."

Lev bawled. "Come here, Leviticus the Levitator," Demeter called.

Instead, Sonya appeared. "I'm bored. I need something to do."

"Apologize to Lev," I said. "That's something to do."

"But he's the one who messed up all the pieces. I was designing him a board game from scratch and I cut out the pieces and I drew on them, because you won't let us leave the house when all I want is to be outside. Fiona's outside. She's at her grandma's today. She's always outside. And we're always doing nothing, because of ticks, ticks, ticks, which aren't even real."

Her bare feet stomped upstairs. She slammed the bedroom door. Knowing his cue, Lev came to my lap and slid his thumb in his mouth. I held him like armor. Demeter rubbed his leg. "I think you've just had a really lucky life, Eve. The luck of health insurance. The luck of parents with money and graduate degrees. The sheer luck of health. You think someone will always provide you with just the right medicine. You can't imagine that anyone you love would be the kind of person to die of kidney failure because they can't afford insulin."

"Demeter, come on. I can imagine that."

"No, I don't think you can imagine what it's like to be me. I never took Persephone to the dentist. Never. She's never been to a dentist. Think about how many years it'll take for Ellen's people to put this plant through their tests, peer-review them, wait until they're published . . . so they can get tenure or whatever. Unethical? I'll tell you what's unethical. By then, Persephone will have spent her entire childhood in the dark. Please, Eve. Please let me take them."

Lev kicked his heels against my shins. "I want Daddy. Where's Daddy?"

I ran my fingernails down his arm to make him shiver. I had no idea what to do. I trusted Antonia and Ellen. I wanted them in charge.

But I hated not giving Demeter what she asked of me. I suppose I chose that moment to tell her about Will being Jeremiah because I was so uncomfortable and so unsure. What were we supposed to do, the seeds and me?

I showed her the man at the Tribeca Ball and the Fashion Scholarship Fund Gala who looked like Will but was called Jeremiah, since her own googling hadn't revealed this. "I see." She nodded. "I get it."

"You do? So why'd he pretend?"

"Some sick reason, who cares. Doesn't matter. He's not coming back. I was hoping . . . Since you were wrong about him being a spy and all. But no. I don't think so."

I couldn't believe her. "But you wouldn't want him to."

"I wouldn't?"

"Everything about him was a lie, Dem."

"He helped Persephone. Nobody ever helps Persephone. Will—or whatever his name is—helped her. He gave us a place to live. He was so kind to her. That's all I care about."

"I'm helping. I'm going to help." Searching for evidence, I told her I'd run into Matty at the garden center and asked him to check on her electricity. "Won't it be a relief to have the power back on?"

Very quietly she asked, "What did he say exactly?"

"He'll fix it. Don't worry, he'll fix it."

She picked up her purse. "I need a ride. Can you drive me home?"

I COULDN'T BRING MY seeds, because I didn't want to draw attention to them, so as I drove—Lev and Sonya in the back seat—fear electrified me. Could they have convinced Demeter to work for them? What if all this was a scheme to get me to leave the house and abandon my seeds? I stared at every passing car. Every driver looked suspicious. Only as I parked in the lot behind Will's apartment did I come back to myself—and to Demeter, who was biting her thumb. "Are you okay?" I asked.

She looked out the window and didn't answer.

"Are you worried about Matty? Is that it? I think he really wants to help you out. Fix the lights."

She turned to me. "He wants that? I think that's your lack of imagination again, Eve. It's August. Will—or whoever he is—I don't think he paid rent past July. I was always the one who dropped it off in Matty's mailbox near the restaurant. So when the electricity went out, I wasn't about to call him. What Matty's going to want is rent, a deposit, a credit score. I don't have that."

It seemed cruel of Will to abandon her with no place to stay. But it was my own cruelty that shocked me. Had I messed this up for her? I thought I'd understood her—how she needed Will and the floor he gave her—but I'd thought only so far. Not about this. Not about no dentist appointments. Not about no credit score. "But . . ." I began and stopped.

"You're wondering what my plan was? My plan was to squat a little longer. As long as possible. I don't want to put Persephone on a bus for three days again. My plan was to stay under the radar like usual." She unbuckled her seatbelt, opened her door.

"But we'll see you tomorrow," I called out with frantic optimism as she left. "I'll come by tomorrow and if Matty . . . if he acts like a dick, I'll help you find another place to live, of course I will, if it comes to that."

PARKING AT THE BAIT and soda shop, I amped into faux humor. What's cold and lives on a stick. I gave each kid a dollar and sent them inside for Popsicles and then I dropped my smile, undone.

If it comes to that. I'd actually said that. But Demeter had been telling me since Will left that *it* was already *that.* Forgetting her phone was dead, I decided to call, to explain, to apologize, to promise to help immediately, *it* being *that.* But when I pulled out my phone, I called Ellen instead, so that I'd know what to say to Demeter about the seeds.

"Way to go, Eve! Antonia says you're bringing them up here. Are you driving right now?"

As soon as I asked her my question, my kids returned, proudly dropping coins in my palm. "Look! I bought a blue one and Sonya got the last red one."

"Oh god, no, whatever you do . . . Not your friend, as good intentioned as she is, and not her healer. I can tell you a million stories about men like him, men who prey . . ."

"Mom, do you see?"

". . . desperation of the ill for personal profit. I can give you statistics if you want about deaths from unregulated herbal remedies. It all sounds so innocent, but we have the FDA for a reason and that reason is . . ." Whatever the reason was lost as another call came in and I accidentally hung up on Ellen trying to silence it.

"Hello? Hello? Yes, this is Ishmael Anderson. I have heard the wonderful news about the seeds, which contain, as so many plants do, their own medicine. Demeter tells me they are sprouting. This is such a good indicator of their health, but time is of the essence . . ."

My kids handed me their sticky wrappers, beaded with juice. "Where can we go now? Can we go to the spray park? Is it open again?"

". . . tells me you're considering giving the seeds to a scientist friend and I must caution you against locking away our plant medicine, that which Mother Earth offers so freely and . . ."

I hung up the phone. "We're going home."

"No. Not home. Why does it have to be?"

I reached for a piece of paper that I'd left beneath my windshield wipers all afternoon, thinking it was an ad for a local weed shop as usual. And it was. But on the other side, I saw now, my name in small block letters. *HI! LONG TIME NO SEE. LET'S CATCH UP! BUT FIRST! DESTROY THE SEEDS. THIS IS THE EARTH'S GREATEST CHANCE TO RETURN TO WILD WITHOUT OUR CARS, WITHOUT OUR LIGHTS. LISTEN TO THE TICKS! KILL THE PLANT!*

No signature, just a smiley face. But who would want the seeds destroyed?

"See, there's no reason, Lev," Sonya said. "It's a thing Mom made up, a home day. It doesn't exist."

I WAS THE DOUBTER. The undecider. The hemmer, the hawer, the flip-flopper, the yes-but-er, the people pleaser. I wanted to ask Nell.

I wanted to ask Will who was Jeremiah. I kept getting Ruth's voicemail. *This is Ruth. You know what to do. This is Ruth. You know what to do.*

But I didn't. Back in my bedroom I knelt in front of the seeds. Who should I give you to? The seeds were mute. I dug them out. On the first two, although I saw no new growth, the sprouts were intact. But the third, the third. A brown, shriveled sprout. Crying, I dropped it into the night guard case with its dead sibling.

Quite late, when the air was listless, rain clouds having settled but not spilled, I went downstairs and sat on the floor beside the couch. I put my hand on Henry James's arm. I wanted so much to lie my head on his chest, to feel his heartbeat, the sour smell of only him. "Hey," I whispered.

He opened his eyes. "Is everyone okay? Are the kids okay?"

"Can I talk to you?"

He propped himself on his elbows. "Yes. I've been waiting. Yes, yes. Let's talk. Please let's talk."

But when I told him it was about the seeds, he rolled away from me, hiding his face in the couch cushion. "Jesus. No."

Lightning lit the kitchen window an alien green.

There once was a woman named Eve who didn't know what to believe.

Persephone

...

SHE KNOWS THE WAY FROM DRIVING BUT WALKING TAKES MUCH longer and the pink suitcase catches on tree roots that buckle the sidewalks. She's feverish by the time she rings the bell.

Joan opens the door wearing a white nightgown that shows her legs beneath it and has lace on the wrists. "What is it? What's wrong?"

Persephone left her house in a rush, a storm rising in her brain, and she didn't think until now that Joan might turn her away. She whispers, "I was wondering, if it's not too much trouble, if I could move in with you."

Joan presses a palm to Persephone's forehead. "Does your mother know you're here?"

She covers her mouth when she says, "She's taking me away. I can't leave. I don't want to leave."

Inside, Joan tells her to wait at the kitchen table, heads to the bathroom, and returns with wet washcloths, one for Persephone's forehead and one to rub on her legs and arms. She flicks on the low-voltage light and makes a peanut butter and jelly sandwich, asking gently where her mom is planning to go and why. She doesn't say anything about Persephone staying, but she also doesn't include her name in the questions about leaving.

When thunder crashes outside, Joan tells her to bring her sandwich and washcloths into the living room. Joan stands with her hands on her hips in the center of the room and asks, "Should we take them down?"

"We should," Persephone says, although she doesn't know who they're talking about.

Joan drags a wooden chair in front of one of the windows and climbs on it unsteadily, gripping the curtain until she gains her balance and can reach up to unscrew the rod. The blackout curtain slides to the ground like a bird shot in the sky. Persephone offers to do the other two windows, and as she's standing on the chair, the rain starts. It pounds against the glass, trying to reach her.

They sit together on the couch and listen to the loud rain and watch the shapes of bushes moving in the wind. It's dark enough but not blackout-curtain dark and Persephone feels a message passing between the outside world and herself. The rain grows louder still.

"A hard rain's gonna fall," Joan says. "Do you know that song?"

Persephone shakes her head.

Joan moves to a little table with a cardboard box and a record player and rips open the box. "I told Eve it was stupid when she brought me this, but maybe it's time."

She puts on a song about a blue-eyed son, a darling young one who has gone away. Persephone searches for an answer to the question of can she live here in the lyrics but there are far too many words. A strange sound starts when the song ends, a looping, crackling noise. "It's the needle against the center label," Joan explains, but she doesn't move to stop it. Persephone feels the crackling in her body. Joan isn't saying yes she can stay but she isn't saying no, all the possibilities are here crackling. Unlike when her mom said they were leaving and Persephone's brain began storming. How could she bear to leave the other Emilys? How could she be all alone again?

She notices that Joan has stuck her legs straight out in front of her. She wears dark socks and her toes point to the ceiling. "Are you okay?" Persephone asks.

Joan holds up a finger. "I'm figuring something out."

Persephone is quiet, thinking that Joan is deciding her future.

"What I'm thinking is why are we doing it the way they do it?" Joan says finally, lowering her feet to the floor. "Why are we keeping ourselves awake in the day? Why aren't we out there in the night when we can go anywhere we want?"

"Like a nocturnal animal?"

"Exactly. Like the owls and foxes." Joan is staring out the window. Persephone looks out the same window, certain they are seeing the same thing: Nina and Kiran and her and Joanie and Marta outside together and maybe some kids or teenagers, too. She doesn't want Emily for kids or teenagers, but it seems like it's going to happen. It might already be happening and she will be so happy to talk to them.

Eventually, Joan lifts the needle and takes more records from the box. "I want you to know that women have always suffered and made something of it, attained a depth and brilliance that would be unreachable without suffering," she says. She teaches Persephone the singers' names. Joni Mitchell, Joan Armatrading, Joan Baez, Nina Simone, Roberta Flack. Persephone listens carefully. She can tell this is a lesson that means a lot to Joan, but she doesn't want to suffer. When she curls up with her head in Joan's lap, Joan must think she's asleep, because she starts to cry. Persephone can feel her shaking. Does this mean Joan will make her leave? But how could she when outside that window is all of them, all night long?

Joan wakes her, saying, "The owls are headed home and we have to go."

Persephone sits up. "Why? Why can't I stay here?"

"She's your mother." She says this firmly, as if the sentence were a stone bench. Persephone doesn't protest, although she can feel something building inside her, growing as they walk in the near-dawn, cats darting away, birds pecking the wet grass, the pink suitcase rumbling, Joan gripping her hand.

Sixth Day with Seeds

. . .

i

YOU CAN'T IMAGINE MY LIFE, DEMETER SAID, BUT I'VE TRIED. I'VE imagined Demeter waking at one A.M., as always. I imagined her stepping into Persephone's room to feel the soft limbs of her daughter who couldn't be angry in her sleep. She touched the sheet, the pillow. What hell then? Demeter had no phone, no car to reach a phone, the nearest place open at that hour was Cumberland Farms a mile away. She couldn't leave in case Persephone returned. They'd fought earlier, after Matty came and refused the cash Demeter offered him, told her the lease wasn't transferrable and she had twelve hours to get out. When Demeter said they were leaving town, going back to Taos or Olympia or Colorado—she wasn't sure yet who could put them up, but she'd find someone—Persephone had gone to sleep furious.

All night without her daughter. An hour and then another hour and another until the door opened. She pulled Persephone inside and shut the door when my mother tried to talk to her.

"You do everything wrong." That's what Persephone shouted at Demeter, according to my mother, who stayed in the stairwell. "I hate you, you're the worst mother. I wish anyone else was my mother."

"I was so sad for her," my mother said. Her call came a little past dawn, when I'd finally fallen asleep.

"Sad for who?"

"For Persephone of course. My heart was breaking for her. To have a mother that deaf to her child's needs."

But I ache for Demeter. I wasn't there to tell her, it's not true what your daughter says.

"I hate everything about you I can't stand to look at you I hate the way you touch me I hate the way you talk to me I hate your breath I hate your hair I hate how you think you're so pretty but you're not pretty you're pathetic. Don't smile like that don't talk to me get away."

I wasn't there to say, she screams because she loves you. I wasn't there to hold her as she cried, she's gone, she's gone, even though she's with me, my baby's gone, and I wasn't there to say, you've given her everything you have to give and Persephone will come back to you. I wasn't there, and I actually don't know if she did.

"I threw up twice on the way home," my mother said. "I'm sure I looked crazy to everyone heading to work, an old woman in night clothes stumbling from shade to shade. Can you believe nobody, not one person, stopped to—"

"We need to tell them not to leave," I interrupted. "They can live in my living room. They can live in your living room."

"Why else do you think I'm calling?" my mother said. "You need to go. She'll listen to you."

I CARRIED MY SEEDS downstairs, and the kids, already awake in their room, followed. I gave Sonya my phone and told her to let Dad sleep unless there was a true emergency. "Is it an emergency if Lev jumps down the stairs and breaks an arm?"

"Yes, but he shouldn't be jumping down the stairs."

"But if?"

"Then yes."

"But what if he breaks a leg, not an arm? What are you doing?" I was reaching in the hall closet for a shoebox. "What are these?"

"Don't touch that, love." I set the two remaining cups in the box.

"But why do you have Elsa cups. Elsa's for babies. That's embarrassing."

Will's apartment was unlocked. I opened the curtains, and a torrent of trash revealed itself. Ants in an opened tub of peanut butter. Toothpaste piles in the sink. Clothes hung over the loom, a chip bag spilled onto the brown leather couch. The postcards, though, were gone. Who sent them? Who missed the Southwest? Who was G?

I was leaving, my box of seeds under my arm, when I noticed a skiff of mail just inside the door. I picked it up, wondering who it was addressed to: Jeremiah or Will? Mostly *Current Resident*—circulars for pot shops and pizza, a furniture catalog for Will Roth. Slipped between the leaves of a Dominos flyer, an unopened envelope with no return address. She never saw it. Inside, a check from Jeremiah Segal-Weiss to Persephone D'Errico. How much? The number shocked me. Delighted me. Enough for them to live anywhere for a very, very long time. Why not here in this green town, with us?

I shoved the check in my shorts pocket with the dead seeds.

"The pretty lady and her friend wearing sunglasses? You missed them by an hour," said a man in the bus terminal. They were on their way to Springfield, but after that, he couldn't remember. I reached the Springfield depot long after the bus from Northampton had come and gone; nobody there remembered a pretty woman with a pink suitcase or could tell me which bus she took.

In the parking lot where we'd waited for Henry James nearly every Friday for two years, I pressed my forehead against the steering wheel. Sweat dripped down my back and stuck my thighs to the seat. I wished clouds for Persephone, a low fog, a drizzle, but the storm had cleared to a blue benevolence. I'd heard about their long ride here, how Demeter had held a plastic bag for her daughter's vomit. Would Persephone let her mother care for her now?

The pain I felt was also for myself. Was I supposed to do this alone? I couldn't. Not just today but tomorrow and the next week and the month after that. Was she not going to watch Sonya and Lev grow, her peapods, her loves, and was I not to know the metamorphosis of Persephone, and would we not say to each other, you are so wonderful, they are so wonderful, thank god I have you, I would hate to be alone?

"Are you okay?" A woman was leaning over my open window. "Fine," I said, finding tears down my face and understanding I'd been sobbing. I started the car and pulled away. My friend was gone. How I hate that word. *Friend.* Send them a card on their birthday. Like their Facebook post. Chat over cabbages in the co-op—We should really grab drinks sometime. Text me! *Lover* or *mother* at least has dirt between the nails, a line of pain in the throat. Don't call it friend. Call it lightning, call it soil. My lightning was gone, my soil swept away, my roots exposed, gripping nothing.

ii

MY MOTHER LAY ON THE COUCH WITH A FLEECE BLANKET OVER HER face despite the heat—the living room curtains were down. When I tried to speak, she made an odd noise, a moaning, and it was a while before she calmed down enough to tell me to leave. "I'm so tired, Eve. I already sent everyone home."

"Wait," I said, as if she were the one walking away. I sat on the floor and told her about Lillian's book, the Sightflower seeds.

The voice beneath the blanket said, "Kiran knew all that. Not that it was found. But how badly his father needed to believe in this plant. How he ignored Kiran's needs in his attempt to swoop in and cure everything. I didn't know you were involved."

I couldn't stand her casual tone. "But look." I patted the box beside me. "The seeds. If you just look. Are you listening?"

"I was up all night. I'm desperate for sleep."

"I need your help, Mom. I need advice." I explained Ellen, Ishmael. Pros, cons, wish, wash, healer, scientist, doctor, mystic. The seeds were sprouting, the seeds were dying. "Are you listening, Mom? Are you sleeping?"

She pulled down the blanket and turned to me with closed eyes. "You didn't stop her, did you? Persephone's gone?"

"What about your other friends?" I asked, like I would of a child.

"What would be the point without her?" She heaved herself off the couch, the blanket slipping to the ground. With closed eyes, she stepped around me, reaching for the back of a chair, the bookcase, the doorframe.

I picked up my box of seeds and followed. "But, Mom . . ."

One hand on the newel post, the other reaching for the banister. "What do I care who you give it to? The group of us, we've been to everybody. Who helped? Not a doctor, not a healer. A cure? We had a cure. It was each other."

She didn't care. My own mother. All I'd gone through to find these seeds, all I'd lost in so doing—my Henry James, my Demeter. I watched her leaden ascent, hating her and the slow way she moved.

When she neared the summit, I called out, "When I went to college, did you celebrate?"

She stopped climbing. "What's that?"

"Did you have a party?"

She turned and sunk onto a step, eyes shut, her nightgown a suspension bridge between the wide balustrades of her knees, hair loosed from her French twist stuck to her forehead. "Who would say such a thing?"

"Irene, actually."

My mother waved her hand in front of her face as if flicking away gnats. "Pssh. What does she know?"

"You're saying you didn't?"

"I need to get to bed."

"You did or you didn't."

She stood and returned to her slow climb.

"Thanks, Mom. Thanks for clarifying."

On the landing, she called, "Why do you always forget who you are?"

"What's that?" From the bottom of the stairs, I could see only her socked feet.

"It's just . . . You don't seem to remember who you are. Maybe it's your children. I didn't want that. I didn't want to forget who I was once I had you. I fought against it. To your detriment? Very possibly yes. But I wasn't capable of another choice. And I haven't forgotten you, Evie. I haven't forgotten what you were like at four and . . . I don't know, seven, ten."

She seemed to lose her balance, her feet doing a quick shuffle, and I rushed the stairs to help. Holding a hand up to stop me, she carefully leaned against the door. "Eleven was something. And then sixteen." She whistled. "Eighteen. You were stubborn beyond belief. You were determined. You were so cocky. Not in a way others would notice, nothing show-offy, but . . . intellectually cocky. You were learning the world, sorting it. It was fascinating to watch. You knew exactly what pulled at your curiosity and you just zoomed off in that direction."

She winced.

"I'll help you to bed."

She told me no, but I put down the shoebox and led her inside and smoothed the sheet over her and adjusted the air conditioner and collected the Vitamin Water bottles and the empty bags of chocolate raisins and carried them to the kitchen where I made toast and washed dishes and boiled eggs and brought up a tray along with a washcloth for her forehead.

When I was leaving the bedroom, she said, "Oh god, Eve, I don't know. Maybe I did celebrate. Maybe I drank a whole bottle of Chablis in your honor. Maybe I invited Irene and she brought more wine. You know, I was in a bad place then. I couldn't make headway after finishing the last *Wormfood*. You did things for me a daughter shouldn't have to. I couldn't bring myself to stop you. But then you were off! Like a horse from the gate." She paused, laughed a little. "No, nothing tamed like that, nothing trained. Like something wild, a wild force. I was in awe of you, actually, so gorgeously alive, Eve, so ready for life."

iii

SONYA IN A LAVENDER ONE-PIECE. LEV IN SHARK TRUNKS. JUMPING at the sight of me. "We're going to the la-ake. We're going to the la-ake."

"You are?"

"You, too. Get on your suit."

Henry James pulled down his headphones and handed me my phone. "Some mother called. Said a group is headed to the lake and did you want to bring Sonya."

"And it's okay if I come," Lev explained. "Because I'm Sonya's brother."

I checked my recent calls. The number was unfamiliar. Sonya didn't know whose mother it was. Henry James hadn't asked. "Describe her voice?"

"What does it matter," he said. "It's hot."

The lake was in Goshen, half an hour north, on land owned by the Daughters of the American Revolution, but how could these daughters really own it, formed as it was by the slow melt of glacier, a declension in the deciduous forest with a diameter so wide that it apparently took an hour to swim across, but mothers didn't do that. Mothers paid the entry fee at the kiosk and parked in a small lot that led through the woods to sand and a lifeguard who would blow a whistle if we reached over the roped buoys to the pine-green water beyond. But even here, contained in a space between cinderblock bathrooms and shore, we had the view and a view can be freedom. Heron overhead. Ducks bobbing over buoys to ask toddlers for bread.

I figured we'd have a respite, a relief. We wouldn't decide today, my seeds and I. I slid the check into the glove compartment, waiting for Demeter to charge her phone and find my texts: She could come home. Crossing the hot sand, Lev asked me to pick him up. "Look what I'm carrying," I said. Two bags strung on my left arm held towels and pails and shovels and snacks and water bottles and extra underwear and a drawing pad for Sonya and sunscreen and bug spray.

"But why, Mom, why do you need to carry the shoebox everywhere?"

"Do you see anyone you know?" I asked Sonya.

Mothers milled around picnic tables. "I don't think so. Where's my group?" she said shyly, pulling on my arm.

"Anyone from camp? From school?"

We walked slowly, hoping someone would wave us over, but all the mothers were busy in a magnificent dance of care. Slicing watermelon, rubbing on sunscreen, spraying bug spray, throwing a ball, lighting the charcoal, nursing a baby with mosquitoes landing on her chubby legs.

It was then that I realized I might be heading into a trap. Who was real and who was a simulacrum? One glance and they all looked false, spies performing nurturance, playfulness, worry, waiting for me to dive into the lake and leave my seeds behind. I rushed the kids across the burning sand to the damp shoreline.

At the water's edge, a mother appeared beside me. "No other place to be. What with all the camps closed." She pointed at a tapestry with a dump truck and cooler. "You're welcome to join us. How old are your kids?"

"No, it's fine." Was she a pharma spy who called me here knowing I would bring the seeds?

"I really don't mind sharing," she said, laughing. "At the very least put down your load. I'm exhausted just looking at you carrying all that."

I set our bags on dry sand. "Swim with us," Sonya and Lev pleaded, pulling me toward the water. "Carry us to the deep part." Refusing, I held my shoebox and watched my children in the shallows. I could see a very young mother—older sister?—holding the hands of a toddler who squealed with pride at the new thrill of walking, at the roughness of sand on a foot. They looked so much like Corin and her baby Indigo, but Corin wouldn't be here, hours from her home. I could hear two women talking: "I mind the loss of income, don't get me wrong, but I'd rather camps close than kids get sick." The other said, "But how will it be better next year?" "Well, they'll need to spray." "Spray the whole woods?" "Well, maybe something organic, can't they? Annabelle, don't go any deeper." "Sinead, no splashing. Do you believe in Emily?" "I'll put it this way. I really don't want to, but I mean, who would make that shit up?"

I wanted to nudge them, look what I'm carrying. Gather round. I wanted all the mothers to come running. I wanted to be crowned queen of mothers. I wanted to keep the seeds forever, to grow them in Elsa cups, to heal everyone from these seeds, although all I had done thus far was allow two to die.

I felt hot, so hot, my face burning, arms flushing, sweat dripping down my back. I longed to run into the water where some mothers stood. I watched the sublime flesh, the shank of back-of-thigh, the asses, so many breasts wagging with intellectual cockiness, and the slim diagonal scars of top surgery because some of the mothers were not mothers but fathers or nonbinary parents. Sonya and Lev lay down so the water would lick their stomachs. I had not, I realized, applied sunscreen from any of the four bottles I carried with me, some that contained one chemical and some that contained another. We'd all read that sunscreen was killing our children and without the sunscreen the sun was killing our children who were heading deeper now into water that could kill them. I was woozy, dizzy. I wanted to lie back and float, and weren't we all weary, all of us mothers? Didn't we need to lie down, to be held by green water, surrounded by trees of darkest green? I looked around for someone I could trust with my seeds so I could lie in the cool water, so I could be held. Why weren't we all, all of us mothers, lying down and saying, no more? No more. Why weren't we lying down like Jessie in front of the oil pipelines, saying, no, no, no, no, no? But if we did, they would take away our children. They would separate us from our only want. We couldn't do that. We were a thousand compromises. We'd compromised for so long that we forgot that what we were feeling was compromise. We thought we were just tired, fatigued, energy cratered. I was tired of carrying my seeds, the seeds I'd wanted to find by myself. But who was myself? Nobody. Or everybody. I saw that now, as I watched the mothers. We weren't separate from one another or from our children, although we lived in fear of this separation, but how could they separate from us when we were we. We were the water that held them, the minnows beneath their legs, the floating watermelon rinds. We were everything altogether, and I wanted to tell them all, these mothers, all these beautiful mothers ashamed of their flesh and ashamed of their compromises and ashamed of the sunscreen that would kill their children, I see you. I wanted to say that to them. I see you. I am you. We are everybody.

As I thought all this, growing ever more feverish from the rising heat we had created by driving our children around to keep death away, death from drowning and electrocution and choking and boredom, my own name was called. I didn't hear it, because I was all of them. I was the mother lying in the shallows with her baby against her breasts and belly, her legs spread to let the water lap her. I was the mother at the picnic table bleeding into a super pad, because a long-awaited blastula had fallen like a twisted fairy into the toilet bowl yesterday. I was the mother saying, "Stop asking, just stop asking," and the mother saying, with great anger disguised as patience, or patience disguised as anger, "Do you think you could use your words?"

No. We were beyond words in this heat, holding our boxes of dying seeds in this last summer when we weren't afraid to go outside. I was the seeds, too, buried beneath dry dirt and growing thirsty and

I couldn't recognize my name being called because what was my name? Who was I without my friend, my lightning, my soil? I needed to tell her that my mother's depression had returned and I didn't know my own name when the depression settled on her. I was standing nameless outside her office door waiting for her to see me, to listen to me, to name me, but was that true? She remembered me differently, a stubborn, decisive girl with my own mind, my curious mind. Did I remember that girl? Was she somewhere nearby like Sonya who I'd seen bouncing in the water and telling herself a story a minute before, or maybe five minutes before, it was hard to know because time slid on sweat-slippery thighs.

Sonya wasn't bouncing anymore. She wasn't pouring mud on Lev's arms at the water's edge. Was she below the surface? I started to run into the water with the seeds held high in my hand. I would let them wash away, because nothing mattered except Sonya. No seeds mattered except my own. In the end, I would give it all up for me, for my child, and so I splashed deeper, looking for her body beneath, until I felt hands pulling on me. Somehow, Sonya was behind me, water dripping from her limbs. Was she laughing or crying? There was so much water on her face I couldn't tell. But she was here, she was here. We stumbled together to the dry sand where I put down the seeds to grab her with both arms, to hold her wet body to mine.

"Mom, Mom, I've been trying to tell you, but you're not listening. There's a man here calling your name."

"Eve! Eve!" A lone man on the sand bugled his hands.

"See, it's you he wants!" Sonya looked worried for me.

He caught us looking at him. "Of course," he said, coming toward us. "Of course, just as she described. And you are the daughter? She told me about you, too. Sonya."

Ishmael gazed from Sonya to me and back again. I recognized him from his website. His light blue eyes looked as if they might fly away and return to the sky. But I was no longer feverish, no longer lost. I'd been cooled by Sonya's wet arms and chest. He reached out his hand. His fingernails were bitten short. He wasn't frightening. He was just a white man in baggy beige pants and a faded T-shirt that said *James Taylor Fire and Rain Tour.* He scratched his nose and said, in a stilted, bedside singsong, "I know from Demeter that you have the obligation of childcare. When you didn't call me back, I thought, well, she is a mother and mothers operate in another time. I decided to spare you the burden of travel, so I went to your house and your husband was kind enough to tell me where you were today, at this lovely lake." His eyes dropped to the ground. "Are these . . . ?"

"There she is," I heard. I picked up my shoebox and saw, crossing the sand, Ellen in her sharp-cornered blazer over a tank top and Antonia in long basketball shorts.

"Pardon the interruption of your idyllic afternoon," Antonia said, "but Ellen here is paranoid. She made us haul ass."

"We met your adorable and rather grumpy husband," Ellen said. "Just missed you, apparently. And we might have been here ages ago, except Antonia was starving and insisted . . . Wait . . . is that . . ."

We turned to see a young satyr galloping, his arm holding out a carton as if it were an Olympian torch. "I got Indigo's milk," he called, panting. "Nearest store was like half an hour but . . . is she here? Just saw two cars like hers in the parking lot."

"DJ?" Ellen called. "Is that you?"

The young mother who actually was Corin took the milk and jutted her chin toward me. Indigo raised her hands to DJ, who lifted her high against the sun, spinning her around. To me, he said with delight on his face, "Did you get my note? I put one on every blue Subaru I saw, but man there are massive amounts of blue Subarus. We've been looking for you. Someone at the coffee shop said, 'Try the lake. Moms like to go to the lake.' Did you destroy them? You can do it right now. Just throw them in the lake, just be free."

"Are you talking about the seeds?" Ellen asked.

"Mo'," Indigo insisted. "Mo'!"

DJ set a hand on Indigo's flaxen hair. "I figured it out. Okay, listen. The ticks want to save us. First, they stop us from eating red meat. The whole destructive cattle industry. Now they stop us from, you know, turning on the lights. Driving! It's wicked awesome. We refuse to give up fossil fuels, so they force us. Let them!"

Indigo stomped her small and newly proficient foot. "Mo'!"

"No," Antonia said. "DJ, no."

"How will you fetch Indigo's milk if you can't drive?" Ellen asked.

"Are we talking about the same seeds?" Ishmael smiled at everyone in turn. "Let me introduce myself. I go by the name Ishmael."

"Is this the guy you were telling me about?" Ellen asked.

Behind Antonia, a flock of children ran onto the beach followed by three mothers I recognized from camp pickup. They carried bags and swim floaties and coolers and a stack of pizza boxes. "Hi, Sonya! Hi, Eve!" one mom shouted. "You came! Yay! Sorry we're so late. We stopped for pizza and it took forever. It's so hot out!"

"Eve, you will note that I was here first," Ishmael said.

"Come on, Eve," Ellen said.

"Mom? They're all talking to you. Can you hear them?"

I looked at my daughter. I had done it, hadn't I? I had wanted something again, even as a mother. "Just get rid of them," DJ was saying. "Let the wild take control." I looked at Ellen, her concerned expression, and at Ishmael's eager one. Antonia was brave just by standing here, just by leaving her house with all she knew of the future. I looked at the mothers. We were all brave. All lightning, all soil, all ticks, all water, all heat, all children calling out, *are you listening?*

"Eve?"

"Mom?"

Belief is a choice, but how do you know what to choose?

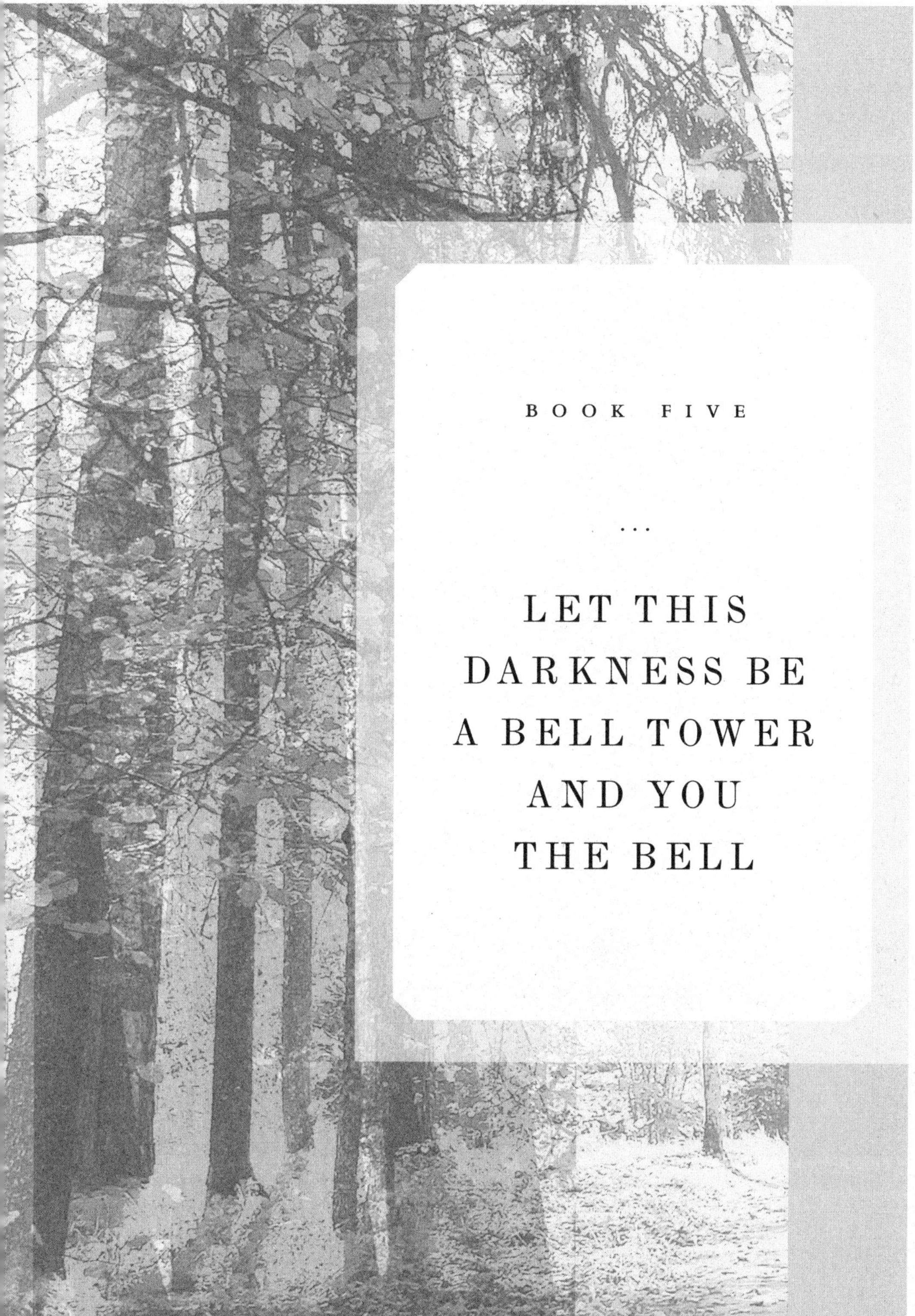

BOOK FIVE

...

LET THIS DARKNESS BE A BELL TOWER AND YOU THE BELL

This April, 2036

...

WANTING TO BE HOME BY THE TIME SHE WAKES, I CUT THROUGH the elementary schoolyard on my way from the Underworld House, but my timing's off. Soon I'm overrun by children saying goodbye to their parents and heading inside. I feel a small ache to have a child hanging off each arm again—and then I'm filled with delight at these small bodies, the way they jump and cling, their friendship bracelets, fuchsia hair streaks, orange shoelaces: little protests against the monochrome of required white pants, white socks, white shirts, white shoes.

I make it through the swarm, but by the time I get home, I've missed my slim window to talk to her. Jam and bread on the kitchen counter. She's made breakfast and returned to her room. I talk to her closed door. "Hey, hon! Want to walk the track with me? It's gorgeous out."

No answer.

Sonya was happy in her teenage years. All my worry. Why did I bother? She had a flock of friends through high school. They drank tea in town with their arms around one another. And she and me and Lev? We were close, the three of us. She chose a college far from the ticks and found others to love there.

She called six months ago to talk about the trip to Target with Ellen. Did we really drive an hour each way for no reason? For plastic from China? Why would I do such a thing?

I laughed it off. It was a shitty day, did she remember? Persephone mooning after DJ?

What about the plastic pool? The Slip 'n Slide? Why'd I feed her burgers? Pack her snacks in plastic? Drive them into the hilltowns just to drive. We visited Antonia every *month*? We flew *each summer* to

Ruth and Jessie? Couldn't we have just FaceTimed? I drove her to dance classes. What had I thought would happen? That she'd become a dancer?

Soon she was home, five weeks into her senior year of college. The therapist calls it depression, but there's another element, something less singular. Is it the world's pain? Solastalgia? Climate anxiety? A yearning for an unchanged world.

She wants to live differently than me, as light on this earth as a dried leaf. After she uses electricity, I hear her yelling at herself. She has marks on her arms from where she's flicked rubber bands to keep from opening the fridge. She wishes she had Emily, she says, to remove the temptation to turn on the light, charge her laptop, get in the car.

My desire for her to leave the house is as great as my worry that she'll head into our woods in that black CBGB shirt and shorts. It's painful to watch a child stall out. A child on the cusp of adulthood slipping back to her room.

BEFORE SONYA CAME HOME, I'd been in Oregon researching a new book. Jessie had introduced me to a group of retired teachers creating a roving school for kids whose towns were cindered by fire. But now I can't leave Sonya. What to do while homebound? Recently I sat down at my computer and started writing about the warm spring day I found Demeter in the park. I changed the names of my ex-husband and Demeter's daughter. And then I kept going. I'm calling the document "Tickfood," which amuses me. That's us. Tickfood.

But what will the ending be? Ishmael's seed died soon after I gave it to him at the lake. I did give him one, although I regretted it later. But Demeter trusted him, and I had to do something for her on the day she left. Ellen's seed languished for two years in a greenhouse, never blooming, denied this grant and that. It drowned when the sprinkler system misfired. Stephen's biotech bros sent botanists to look for four-petalled white trilliums. No luck. They lost interest once the border walls and deer slaughter contained Emily's epidemic reach.

The town has also used a pesticide spray made from fungus, bait boxes that drop fipronil onto rodents. Soon, pregnant mice with genes altered by CRISPR to be resistant to ticks will be released into the woods.

Thanks to the tick scientists who swarmed our town that fall, cause and effect is firmly linked. Camps drive kids to sandy lakefronts. Sports on Astroturf. Laps around the new town track. We're safe biking and kayaking, skiing in winter when there's snow.

But the workers hired to maintain paved yards, pull up creeping pachysandra, repair the concrete borders—they keep getting sick.

I don't want to sound complacent. I've grieved, raged, like everyone. What is life when we no longer lie on grass, pick a dandelion, slap a passing leaf? We largely ignored the plants when we had them, but so much depended upon them. We were living with a flat-out miracle, this green earth a wonderment.

I WAIT UNTIL THE midday jackhammering ends—repairs to border walls corroded by winter's violent stun—and then knock on her door again. "How's your day going? Come outside! I'd love company." No answer. Greentime is me in a white plastic chair on the concrete barrier where I watch the woods like an ocean too dangerous to enter. My mother tells me that the woodlands and meadows reclaimed themselves, growing wild over our former paths.

I settle for birdsong. My heart races when I glimpse woodchuck. I imagine myself across the barrier. Sugar maple leaves against my face, lick of jack-in-the-pulpit on my shin, whisper of unfurling fern at my ankles.

When the seeds died, I was devastated. I thought I'd failed. But I'm not the end of the story, I know this now. The story started long before me. Back when all this was glacial lake. And the story will go on far beyond me. I moved it forward a little bit, which is all we can do. I want to see what happens next.

Sitting here, I'm often overcome with joy. I can't explain it. Everything is shit, my daughter is frightened and furious, my son is in New York with my husband who is not my husband anymore, the ground beneath me is paved, and yet I look at the woods and I'm bursting with curiosity.

IT'S POSSIBLE—IF INCONCEIVABLE—THAT I'M LEARNING HAPPINESS from my mom. *Eve Yalen? Any relation to Joan? Joan Yalen? God, I adore her. She's just incredible.* I hear this at the ophthalmologist, the bank, the post office. Everyone knows someone at one of the four Underworld Houses. Her creation. If we're to be relegated to the kingdom of the sick, she says, let it be a kingdom indeed.

I visit every day before dawn. It's lively then—as it is after dusk—with others from the Overworld. The diurnal world. Mothers, lovers, friends, grandchildren, all of us in our regulation whites. Rabbi Riqqi comes, as do ministers, dentists, haircutters, manicurists, physical therapists, and so on.

Spring and summer are hard. You have to stay up late or come early to see anyone.

You have to stay up? my mother asks in my head. Who is *you*? What if *you* are an Emily? Then it's not late at all, is it?

She writes about this now, how our very language is frightened of the night and those who inhabit it. Bats and vampires all. Dark looks, dark deeds, dark visions. Our darkest hours. These dark days. Dark years ahead. As opposed to enlightenment, illumination. Why is a clever child bright? Why is stupidity dim?

And if we weren't afraid of the darkness, of what's hard to see? Of illness? What world would we make then? She's no longer Joan Yalen the author, but Joan Yalen the seer of night. I try to forget our difficult years. It's not easy. Can we have a relationship without a backstory? It's possible such lack of sentimentality is required to move forward in this changing world.

I'VE BEEN UP SINCE FOUR A.M. and I doze a little in my chair, waking past sunset when I think I hear the front door shut, but Sonya never leaves, so I suspect it's a neighbor's house. I turn on the patio light and use the lint roller to check for ticks while looking at my phone, which has filled with gifts:

A selfie from Lev trying on a suit at Goodwill for prom. He's here on weekends, living this year with his dad in Bed-Stuy, dating a senior named Olivia. Lev has my height, his dad's smile; lucky Olivia.

Flowers from Ruth, as usual. Larkspur and lupine from the Oregon coast where she and Jessie are visiting Ryan and his wife and sons. Miss you!

Ellen wants to know if I've caught up with her and Antonia on our new murder mystery. I remember the last time all three of us visited. Sonya, newly licensed, was driving, claiming her right to choose the music, humming with power and freedom, while Lev stretched his long legs across the back seat.

The last text is from Stephen asking me to buy beets. Everyone loves my borscht.

"We don't have the heart to tell him how awful his cooking is," my mother has said to me.

WHEN I HEAR THE front door again, I rush inside. "Sonya?" I find her in the living room with the lights off, looking dazed. "Hon? What is it? You need some food?" I stand next to her. Her hair is short, her septum pierced. She washes her clothes in the tub and always smells slightly of mold and my coconut lotion. "Let's eat together. I made chili."

She doesn't answer. As always, I want to shake her. I want to stroke her arm, kiss the top of her head. I heat up dinner. She hovers nearby.

"You doing okay?" I ask when we're at the table.

"Persephone came by."

I don't believe her. It's been twelve years. "What do you mean? Persephone?"

"She came up to my room. You were outside. Says she's staying with grandma."

Is she hallucinating? What's going on? I ask if she's feeling okay. She takes her bowl and heads upstairs. I follow. "Did she really? Are you serious? Are you sure it was her?"

"Go away, Mom." Sonya's upset. More than usual.

—

I'D LIKE TO DRIVE, BUT I AGREED TO SONYA'S TERMS, SO I WALK fast, thinking of Demeter. Has she forgiven me? Did she get Jeremiah's check, which—after failing to track her down—I sent general delivery to the town in Colorado where Mary Katherine lived? Will I see her here, my lost friend? At the Underworld House, I hurry past the dark kitchens, the dark health clinic. I don't stop when I hear Caleb in the podcasting studio, even though his voice thrills me (even more so when I'm in his bedroom—the reason I was home late this morning). I find my mother with a friend, weeding lettuces in their metal beds. Today her cane is purple; residents and their families are always carving or buying them for her. She raises it high, like a baton. "Incredible, isn't it? A true spring miracle!"

"She's really here?"

"You just missed her, darling. She went to the farm."

All the Emilys spend their days (our nights) outside, researching in the woods or farming in the meadows. They've nothing to fear.

I chat with Kiran and his boyfriend, who have recently moved in together and are preparing lunch for the farmers, until Stephen returns. He's a cabby, chauffeur, drives their van all day (night).

He drops me at the edge of the farm. I pull up my socks, tuck in my whites, cross the field, interrupt an intense discussion about soil pH for tomato varieties to ask for Persephone.

I don't recognize the woman standing there in boots and shorts, hair shaved on one side.

She flings her arms around my neck, and in her grip I know her. She's gloriously un-thin. Calf muscles like grapefruit, breasts, belly, her same smile. We hold hands and walk. I don't want to stop touching her. I ask about her mother. She answers about herself. She's studying botany and medicinal plants, started online college early, already finished two semesters of graduate work in Albuquerque.

"So, your mom's in New Mexico?" I'm grasping.

"Yeah, she is. Look, I've done the research. How plants are moving north, up into Canada. Escaping the heat. I've mapped the microclimates."

"Is she okay? Your mom?" I try again. "Is she angry?"

"Sightflower, Eve. I want to find it."

I stop walking. My chest burns. That old urge. My seeds.

"Oh, honey, people looked," I say. "They took Abiah's pressed flower. They searched all over. Too much shade too early, that's what they say."

"Not everywhere. They didn't look everywhere." She traces a figure eight in the dirt with the toe of her boot. "Plants migrate. I've mapped the likeliest spots, the type of soil, sun, rainfall, leaf cover. But I can't drive. I can't buy groceries. I can't do shit on my own. So I took the bus here and asked Sonya to come."

I'm stung with fear and excitement and can't tell one from the other.

"Can you convince her?" she asks. "If it exists, it'll be far northern Canada, where the trees leaf out at the time they used to here. But it only blooms for a few weeks. . . . Well, you know."

"Spring ephemeral."

"Talk to her? Please?"

SONYA SAYS NO. HOW could she justify driving? How could I ask her to?

I tell her that she was born into a historical moment in which human connection is predicated on oil and electricity, that she depends upon that energy ecology just as she depends on water to drink and air to breathe and plants to eat. I tell her that she needs to turn toward connection no matter the cost, as a plant turns toward sunlight.

I'm desperate for her to take this chance at happiness. I yell. I plead.

THE SUN RISES EVER EARLIER. The Underworld days shorten while mine lengthen. Soon the trees far north will leaf. "I'm running out of time," Persephone says when I visit. "Please convince her."

But Sonya stops talking to me. When she leaves her room for food or to go to the bathroom, she's wearing headphones. She can't even hear me.

I empty my closet searching for the blackout curtains; eventually I pull them out of a box in the basement under the plastic pool. I duct tape all four sides to my bedroom windows and the bathroom window.

"She won't listen to me," I say to Persephone, and we leave the Healing Hut together before dawn. She sleeps during the day in my room.

All day I try to write a note to give her to take to Demeter. Persephone hasn't told me much, just that she's fine. She's good. She'd rather not talk about her. *Dear Demeter,* I start. *My dearest friend.*

When the sun sets, I haven't gotten any further. I'm too nervous. I bring Persephone breakfast and she takes it outside Sonya's room. To give her privacy, I go back downstairs, start washing dishes with the lights out. But of course I turn off the water to listen. Persephone's talking about a play they once wrote together. She's trying to remember the names of the characters. It's all monologue. But then Persephone pauses and says, "Wait, really? Was that true? Oh my god, you're right. We always made Lev be the dog."

Sonya's door opens. Shuts again.

I wait a moment and then creep up the stairs. From the landing, I can hear only a low murmuring.

Persephone saying, "No, I get it. I do."

More murmuring.

And then Sonya's clear voice, loud and emphatic. "I just don't know! What *do* I want? I don't know. I don't even remember who I am anymore."

Oh, honey, I think, I remember you. I remember you at three, seven, nine, fourteen. Always fierce, never scared of the darkness.

I want to run up the stairs two at a time and tell her this, tell her who she is, but I'm not the one she needs right now. I hold on to the railing, thinking of her at every age, all at once. And then I hear laughter. Persephone's laugh is just like Demeter's. And I can exhale at last.

I'm back in the kitchen when they finally head downstairs. A spring wind has come into the night, the way that two friends together can create a weather neither could alone. "We're famished," Sonya says, laughing and opening the fridge. "We need all the food."

I cook and we eat together and I pack them the leftovers and all the snacks I can find. It's long after midnight when they're ready to leave. Sonya's not wearing whites. I hand her two sets in a bag along with mirrors and lint rollers, although Emily hasn't made it past southern Vermont. "Be careful. Check yourself." A brief moment when I want to tell her to stay, get back in her room. What if she misses a speck, an ick, a tick? Instead, I kiss her again. "Antonia says the outbuilding is all set for you," I tell her. "Windows are covered. Don't even worry about saying hi. Just get some sleep and they'll see you in the evening."

"It'll be morning," Sonya corrects me. "Our morning." Persephone leans her head on my shoulder just like her mom always did.

Surprising us, the rusted car starts.

And they're gone, off like wild horses. The night air is green and the leaves shake behind the barrier and I'm alone. I hear them now, Demeter. I hear the inner voices. They're no longer scolding me, although they're sometimes exasperated as they try to get me to look up from my computer or stop worrying about Sonya and Joan, and to notice that the world is still unfathomably beautiful. I listen. I hear the proud coo of a mother tick sending off her nymphs. I hear a plant, my seeds. Can you find me?

Acknowledgments

. . .

I'M GRATEFUL TO MY BRILLIANT EDITOR, CAITLIN MCKENNA, for believing in this book and having the vision to see what it could become, and to my intrepid agent, Doug Stewart, who is the kindest and quickest, for making it all possible. All my thanks to the Random House team: Andy Ward, Alison Rich, Ben Greenberg, Naomi Goodheart, Erin Richards, Madison Dettlinger, Sandra Sjursen, Annette Szlachta, Elena Giavaldi, Barbara Bachman, Nicole Ramirez, Erica Gonzalez, Alice Berndt, Leah Sims, Rebecca Berlant, Lynn Wu, and Samuel Wetzler. Thank you to the fantastic Anne Tate Pearce for all her support.

I've made this valley in western Massachusetts my home for two decades, and while this novel takes place here, I've changed a few details of its past and present. I'm grateful to its real people and plants, its animals, rivers, and libraries. I'm indebted to the work of writers and scholars who helped me understand its history, in particular *Devil's Den to Lickingwater: The Mill River Through Landscape & History* by John Sinton, *Changes in the Land: Indians, Colonists, and the Ecology of New England* by William Cronon, *A Place Called Paradise* edited by Kerry W. Buckley, *Wash and Be Healed: The Water-Cure Movement and Women's Health* by Susan E. Cayleff, "Historical Erasure and Cultural Recovery: Indigenous People in the Connecticut River Valley" by Margaret Bruchac, and "44 State Street, Northampton" by David Fleming. Thank you to the David Ruggles Center, Historic Northampton, and Thomas Cole's painting, *View from Mount Holyoke, Northampton, Massachusetts, after a Thunderstorm—The Oxbow.*

Thank you to Susannah Abel-Zucker for Eve's name, Will's limerick, and on-the-ground research. Thank you to Ash Abel-Zucker for telling me I got this.

Johanna Ravenhurst spoke to me about epidemiology when I was just getting started. The coaches at Guide kept me going. Aruna Goldstein gave me a home in Hagsville with the best compatriots: Abbie, Alex, Amanda, Amber, Blake, Eliza, Justine, and Melitta.

For insight, artistry, inspiration, and generosity, I'm grateful to Jessica Bacal, Ingrid Binswanger, Matthew Brookshire, Emily Chenoweth, Rachel Cody, Oona Coy, Jenny Gotwals, Alison Hart, Melissa Hersh, Luis Jaramillo, Maud Macrory, Lisa Olstein, Ruth Ozeki, Scott Rosenberg, Gabriel Roth, Tali Woodward, and Leni Zumas.

Thank you to my students for their stories and bravery. I'm excited for all I'll get to read in the future.

Thank you to Lila Cecil, whose wisdom and compassion made this book wiser and more compassionate.

Thank you to Erin White for all the words, all the walks, every day.

Thank you to my parents, Emily and Rick Abel, who are nowhere in this book, but everywhere in my heart. Thank you to my sisters, Laura and Sarah, for traveling this path with me.

My wildest thanks to Adam, for this life together, for your heart and mind, for being my favorite place—and to Ash and Susannah, for the joyful and profound gift of loving you and being your mother.

ABOUT THE AUTHOR

...

HEATHER ABEL is the author of the novel *The Optimistic Decade.* She lives in Northampton, Massachusetts, with her husband and teenagers, and teaches creative writing at Smith College.

heatherabel.com
Instagram: @heatherkabel

ABOUT THE TYPE

. . .

This book was set in Bembo, a typeface based on an old-style Roman face that was used for Cardinal Pietro Bembo's tract *De Aetna* in 1495. Bembo was cut by Francesco Griffo (1450–1518) in the early sixteenth century for Italian Renaissance printer and publisher Aldus Manutius (1449–1515). The Lanston Monotype Company of Philadelphia brought the well-proportioned letterforms of Bembo to the United States in the 1930s.